1511.77.79

New
10.99

D0283728

A SAFE HAVEN

— A NOVEL —

SUMMER ALLMAN

Thomas Nelson Publishers
Nashville • Atlanta • London • Vancouver

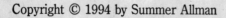

Copyright © 1994 by Summer Allman

All rights reserved. Written permission must be secured from the publisher to use or reproduce any part of this book, except for brief quotations in critical reviews or articles.

Published in Nashville, Tennessee, by Thomas Nelson, Inc., and distributed in Canada by Word Communications, Ltd., Richmond, British Columbia, and in the United Kingdom by Word (UK), Ltd., Milton Keynes, England.

Scripture quotations are from the NEW KING JAMES VERSION of the Bible. Copyright © 1979, 1980, 1982, Thomas Nelson, Inc., Publishers

Library of Congress Cataloging-in-Publication Data

Allman, Summer.
    A safe haven / Summer Allman.
      p.   cm.
    ISBN 0-7852-8319-6 (pb)
    1. Wilderness areas—Cascade Range Region—Fiction.
2. Women psychiatrists—Oregon—Fiction. 3. Widows—
Oregon—Fiction. 4. Solitude—Fiction. 5. Grief—Fiction.
I. Title.
PS3551.L467S24   1994
813'.54—dc20
                         93–49861
                         CIP

Printed in the United States of America
1 2 3 4 5 6 7 — 99 98 97 96 95 94

Dedicated to

    all who struggle with the blank spaces in their own being, who by the will of God will find their way,

    and, to the helpers in my life—most gratefully to my husband who has given of himself every inch of the way that I might be all God created me to be.

A special thanks to Katie Androski, friend and author, who challenged me to write.

---

*I have come that you might have life,
and have it abundantly.*

Chapter 1

The twin engine plane banked left, leaving behind the last fragment of civilization she would contend with for a long time. Katherine kept her eyes to the window to avoid encouraging conversation with the pilot and to drink in the source of her solitude. Giant emerald firs, dusted in mist, pointed to her, reaching, welcoming. This would be a good place to hide. *And good hiding places don't come easy,* Katherine thought. If it didn't work out, perhaps the peacefulness of the outside would squeeze the inside torment into a small compact emptiness.

At the edge of fifty, life had become for Katherine Allen a cruel exposure, an accumulation of explanations, justifications and criticism, etched into every wrinkle and bit of sagging flesh—identifying marks betraying a truth within.

Sunrise exploded across the nose of the plane. The logging roads lay below like discarded ribbons, scattered over the forest floor. They led to and from the clear cuts, great expanses of raw mountain covered with the remains of devoured wilderness. From this height, the slash heaps made her think of the child's game of pick-up-sticks. All the hours she'd spent delicately lifting one stick without disturbing the others. Maybe childhood was practice for real life, after all. But now, with the stakes higher, Katherine wondered if it was even possible to claim the dry twig of love that lay wedged between the rage and the betrayal.

The motor rattled and vibrated its way deeper into the Cascades. Ahead and below, vultures circled. She envied them. *They fly in silence. They float the wind. Fighting is so loud. But soon I'll be part of it. I'll be quiet, too.*

That incessant rattling stuck in a worn groove in her

brain . . . the same city-sound she was fleeing. *How much longer?* Wind clawed at the craft, threatening to shred the man-made intruder. As the war between the two worlds pounded—the outside clamoring against the inside, the inside screaming to be out—a burning fear rose in her throat. She stared at the trees racing beneath them. *How much longer?*

It had been over an hour since she and her meager possessions had been loaded into this rickety cockpit. Her only concern had been whether or not she would have to converse with the pilot. She had smiled just enough to be polite, not enough to be encouraging. He had given some perfunctory instructions above the propeller roar. Then they'd ambled down the runway for what seemed like an eternity before she'd felt the familiar weightlessness.

Now, Mrs. Katherine Allen sat motionless in a tin box slicing its way eastward into the wilderness sunrise. As always, the noise unnerved her. Soft music and night sounds were her preference. She longed deeply for the quiet and, for a fleeting moment, tried to retrieve her lost memories of it, to no avail. Years of longing seemed to rattle against the dry bones within her.

Maybe some needs are so primitive—like the need to be safe, to be touched or loved—that they don't arise of experience but of instinct. Katherine had a need to be alone. She'd always had it. As long as she could remember, her childhood had been a constant search for hiding places and waiting for opportune moments to sneak away.

She had hidden in closets and in alleys and in the cool of the wood lot that sprawled behind the house. She had hidden behind walls and drapes and work and laughter and streetwise veneer. Although rarely caught, the few discoveries had been shattering experiences, events she found very difficult to think about, even now.

For the past nine months Katherine had felt hidden in someone else's dream. Nothing mattered because it wasn't real. It wasn't hers. She had tried her best to bury herself in church work and exercises of faith and praise, but the joy never came. Instead, each succeeding day was a steady slide into a gray nothingness.

John had died the night the tea roses froze. Afterward, she

had been surrounded by comforting family and friends, some of whom knew her well enough to know she was gone, too. The months of finishing that life, "putting things in order," and planning her escape, had been carried out by a smiling, nodding mannequin. When their best friend, Adam, finally drove her to the terminal, he had threaded his way through the O'Hare traffic without a word. He'd already said them all. They had not budged her an inch.

Her bags safely in the hands of the skycap, Adam hugged her close and whispered, "Don't go, Kate." It all came back to her now.

Katherine's arms hung limp, her eyes vacant reflections behind the iridescent one-way sunglasses. It was useless, he knew. She was already gone. Her numb face did not feel the kiss he placed on her cheek, nor did she hear him whisper, "Come back to us, Kate." She just turned and walked up the boarding ramp.

Adam watched her go, as he had known she would, from the first moment she had told him of it, when he'd shouted at her, "This is nuts! You can't just go off in the woods someplace. People are made for fellowship. Kate, think!"

But this woman was probably the most stubborn individual he'd ever met. Not that she was belligerent about it, just matter-of-fact when she finally made a decision. He could not recall a single time when he had been able to change her mind.

The only one with that prerogative was her husband and, Adam gathered, even John had needed to bring his lunch for that battle. But as far as he knew, John was the only human being who had ever been able to get Kate to do something against her better judgment . . . for him . . . just because he wanted her to.

When she was younger, Adam knew, Katherine had been impulsive. Numerous emotional scars and scraped feelings later, she was a woman of extraordinary thoughtfulness. Trying to reason with her was like reading from the answers she'd already discarded in a multiple choice exam. You had to prove to her that she was wrong.

Katherine possessed the rare quality, openly visible in her relationships, of piercing insight and generous acceptance. She was seldom fooled by anyone but frequently chose to blatantly ignore what she knew. She was seldom disappointed, because she had very low expectations of people.

Dr. Kate, as she was known, worked in a psychiatric clinic with a staff of other psychiatrists, social workers, and psychologists, as well as a cadre of supporting office people. She was well-liked by most, adored by some, respected by all.

Once Kate was on track, she didn't let go. Staffings were challenging, especially if she thought some child wasn't getting a fair shake. For at those times, her loving demeanor could take on the endearing quality of a mama lion. No one would deny that, as a therapist, she was brilliant.

Many people vied for Kate's friendship, but she guarded her relationships, so she had few real friends. She had married her best friend, John, and had worked with the other, Adam Silvan. Adam had come through residency with her, one of the only students sympathetic to her faith. Though an orthodox Jew himself, Adam understood Katherine's passionate quest for the truth and defended her right to her beliefs. In fact, during their residency, they had sat up many a night encouraging each other, like a flickering flame of life almost extinguished amidst the cadavers of anatomy class. Together, they had speculated about the lives of the people whose bones they picked and had felt something unholy about the whole thing. Probably it was that experience that had written more indelibly than any other of the sacredness of life and of her grave responsibility in her service to the Master and mankind.

It was also in those late-night sessions that they had begun their practice on each other, fine-tuning their skills of analyzing the human psyche, of probing the soul, mindful of its eternal worth. In the classroom, faith was not validated nor God seen as relevant to healing or even health. So Katherine clung for validation to Adam, who at least knew the same Heavenly Father.

To others, Kate was a loner, seeming to elude everyone's probe. Although appearing genuinely warm and open, Adam knew she was, in reality, implicitly private. Through the years, he had learned by osmosis that she was also a very disturbed person on the inside, with remarkable exterior coping skills.

To his irritation, he was never able to maintain an objective attitude toward Katherine. He seemed to get lost in her piercing navy-blue gaze. When they were both hired at the clinic, one of *the secretaries had asked him if he was in love with her. He'd answered, "No, she's my friend." Later he wondered what that meant.*

Of course they were friends! Didn't he know some things about her that others didn't know. For one thing, he knew that Katherine was not as self-assured as she appeared to be. Nor was she open in any sense of the word. But, Adam realized, she was incredibly courageous, the kind of courage only a coward knows.

He knew something of the intense fear that gripped her life and the effort it took for her to keep functioning. For months, he'd spent Wednesday afternoons locked in her anguishing struggle, trying to pry open the isolation in which she lived. Adam had shared that inner sanctum where the fear ran rampant, the fear that reduced her to a whimpering child. But, remarkably, at the end of such a session, he had watched her stand up, straighten her shoulders, and walk out into the world—a terrified little girl in a competent woman's body.

Professionally, Adam questioned the wisdom of taking her on as his client, wondered how objective he could be as her therapist, and how much "counter transference" he had going with her. But the relationship had begun so early in their med school days that it had continued like a habit. Besides, it was her idea. Starting over with someone else would take too long. And it did seem to be working.

Their friendship, however, left him with the sense of never quite being received. She always held him at arm's length as, he suspected, she did most men. One of the most difficult tasks for a therapist is teaching incest victims to trust again.

Adam wrestled with exactly what he wanted from her. Maybe it wasn't possible to love Katherine Allen. Maybe she would never really let anyone in. He knew it had been the struggle for John, too.

There was a vulnerable side to Kate that she had revealed only to John. Perhaps, Adam surmised, because they shared the same faith. Probably no one else would ever have guessed how dependent she was upon him . . . .

Now, on the last leg of the journey, things were beginning to matter to Katherine. Encapsulated, without breath, sleeping nerve fibers prickled awake. As the noise became louder, the old longing pounded harder.

She peered out at the silent world beyond the windshield. Was this engine noise or the violent surging of her own blood? It seemed they were suspended in the air, motionless. She could not feel the plane moving. She could not remember how to inhale. A clammy panic slid down her spine and squeezed through her skin. Louder and louder! *Let me out! God, please get me out of here! Stop this noise!* What ripped like a silent scream through her was heard as a moan to the pilot.

"Are you okay, ma'am?" Katherine's head snapped involuntarily to the left. Wild-eyed, all she could do was nod. "Are you afraid of flying? It'll only be a few more minutes. Think you can make it?"

I can make it! I can make it, she thought, although she wanted to scream at him to "Shut up!" Instead, she faced the window and, pulling herself as far from him as possible, waved him off with her left hand. *Soon. Soon,* she thought. *Very soon, it will be over.*

Now they were passing over trees, ancient timber that had never been cut. Looking ahead, she could see that here the forest was clear of scars, those ugly patches of baldness that marred so much of America's great forests. She forced breath into her lungs as they entered the place where the steel teeth had never ripped, where the cycle of life and death bent together, caressing and nurturing each other. Where it was all left to Nature.

John's death lay like a marble slab in her stomach. *Where is the nourishment? Where is the purpose?*

It had taken twenty-one years to approach his love with a sense of trust, to bend together with him. His death fed nothing in her. It was a dry incision that left her unable to talk, to work, even to pray.

Katherine had not wanted to share her grief with anyone. So she'd spent hours in the dark of their apartment, hugging his brown tweed jacket to her, letting the tears disappear into the fabric, the same jacket that now lay carefully folded in the bottom of her suitcase.

As they began their descent, she squeezed her eyes tight, afraid to look. Clutching the arm rests till her knuckles turned white, Katherine resolutely wrapped her mind in John's tweed jacket for safekeeping. He had always held her hand whenever they landed because she hated the going down and down and down. Now it seemed an eternity before she felt the ground, bumpy, beneath them, then the plane braking to a stop.

John's death had fallen on her like the snowstorm of '79 that had brought the arrogance of Chicago to a halt. *There's something about a seed,* she thought, *falling to the ground and dying . . . don't fall. Don't fall.*

"Watch your step, ma'am," the pilot was saying. "Wouldn't want you to fall."

Startled, Katherine opened her eyes. The pilot's hand was extended to help her from the plane. They'd landed. Thank God, it was finished.

Chapter 2

"I'll just unload your stuff here. There's not very much. How long you planning to stay?"

"A year."

He turned to gape at her. "A year? Alone?"

Working in the woods was all he'd ever known, and his father and grandfather before him, till he'd learned to fly in Vietnam. Now flying was a skill he used to earn a few bucks when the woods shut down. He had never considered the woods a recreational activity . . . certainly not a place to be alone. And a woman yet!

He shrugged his shoulders in a live-and-let-live attitude that was typical of Northwest loggers. As a breed, they didn't much care what anyone else did as long as they did it in their own backyard.

A year alone, Katherine thought, *one entire year.* She turned it in her mind. *Maybe it isn't enough.* How long does it take to wash off the filth of coping? How long does it take to reach a soul, to find what is real, to be at peace with yourself, to remember what you never learned, to coax a self out of hiding? *Maybe I'll never go back,* she thought.

Together, they pulled her things out from behind the seats—two suitcases, a duffel bag, several boxes tied with twine. What do you pack to disappear? She had assembled these things with a calm expertise, as if she'd been planning this trip her whole life. Perhaps she had.

From somewhere the pilot retrieved a flatbed wooden wagon that looked like part of the Lewis and Clark expedition. They piled her stuff on. He pulled. She followed. It was nearly fifty yards to the end of the makeshift runway, a fairly level grassy clearing beside the river.

Apart from the runway and the river, they were engulfed in trees, Douglas firs that reached a hundred feet in the air. Snow still clung to the north side shadows, although the sun was warm. The last of the night mist floated halfway up the timbers.

Water tumbled across the river rocks, stroking the banks with a hissing song as a jaybird streaked above them, announcing their arrival in an echoing shriek. Everything else was still. Over her shoulder, she surveyed the spot where they had just landed, grateful her thoughts had been elsewhere. She had new appreciation for the pilot.

She saw that he had already begun his routine procession toward a dirt road that wound to the left through a band of trees. As he led the way, the wagon bumping along behind him, he lectured the air with sounds as crisp and clear as the water that ran the river.

Katherine felt she had arrived at the quietest place in the universe. She was captivated by its depth of stillness, where every sound echoed against the silence. As they moved away from the river, there was even less competition for his words. Only the groaning old wagon that seemed to provide a kind of ancient accompaniment for his lecture.

The pilot marched on, the vaporous words curling around him as he went, then disappearing into the cool morning. Katherine watched, mesmerized. Words she could see. Words that dissolved in the quiet. Words that fell in crystal slivers on the forest floor in front of her. Words that held no surprises. Words that didn't hurt.

She was completely lost to their meaning, so fascinated was she by their visibility. For several minutes, Katherine stood mute, watching him. Then she ran to catch up to him. He'd cleared the runway in squished tracks that led into the dark tree line beyond. She felt the ground turn to sponge, as millions of years of compost absorbed the sound of every step. The primitive road, which was nothing more than two narrow worn tracks laid out like parallel dotted lines, was lined along the edge with brown skeletons of lacy maidenhair ferns, waiting for the sunlight to fall between the trees and bring the spring.

The trees. Slowly, her eyes traced the wet bark up and up

to the sky. The mist of morning still dripped from their tops, gently swaying. Their green was dark and cool with silence.

She'd heard of them, read of them. The old growth, they called it. Some spoke of it in almost reverent terms, some with greed. Never had Katherine seen anything so awesome. It made her dizzy to look where they pointed. She felt a desire to touch one, but not the permission.

So she tiptoed past them, hurriedly covering the tracks the pilot had laid out. He was now out of sight. Once in view again, she could see he was still giving out his memorized oratory of all she must know about staying here, oblivious as to whether or not she took it in. How comfortable he seemed with his part. How lacking in responsibility for her. What a refreshing difference from all the hours she'd spent taking very personal responsibility for what others heard her say. Here, Katherine thought, was a man responsible only for himself!

He lurched forward like a pack mule hitched to the wagon tongue, leaning against its weight, his knit cap cocked forward on his forehead. For all he knew, she might have already changed her mind and returned to the plane.

"It all works with flags," he was saying. "You run 'em up the pole. The pink flag will bring help. You may feel very isolated, but actually you are quite safe within the range of the ranger station. They can see it from the fire lookouts and get here within an hour or so. Remember, your drops are every other Friday. It's best to pick up right away 'cause of animals. The two-way inside can radio to the plane when it's overhead. So if you need anything on the next trip, you can let us know." There. He'd said it. The rest was up to her.

The trees gave way to another clearing, more than a football field in diameter, a meadow with a slight grade uphill to the east. Last year's grasses and camas weeds filled the entire circle, bent with tufts of lingering snow, melting in shiny streams of sweating earth that betrayed the cool temperature.

The wagon groaned along, delivering the crushing blow to the bent grass in its path. Katherine followed in its track, wishing she could avoid trampling on them. She knew what it was to be dry and bent. Was it true, she wondered, as the prophet Isaiah promised, that God would never crush the bent reed?

They proceeded on, a sloppy, slushy parade, over sucking mud and snapping grass, in the direction of the sunrise. The meadow still lay in the purple shadow of night, not yet erased by the climbing sun, which was just spilling over the lowest eastern treetops. Here and there the sun found passage between the trees, shooting a golden ray across the meadow, guilding the tips of the giants on the western edge.

Barely noticeable, tucked against the far rim of the woodland dish, was a very rustic log cabin that looked as if it had been painted into the landscape or discovered growing up through the underbrush, completely rejecting any notion of its ever having been built there. It was perfectly camouflaged, dwarfed by the ominous trees and the silence. At first, Katherine thought she might be imagining it.

As they approached, the fairy tale cabin grew to life-size. The logs were weathered gray, matching the shakes on the roof. A column of smooth river rocks, painted in green moss, piled high against the west side, composed the chimney. The roof sloped forward, overhanging the porch, which might have railings beneath the tangle of blackberry vines, she couldn't be sure.

The cabin looked as old as the trees and just as organic, remaining visible only by the routine efforts of someone chopping away at the new growth. Katherine moaned to herself. She had the delirious sensation of having found her place—a place to hide, so secret it must surely be a safe haven.

"You alternate the white and yellow flags every day. If you forget, you'll have company. It's in case you get lost or sick or something." The pilot pulled the wagon to a stop, in line with the rough-hewn planks that composed the steps.

She could just see the corner of an outbuilding on the other side. The pilot unhitched himself and stomped his corks up the wooden planks that sprawled to the landing at the door. Katherine noticed the hollow sound his cleated boots made against the wood. Why they called them "corks" she didn't know, only that these were the special boots all loggers wore to give them footing. She had learned that bit of trivia from a magazine in the airport while waiting for her bags.

"You'll find all the wood you'll ever need in back under the carport." He fumbled with a key in a padlock on the door.

Then two more keys for the door locks, one above the other. Katherine wondered who was being locked out of this place that had taken months to locate and two hours to reach!

It made her think of the story of a young Chinese peasant who was asked why, after years of tutelage by a missionary, he had not wanted to convert to the faith. Yes, he agreed, the missionary was a kind and admirable man, but, "I don't think I could have the faith of a person who has so many keys!"

Every night for the past twenty some years, she had closed her eyes to the ebbing question, "Did I lock the doors?" And more than once, Katherine had tangled the separate threads of faith and irresponsibility. Sometimes, she was not sure she knew the difference.

Bits of forest debris, twigs, and some chewed pinecones cluttered the porch with a "nobody lives here" look. Sure enough, the berry vines had swallowed the log pole railings. Two shuttered windows stood gagged on either side of the massive entry. Katherine wondered how long the cabin had been empty and what stories it could tell.

As the pilot swung wide the bulky door and politely stepped back, Katherine peered into a dark room. A stale blend of aromas welcomed her—charred wood, bacon, dill. The air was cold and sealed, uninhabited. Suddenly, she felt embarrassed, like an intruder. Too polite to barge in, she could not get past the threshold.

"Excuse me." The pilot brushed past her with an armload of boxes. "So, what do you think? Not bad, huh?"

He set the boxes in the middle of the room and proceeded to open the window shutters that formed an added barrier of security, matching those on the exterior. From the exposed spiderwebs on the outer shutters, it was obvious that someone had recently "opened" the cabin. Light streamed into the sallow environment, unsealing the tomb.

Katherine's eyes strained to adjust. As the interior came into focus, she could see that it was one large room, embodied by amber logs shining with years of shellac.

The stone fireplace claimed the centermost of the wall to her left, holding a rough-hewn log mantel above its generous hearth. Long paned windows hung like paintings on each side. A green and gray braided rug, perfectly centered, reclined on the floor. There were scattered burn spots both on the rug and floorboards in front of the hearth.

The floorboards were of oiled fir, about five inches wide, and ran, seamless, for the entire length of the room—a distance she guessed to be about thirty feet. This cabin had been built around the turn of the century when it was still possible to plane lumber in that dimension.

All the furniture, sparse as it was, clung to the walls, creating a dance hall effect. A frayed, yellow plaid, Colonial-style sofa without legs squatted to the left of the door. It stuck out like a fake from the wrong century.

There were no curtains, just the wood shutters, which the pilot was noisily flinging open as if duty-bound to douse the quiet as much as possible in the brief time he had left.

Something about him had annoyed her, like the irreverence with which some nursing home aides bang about the rooms of the elderly. She wished he would leave, trusting her own capacity to figure out the necessities.

To the right a shellacked wood counter surrounded an ancient porcelain sink, once white, now decorated with years of rust stains from the water pump anchored to one end. On the dusty windowsill above the sink, someone had left a small bouquet of what appeared to have been crimson clover, now a dried colorless anchor for the elaborate cobweb that reached to the pump spout. The dust and spiders colonizing the water pump made Katherine calculate how far it was to the river.

"There is water? This does work?"

He answered by jerking the handle up and down so fiercely she thought he would yank it free of its bolts. The old pump yawned and squeaked and sent a gush of brown liquid into the sink. Satisfied, he moved on.

Pointing to a square black cast-iron box on legs, centered on the north wall opposite the fireplace, he began a dissertation about the Fischer stove, which, he informed her with some pride, was the creation of an unemployed logger who had cleaned up on an invention of necessity. Systematically, he opened and closed the door, turning the intake valves, demonstrating the work of genius it was. Built with an airtight firebox, it allowed burning for up to seventy-two hours without reloading. He wrenched the damper on the stovepipe it shared with a small wood cookstove between it and the sink. Every joint grumbled in protest before yielding in an arthritic fashion.

"You ever cooked on a woodstove before?"

She shook her head.

"Well, it's an experience. Some people get real good at it with practice. Guess you'll have a lot of time to practice, huh! What are you gonna do here all by yourself for a whole year?"

Without waiting for an answer, the pilot continued around the room, opening cupboards, shutters, swiping at the dust and spiders. At the far corner of the room, he abruptly stopped, turned and faced her, as if waiting for her answer.

Katherine flushed, stammering, in the midst of a response, when he suddenly flung open another door and pointed enthusiastically into what appeared to be a dark closet.

"And here's what really makes this place the Ritz!" Katherine stepped closer. "A compost toilet! See, you never have to leave the cabin. A godsend in the winter. It's all right here." He banged the wooden lid up and down. "Odorless. Flushless. And you throw your kitchen scraps in, too! But no water," he said, accenting the latter. "Then in about six months . . . voila! . . . you have compost," he reported triumphantly. "Great for flowerbeds and vegetables. Well, I don't suppose you'll be planting any of those," he said moving on. Clearly, this amenity was his favorite thing. It sounded good. She only hoped it worked.

"And another thing, as long as you don't throw any kitchen stuff outside, you won't be bothered by bears. It's all right here in this manual." He waved a stapled booklet in the air and let it drop on the table with a resounding smack and a flurry of dust.

"Tells you everything you need to know. How to work all the stuff, including the pipes that run through the cookstove so you can get hot water. There's a map in there . . . follow it. Shows you where the trails are. They're all color-coded. Stay on the trails and you won't get lost." He stopped and faced her, "If we don't see your changed flag, we'll come looking for you, You're pretty safe here. We never lost anybody yet," he added with a grin.

It had never occurred to Katherine to worry about being

lost, so she marked the advice to avoid visitors. She made a mental directive never to forget the flags.

The pilot began fumbling with two more padlocks on the back door directly opposite the entry. Once open, Katherine could see it led to a covered carport, stacked higher than her head with split logs. She followed him out through the wooden tunnel to a metal shed, resembling a small barn. More padlocks.

Inside, the shed was lined with shelves of canned food and other supplies. Like magic, she noted the materializing of a rather exhaustive list of her estimated needs, sent at the request of her landlord. It was all here, neatly stockpiled. Her own grocery store. Attached to a clip, hanging on a nail, she recognized her own handwriting.

"Do you want to go over the inventory?" he asked.

Surveying the shelves of cans, toilet paper, and labeled five-gallon tins, she shook her head, "No, I trust it's all here."

He seemed relieved. "Well, if you find anything missing, you just let us know and we'll drop it next Friday. Keep the tins closed. Keeps out the mice and bugs." He snapped one of the tins, producing a metallic ring. "They're all labeled with the bulk food you asked for. It's easier for us to just fill these instead of dropping that stuff." She could see the contents listed on each one—wheat flour, powdered milk, cornmeal, powdered eggs, sugar, rice, salt.

"Shoot, I think the last people were here a month," he commented, scratching under his cap. And there were two of 'em. What you gonna do alone for a year?" Again, he didn't wait for an answer but lit a propane lamp mounted on the wall beside the door.

As the light poured over the shelves, a sense of security rode up her body as if she were wading into it. It appeared as if everything she could possibly ever need was here. Besides the goods she had ordered, the room was stuffed with assortments of everything imaginable, tucked into nooks and hanging from crannies.

There were axes, long- and short-handled, and a saw leaning against the lower shelf. Some other tools and hardware lay on the shelf next to them. She noticed fishing gear, batteries for dusty flashlights, cans and jars, rope, and a large metal box with a red cross painted on the top.

Altogether, the space resembled a combination general store and a grandfather's garage. It looked like a place in which she could rummage for hours, but the pilot was already outside, holding the door, her signal to move on.

Passing through the doorway, he thumped a large washtub with a washboard on the side, the kind she'd seen in antique shops, "Your washing machine, madam. Runs on elbow grease and biodegradable soap."

Figuring she had looked long enough, he extinguished the lights and dutifully locked the padlocks, top and bottom. Katherine obediently followed him back inside, where he unloaded some wood he'd grabbed on the way.

The pilot never really looked at her when he was talking but kept busy making every effort count. He seemed very sure of himself, perhaps a little ill at ease with her. She felt a certain condescension coming from him, as if he expected her to fail. Each instruction seemed prefaced with, "This is useless, but here goes." Katherine concluded that he was no more interested in conversation than she was.

"Almost forgot!" He pushed past her. Kicking aside a rag rug in front of the sink, he pulled up what appeared to be a small trapdoor. Katherine moved closer. "Your refrigerator. Actually it's a pretty good root cellar. Keeps stuff cool even on the hottest days. I oughta know. I grew up with one." He descended the ladder and disappeared into the dark cavern below.

"You can keep meat and vegetables for a few days anyway." His voice echoed up. Within seconds he lit the lamp, revealing a damp, cement-encased room about six feet square, with nothing but a ledge around the sides and a cricket in one corner. Katherine wondered how the cricket had gotten there.

"We'll drop some fresh stuff. Milk and meat, fruit. Stuff like that. You'll be surprised how long it'll keep down here, especially if you throw a bucket of water on the floor," he added. He hauled himself up from the hole and let the door fall with a bang that made Katherine jump.

"Well that's about the long and dumb of it," he said with a wave of his hand. He grabbed a handful of kindling and started a fire in the cookstove, giving instructions about the water pipes. "Just to make sure no critter's moved into your chimney." The kindling crackled and spit and the smoke rose just as it should.

"So, I'll be off. Everything else is in those cupboards—blankets, some pillows. There's some books on that top shelf, if you like to read. Don't know what they are. Somebody left 'em here. Like I said, all the directions are in there. You got a full tank of propane. All it runs is lights, so you should have plenty. You can do what you like with the Decon. There's more in the storage shed. Keep it locked. Animals. Actually," he added, trying to sound reassuring, "we don't have much trouble up here, except with raccoons. They'll steal you blind if they get a chance." Then he stopped.

For an awkward moment, neither of them spoke. "So, you got any questions? I can check back in a day or so . . . if not . . . I gotta take off. Sure you don't want to change your mind?"

"No, I'm sure. I'll be fine. If not . . . I just signal you with the flag, right?" They both shifted their weight and looked at the floor.

"Well, like I said, I gotta take off." Heading for the door, he turned to look at her. Planted in the middle of the room beside her boxes, she looked like an orphan. *What kind of a woman wants to spend a whole year alone in a mountain cabin?* he wondered.

In the past years, he'd flown numerous hunters and other wilderness enthusiasts into these mountain retreats owned by his boss. It was the nearest thing to a real pioneer experience for people who were into that sort of thing. But never one person for a year. A month maybe, but not a year!

Pouring through the east window, the shaft of light that canceled the dark lit her auburn hair at each unruly strand springing free of the tight bun at the nape of her neck. In rust suede boots and a tan corduroy skirt covered by a three-quarter-length green leather coat, the woman reminded him of someone.

Her fancy "uptown" clothes looked quite out of place here. *Still,* he thought, *if she ever let that warm brown hair loose of the uptight bun . . .* Katherine stared back with those big purple eyes, clutching her leather shoulder bag and looking helpless. But any momentary sense of masculine protectiveness withered when she lifted her face and set her jaw against him.

"Is there something else?" she asked in a cool voice. Her eyes leveled, uninviting.

"Guess I'll be going," the pilot responded, trying to sound at ease with just having been dismissed. "Sure you don't want me to start a fire for you?"

"Thank you, no. You've been a big help already. I'm sure I will be fine."

As he stepped out into the morning, he wanted very much to turn and lower his voice and say, "Lady, why do you want to do this?" But he didn't.

Katherine watched as he pulled the wagon in a wide circle in front of the cabin, then back on the return route along the perimeter of the clearing. Motionless, she waited in the doorway, shoving his retreat with her eyes.

When he disappeared in the trees, she shifted her weight. Leaning against the door sill, she listened. Nothing. Minutes passed.

Aware that she was barely breathing, Katherine stared at the spot where he had been swallowed up by the dark green. He was still out there, somewhere

What is he doing? What is taking so long? Her mind shouted, *Go!*

She strained harder to hear him. A slender band of fear began to squeeze her ribs. *What if he comes back? Something is wrong. It's taking too long!* The silence was loud. Katherine could hear nothing but the high wind moving the tops of the trees. Minutes passed.

Snap! Like an alarmed animal, she froze. Without a sound, eyes wide, Katherine moved to her right, feeling her way along the exterior of the cabin. With the stealth of a cat, she eased her body into the undergrowth at the end of the porch.

She waited. And stared. Between the limbs of the bushes, she had an unobstructed view of the clearing and the porch.

Her mind raced with strategies of what she would do if she saw him. No way would she let him corner her in that cabin. At least out here, she could get away.

Bang! Katherine's insides jumped so hard every part of her

hurt. Then she heard it again. The hollow bang of the plane's side panel.

When the motor began its sputtering, Katherine closed her eyes. She listened anxiously as the engine rattled along the river edge and gradually lifted above her in a wide circle west. As the sound slowly faded into the morning fog, her shoulders relaxed. Then everything was still.

She felt a little foolish, crawling from the bushes. Inwardly, she cursed her irrational fears. But she also prided herself on her ability to think fast. *After all,* she rationalized, *he could have been up to no good.*

Dusting off her clothes, she rounded the corner of the porch and climbed the front steps for the second time. She entered again, through the door she'd left open, and shut it soundly behind her, feeling its weight.

A giddy sensation scampered across her pelvic floor, the way it had when, as a child, she had watched her parents' car back out of the driveway—a feeling of freedom, when she claimed ownership of her own life. Then she would create all sorts of scenarios, as she had sipped juice from her mother's long stem crystal and carried on weighty, imaginary conversations with invited dignitaries. The charade would continue until they returned and she had to relinquish her life to them again.

Standing inside the empty cabin, Katherine had the strange sensation of watching herself. What was she supposed to do first? Look relaxed.

Katherine pulled open the door again. What do you do when no one is looking? There had always been someone watching. Or if not at that moment, there would be soon.

Chapter 3

"What were you doing? You were talking to yourself! I saw you. You were just walking along having a conversation with yourself, weren't you?" Katie twisted her hair and felt herself turn scarlet beneath her plaid cotton dress, all the way to her white anklet socks.

"Tell the truth," chimed her mother. *"I saw you."*

Katie stood mute, peering up at her mother from large round eyes. All the magic of her previous dramatic monologue sank into the mire of humiliation.

"Someone is going to think you're crazy if you keep talking to yourself!" Laughing, Janice turned away.

"So what!" Katherine started at the sound of her own voice. "So what if I talked to myself?" she whispered.

She crossed the room and sat gingerly in the wooden rocker that stood beside the bed. Suddenly she felt tired. She felt like crying.

Why had they always crashed in on her private world? Sometimes it seemed to amuse them. Sometimes what they found enraged them.

Always it was another nail in the lid of her inhibitions, creating in her a hunger to be free of the prying eyes. She skimmed the room. *No one is watching now, but me,* she thought. It began to sink in that she could do anything she liked, in whatever order, and there was not a soul around to correct her.

By the age of fourteen, Katie had "learned" to wash the glasses first, to always dust the baseboards before the floors, never to mix darks and lights in the wash, to set the table with the knife's cutting edge toward the plate, never to let a boy touch your breast lest he become a lusting animal, never to talk back, never to talk to yourself, never to talk long on the phone, never to tell other people the family business, never to ask for anything at the table without first saying "please," never to be caught just having fun or "doing nothing," never to be late, and never to be caught wearing lipstick.

"Katherine Henry! Don't ever let me catch you doing that again!" The tops of her hands stung where the ruler had landed with a crack. She stared at the teacher and fought tears.

"You know better than that! Take your seat, young lady, until you are prepared to do your problems at the board correctly." The children snickered as she threaded her way to the second to the last seat in the third row.

I'll never do it again, she pleaded in hollow thoughts. I'll never do it again, I promise. She was holding her pencil so tight in her fist that the point pushed into the fleshy part of her thumb. She wondered if she would die of lead poisoning.

Later, she had linked that little piece of trauma with her hopeless bungling of anything having to do with mathematics. From grade school to high school, she had managed to barely squeak through the required courses, even despite massive amounts of time and effort. Her grades did not reflect any real comprehension on her part. Katherine always suspected that the teachers were given to gracious concession that she was quiet and polite.

As for her promise never to do it again, it was with all good intention. But, to this day, Katherine had not the slightest idea what she had done to incur such wrath from the teacher.

Ironically, it had been the impetus that originally sent her into group therapy, for math phobia, in college. And fascination with the therapy process had snagged her ambitions, sending her down the long road of medical school and residency that had resulted in the mounted bronze plaque that hung in her office of psychiatry high above the streets of Chicago. Probably, like most in her profession, she went looking for the answers to her own problems and ended up staying for the duration.

Katherine rubbed her middle finger over the grayish blue spot of graphite still visible beneath the skin. A dry squeaking noise came from somewhere in the distance. Katherine rocked, hugging herself. With each gentle motion, the chair squeaked again. For a long while she just rocked, cautiously, inhaling the tranquility.

The interior began to assume a soft peacefulness. Silver flecks of dust danced in the shafts of sunlight. Pulling her foot from its boot, she stuck a toe into the beam of light. It was warm.

Katherine slid from the chair to the floor to immerse herself in the warmth. The golden light flooded down from the top of her head, across her shoulders, and down her back. She could feel the gentle glow radiating through her coat, penetrating the invisible shield that encased her.

Sadness lined the edges of her heart—a sadness too heavy to rise to a lump in her throat. Too solid to squeeze out through tear ducts.

Katherine sat on the floor, hugging her knees, and continued to rock. She could hear soft humming.

"What's the matter, honey?" Grandma held up the covers for her to slide into the warm bed. Grandma always made her feel safe. She would pray and hum. She would hug her and speak gentle reassurances.

Always she welcomed her when Katie stood tearful beside her bed, "I can't sleep, Grandma," and she never pressed her about why. Sometimes she would ask if she'd talked to Jesus about it. Katie always said she had. But really she just wanted the comfort of her grandmother's warm reality.

Still hugging her knees and rocking, Katherine realized it was she who was humming.

Deliberately, she began to survey the cabin a second time. It seemed more open to her scrutiny this time, like a hesitant friend. Instinctively, she knew that she would never again see it like this. The room still maintained its own identity, separate from what she would make it.

Katherine looked across the ribbons of morning, angling from the windows like curtains waving in a windstorm. The cabin was recovering from the clamor of the pilot with his intrusive noise and unsettling swipes. Quietly, confidently, each particle of dust settled into its nest again. Katherine liked the sense of permanence in this place. She knew she would rearrange the room and scrub its contents, but would never really change it. Some things never change.

She tried to record the room with a series of mental snapshots, knowing it would not be long before her quaint abode would lapse into a familiar "taken for granted" space. Then she wouldn't see it anymore. Funny how sometimes the most invisible hiding places were those in plain sight. Certainly the day would come when she would want to pull this memory from the file drawers of her mind.

Great Scott! I'm already thinking about leaving, she thought. *Why is it so hard to just be here now? Why must I always fall backward into the past or race ahead to some imagined future? I have a whole year. I want this year! I don't want to remember it. I want to live it!"* She could hear Adam admonishing her to work on staying present—to focus on what she felt in the now.

Maybe memories are a way of holding life's events out, turning them carefully with our fingers so the rough edges don't cut. To live it means to risk the pain. And the joy. To become it instead of remembering it. Katherine considered the possibility. Perhaps here, in this place left out of time, she could finally open the vault of previous moments, saved, not consumed, and eat of them, the bitter and the sweet, that she might be whole. At last she would have the time to sort the meanings and assemble herself, instead of always postponing her needs for those of others.

Her deep-seated feelings of unworthiness had always been the excuse for her to tend to the needs of others at the expense of herself. And, although she knew better, she could misconstrue Christian teaching to see purity in her motives for self-sacrifice rather than the pride it probably was. Consequently, Katherine had lived on the edge of exhaustion, constantly depleted, and had thought of it as a virtue, maybe even a Christian virtue.

But any hope of labeling her denial as a virtue had come to an abrupt halt when John died. Suddenly, she cared nothing for the plight of others. Try as she might, she could not resurrect an ounce of compassion. For the first time, the hungry faces etched in the suffering that lined her waiting room stirred nothing in her save weariness and disgust.

Worse than the lack of empathy was the accompanying guilt. She tormented herself with accusing questions, imagining the same writ large in the minds of others: Where is your victory? The victory she had preached to others? How could she lead others on a path she could not find for herself? Her prayers became a steady litany of "Father forgive me," which bounced off the ceiling until at last she was silent.

In the end, Katherine packed without knowing whether it was grief or shame that compelled her.

Chapter 4

Standing in the center of her new life, the present leaned against her from all sides. Inside, too, there was the present moment, begging for attention.

It was time to try out the wonderful compost toilet. It was built into the wall like a closet and looked for all the world like an outhouse with a modern porcelain fixture. Strange, though, there was no noise. "How will I know if it works?" Katherine got up and peered down into the dark hole. Flushless, odorless, a compost-maker. "I hope it works."

Katherine wondered what time it was and then wondered what difference it would make. She considered digging out her windup clock to set it by her watch. Then, she decided against it.

She looked around the room again, at the boxes in the middle, waiting to be unpacked.

She could start a fire. She could rearrange the furniture. She could make the bed or fix something to eat. She could go for a walk. Or maybe just sit on the porch until dark. She could laugh or cry or talk to herself out loud.

Perhaps she had always attended to what she should do in order to avoid deciding what she wanted to do. Now Katherine found it disconcerting to sift the possibilities for the satisfying choice.

Finally, she decided to eat. That meant she would have to build a fire, stoking up the woodstove from the embers left by the pilot. Also she would have to make a trip to the storage shed to retrieve whatever supplies she wanted in the cabin. So she decided to look at the books instead.

Standing on tiptoe, the dusty volumes were barely reachable on the top shelf of an open, otherwise empty bookcase. The meager library consisted of: *The Nature and Scope of Social Science, A Critical Anthology,* published in 1969; *The Universal Classic Library of Oriental Literature;* a child's book, *All About the Weather; The Politics of Aristotle,* by Baker; *A Manual of Home Repairs; The Psychedelic Experience, A Manual Based on the Tibetan Book of the Dead;* for light reading, *A Reader's Digest of Condensed Books,* Vol.2, 1979; George Orwell's *Animal Farm;* and *135 Group Interaction Ideas,* by Earl P. McQuay.

"Well, Earl, you just never know where your work will end up," she addressed him aloud. "What a library! Oh, well, I've never been real fond of libraries anyway. They make me want to laugh or do some other inappropriate thing when the prune-faced librarian isn't looking. Libraries have a kind of artificial quiet that makes my skin itch."

Blowing off the dust, she carefully lined up the books on the middle shelf, eye level. Then she sat down in the rocker to look at them. She got up again and rearranged the order to better suit her sense of aesthetics. There. Her first mark at making this home. And, as always, one change led to another.

Katherine did indeed build a fire, after splintering off some kindling and wrenching the flue handle till she could see light at the top of the chimney, then having to go back to the shed for matches, not finding any in the cabin. At last, the flames crackled and sparked and filled the space with warmth and friendly sound.

On the next trip to the shed, the inviting fragrance of burning wood penetrated the dampness. A soft curl of smoke rose like incense, offering thanks. For the first time in months, maybe years, Katherine felt the mellow stirrings of gratitude. She stood very still between the cabin and the shed and watched the offering rise. And listened.

Nothing came but the faint clicking of life against life, the gestating of new birth deep within the earth's womb, under the melting snow. Turning the key in the lock on the shed door brought an assault of metal on metal. She resented it and vowed to find another means of security.

With some Spic and Span and a bucket of rags from the shed, she set to work scrubbing dust and soot, spiderwebs and old grease. Everything yielded except the grease. It would take hot water. She decided to save that production for another day.

As the fire consumed one log after another and the hours passed, Katherine claimed every inch of the cabin—shelves, mantel, shutters. She changed the water repeatedly, throwing the murky remains of previous tenants out the front door.

What she could not reach with the rag, she attacked with the broom. It was a wrestling match to get the braided rug out the front door and up over the porch railing. On hands and knees she crawled over the entire floor, scrubbing and moving furniture as she went. Vinegar and some old newspapers made the windows transparent again.

She found sheets, towels, blankets, several old quilts with frayed edges and a hand-crocheted doily in the drawers beneath the wardrobe. They were packed in black plastic garbage bags and smelled faintly of mothballs.

She hung them to air over a line she had discovered stretched between the cabin and a tree out back. Then she carried the drawers outside to empty the rat poison, and scrubbed them clean.

Waiting for the floor to dry, Katherine sat on the porch with a tin cup of water. It was icy cold, sweet and deeply satisfying. *Like a deer panteth for water, so my soul hungers for thee,* wandered through her mind.

Jesus had once told a woman by a well that He would give her living water and her soul would be satisfied forever. *What would it be like to be satisfied forever?* she wondered.

With that thought lingering in her mind, she attacked the braided rug with a broken broom handle, till the dust ceased to fly. Once she was assured that it was clean, she fought with it again till it was settled in a spot in front of the fireplace, off center, much more to her liking.

She moved the old sofa to the middle of the room, facing the fire. A careful search yielded two logs of equal proportion which served well as legs to lift the sofa to its appropriate height. Katherine soon discovered why chair legs were square. Several "log legs" became kindling before her pitiful carpentry skills managed to hone out two reasonably similar in size.

The faded blue and white quilt, retrieved from the clothesline, smelling of fresh air, all but eliminated the gaudy yellow plaid. As she straightened and tucked it around the pillows, she could not help noticing the tiny white stitches so precisely placed by some unknown hand. Gingerly, with her fingertips, she traced the delicate design stitched through the layers of batten, matted flat with the weight of years.

She imagined the old hands, like her grandmother's, tanned from gardening, callused and unmanicured, that must have fingered it so many years before—passing the needle back and forth, pricking the cloth, setting each regimented stitch in the exquisite pattern.

Katherine wondered about the invisible hand that orchestrated her life. She had always believed there was one, a fact one might have taken for granted, growing up in Grandma Henry's house, where His presence was in abundance.

Katherine followed the tiny stitches across the cloth and wondered how many strokes of the sharp steel had passed back and forth through her life. And did it compose such a lovely design, after all, or just random puckers between dry punctures?

Grandma Henry had been a cornerstone of her faith. She was the godly woman who had rescued Katie from the uncertainties of life and who had provided what comfort was afforded along the way. Suddenly Katherine wondered if she believed in God, or if she really just believed in her grandmother! That thought caused a sick feeling in the pit of her stomach. Never had she entertained the possibility that her atheist colleagues might be right. Katherine lowered her eyes, ashamed at the new low to which she had slidden.

Uncle Sel, her mother's brother, the other person who loomed large in her life, did not believe in God. In her little girl's mind, she could never picture him "fearing God." His near six feet of stooped height carried about an impending figure—a man who surveyed the world from the intensity of his steel-gray eyes, recessed beneath heavy brows, a man whose judgments were not to be questioned.

According to the family story, he once had believed but had left the church when the pastor was caught in an indiscretion. It was reported that Uncle Sel would not tolerate that kind of hypocrisy and left, taking his money with him.

As a young child, Katie always liked that story. It gave her a hero and a laudable reason for why people didn't like Uncle Sel. It also made her understand why everything that took place at Vida Baptist Church was puny. She, like everyone else,

had grown to believe that whatever Selinus Hileman blessed prospered; and what he didn't, didn't.

As for her mother and father, they were sporadic church-goers, making their appearance at those times when it was what good citizens did, like voting and keeping their grass cut. The "practical" realities and routines of life necessitated that they be "realistic" about their commitments. Still, they taught her that Jesus was a wonderful man, a sort of Abraham Lincoln, who should be remembered. And if everyone did what Jesus said, the world would be a better place. However, to raise His name at the table in any personal way was tantamount to open-ing the topic of sex—it was a private matter.

All her life, she'd heard such under-breath statements as, "They're good Catholics," which meant they had a lot of kids; "He's an elder in their church, you know," or "They're very active in the church," which meant they were good people; or "They're in church every time the doors are open," which meant they were a bit fanatical, a definition also ascribed to the "Tithers." It was as if they were describing personality types, as if this single piece of information revealed everything one needed to know.

The other sizing-up came in the form of "He's a Democrat, you know!" Katie could tell from the way they pronounced "Democrat" that it was something undesirable, the same way they might have said, "He has lice, you know!"

She never forgot those lessons. Years later, she noticed that candidates aspiring to hold political office always had their church affiliation proudly displayed on the back of the brochure, just above the disclaimer. "Yep, a good citizen!" she would register. It was not until she was well into adulthood that Kath-erine discovered all who warmed the church pews did not know the Lord as her Grandma Henry did. In fact, she feared that her parents might be among those lacking.

Deliberately, Katherine stood up and smoothed the sofa back. She had to this point avoided the bed. With set jaw, she laid hold of the antique rope bed, pushing and shoving it around the corner of the room. She muttered when it slammed to a halt, stuck in a crack in the uneven floorboards, leaving bruises in the skin across her pelvic bones. Katherine was irritated

with this setback, then disturbed by the intensity of the anger that welled up within her.

Exerting an effort to breathe out, she lifted the bed to free the leg and began again. Nothing suited her. She could not find any position in which she could imagine sleeping. Something was wrong with every spot. Back and forth, the bed groaned as it bumped across the irregular floorboards.

Wait a minute, she thought. *Why is this such a problem?* Standing at the foot of the bed, facing the room, the answer occurred to her. *Sleeping has always been a problem for me, so no wonder I can't figure out what to do with the bed!*

She sat down on the bed again, and a startling realization came to her. *I can't sleep here! I can't see both doors! I've got to face the doors.*

She pushed the headboard into the corner where she could watch both doors at once and searched her memory to see if her other bedrooms had been so arranged. They had. On hands and knees, she carefully dusted all the spooling and connecting ropes and tried not to imagine who might have slept here before her. For some reason, she felt squeamish thinking about it.

The rolled mattress was cautiously extracted from its plastic bag after dragging it out back, for fear it might contain some unwelcome critter. There was none. Just the same faint odor of mothballs.

The mattress seemed to be in good shape, despite what it lacked in firmness. Its striped ticking was so clean Katherine guessed it might even be new. She preferred to think so.

When it was again settled atop the rope supports, the mattress sagged severely in the center. Katherine eased herself onto it, expecting it to let her down with a crash. In fact, this bed held her quite securely. Katherine remained squarely in the center, her arms and legs held snug to her body, a far cry from the wide expanse of her king-sized bed at home. *But,* she thought, struggling to get up, *one does not easily fall out of this bed!* Katherine studied the bed with its mattress clinging to the sides and sagging in the middle. *It will be like sleeping in a cocoon.*

She shook out the sheets over it and tried to make it look flat, finishing it with the more colorful log cabin quilt. Sliding one of the small wooden tables next to it, she placed the

crocheted piece in the center. The little corner which was to be her bedroom looked comfortable enough. She quickly pushed away fears of sleeping there. There was always the yellow plaid sofa.

Still, from the bed she would be able to see the stars through the window at night, she decided. Sleep was a great challenge for Katherine and had been for as long as she could remember. Somehow, watching the stars made the time pass. Slow as it was, at least she could trace some progress through the long nights.

The dishes were an odd collection of tin plates and old discolored ironstone. There were some pottery bowls, four blue canning jars with lids, the old zinc ones with the porcelain insets, and an assortment of mismatched silverware. She washed and dried them all.

One piece, a grape-patterned sugar spoon, was real sterling. It was worth a special trip to the shed for some baking soda for polish.

Scouring the blackened cast aluminum pans proved most difficult, finally requiring her to build a fire in the woodstove.

Rehearsing what the pilot had told her and following the directions in the "everything-you-need-to-know manual," she managed to wrestle forth some real hot water from the copper pipes that passed through the fire, along with the curled corpses of flushed-out spiders.

This turned out to be such a dirty job that she put the pans in a washtub outside and poured boiling water over them to loosen the grease. Somehow, claiming these utensils had become of utmost importance.

Katherine thought of the hours of therapy—searching the fragments of memory, piecing together the pain, owning the incest—and scrubbed the pans harder. Adam had been her friend, and, every Wednesday for as long as she could remember, her therapist. Katherine did not know for sure which had come first—the friendship or the therapeutic relationship.

In any case, in the end they had managed to jigsaw together a picture of her past that filled in most of the gaps and provided some necessary explanations. But somehow it hadn't been enough. It was as if her life had remained a flat, two-dimensional thing.

Frequently, Adam pointed out that she lived at a breakneck pace, pouring her energy into her clients, transfusing their lives with the very essence of herself. He accused her of never taking the time to incorporate or investigate their marvelous, hard-won insights. And he was probably right. She gave away more than she took in—a costly imbalance.

When John got sick, she worked even harder, ran faster. All the while playing in the back of her mind was a siren song, luring her to come aside, to stop, a longing for a quiet time and space to sit down with the meaning.

The old pan began to shine beneath the steel wool. Whole patches of warm silver flesh appeared as years of accumulated grime were removed. The aged black grease did not easily let go. Katherine's fingers ached from the pressure. It was the last of her professional manicure.

She was more careful with the black iron skillets, not wanting to remove the seasoning which made the cookware superior to anything in her own modern kitchen.

Back to the shed again, she retrieved three kerosene lanterns with the necessary fluid. After cleaning them up, she carted them into the house and spent some minutes rearranging them until selecting their final resting place—one on the mantel, one on the table next to her bed, one hanging from the beam between the cookstove and the counter. The propane wall fixtures would wait for another day.

Each time she encountered another spider scrambling to escape her frenzied cleaning, it pleased her to think, *I live here now.*

As the last light fell across the trees, she was done. Katherine stood by the sink and inspected the results of her labor. It pleased her. The little kitchen table stood in front of the east window, with the two chairs at either end. She walked over and moved the far chair to the other side of the room.

The meager environs had an innocent aura, like she had always imagined a monastery to be. Katherine repositioned the single polished sugar spoon she had left on the table. It added a note of elegance.

Flickering firelight danced upon the amber log walls and made the fir floor glow with the same rich reddish brown that carpeted the forest. Now it was clean of all ghosts of the past and previous tenants. If only a soul could be so washed.

Reaching up to light the kerosene lamp above her, Katherine felt every muscle complaining. A weariness far deeper than the exertion of the day welled up from something fathomless within her. The tin cup of water hours ago had been her only act of kindness toward herself.

She was tired and hungry, but she could not shake the urge to push herself further, to complete the task of unpacking and bringing in tomorrow's supplies from the storehouse out back.

She'd always had a difficult time knowing when to stop. John used to ride her about it, saying it was her compulsivity.

She sat down on the sofa and stared at the fire. How she wished John would bring her a plate of food, some offering he'd prepared while she was caught up in her own world, to help her return to this one. John had been an anchor that kept her from floating away.

Katherine rose and began closing the shutters. It was then that she noticed how dirty she was. Grime clung to the space under her fingernails, and her knees were black and sore. The hair at the nape of her neck was damp and the stray strands were stuck with dust and spiderwebs.

Somewhere in the process of cleaning the cabin, she had shed her boots and coat; the corduroy skirt looked like it should be burned. She wondered how much soot and dust must cover her face.

That moment brought a startling realization. In this entire cabin there was not even the smallest mirror. She was dumbfounded as she turned in place, scanning the walls. The thought of not being able to see herself for a year, except in the one-inch diameter attached to an eyeshadow compact in her purse, was unimaginable.

As she slumped to the sofa again, she thought numbly about putting another log on the fire. But she was too exhausted to move. She closed her eyes, reminding herself that she had not turned out the lamp. Then her aching body slid into the oblivion of sleep, and she did not hear the diving whistle of the nighthawk or the mournful coyotes. She did not stir when the soft rain fell upon the spongy world around her. No murky figures warred in her mind and no city noise unnerved her peace. Katherine slept.

Chapter 5

Daylight spilled across the eastern slopes and filled the crevasses with morning, as it had for millennia. That amazing conversion from dark to light had once again transpired. It was the signal for life to begin or end. A signal without a sound.

Katherine awoke with a start. Her eyes flew open, but her body lay still, crumpled on the sofa where she had fallen sideways in her exhaustion the evening before. Only a charred log remained of the warmth of the hearth. A brilliant daybreak pushed against the closed shutters, pressing sparkling threads of light through the cracks. Overhead, the lamp still burned. Both doors stood agape with a cool breeze sighing between them.

She tried to sit up. Hot fingers of pain dug into her neck and shoulder. It felt as if her whole body had petrified in this position. Everything hurt. Her throat was dry, and it was painful to swallow, her mouth welded shut.

In a series of jerky motions, she carefully unfolded herself and stood. Wincing at the needles in her feet, she hobbled to the cookstove. It was cold. The water was cold, too, but wet.

With the grace of an arthritic old woman, Katherine managed to start a fire, and in a few minutes, warm water poured from the spout into the sink, held fast by the rag stuffed in the drain. The warm water soothed her aching fingers. She submerged her arms up to the elbows and leaned forward to let the warmth pull the soreness from her body. With aching hands, she washed her face and watched the gray drops drip from her elbows to the white porcelain edge.

Pulling the large hairpins from her hair, she rewound the

knot and secured it, drying her hands on her hair in smoothing motions from front to back. She tried to imagine washing her hair in this sink . . . and failed.

At that moment, she missed her Michigan Avenue apartment. Well, not actually the apartment, just the Jacuzzi with the hot water at the turn of the faucet. It would have been heavenly to sink into it about now.

Amazing, this was the first time in all the past sixteen years that Katherine had ever thought of anything associated with Chicago as heavenly. Generally, she detested the city and considered it a special act of martyrdom that she had lived and worked there. Never before this moment had she acknowledged a single good thing about the place. It had been a source of pain and disgust since her earliest encounters during her med school days in the sixties.

In 1968 she had been in Chicago when the infamous Democratic National Convention took place. For months previous, Katherine had walked to and from classes, past the long tables of protestors with their urgent petitions, books clutched to her chest, facing straight ahead as if she wore blinders, the kind city horses wear to shut out any distractions lest they become frightened. She was a-political then, fearful of telling the anti-war protestors that her father was in Vietnam. Not only was he there, he was a self-admitted part of the military industrial complex they so adamantly detested.

In the years since, Katherine had been over and over the terrors of that week. The rioting, the tension, had produced in her a reaction which still made her shudder. It had begun as a nightmare in the August heat, from which there was no dawn breaking. As the world outside went mad, with two armed camps squared off across Grant Park and the military in the streets, something came loose inside her.

Katherine truly thought she was losing her mind. Images of blackness swirled around her; grotesque, dark forms, pulsing triangles erupting out of everything that had, at an earlier time, been a source of pleasure or enjoyment. Trees became frightening figures, looming and threatening. People were monster-like, disfigured. She was terrified to be alone, fearful of going to sleep but hating every waking hour. Somehow she managed to stumble through those agonizing months in robotic fashion.

Her friend Adam had "been there" for her, but she had had no confidence in him then. It seemed that the misery just gradually wore off over the next two years. But the fear never did.

It was terrifying and disillusioning. But since that time, something worse stalked the halls of her imagination. Or was it her memory? That week in Chicago haunted her. When she tried to think about it, she got lost in it. True, she was generally uneasy with the city, the crowds, the dirt, the noise, probably because all her good memories came from the serene flatlands of Iowa—that abundant green breadbasket that stretched its arms across the Midwest. Living there during that violent week had set off an alarm that continued to sound.

Her friends and colleagues volunteered all kinds of reasonable justification, but nothing which placated her fears. Out of Chicago she had bought passage on a train of self-destruction. It was a time when the foundation beneath her seemed to unravel until, at the end of it, she was not only afraid but afraid to be afraid. Somehow the war in the streets moved inside her. She stopped going to church, her prayer life dwindled to a meager mealtime ritual, and her letters to Grandma Henry became sparse in number and content, justified in her mind by her overwhelming studies.

In order to avoid the dark fears, Katherine kept to a rigid and exhausting routine. Gradually her sparkling eyes retreated into dark hollow sockets, betraying an alarming lack of sleep. Living on Gyroes and doughnuts left her complexion like pale parchment stretched over bones.

It was in the midst of this that she met the solid professor of religion in an all-night Greek restaurant, her retreat from the shadows of the apartment, where the coffee was as burnt as the stains on the orange carpet. Katherine did not actually remember their first encounter, a fact John never let her forget. But somewhere during these chance meetings, which may have been anything but chance, he offered to buy her a salad. When she refused without looking up from her book, he offered to buy her a vitamin. So began their relationship.

It was a whirlwind courtship that resulted two months later in an intimate ceremony, witnessed by a few close friends. By the third month Katherine was with child. All under the cloud of the political upheaval that had stirred turmoil in her soul, a turmoil that seemed to retreat under the loving command of her new husband.

Still, Katherine could never quite shake the memory of those nights when she had lived on the raw edge of fear. What had been triggered in Chicago? What lay buried in her subconscious, just beyond her reach? She had turned it over a hundred times in her mind, searching endlessly. Searching for what?

Perhaps that's why she had taken the clinic job in that wretched city. What was there about Chicago in '68 that she could not shake? Why had it frightened her so? Why did she lie awake at night, listening? Why did she stare at the doorway? What dark form did she expect?

"Kate, give it a rest!" She could hear Adam's exasperation. "Some things you're not going to understand. Just let it go!"

Adam was a good friend and an able colleague. She had never doubted that he genuinely cared for her and John. He was not just trying to dismiss her. Rather, he hated to see her torment herself. Other than John, he was the one person who had seen the most.

"But it's not supposed to be like this, Adam. I'm a psychotherapist! It says 'Doctor' on my door. If this physician cannot heal herself, then who can?"

"Look, Kate, you're a good shrink. Nobody's perfect. Want me to go through your files? I know what you've done for those people. Where do you want me to start? With the A's?" Adam was pulling open file drawers, "Let's see. Pick a name. Any name."

Kate slammed the drawer shut, barely missing his fingers. "Adam, I don't want to be perfect. I just want to be well!"

"Define well."

"It's what I'm not!"

They had gone around this bush too many times to count. Katherine could absolutely rage when Adam started the academic game of "define this and define that." Only once had they really come to blows. That was when Adam had answered her in absolute frustration, "Kate, where's your faith?"

Katherine had not given him a chance to finish. Instead, she had shouted, "That's not fair! You, of all people, have no right to raise that issue!" And, for several months, their friendship had chilled—the same months that she had plunged into the crevasse of terror.

The wonderful thing about Adam was the fact that he had come to the wedding as if nothing had happened, his presence that day, tacit confirmation that all was well between the three of them. They never discussed it again. And since that time their friendship had remained intact, aided by Adam's marvelous capacity to never "take it personally."

Or perhaps Dr. Adam Sylvan was actually one of those "healthy" individuals, after all—the kind whose very existence Katherine had doubted.

Katherine stared into the sink, watching the dirty gray streaks drip down the sides, swirling into the water at the bottom. Instinctively, she darted a glance behind her, as if to reassure herself that no one had caught her daydreaming. The water had become cool. She pulled out the rag and watched the murky liquid go down the drain, remembering it only went as far as the bucket under the sink, which must be carried out. Somehow that seemed a just penance.

The last substantial meal Katherine had eaten was the one she'd relished alone at Sylvia's in Portland, a lasagna fit for a last meal. Now pangs of hunger squeezed her insides. That was the night before last. Yesterday she had buried herself in arrival and then in the frenzy of digging in.

It seemed ridiculous to have been in such a hurry. Now, turning to survey the cabin, she felt ashamed at the shabby way she had treated herself. A little light-headed and still thirsty, she headed for the storage shed.

The morning was clear and cloudless. The air had a clean feel, devoid of the soft humidity that invaded the midwestern June. She could see her breath. The surviving patches of snow had turned to a transparent slush from last night's rain. As she turned the corner of the woodpile, something darted under a log.

Once at the shed door, it dawned on her that she'd forgotten the key. Katherine returned to the cabin, muttering about locks and keys. Was it not possible ever to be free of them? Must the whole world be locked?

In Chicago, there was the constant fear of theft. One had always to be on guard against the loss of precious stuff, material or personal. Now, even here, she must lock up, or the raccoons and whatever other marauders were about would steal her blind of the only possession of any consequence in this place—food!

At least food is worth the effort, she thought. Food meant survival. There was nothing in her apartment she could not do without. While theft of possessions would pose expensive losses and considerable inconvenience, these were nothing compared to the contents of this shed.

Katherine fumbled with the padlocks, top and bottom. Finally the door swung wide. Carefully she began the decisions as to which items to stock in the kitchen. Her increased hunger made her put the armload down in the middle of the floor to choose, instead, some canned juice, biscuit mix, beef stew, and coffee beans.

She was dying for a cup of coffee. Back inside, the stove was hot in minutes, water boiling for the coffee. Now where was the grinder? There was no grinder!

First, she placed a few beans in the bottom of the cup and poured the water over them. Nothing even remotely resembling coffee resulted.

She dumped the contents of the canned beef stew in the skillet and plopped some of the biscuit mix on top and set it, covered, on what seemed to be an appropriate spot on the stove. Settling for the apple juice, Katherine sat down at the table to think how she could make coffee. The juice helped.

That simple breakfast tasted like a loving meal. She could feel her body grabbing the nourishment. She ate slowly and deliberately, sensing that it might have been the first meal she had really enjoyed in a long time. Maybe since John died.

Katherine set her fork down and stared out the window. A wave of loneliness hit her and then another as she pushed away from the table.

John had so enjoyed food. And he was a good cook. When she was buried in work, he would bring her offerings—delicious morsels to remind her to "have a life."

The lump in her throat ached and her heart was so heavy

she felt it breaking. Katherine threw the big leather suitcase on the bed. There, at the bottom, her fingers closed on the familiar wool tweed. She laid it carefully beside the suitcase while she dressed in clean clothes.

Then quietly, she slid her arms into the jacket. Letting it wrap around her, she closed her eyes and caressed her arms, trying to remember how it had been to touch John, when his warmth and strength were inside that fabric. Pools of loneliness blurred her vision as she headed for the door and stepped outside.

"I don't think I can do this, John," she spoke softly as if he were standing next to her. There was no answer. Katherine looked left and right and across the meadow. A gentle breeze moved the puffs of white against the blue sky. She could hear the constant liquid of the river that sounded like distant applause, as the high rift of a bird's song drifted across the quiet.

Katherine put her hands in the pockets and walked toward the river.

Chapter 6

"When I was a little girl, I lived in Vida, Iowa,"

Katherine wrote. She had begun journaling, which seemed somehow preferable to talking to herself. Time spent absorbing the stories of needy strangers, albeit the handsome price they paid for her ear, left her too exhausted to tell her own. Now she would listen to herself.

"Vida was a four-way stop in the middle of nowhere. The cornfields had sacrificed just enough acreage for about twenty families, two gas stations, Smith's Insurance Agency, and the Grange Hall, where they held ag extension meetings, Catholic wedding receptions, and Bingo. The white frame Baptist church with its bell steeple stood watch over the fenced cemetery with the sign on the gate that read *Vida Cemetery* in case anyone wondered. Jewel Gancy's Grocery Store, with the beauty parlor in back, marked the corner of the crossroads.

"It was not the charming farm community pictured on the Farm Bureau calendars. If there was anything charming in Vida, it had been 'remuddled' before I ever saw it.

"Vida had been on a downhill slide since before I was born. The last time I passed through, all that remained were a few peeling buildings and some skinny cats.

"Vida's last attempt at a comeback consisted of a tavern with a house of ill-repute in back to attract the city folk. It never became a bedroom community . . . it was left to the jackals.

"Nonetheless, it was the home that received the baby Janice pushed out one hot September day while Preston was away fighting the war. For the first four years of my life, Vida, Iowa, might as well have been the entire universe."

Katherine shifted positions on the step before continuing.

"I remember Uncle Sel giving me a nickel to pull a bottle of Nehi pop from one of those antique pop machines . . . the kind with the water in . . . you slid the bottle along a row to the spot where you could lift it up and out. I guess that's why bottles are shaped the way they are . . . so the neck sticks up through the bars, but the wider bottom keeps you from pulling it out at the wrong place."

Pen and journal in hand, Katherine left the porch and followed the trail of yellow tags along the river, while the morning turned from pink to silver. The marked trails were indeed as easy to follow as the pilot had told her.

The trail passed close to the river, which filled the air with sound, a soothing sound, not the cacophonous sounds of the city. She was grateful for the presence of the river with its constant voice and steady life. It seemed to have an eternal quality, an indestructible nature that was comforting and reassuring.

Katherine came to her favorite spot, where she settled in the sun on a jutting rock that overlooked the westward flow. In the warmth of the sun and John's jacket, she opened the journal again.

"It really wasn't much of a security system though. You just dropped the money in a box. Then you were entitled to get your pop. Kind of an honor system. I don't think it ever occurred to us to take more than one or to steal anything, for that matter.

"To me and my country cousins, stealing was the gravest of sins—the kind that caused judgment to fall out of heaven and gave authorities the right to chop off the fingers of little children. Also, I was certain it would take more courage than I possessed.

"I can still see that dented old red cooler with *Coca Cola* scrawled on the side in big white letters. It stood in the corner of the shop, wedged up against the walls.

"The men would congregate around it. Talk. Drink pop. Tell their lies and make each other laugh. And they thought it was really fun to scare kids. I remember they'd say things to me like, 'You want me to take you home with me?', or 'One of these days when nobody's lookin, I'll jus' snatch you up!'

"It always amazes me the ludicrous things old men say to children."

Katherine thought about the children she had seen bury their faces in the grocery line at the suggestions which, she supposed, were intended to convey some tenderness and good will, but which she knew children took literally. "I don't have no cute little girl at my house. You 'spose your mama would be willin' to trade you for some of them raspberries I got there?"

"There was one guy who really scared me, though. Casey Putney. During that time, amidst its ordinary citizens, Vida boasted a family of idiots, as they were called. Or sometimes my mother referred to them as 'mongoloid idiots,' or worse, 'pinheads.'"

Katherine shuddered, *Horrible term!*

"But whatever they were called, Casey was one. He was the eldest of nine, the only son, and a grown man at the time—probably the *ugliest* man I'd ever seen. His pointed head was thrust forward, and his little round eyes were set too close together under heavy, cave-man brows, exactly like the pictures of a Neanderthal man I later saw in school. Huge, fuzzy hands dangled limp from his shoulders as he lumbered, like a bear in overalls.

"They told me he was retarded. I had no idea what that meant. I was told it was the result of a terrible sickness his parents had—syphilis was the word they whispered—and it had caused three of their nine children to be 'different.'

"The other two, twin girls, were about my age. No one saw them very often, but they did come to Sunday school at the little Baptist church.

"I never liked going to Sunday school there. Although it was cool in the basement on hot summer days, it was also damp and uninviting, and I was always worried about being seated next to one of the twins."

Katherine leaned back, thinking about the church basement, then wrote:

"The only other occasion to be down there was for funeral dinners served up by pasty ladies with bulging middles and short frizzy hair they achieved at Gladys's Beauty Parlor. Those dinners always contained some exotic Jell-O dish the women raved about.

"I was a tagalong, rarely speaking at funerals, since the day I was sharply shushed for asking which side had the liver cancer, when viewing the dead body upstairs in the church!"

Katherine scribbled an exclamation point in the margin, noting the obvious incongruity of having been punished for being insensitive. How often the curiosities of a child are misinterpreted.

She turned the page and continued.

"I remember that all the Bible pictures were pasted up high so we couldn't touch them. Of course, we couldn't see them either.

"I never felt like I belonged. I was just relieved when it was time to go home. Then I would walk or run to keep up with Aunt Elsie, who had a stride longer than most men.

"Aunt Elsie was a simple Swedish woman who clumped through life like a peasant. She was hard-working and slightly homely, with large bones and ragged fingernails. She couldn't read much English, snorted when she laughed out loud, and baked the best raspberry cakes in four counties. What she lacked in sensitivity, she made up in goodwill.

"I never heard my uncle call her by name. He just barked orders at her in a sour tone. As a child, I felt sorry for her and thought it a wonder that she never complained. Even more remarkable was her willingness to allow me to make cakes from my imagination with real ingredients. Some of them weren't half bad."

Katherine could see her tall, homely aunt yet, apparently unfazed by her husband's brutish behavior. Later, Kate surmised that her cheerful demeanor was something else.

"Anyway, when the two retarded sisters came, everyone tried to be nice and not notice how they smelled. It was hard.

"Sometime—I can't remember when—we heard that one of them was pregnant, and no one knew who the father was. She was unable to talk, so they never found out.

"I remember hearing them talk about what a disgrace it was and that she should be sterilized. Through the years, I turned that remark over and over, trying to figure which was the disgrace—that someone had so exploited the poor girl, that there would be another mouth to feed, or that she should be rendered Vida's relief receptacle without any consequences. I'm not sure I know yet.

"I heard the sighing whispers and saw knowing glances hidden behind people's hands, but I never got it. And I knew better than to ask. When finally I learned how babies were made, in a white-knuckled lecture from Janice, whose upper lip matched her knuckles, my first thought about this 'wonderful plan of God's' was: How could anyone stand to get that close to the mongoloid girl!

"But what really frightened me was Casey Putney. Uncle Sel would threaten to have Casey kiss me if I wasn't good, that if I didn't stay out of trouble, he'd turn me over to Casey. Casey would grin at me with his toothy grin and grunt.

"I could not begin to imagine what it would be like to be turned over to him . . . certainly the most repulsive and horrifying of possibilities. To this day, the very idea makes me shudder."

Katherine flicked a dry twig into the river and watched it float away.

"The saddest thing, though, is that I'm sure this is why I avoid retarded people. I feel disgusted and have the rather ludicrous fear of being drooled on. I still remember how he smelled . . . of liver and woodsmoke, like his sisters."

As an adult, Katherine was deeply ashamed of her uncaring and bigoted reactions. She had become very accomplished at hiding her disgraceful feelings. And she was angry that she'd been taught those responses.

Katherine put down her pen and watched a pair of swallows swoop in uniform precision over the water. Above her, a gray squirrel chattered nervously, flicking its tail. The river raced beneath her—fast, clear, and cold—carrying melted snow from the mountains through sharp ravines and rocky flats to be lost in the salty blue Pacific and await the becoming of rain again. The exhilaration of this river was so unlike the lazy, bug-infested, thick chocolate rivers of the Midwest that she was reminded again of how far she was from "home."

She watched as the river danced in the sunshine and listened to its song, rushing, tumbling over and around boulders, spraying low-hanging branches. Farther on downstream, the river widened and flattened some, providing a suitable place to wade.

Better to wait for a hot day, she decided. Though this was early June, it was still cool in the mountains. The radiating cold of the frozen ground had not yet yielded in the struggle with the sun. And Katherine had already discovered how cold melting snow could be. When she tried wading, it made her inhale sharply and hurry to get her numbed feet back to dry land.

Leaning back on her hands and tilting her face toward the sky, she closed her eyes and listened. She opened herself to it, wishing it could scrub her mind. This had become a favorite spot, one of the few which seemed to ease the grip of the past, allowing memories to bubble to the surface painlessly.

For many minutes she sat motionless, until her wrists began to hurt. Then she moved forward, holding her knees close to her body, resting her head sideways. Through a crack between the boulders, a yellow flower gently swayed. Katherine leaned closer.

It was a cluster of four buttercups on a stiff homely stem. The little petals drank the sunlight into their centers, fuzzy with pollen-filled stamen.

"Katie loves butter!" Mama brushed the miniature bouquet of buttercups under her chin. "See, baby, how the yellow powder sticks to you?" She opened her chubby hand and sprinkled the dust in her palm. It was lovely in Mama's lap, sitting in an orchard on a blanket, having a picnic.

An insect buzzed the flower, jarring Katherine back to her place by the river. She gently touched the flower's center. Yellow dust clung to her fingertips. She picked up her pen.

"For as long as I can remember, I have felt sad. I'm not sure what about. What makes a child sad?"

The faces of some children she had worked with floated before her. Kent, whose mother had run away. When she asked him if he had any idea where she might be, he had looked up at her, his little face tense with tears. "Missus Katrins, did she go to crazy?" She remembered rocking the child's slender body, trying to comfort him, to reassure him it wasn't his fault she was gone, even if she had told him he was driving her crazy!

And stringy five-year-old Justin. His father had abandoned his family, and Justin had tried to be brave and "take care of" his mother. But it had all fallen apart in Katherine's office one day when he confessed his great failure: *I don't know how to get a job!*

How many children try to carry their parents? she wondered. *Is that what makes them so sad? The hopelessness of responsibility, of never getting it right, of never doing enough?*

Suddenly the face before her was her own—a photo she'd seen of herself, standing on a porch next to her pink-clad sister. She was wearing a gray corduroy skirt, with dirty anklets sucked into brown oxford shoes. How often she had wanted pretty feminine shoes instead of the "mountain climbers" her mother bought her. Her tan face squinted against the sun, fingers picking at each other. Standing on the side of her left shoe, she peered out through dark circles.

It was a child of fallen countenance, a child of woe, the same look she'd seen in so many other children in her office. Abandoned children. Some of them abandoned physically, some emotionally, some spiritually. Those haunting empty little bodies with the sad eyes.

"I am one of them,"

she wrote. Katherine looked toward the river again, trying to draw some comfort, some moisture for the dry tears buried in the unknown. Her throat began to burn with the unnamed but familiar fear. It was like a fear of being trapped. But she could never tell if she was trapped on the inside or the outside.

In times past, Katherine had felt her way along this invisible barricade, fingering for a crack, a handle, anything that would afford an opening. The old dreams, or were they hallucinations? A small pinkish sphere tumbled amidst huge pinkish spheres; a huge pinkish sphere tumbled over small pinkish spheres. Pink, not the lovely baby pink, but the sick orangish pink of raw flesh.

It was an image that constricted her lungs and turned her

sweat to frost. It made her throat tighten and the saliva run before the urge to vomit.

And the other one. Worse. The triangles. Black swirling triangles that sent her into raw terror, hurling her from her bed, reducing her to a whimpering child.

Katherine pressed her wet palms against the rock. She could barely feel its cool. She could barely feel her body . . . just the rising burning in her throat and somewhere from the back of her brain the urgent message, *Katie, talk! Katie, talk!*

Chapter 7

"I remember how the machine shop smelled."

The words looked hollow and far away, as Katherine strained to deliver the brick syllables to the paper.

"It smelled like hot metal and grease and tires. And one corner far in the back smelled like an outhouse. It was a cubbyhole with a toilet as dirty as everything else in the shop and a sink perched on chrome legs, with a cake of blackened soap that stuck to the slime between the faucets."

Little beads of perspiration oozed through the flesh of her upper lip as she wrote in her journal.

"Uncle Sel worked there. Three or four men worked for him. In that place, those men, with years of embedded grease under their fingernails, fashioned whatever odd metal pieces the customers required. What wasn't ready-made and stored in the parts room, they produced at various machines anchored around the room. I thought those machines were monsters that screeched and spewed hot metal sparks that could reach out and grab me. I always tried to keep as far away from them as possible when it was necessary to pass among them.

"I can still see Emmit somebody, way in the back, hunched over a glowing white spot (they told me never to look at it, or I would go blind), where the flame from his welding torch touched the metal and glowed red hot. He wore a black square helmet that covered his whole head and heavy asbestos gloves. I always associated this with what hell must be like.

"At one time Uncle Sel had sold gas. When I was little, the pumps were just for his own use. They were the decorative old gas pumps—two out front—with glass crowns on top and the window with the whirling balls inside that turned as the gas passed through. There were enormous doors in front of the shop, like French doors, that folded to the sides. They usually stood open in good weather.

"In the far left corner was a narrow stairway that led to his office above. I remember an enormous rolltop desk pushed against one wall. The desk was piled with papers and assorted other bits and pieces of grown-up stuff I didn't understand. Uncle Sel sat in a big leather desk chair that squeaked when he leaned back. It was in that room that he met with his business associates and carried on whatever it was he did to earn a living. The floor was bare. There was a closet that was always kept locked, which I was told held his important papers. A door next to the desk led to the house which faced the other direction on the corner of the street. Windows opening in three directions gave him a perfect view of the town—east, west and south—including anyone going to his front door. It gave me the impression that nothing happened that my Uncle Selinus didn't know about."

Katherine wiped the moisture from her face. Some part of her brain questioned the wisdom of all this, but as long as she kept writing, she seemed able to remain connected to her body.

"Also, in the shop downstairs, there was an enclosed room in the left corner of the building . . . a parts room, I guess, where he stored auto parts and new tires."

The burning, rising from a sick slime in her stomach, was now decidedly painful.

"I never went in there,"

she wrote, which sounded like denial, even to her. She took a deep breath and put her pen to the paper again.

"I knew I wasn't supposed to go in there. It was one of two places I couldn't go, the other being a closet in his office with secret stuff in it . . . I don't know what was in there."

That seemed like denial, too.

Dr. Kate was very accomplished at noticing the slightest details. Now she was practicing her own medicine.

"I really don't know what was in there," she said aloud. "It was a secret." She paused, then whispered, "But what secret?"

This was not the first time she had stepped to the edge of this precipice and peered into the oblivion. Under Adam's direction, she had groped and grabbed, desperately trying to retrieve something from the darkness. It was a frustrating game of blindman's bluff, in which she was apparently destined to be "It" forever.

She sat on the rock, clinging to her knees, her journal beside her. The perfume of rubber tires whirled in her head. "The smell of rubber . . . it reminds me of something. What?" Katherine thought hard. "Did I ever go in there? I can't remember."

Leaning back, she closed her eyes. It was easy to envision the door, made of wood with grooves like wainscoting, painted white with smudges of grease around the doorknob. No! It was not a knob, but a spool! A large wooden sewing spool with the thread gone, held fast to the door by a wooden screw.

A new piece! Katherine's heart pounded with dread. She wanted to stop, to run. "Stop, Katie! Don't go in there. You mustn't go in there," Uncle Sel had said. . . .

"Open the door, Katie." Her little hand reached up to pull the spool. The door swung open, squeaking against the spring that held it. She peered in, stepped inside, carefully preventing the door from banging shut behind her. Katie stood perfectly still and waited. No one came.

In front of her, stretching from floor to ceiling, a wall of cubbyholes stored auto parts. Grimy black handprints marked the walls and shelves, drawing attention to the most popular parts by the evidence of grabbing left around their openings.

Fan belts hung from hooks near the ceiling like wilted circles. Next to the door, a bare lightbulb protruded from the wall, drooling a pull chain with a key on the end.

The streetside windows were sprayed with silver paint, giving the effect of a perennial gray fog outside. Sticky dust was everywhere. Dead flies clutched the cobwebs, and the odor of tires permeated the muggy heat.

Katie followed the handprints to the end of the wall where they clustered at the side of an opening to another room, dimly lit, with stalagmites of dusty tires sprouting from the floor to the ceiling.

In the center of that room, wedged between the black columns, stood a square oak rocker with a split leather seat. Katie stepped closer and gingerly stroked the arm, her fingers skidding over the sticky surface. The chair was painted in dust except for the arms and seat.

Katie stood in the middle of the room. Around her, the floor was filthy with city dirt—crushed cigarette butts, bits of metal and grease, and dried stains. Katie turned to go.

It was then she saw them. Ripe, dripping red lips flew at her! Lips pursed to kiss! Sassy, laughing, sticky mouths! Katie covered her face, gasping.

Trembling, she sucked air as her eyes widened to peek out through her fingers. She stepped back, bumping into the rocker behind her.

Covering the wall before her were hundreds of "girlie" calendar pictures—colored photos of scantily clad, big-busted women with crimson smiles and high heels, lounging in lewd poses. Welded to the wall, dozens of gaudy mouths, oozing red, laughed their silent laugh at the red-faced, skinny little girl.

Each glistening body seemed to challenge and taunt her, unabashed. They had no secrets, they carried no shame. These writhing ladies were someone else's secret, someone who sat in the rocker. Now they were Katie's secret, too!

In Katie's world there was no nudity. People kept their clothes on, their buttons buttoned. Doors were locked and the night was full of whispers.

The only exception had occurred once when she was five. Katie and her mother and aunt had gone to a beach with a public bathhouse. Inside that cedar box was a room of flesh—women in various states of undress, squeezing their doughy abundance in and out of tight spandex suits. Most of them turned and faced the wall as if that provided them some privacy.

But they might as well have covered their heads! Katie's face was flooded with scarlet as she fumbled with her own clothing and tried not to look!

Chapter 8

The breeze swirled about her, blowing some of last year's birch leaves into her lap. Katherine blinked and stared, unseeing.

Suddenly she jolted upright. "I had completely forgotten! That room was full of pornography! Well, soft porn, I think . . . yes, I remember now. And every time I passed that room, either inside or outside the building, I was embarrassed, afraid someone would find out I knew what was in there."

She grabbed her pen again and began frantically writing.

"I recall standing in the driveway outside the faux cobblestone building, on the outer wall of the parts room, staring at the cement, watching a daddy longlegs scamper over the entombed secret. As a child, my discovery made me feel personally responsible and enormously guilty.

"I can still see the men going in and out of the white door, with the same absence of shame as the ladies they cavorted with inside. After that day, I went in and out of the white door, too, though not openly, to gaze at the wall and wonder what strange meaning was there. I wondered about the brassy women and how they could be so free, so uninhibited in a room that smelled of rubber tires.

"And fascination with such *freedom* became a titillating fantasy that remained locked behind that dirty white door. I suppose it's why I grew up believing, however unconsciously, that lack of inhibition was something obscene, severed from any loving context."

Katherine let her shoulders relax. It felt good to her to make sense of things. She turned the page and continued:

"The machine shop had once been a still . . . back during the prohibition days, the kids said. It was a place of secrecy, where they made illegal whiskey. I didn't know anyone who 'drank,' although I'd overheard some people referred to as 'drunks,' who spent all their time in the 'beer gardens,' which conjured in my mind strange images of weird plant life and evil dripping down the sides of thick yellow glasses.

"Selinus Hileman, my uncle, who had raised my mother after the death of her parents, had converted the building to a machine shop, with his office upstairs, and had built his house, connected by an enclosed porch that formed a hallway entrance to the front door, as an addition on the north side. The house sat on the hill, slightly above the level of the machine shop, which was street level and faced the other street on the corner of Vida Road and Bently Street. There was nothing attractive about it. Actually, it always looked to me like a fort planted on the highest spot in Vida, surrounded by a grassy moat.

"One green strip separated us from the post office on Vida Road. Beyond that was Jewel Gancy's store, a threshold Uncle Sel never darkened. Apparently he'd had some feud with Jewel sometime in the past and had never gotten over it.

"Old man Guston lived next door on Bently Street, jealously guarding the drooping branches of his weeping willow trees from the covetous hands of the town kids who loved to use them for whips. That required full-time vigilance on the part of the old man, since the trees flaunted their tempting boughs over the sidewalk, forming a cool tunnel to ride bikes through. I didn't have a bike, so I couldn't grab one and make a fast getaway like the other kids did.

"Our landscaping was simple—one hard maple planted on the west side and its twin next to the driveway on the east side. They were dense trees that made wonderful umbrellas against summer deluges. The east side of the shop, next to the front steps of the house, was also privy to a row of peony bushes. But my favorite flowers bloomed on the hollyhock stalks around back by the fuel oil tank.

"They circled the cement well cover with bright ruffled flowers that could be plucked and inverted to make lovely princess dolls with little green caps, an enchanting pastime that was frequently interrupted by, 'What are you kids doing? Get off that well cover! Get out of there!'

"That was another thing I never understood! Since the well cover was a slab of cement that must have weighed a ton and would have taken six men and a boy to move, it was highly unlikely that a forty-pound child could hurt it.

"But in the days before I started to school, I merely accepted it as the way things were. My playmates thought Uncle Sel was mean. Actually, even then I think I realized that everyone in those parts had a healthy respect for Selinus Hileman. They moved around him carefully, like he was a junkyard dog. But to me he was a benevolent dictator, the dispenser of nickels and other treats. I suppose it gave me a certain status that everyone was afraid of him.

"At noon each day, Uncle Sel would scuff his way to the house from his office across the enclosed porch. That porch always smelled like heated dust, and it led to everything. It connected the house with the machine shop, had a room on the back which we always called the oil room, and opened to the front stairs outside, which accessed the garage built under the house like a basement.

"Thinking about it now, the layout of the house was extremely odd. The big front door was so heavy that it took all my strength to push it open, although it swung freely on brass hinges.

"Entering the house was like entering a war museum. The hall was lined with photographs of military men, airplanes, and other war machinery. The floor was littered with big brass artillery shells and mysterious metal objects. Uncle Sel had lost his leg in the first World War and my father had served in the second. As young as I was, I knew war was important to them, full of glory and pride.

"Other than hunting stories, it was the only thing I can ever recall the men talking about at any length. Apparently, war settled things, gave them purpose, and distinguished black from white.

"Once past the military zone, the house was like any other, or so it seemed to me, furnished of familiar smells and memories—some warm, some strange, some dark. Directly opposite the front door and across the hall, was an L-shaped bedroom that we called the guest room, although I never remember having any guests. It was the room where my parents slept when they came to visit, the room my mother and I had when I was a baby and my father was off in the war. Later, it was the empty room with the black and white framed photo of a World War II fighter plane looming above the bed. It was the room I always avoided, watching the door over my shoulder as I rounded the corner to the rest of the house.

"The long oak-paneled hall extended to the right, with a row of windows running the entire length. Halfway down on the left was the kitchen, with the bathroom behind it. The dining room was off the hall, beyond the kitchen. At the far end, the hall opened to a large living room with another hallway to the back of the house. The bedrooms were back there—Aunt Elsie's room first and Uncle Sel's room at the end—with the bathroom between them. Aunt Elsie explained once that his snoring kept her awake, so they didn't sleep together anymore.

Katherine rested the pen in the crack of the book binding and lay back, closing her eyes.

The sweet aroma of freshly baked pumpkin bread drifted all the way to the shop, enticing them to the dining room table which was set for lunch. Katie yanked open the side door of the buffet for a fistful of butter mints.

"You'll spoil your dinner," Aunt Elsie chirped from the kitchen. No was not part of her vocabulary, but she never failed to pass a judgmental comment on whatever Katie did. Aunt Elsie never told Katie not to get dirty, just scolded her when she soiled her new dress; she never told her when to go to bed, only that she would be tired in the morning if she stayed up late. When Katie came home with storebought candy from Jewel's store, Aunt Elsie warned her not to eat too many or she would get worms; and when on rare occasions they took her to the County Park to swim, she told Katie not to drown.

Consequently, Aunt Elsie was an enigma to Katie as she was growing up, not someone she looked to for advice, certainly not a protector. Her aunt was just there, like the other comfortable furnishings in the house.

Uncle Sel hung his hat on the back of a straight wooden chair that stood at the end of the hall. He always wore a European tam, decorated with a dark smudge on the right side of the brim where he fingered it. It contained his bushy gray hair, that sprang in all directions once freed.

In the bathroom, he used the toilet, then washed his greasy hands in Lava soap, leaving spots of one or the other wherever they happened to drip. It was a good thing Aunt Elsie was a fastidious housekeeper.

Then, as he did every mealtime, he went to the oak bookcase next to his chair in the living room and opened a bottle of pills, discreetly dumping one in the palm of his hand. That was about the only thing he ever did discreetly, and it was never clear to

Katie why it was so. It was simply a ritual he performed three times a day so he didn't have to worry about his health, so he said. Every motion was exactly as it was the time before—shaking the tiny pills into the giant paw, throwing them at the back of his throat, and downing the glass of water his wife had placed there for his convenience. That was the sum total of all he ever did to take care of himself. His philosophy was that if he couldn't do as he pleased, he'd rather be dead anyway. I figure Uncle Sel's "doctoring" was probably something he'd cooked up to counteract some legitimate advice he'd been given about his blood pressure.

On his way to the table, he turned on the noon news that spewed from the Philco on the buffet. Katie didn't pay much attention to the content since it never made much sense to her. She just heard the droning voice that carried a hint of alarm, blending the events of the day into one long stream, like a spit in slow motion, ending with the familiar Lowell Thomas sign-off.

Uncle Sel plopped himself in his chair at the head of the table, his elbows on the table, and drank another whole glass of water before announcing, "I'm going to Baker's Grove this afternoon for some liver." That meant if she wanted to, his wife could get in the car and ride along.

"Katie, your elbows are on the table," Aunt Elsie answered noncommittally, a cheerful servant who did whatever was necessary to keep her husband satisfied.

Her uncle bought his meat at a butcher shop on the other side of the county because he liked the best. The only liver he would eat was pork liver, which his wife floured and fried in lard until it was hard, then served with vinegar.

"Can I go?" Katie chimed, secretly craving the black and white soda she always got when they stopped at the ice cream parlor next door.

She knew Uncle Sel wouldn't say yes or no; the answer would lie in whether or not he waited for her and let her climb into the front seat next to him. That made it important to stay close to him and watch his every move for the next hour or so.

Dinner was home-canned corn, roast beef and potatoes—the beef so well done it fell apart in strings—freshly baked chewy white bread, and fresh raspberries with sugar and cream, served in pink depression glass stemware. For dessert, there was always *pie, usually fruit, but sometimes lemon meringue, cradled within the most delicate lard crust.*

Elsie was an exceptional baker, preparing everything from feel and instinct rather than recipe, because she couldn't read a recipe, or anything else for that matter. Except for the baked goods, she overcooked everything, in spite of the ag extension lessons at the Grange Hall, where a pale home economics major tried her best to push the traditional farm wives toward a healthier diet. She begged them to abandon the lard and butter in favor of the tasteless yellow grease she called "oleo" and to cook green beans only to the crisp bright green stage which they considered blanching.

What the teacher, frustrated by her lack of success, failed to comprehend was that she was educating the wrong spouse. Since she herself was unmarried, she had no way of knowing that the women cooked what their men would eat, or, in Aunt Elsie's case, what her husband would buy.

Gradually, Katherine's thoughts returned to the present. As night becomes day, as the flowers open, she found herself lying on the rock, staring at the sky while the river went by.

Relief set in. Somehow she had expected something much worse in Vida. "I suppose it was shocking for a little kid, especially one who grew up with neuter parents," she mused about the revelation of the parts room. Funny, how she and Adam had not uncovered that. It made her wonder what else they had missed.

She watched the river cut its way through the green, trying to feel at ease now in these comfortable surroundings. Still, something else nagged her, something about the smell. Why did the smell of rubber make her feel strange? And why did she stare at doorways? Katherine's trained mind knew she had not found enough fire to account for all the billows of smoke. And she knew that for all the work they had done on the incest, she was somehow not free of it yet. Maybe they were right—those colleagues who believed that incest causes damage so severe that one never fully recovers, only survives.

Katherine had doggedly refused to believe it was that hopeless. Besides, her own practice was evidence to the contrary.

People did get well. Healing was possible. In Christ, there was a way.

She reckoned what she'd known for years, that inside the self-assured, professional woman, an orphan child whimpered in the dark. Kate did not know how to help, and all her efforts had come to nothing. Was she to bow her head in simple obedience, believing that His grace was sufficient? Did she, like Paul, have the one infirmity God would not heal?

I have come that you might have life and have it abundantly. Katherine sat up. What could that mean now? It was inconceivable that life would ever again be abundant. Just coping was all she could hope for. She had lost the Savior who had given His life so she could live, not just in the hereafter, but now.

Katherine thought again of the women behind the pictures, those desperate souls caught in their own circumstances. She had treated some of them and knew them to be anything but happy or well-adjusted. But, then, what was their appeal? Perhaps just the illusion they represented—total abandonment. Complete freedom. No inhibitions. *Perhaps we would all like to be what they appeared to be,* Katherine thought.

She opened the journal and began to write:

"Can innocence and sexuality ever be joined? Eve knew innocence. Then she was sexual . . . after the fall . . . after the innocence was spoiled. Is there no reconciling the two?"

All her adult years, Katherine had struggled to wed sexuality and pleasure, without the baggage of fear and guilt she hauled along. But was it possible?

Chapter 9

With that, Katherine closed the journal, stood up and dusted off her behind. It was time to head back to the cabin, perhaps fix something to eat.

Pulling herself along the steep path, holding to the underbrush, she realized she'd been crying. The pathway swam in liquid before her. She still had the strange sensation of being watched, of not wanting to be caught crying and having to explain herself. It had been nearly a week since the pilot left. She had not seen another soul since. But still she listened. Still she looked over her shoulder. Still she stayed to the edges and shadows.

Gradually, the meandering path abandoned the river for the trees and the cabin beyond. A dense line of mature growth for a distance of about a quarter mile stood between her and the clearing at the cabin. It was dark. Precious few coins of sunlight fell among the giants, immense wooden columns that lifted the green tufts up to the mother sky.

The air was as still as the ground, clear of undergrowth, covered with a smooth blanket of compost—the accumulation of the droppings of millennia—forming a soundless carpet beneath her boots.

Katherine looked up, steadied herself against a trunk. All the dark green boughs seemed gathered together, pointing to the same place in the sky, their tops gently swaying. The sky raced by, creating the sensation of standing on a whirling planet. It made her insides weightless, like the carnival rides she hated. But from this day forward, she would never fail to stop and look up when she passed this way.

Nothing marked time here, just the steady hissing growth.

This could have been any moment in the previous centuries or one to come. The trees held the hushed wisdom of the ages, as the forest floor yielded to her heel and recovered like a dented sponge, leaving behind no trace of her.

She remembered her Grandmother Henry reading to her that the cedars of Lebanon were used to make a temple for God. These giant Douglas firs seemed to personify their own holy place—perhaps God's private place where He escaped in the heat of the day.

As she approached the west rim of the clearing, silver threads of morning spun the darkness, glistening like dew-laden spiderwebs. Entering their domain, warm fingers of light caressed her shoulders, igniting sparks in her auburn hair and tickling her eyelids.

Katherine smiled and softly whispered, "Hello." Black-capped chickadees darting between the branches answered back in an unknown tongue.

Here at the very border of light and dark, at the edge of both and neither, where the sunlight could make the darkness dance, where it was possible to stand on a hypothetical spot—like the line of the horizon, or the end of a rainbow, exactly here—the lacy maidenhair ferns unfolded their feathery praying hands.

Scattered across the forest floor, Katherine noticed trillium about to bloom. Here and there a delicate white flower already floated on a triple leaf.

Yesterday, when she passed this way, she had seen only the ferns. Could they have sprung up overnight? Katherine turned to look behind her.

There, where the shafts of silver blue sky pierced the ground, thousands of tiny white orchids danced, uninhibited, on the end of green spikes poking up through the silence, like impaled teardrops stolen from a thousand souls. Houndstooth, she would later learn.

It was a vision of such immaculate innocence and frail purity that she feared it might wither at the watching, never intended for human eyes. How had she missed it before? Gingerly, she tiptoed through the fragile breach between the light and the darkness, sensing it was doing something to her, knowing this would never be a memory, like being born.

Just inside the clearing, something caught her eye to the left. She froze. There, about twenty feet from her, a young doe stepped with fluid motion, cautiously placing one dainty foot after the other, quietly maneuvering her golden body into the sunshine. Ears alert, she lifted her head, sniffing the breeze. Downwind, Katherine didn't move. The doe continued her meticulous approach. The slightest movement, Katherine knew, and the animal would be nothing but a flash into the darkness again.

The elegant creature moved along the edge of the open space, ready to run, to disappear, suspicious of every drift and flow. Her progress through the clearing was that of a prima ballerina. It was only when she turned away in the direction of the cabin that Katherine slowly exhaled.

The doe flicked her white tail and lowered her head to nibble at the glowing green spikes of spring, then raised her head, moving her ears like antennae while chewing the tender shoots, then down again.

Katherine had always been fond of deer, believing them to be perhaps the epitome of grace. Never had she been so privileged to watch one in the wild for so many minutes. Usually, they were caught in the headlights by the roadside at night or standing far off in a field at dusk, too distant to hear the, "Oh looks".

All at once, some jaybirds screamed through the trees above her and in one sideways bound, the doe was gone.

For a minute it made Katherine's heart pound, too. But since she could not read the meaning of the signal, she resumed her trek toward home. Perhaps the jays had noticed her and warned the doe.

Katherine began to think about coffee. She still had those infernal beans, but she had not yet engineered a way to extract from them a decent brew—the single challenge occupying her mind this past week. Funny how the wilderness coping had come easy, but the thing she'd always taken for granted, like a morning cup of coffee, still eluded her.

She had tried boiling the beans and soaking them, then crushing them with the hammer. It was a step in the right direction, but much too slow and wasteful as most of the beans went flying.

On her morning walk Katherine had discovered two rocks that seemed to fit together like grinding stones—a flat one with a bit of a dish in it and a round river rock she might be able to hold and turn. She stuck them in the canvas sack she had learned to lug along on outings.

On the porch, she carefully lifted them out, like fragile garage sale treasures. Quickly she retrieved the can of beans from her tidy pantry, twisted off the lid, and slowly poured a layer into the indentation of the flat rock. She set the other rock on top and turned, pressing it down hard.

The beans crunched and popped and scraped and broke open, spilling their fragrance. Katherine lifted the top rock and inhaled the delicious aroma.

"This is going to work!" she crowed triumphantly. She ran back to the kitchen for her gold coffee filter, the one possession she had refused to leave behind. In spite of the filter, jealously guarded all the way from Chicago, she had now gone six whole days without coffee.

Back home, Katherine drank a lot of coffee—six cups a day, sometimes more. It was a flavor of which she had never tired, since Grandma Henry had first spooned Nescafé into her milk. She could not remember going a whole day without it.

Wednesday, two days ago, she had become so desperate she had tried chewing the beans! Sucking on them wasn't too bad, but chewing them up was about like eating gravel.

Carefully, she dusted every precious granule into the filter and ground some more until it measured enough for a pot. Inside, the water was coming to a boil in the remains of the sunrise fire. When she heard it hiss, her patience dissolved. She poured the steaming liquid into the filter and listened as it splashed its dark hot stream into the hollow thermos.

As the cabin filled with the wonderful enticement, Katherine selected the largest stoneware cup in the place. Grinning with anticipation, she carefully lifted the filter so as not to spill a drop, tipped the thermos, and let the auburn liquid slide down the sides of the cup, leaning forward to breathe in the vapor. She sprinkled the powdered cream lightly on the surface and watched it slowly melt into a tan swirl.

Like an offering, Katherine carried the cup with both hands to the porch, where she deftly lowered herself to the top step, engrossed in the lovely contents. Oblivious to etiquette, Katherine lifted the cup to her lips and slurped in the hot bitterness with sloppy abandon. The delightful bouquet blended with the morning freshness, filling her with a feeling of euphoria.

"Now that is a good cup of coffee!" She took another sip, "Wonderful!" She sat on the step and drank slowly and deliberately, sharing its warmth with her hands.

The meadow was in full light now. It was probably somewhere around nine o'clock in the morning. Katherine didn't know for sure, since she had decided not to set the clock. It seemed appropriate somehow to divorce herself from that imposition of society, although twice in the past week, she had peeked at her quartz watch lying on the bookshelf.

Periodically though, it occurred to her to wonder what time it was. Sometimes, not knowing, she got an anxious feeling in the pit of her stomach.

"This must be how a child who can't tell time feels. The day just rolls along. You do what you please, when you please. You don't know whether you have time to start or finish something, and you don't know how long you'll have to wait. But then, if you're not waiting for anything, it doesn't matter anyway." Katherine poured another cup of coffee and continued her soliloquy. "So . . . do I feel like a child facing the unknown or like a free adult? Am I excited or afraid?"

She didn't know. She knew only that at this moment she was drinking deeply from the cup of well-being, a most unfamiliar flavor.

"Well . . . no one is going to call me in or tell me what to do. No one is going to define my time. I don't have to hurry up." Katherine opened the journal and began writing again.

"I came back from the walk this morning because I wanted this cup of coffee. And a wonderful cup it is!"

She sipped again, holding the warm mouthful for a moment before swallowing.

"I wonder if this is the first thing I've ever done just to please myself. What else could I do here but please myself? I suppose I could try to do what is right. Or I could try to come up with a project, a challenge, something to pass the time . . .

Katherine looked up from her writing. *To pass the time*, she thought. *You mean to waste the time*. Her thoughts darkened. She hurriedly scrawled:

"Most people waste most of their time wanting to get on to something else. Most people want to finish—breakfast, assignments, days, lovemaking, life—everything. I don't want to finish. I just want to live!"

She slammed the book shut, like an exclamation point.

Beyond the far edge of the clearing, toward the river, a vulture, joined by two of its fellows, floated on the wind. "And what does it take to sustain life?" Katherine whispered. "Must some things die? What must die in me?" She idly swirled the coffee in her cup as she watched the vultures circle and dip.

Chapter 10

Eyes riveted on the great black birds, Katherine whispered, "Today I have lived. I have heard the river. I have seen the flowers. I have felt the sunlight. I have watched the deer graze, then flee. I have made this coffee. And absolutely none of this has any purpose, except that I have experienced it. It's just for me." She could not recall the last time she had done anything for the mere pleasure of it, for the celebration.

From a far distance, the low drone of an engine drifted within earshot. Katherine jumped as if she had been shot. "Great Scott! It's Friday!" She ran into the cabin and slammed the door behind her.

Her mind raced, frantic thoughts banging against her brain. *Get hold of yourself! It's only the plane . . . they'll drop the stuff and leave. . . . But what if they don't?* Where should she go? What should she do? She didn't want to be seen. It was too early. Had she put up the flag? She had been so careful to alternate the flags each morning. *But what if I missed one?*

As the rattle of the engine vibrated its way through the heavy door, she mentally ticked off the days, the color variations: *Monday, Tuesday, Wednesday, Thursday, Friday . . . white, yellow, white, yellow, white . . . today is a white day!* Rushing to the window, she looked up. At the top of the pole waved a white flag!

Forcing herself to breathe, Katherine collected her thoughts. Remembering that the radio was still in the shed, she dashed for the back door, grabbing the keys off the nail as she went. Fumbling with the locks, she could hear the short wave inside, hissing and crackling. Someone on the other end would be wanting a response. Not that she cared to give one, except to assure herself that there would be no surprise visitor.

"This is Ranger One to Ladybug. Come in." Overhead, the plane made a noisy pass. "Ranger One to Ladybug. Do you copy?"

Katherine located the switch. "Ah . . . yes. Ah . . . this is Ladybug," she answered him, resenting that label. "Ah . . . over." She flipped the switch again.

"Ladybug, how are you doing? Over." She could recognize the pilot's singsongy voice.

"I'm fine. Everything is fine," she spit the staccato words into the silver microphone. "Over."

"We're making our approach for the drop. Do you need anything?"

"No. I'm fine." Katherine was annoyed that she couldn't think of anything else to say.

"Is everything working down there? Over."

"Everything is working just fine. Over." The plane rattled overhead, and Katherine stared anxiously at the ceiling of the shed.

"We can come down. Do you need anything? Over."

"No!" she shouted a little too emphatically. *You're supposed to leave me alone! It's part of the deal,* she thought. "No, everything is fine. Really!"

"Okay," he sang. "Have a good week. See you in a couple. Ranger out."

Katherine left the shed and ran for the clearing in time to see two packages hurled from the plane, tumbling end over end toward the runway. At least, she hoped they would land on the runway. From here, it looked as if the cargo might land in the river.

She ran for the break in the trees. It was exhilarating. Her hairpins had loosened and her hair was flowing free about her shoulders. She could feel the strength in her calf muscles, pushing her forward.

Breathless, she approached the runway. Dead center, within six feet of each other, lay the two packages. As she walked over to retrieve them, Katherine had a new appreciation for the pilot.

She grabbed up the bundles and headed home. Walking the trail back to the cabin, Katherine felt a surge of delicious accomplishment. She had really pulled this off. Everything was going according to plan. It would be two weeks before the next drop.

The contents revealed what she expected—three servings of frozen meat, a cabbage, carrots, onions, potatoes, a package of longhorn cheese—a chunk of which Katherine immediately devoured—more boxes of matches, some extra batteries, and six Baby Ruth candy bars, not on her list. The other package contained two quarts of milk, a dozen eggs—so miraculously packed that only one was cracked—some real butter, a bag of apples and oranges, two grapefruit, and a bag of sunflower seeds. The cabin was filled with an aroma of freshness. And she was as excited as a kid in a candy store.

On the very bottom, Katherine spied a copy of the Sunday paper, nearly a week old, and a copy of the current Friday edition. She laid them aside, not having made a decision as to whether or not she would allow that intrusion from the outside world.

Katherine hurriedly lifted the cellar door and pushed the groceries to the edge, as if every moment was crucial in the race against spoilage. Carefully, lantern in hand, she descended the ladder. She felt a twinge of pain. Putting away groceries made her think of John.

"Kate, did you get mushrooms?"
"No. I thought you got them."
"I asked you if we needed them. You said we had them."
"No, I shook my head yes. We need them."

It seemed impossible that after all the years they'd spent together, they'd still miss each other's signals occasionally, mildly irritated that the other could not understand simple English or comprehend the obvious.

But John loved to buy groceries and they both loved to eat. So this was a compatible ritual, perhaps the reason they invested so much in it, taking on an aura of seriousness. Now and then they would stop to admire an item or comment on how clever they were for finding that particular bargain, or anticipate together how they would prepare it, especially if it was something exotic, like bitter melon.

In the store, Katherine could fill a grocery cart in the time it took John to decide what kind of mustard to buy and for what price. She never thought it was worth ten minutes of label-reading and ounce-pricing to save three cents. She figured if she wanted it and could afford it, then why not? If she didn't want it, she didn't care what it cost, and if she couldn't afford it, she didn't care to waste any more time.

John, on the other hand, was much more selective. He was the one who kept a running total in the checkbook, was not willing to be cheated, and bought shrimp by the count. In spite of all this, at any given time, their larder probably contained enough ingredients for a seven-course meal to delight the palate of any discerning army.

She and John did nearly everything together. Reflecting now on these simple pleasures, it was painful to think she would never know his touch again.

Shaking off the memory, her thoughts returned to the items now neatly stored in the damp cellar. Stocking up brought such a lovely sense of security. "John, you would love this," she said, lowering the trapdoor over the lingering aroma of fresh vegetables.

For the past eight months, Katherine had postponed thinking too deeply of John. She touched her grief ever so lightly and with rigid brevity. Somewhere in the back of her mind, she knew it was a pain and a loneliness she must claim, but she was not yet certain she could endure it. Besides, the agenda was so long.

Katherine looked at the brown tweed jacket hanging on the peg beside the fireplace. She couldn't be sure whether it still smelled of him or if she just imagined it. She remembered the first time she'd seen him. At the café. His eyes sparkling, he'd smiled at her, lifting his cup in salute across the room. She had always been taught not to talk to strangers, but when he approached the table, offering her a vitamin, he seemed so safe. When he finally introduced himself, the resonance of his voice, deep and rich, made her dizzy. No other man had ever affected her that way. It was as if he had touched some forgotten essence in her or sparked some life she hadn't known existed.

Katherine set the armload of vegetables in the sink. Suddenly everything seemed deathly quiet. She lifted the pump handle up and down, splashing water over her soup ingredients.

She tried to pretend John was sitting on the sofa behind her, with his feet up on the coffee table. She would make soup for them, although he usually made it for her. She tried to think that he had hung his jacket there and that after dinner they would go for a walk.

Katherine began cutting the vegetables, clinging to the imagined presence behind her. "John, you're going to enjoy this soup. It's all these very fresh vegetables, better than we can get in Chicago." Unexpectedly, she started to cry. "And after dinner, I'll fix you some of my wonderful stone-ground coffee . . . and . . . are you listening?" The tears were splashing down the front of her shirt. *He's there,* she thought, *I can feel him . . . as long as I don't turn around.*

She kept cutting and crying and wanting desperately for him to see. Then he would come up behind her and put his arms around her, and this time she would tell him anything and everything. She would hold nothing back. She would let down her guard.

"Don't you know how much I need you?" she pled. "Why don't you say something? You always know what to say. I can't work this out, John! I can't do this!" Katherine stared at the sink. "John, please. I'm sorry. I should have listened to you when you wanted to talk. I'll listen now . . . John?" Katherine turned toward the empty room.

She held her breath as the tears dried on her face. John was gone. He'd left his jacket and gone. Katherine took a deep breath and squared her shoulders.

She thought then of his journal at the bottom of the wardrobe drawer. All she knew about the leather-bound volume was that it was in John's handwriting, recorded over his last year, and that he had wanted her to have it.

The night he died, she had stumbled home alone and sat on the floor in the dark, hugging his brown tweed sports jacket, burying her face in his scent. By the time the flowers had wilted across the damp earth that covered John's body, Katherine had begun her search for some place to mourn. She knew the emptiness within her would not lie in its dull apathy for long, and she had no intention of sharing this last remnant of her husband with anyone.

For the first time since arriving here, Katherine felt alone. She considered getting out the journal, but pushed it down. Instead, she puttered about the primitive kitchen, setting a pot of homemade soup to simmer and assembling a lunch, all the while conscious of the hollow sound of her own footsteps.

When the soup was done, she sat down at the table to eat. The east window held a narrow view of the top of the meadow, which sloped up and away, holding the cabin in a protective hollow. She could see the gradual tree line beyond a rich growth of blackberry bushes, just beginning to leaf out. The new life glowed like chartreuse flames against the emerald firs. Here and there, tucked among the shadows, drifts of lingering snow were mute reminders of what had been and what would be again.

There was nothing phony here. Everything was just as it appeared, without shame or inhibition of any kind. It occurred to Katherine that if she stayed long enough, she, too, might absorb her surroundings. She had the urge to pray, but resisted it.

She was weary of hiding. Perhaps she had found the perfect place. She could not recall a time when she had not felt watched, self-conscious. Here, there were moments at least when she felt safe.

As she sat eating and enjoying the pastoral scene, a peacefulness settled gently on her mind. It seemed that for the entire week prior to this moment, she had been racing from one duty to the next, running, running. Now she could not remember what had kept her so busy.

Why is it so hard to be what you are? she mused. Could she not shed the inhibitions like old clothes? And what was so difficult about staying now . . . in the present. It made her slightly anxious to realize five days were spent, with only a few living moments to show for them.

She poured another cup of coffee, the last of the pot. It was a cool damp day that called for another log on the fire. At night, while she slept, she let the Fischer stove keep the place comfortably warm, since it could go for hours without restoking. But during her waking hours, keeping a fire crackling on the open hearth was her preference.

Coffee, a crackling fire, vegetable soup—all blended, filling the room with kindness. Katherine adjourned to the sofa and picked up the crocheting she worked on just such afternoons.

The creation of lace—twine looped and knotted into a work of delicate utility—this one was an elaborate pattern of squares that would someday form a coverlet, a woven diary of her days here. It was the only thing resembling a project she had brought with her, other than herself and the journal she vowed to keep at Adam's suggestion.

As the remaining light dwindled, it became more difficult to see the tiny stitches. Katherine laid her needlework aside, stretched, and sauntered out to the porch. It was her favorite time of day, when everything green seemed to glow with the accumulation of the day's sunlight.

The rain had stopped and the sun was a brilliant fire, glowing just beneath the trees, casting soft purple shadows across the meadow. She wondered if the doe might return to feed in the evening and decided to walk down the lane toward the river.

Out of the windbreak, the gentle afternoon breeze was giving quarter to a steady wind out of the northeast, and the temperature was dropping. Katherine pulled John's coat closer around her and turned up the collar.

She walked slowly, letting the wind have its way with her hair. When she reached the south end of the meadow, two raccoons scampered around the bend toward the river. She abandoned the idea of a river walk, turning back toward the cabin instead, following the far eastern rim.

The rustic log house hugged the green evening shadows. A curl of smoke filled the air with an inviting lure to the glowing windows.

Katherine stood several minutes just to take it in, then slowly resumed the long way around. By the time she reached the steps, the sky was a deep purple, sliding over the last patches of light blue trailing the sun. A dark navy curtain of clouds rolled across the window of heaven.

Another storm was coming. The wind bit her face. Inside the cabin, the warmth was a welcome relief. She felt at home.

She was about to bolt the doors when she remembered she had never closed up the shed from this morning. Out back, the evening had been devoured by blackness—the kind that makes you blink and stare and wonder if you're blind.

Groping her way back into the cabin for a lantern—her instant security—Katherine again sensed her aloneness. Once the light was in her hand and the shadows subsided, courage returned.

Sure enough! The door stood wide open! She tried to remember if she had left it that way or not. She thought of the raccoons and wondered if they had been stealing her blind.

Preferring not to surprise whatever might have wandered into her storehouse, she began whistling. With each step, anticipation skittered around the edges of her ribs. Still, whistling nonchalantly, she snuck up on the open door and jerked it back.

There was no outburst from within. No scurrying sounds. No yellow eyes peered from behind the tins. Just the mournful song of the wind making love to the trees.

Shining her light inside to assure herself that it was empty, Katherine quickly snapped the padlocks. Then she darted for the cabin, sliding the heavy wooden bolt behind her. Night in the Northwest woods was black. Katherine Allen had finally escaped the artificial glow of civilization.

Once inside, the warmth engulfed her. Katherine embraced the soothing peace without reservation, surprising herself. She felt at home and safe. She floated in the lovely pool of belonging, a feeling she thought she'd left on the Henrys' dairy farm, somewhere between the milk house and the barn. Many places were familiar to her, but her Grandma and Grandpa's dairy farm was the place she had called home, the place she always returned to, the place she missed.

Now here it was again—that delicious feeling—returning as if it had been only momentarily misplaced. Had it really been twenty-five years? And what was it the Lord had said about returning the years the locusts had eaten? She remembered having shared that promise with a client once, but she had never taken it for her own.

She sat on the sofa, watching the fire and drinking milk. Then she went to bed. She had loaded the Fischer stove to carry her comfortably through the night and had dampened the lanterns. Only the dying hearth held back the night tide, as she pulled the old quilt up around her shoulders.

Sleep came easily, miraculously, as it had each of the past few nights. She did not think about watching the doors, nor did she hear the rain pelting the windows. Her fading memories were only of the lovely white houndstooths dancing in the silver sunlight.

Chapter 11

Katherine had found living the life of a hermit to be infinitely manageable. For the first time, she did not have to put up a front or wonder how she might be perceived by someone looking on. There were no explanations to be made or criticisms to swallow.

She had easily acquired the skills of a pioneer woman, washing clothes in a tub of boiling water outside and discovering that fresh air made a wonderful dryer. When a week of rain fell, she dried her clothes on a rope strung from the beams inside the cabin. In the shed, she had found an iron tripod in which she could balance the washtub and build a fire under it. She set a bucket of cold water next to it for rinsing.

Now that the days were warmer, bathing was easy. Off the trail behind the cabin was a pool where the water fell some fifteen feet over a ledge as it coursed its way down the mountain to join the river below.

At first, Katherine had the sensation of doing something quite risqué, maybe even immoral, as she hung her clothing on the bushes and waded in, much as Eve might have in that first garden. Each time the water welcomed her, baptizing her in acceptance, until at last, on an especially bright day, she was so at ease with herself that she crawled out and fell asleep on the smooth warm rocks.

Lord, this is good. I want to feel this way forever . . . and to walk with you in the cool of the day. The thought floated from her being. She could not remember when anything resembling easy conversation had flowed from her to God. Perhaps it was the Holy Spirit speaking for her. Perhaps there would be healing, soothing, comforting—everything she believed was gone.

Katherine opened her eyes slowly against the filtered sunlight. A tiny bird hopped within inches of her face, pecking at the moss between the rocks. It was as if she had been accepted. The jays and the crows no longer sent alarms ahead of her as she walked the trails, invading their territory. She was part of this world now.

Buttoning the last button on her shirt, she recognized another change. Clothing had become a thing of protection rather than a cover of shame. Katherine had whiled away the summer hours unfolding, accepting, being comforted, sensing the abiding presence of God, as if he walked with her.

By the end of August, the nights were growing cool, signaling the end of summer. Fall in the Northwest woods was contained within the briefest of days, wedged between blue summer skies and the white drape of winter. The firs and hemlocks never changed. It was left to the underbrush to produce the showy colors associated with fall.

Along the river, thin rows of poplars and aspens were flashing gold. The poison oak was turning a brilliant red, inviting her to gather the leaves for a table arrangement. But she had been warned about this in the handy manual.

Fall would also bring the rains that quenched the summer thirst and the long days of summer. Katherine took advantage of the dry days to venture forth in search of dried weeds and grasses to decorate the corners of the cabin.

On one such gentle day, as Katherine walked along the river with her journal under her arm, the sun caught the aspen leaves, spinning them in place. A gust of wind sent a few of the glittering gold coins twirling earthward. They settled lightly on the surface of the water, riding the current to destinations unknown.

Settling on the grass, Katherine opened to a new page:

"Twenty-one times, John and I watched the leaves fall, holding hands and sharing. Now I walk alone."

She shifted and kicked the leaves, then spoke aloud into the air. "I wish I could return to the days of a year ago . . . to live them over again with you, John."

She had the aching sense she'd missed something. She had insisted upon discussing Christmas plans with him, pretending not to see his strength dissolving, all the while fearing that somehow she would be jerked away as she had when she was a child, living that disjointed existence between the farm and her parents.

It was as if their lives—hers and John's, like the spring planting—were leading to something, some culmination. But it was cut short. The time had run out, leaving her like the unharvested Midwest cornfields that stand through the winter, bowing their heavy heads to the ground in disgrace . . . not worth the picking . . . abandoned.

Katherine watched the river and wondered what John had been trying to tell her. Through all of their relationship, he had fussed at her about not listening to him, about looking out the window or finding other distractions. To Katherine, it seemed she listened until the thoughts coagulated in her brain. But he had an insatiable ability to spin intellectual fabric, weaving concepts and ideas—everything from the concrete to the abstract. John was fascinated with the meaning of things, which he wrung from every event. He lived in a constant dialogue with God, and so he was a willing sojourner down any interesting path. His faith in Christ provided him security and freedom, believing the Lord led him and would keep him from paths of unrighteousness.

Katherine, on the other hand, struggled with legalism. It was far easier for her to follow the rules and do good works than to trust in grace.

She tried to follow his conversations, mentally sorting out how this or that might apply to her life. What difference did it make to know this? What did that imply she should do or not do? At the end, she now realized, he had been trying to prepare her for his death—a fact she had steadfastly avoided considering until there was no longer any way to avoid it.

Katherine lived life as if it contained a vast number of events that shouldn't be permitted to happen—things she herself must prevent or that must be instantly redeemed. John was content so long as he could glean some wisdom from the event. And their friend Adam simply shrugged his shoulders and said, "That's life!"

Adam, it seemed, was along for the ride. He possessed that rare ability to take things as they came without question—to get on the roller coaster and go where it led—with no concern for the future.

Not so John. Even though his ride had been cut short, he had wanted to know the meaning. When the doctors brought bad news—one series of failed attempts after the other—he had tried to reassure Katherine that there was a purpose in it, a meaning.

"I do *not* see the meaning," she now protested out loud, a bitter note in her voice. "But I'll tell you this, John. I've found a place where nothing more can be taken from me. Where I can be at peace. Where there are no surprises . . . and I like it!"

Katherine turned the thought. Maybe she had found the place where pain could not enter, where nothing more could be lost.

She could almost hear John saying, "Kate, you can't hide from yourself!" Startled, Katherine looked up. But it was only the drumming of a pileated woodpecker, his red head hammering away at a tree trunk, like a teacher tapping a ruler for attention.

Dangling her feet over the water, she sighed and tried to think of nothing. She sat on the riverbank, wrapped in the August sun, listening as the crows sent messages across the treetops. It was time to head back, to compile the list for the pilot, to make cornbread and stir the soup.

Chapter 12

H*eavy footsteps, running.* Katherine bolted from the abyss of sleep. Her pulse pounded in her ears as she strained to hear the footsteps, fearing to breathe. Were they moving closer or away? Every nerve pawed the darkness. The room was black, her mind as blind as her eyes. She could not remember where she was or how old she was.

Body awareness told her that she was huddled in a corner somewhere with her fists closed tight and her arms covering her head. As her eyes adjusted to the void of light, the contents of the cabin replaced the image of a toddler in white high-top shoes, running, tripping, falling in slow motion, headlong, arms outstretched.

Slowly, consciousness returned from the collision of the dream world with the present reality. With it, Katherine discovered herself wedged in the corner behind the bed, cowering in a fetal position, wrapped in a drenched flannel nightgown that was twisted like a rope around her.

Carefully, unfolding her body, she eased her legs forward, feet to the floor. She pushed the wet hair from her eyes, holding her face with both hands. Then, reaching out with tentative fingers, she touched the smooth, round logs on either side of her. And bracing against the corner, she pulled herself up.

Dry screams still stuck to the back of her throat like popcorn hulls. Her body trembled beneath its own weight. She squeezed herself between the wall and what she dimly discerned must be the bed, feeling the blackness with blind hands, remembering there was a lantern on the stand beside it.

In the dark, she bumped the table, skidding it some inches

closer to the wall. Fumbling for the lantern, her fingers closed around what she knew must be the box of matches.

After several uncoordinated attempts to connect the head with the rough strip on the side, success came in a bright flash, instantly shattering the dark void, ending the uncertainty of her whereabouts.

"I must have been dreaming," she breathed in relief, securely back in the mountain cabin. Trying not to think of the image of herself cringing in a corner, she peeled off the clammy nightgown and quickly put on a warm pair of sweats. Even though she was standing next to the stove, her teeth were still chattering audibly.

It wasn't clear whether the chill came from outside or was radiating from her bones. Or was it the chill of reality? She trembled with the realization that John was right—she could not hide from herself. Even here in this place, her fears had finally found her.

"Oh, God," she murmured, "is there no place to hide? No safe place?"

Digging through the drawer again, she grabbed some heavy wool socks. Donning them seemed to help. Then she padded about the cabin, assembling the ingredients of a hearth fire, as ghostly shadows of herself hovered on the walls and ceiling.

The new flames were soon licking at the logs, further igniting the kindling, and she settled back against the old quilt covering the sofa and stared into the popping blaze, still trembling. There was something reassuring and comforting about a fire, something more than the heat.

"What is it?" Katherine spoke aloud, trying to sound brave. "What am I afraid of?" Something very dark lurked behind a curtain of consciousness, she knew, something that propelled her from the comfort of her bed, something so frightening that in all these years, she had not been able to convince herself that it was permissible to remember.

All the hours she had spent calmly bolstering the courage of clients locked in the vice of repression had failed to lift her own iron veil. All the Wednesday afternoons with Adam had not exposed all the dark secrets. Katherine stared at the fire, mentally sorting the reasons that might account for such a memory loss.

Professionally, she understood that one does not remember either because one does not *want* to remember or does not *dare* to remember. She tried to imagine what could be so horrible that she would choose to lock it up forever.

"What must I not tell?" she questioned herself. "That the men looked at nude pictures in the parts room? Is that it? Is that enough to screw me up this bad?"

She thought about all the haunted nights, the creeping fear that slithered into the shadows of her mind when the sun went down, only to evaporate by morning. Goosebumps prickled down her spine.

She thought of the nights she'd been awakened by John's gentle touch, his familiar voice calling her back. He'd found her in closets and, whimpering, behind overstuffed chairs. Once he had retrieved her from the balcony, which frightened him. What would she do to herself if left unattended?

"There's something more . . . I'm really scared!" Katherine glanced furtively about the room, crossing her arms to tuck her icy hands in the warmth of her armpits, wishing she could shake the dream.

She thought of Chicago in '68. "Was I scared *in* Chicago or was I scared *of* Chicago? No, it didn't start there. But I felt it there in the nightmare of the rioting. The world was upside down then . . . if it hadn't been for John."

Katherine pulled her feet up, Indian style, and rocked forward and back. "What does Chicago have to do with this?" She'd spent three very crazy years after the convention, suffering from bouts of depression and nightmares. She had raged about Preston and Janice's "life of materialism," though never at them, preaching that nothing mattered but their money and their toys and their military society, and the two hellish months when she had struggled with a dark night of the soul.

"Yes, Adam, my friend, I was totally out of it, and it scared the liver out of me. But that time in my life was a symptom, not the cause!" Katherine stood up, shaking down the fire, watching the sparks fly. She jumped back into the sofa and pulled her feet up as if "it" would grab her from the space beneath.

"Chicago, you're a symptom! You represent something . . . you triggered something . . . but what?" Katherine's mind raced from Rush Street to Michigan Avenue. Finally exhausted, it raced down the same blind alley as usual. "What's the possibility that I've done something unforgivable, something really horrible? But what could I have done that they wouldn't have told me about?" Katherine shifted her position.

"Oh, no! They never had any problem letting me know every little thing I did wrong. Surely, if they'd had any real gripe against me, I never would have heard the end of it!" Leaning back, she pulled her feet up under her and concentrated.

"No, I'm just trying to fix it. If I did it, I can fix it . . . can't I? I'm just trying to be responsible . . . I think."

Katherine knew a lot about the intrigues of the human psyche. For the past twenty-two years, she had earned her living chasing the hounds of hell through the elaborate mazes constructed in the minds of clients in search of the truth that would set them free . . . a memory, a meaning, the tiniest fragment that could turn a lock, opening a way of escape.

And she was good at it. Adam could attest to that. In an ever-expanding circle of her peers, she had gained the reputation for being "the best" at solving the mysteries other shrinks chose to bury under medications.

Katherine had never been convinced that to be symptom-free meant health. She was all too familiar with the Lithium shuffle—that state of oblivion which enabled patients to stumble through life free of hallucinations, mood swings, and tics but in a state of mesmerized stupidity unbecoming any growing thing. She was, as an M.D., not naive to the breakthroughs in modern medicine, but she was equally alert to a world looking for a quick fix. She had long since determined not to be one of them, doggedly refusing the relief that came in little brown bottles with the childproof caps, insisting she would "wait upon the Lord."

Consequently, she had spent precious years fighting the insomnia, the nightmares, the hallucinations—sometimes, she was unsure which—and the deep terror that constantly ate at her gut. She had become accustomed to the distorted perceptions that left her feeling foolish, like the morning the pilot left.

John had done more to rescue her than any other person alive. He had been her champion, her intercessor, the one who saw something of value in her and called her to sanity . . . the one, in the beginning, whose expectations she had wanted to meet, the one who had helped her to function again. And he had never held her weaknesses against her.

Those early years had been an inescapable turmoil for them both as her insecurities alternately slammed them into each other and sucked them apart, repeatedly tearing the innocent bonds that love would grow. But in time, maybe the result of having previously tasted the greener grass, or, as Kate often suspected, a God-given grip in John that would not let her go, they gradually floated a bridge over the shaky foundation of her fears. That bridge had been solid enough to allow the passage between the past and present, necessary to sustain life, to work, to laugh, to cope. But she and John had never really cut the fetters.

Somehow John held her pieces together. His mere presence seemed to remind her of time and space and anchor her in this reality. Yes, she could see it all now. John had really become the anchor for her faith, much as Grandma Henry had been years before.

"Perhaps I've come here to fall apart," Katherine mused, not at all a comforting thought. She preferred so much to see the pieces fit together, to understand what had gone before—the events and the meanings—to complete the puzzle. "I distinctly remember planning this year as a time to 'get it together,' not to fall apart," she said, trying to sound cheerful.

The logs caught, spreading the soft flickering orange light like frosting on the walls. Her body reluctantly relinquished some of its tension, enough so she could stop shivering.

From the kitchen, on a shelf above the sink, behind some cups and plates, Katherine lifted a bottle of Benedictine she had brought along for "cold" nights. She jerked the cork and inhaled the vapor which hit her like smelling salts—just what she had in mind. Sliding an inch of the amber liquid down the side of a small jelly jar, she carried it back to the cozy place by the fire and watched the fire and liqueur mingle in the glass.

The first sip melted into a stinging spice she could trace all the way down to the tight fist in her stomach. The second flooded across her shoulders, gliding halfway down her spine. By the third swallow, Katherine could feel the lovely warmth thawing her chilled ribs and radiating out through her skin. She knew the second glass would carry off the guilt to the same magical land of make-believe that called to her now.

Heat gushed from both the stove and the fireplace. The temperature climbed to an unbearable pitch, until Katherine realized she was again covered in the soft down of perspiration. In desperation, she set the drink aside, stepped out into the Northwest night, and closed the door behind her.

The still, crisp air brought an invigorating wave of clarity. All the murky places in her brain snapped to attention as she located a spot on the step to sit down. Concentrating on her footing, finally out from beneath the canopy of the porch, she lifted her face to the sky. What she saw made her gasp, wide-eyed.

"Dear God!" she gulped, seeing the stars smeared across the purple sky. Thick, bright clouds of diamond dust clung to the emptiness.

Katherine stood up, absolutely enthralled, her head craned back between her shoulders. For as far as she could see in the wide dome casing above her, a brilliant finger painting lit the earth far brighter than any moonlit night she'd ever experienced.

As she stood motionless, inhaling the splendor, it was as if the dark metal sky was melting, sending spears of molten gold cascading from the canopy, hurling themselves toward earth. Light burning itself out in brilliance before it struck the ground, exploded like a whole skyful of soundless fireworks.

An astronomer friend had once told her that there are more stars in the universe than grains of sand on the entire earth, but she had never beheld them like this, one upon the other, in fathoms of milky streaks swirling above her.

A deep and comforting reassurance threaded its way through the light-years toward her. "It has always been like this," she breathed, "only I never saw it!"

"And so are my thoughts of you."

"Oh, Lord," she whispered, "more numerous than all these stars?"

She turned, looking back over the cabin, and the same angelic host sang its vision song, the song without sound that only the soul can hear. And somehow, Katherine heard.

Reaching for the cowering child within, Katherine lifted her hands up, up to the sky, up to the One whose invisible hand paints universes with stars as easily as a child pushes the slippery colors across wet paper. And in that miraculous moment, Katherine felt His hand close around hers. She felt the warmth of it, the compassionate flesh of it. She nuzzled her cheek against it and felt safe.

The mournful bark of a coyote broke across the spell, one and then another, calling from the ridges all around her, up and down the river, echoing her longing, crying to the light and being heard. Then it was still. It had passed.

Katherine exhaled a breath she could see. The ebony where she stood penetrated her sweats with cold needles of night air, urging her toward the warmth of the cabin. For a long moment she stood in the doorway, looking at the sky, marveling at what had happened, something beyond words, having no explanation, something which escaped reason or record.

Whatever it was, it was happening to her and she could do nothing but let it. All her mind could answer was, "Grace. Amazing grace!"

She had no idea what time it was. The lantern by the bedstead had consumed the wick to a smoldering spark, and the fire she'd left in full glory was now dying embers, which she knew for certain had taken more than the few minutes it seemed she had been gone.

She carried the glass of liquor to the sink and poured it, along with the entire contents of the bottle, down the drain and into the slop bucket below. Beside her bed, Katherine turned the crank on the lantern, leaving only her favorite firelight dancing on the ceiling as she lifted the quilt up to her neck.

Chapter 13

Something about the worn quilt reminded Katherine of Grandma Henry, maybe because it was old and used. Maybe because it felt like her. Katherine closed her eyes, allowing herself to drift in and out of consciousness, feeling the softness of her grandmother's hands, old and worn, like fine leather, more supple with use.

"Grandma Henry would have liked the tattered quilt. She never threw anything away, least of all children. Her home was an ebb and flow of grandchildren in various states of disarray. There was Daniel, a gentle spirit who lived there most of the time, for whom, like me, Grandma was really Mother. And Ross, a feisty colt who tried his parents sorely, and when it was beyond their endurance, which was most of the time, they sent him there, too. Matt and Sandy lived across the road, or at least that's where their beds were. And Hal, he was older than all of them. I never did know why he was there, but I loved his clipped British tongue and the way he addressed my grandmother as Aunt Alta. I think he was distantly related, or as she would say, a 'shirt-tail relation,' who had come for a visit and just never left.

"The Henrys seemed to be the hub of a wheel—the center where everyone connected. Their house was also a shrine of personal histories, in which memories were built and treasures kept for each of us, the second generation of children she raised.

"Daniel, eight years older than I, was born on April 28, the same night the peach blossoms froze, I've been told. Aunt Effie cut some branches for a bouquet around his mother's casket, which by morning had burst into bloom. I have as vivid a picture of that bouquet as if I had actually been there.

"Anyway, since he would never know his mother in this life, Grandma

Henry had fastidiously accumulated memorabilia—letters, trinkets, pictures, newspaper clippings that she kept for him in a scrapbook and large box in the linen cupboard. Daniel would spend hours touching the articles. I particularly remember a lace collar that he would turn over and over, pressing it to his face, as if trying to drag from his prenatal memory some trace of familiar scent.

"'What was she like?' he would ask, sliding under Grandma's arm, next to her on the rose sofa.

"'Well, honey . . . ' Grandma always began her stories that way. 'Mary Frances, your mother, was one of the loveliest persons I ever knew. She was tall and straight, like you, with silky blond hair like yours.' She would stroke his hair and tell him all the things she could recall of his deceased loved one, the precious stories that only she could tell in a way that made them so special.

"I would lounge on the floor, drawing or idly listening with my chin in my hands propped up on my elbows, swinging my feet back and forth in the air. I never felt so much as a twinge of jealousy. In fact, whenever Grandma gave time and attention to one of the others, which was often, it gave me a warm sense of security. In Grandma Henry's house, love was not a scarce commodity. There was plenty to go around. As I watched them together, I knew my turn would come.

"In fact, Grandma Henry had assembled a very similar box for me. The box contained bits of history from my father's life—military medals and insignia that were made like tacks, with brass sticks on the back and little brass spring caps to keep them from poking in your skin; a picture of him in high school, looking very young; some 4-H and FFA badges he'd won; some newspaper clippings, one telling about his prize cow and another about him going to some farmer's convention; more ribbons he won at the fair for animals and oats; a little embroidered baby hat that had darkened with time to a mellow amber. I would hold up that little cap, trying to imagine my father that small.

"Of all the artifacts, there were three things I treasured most—a packet of letters addressed to his mother and father from the strange places he had served on the other side of the world during the war; a tiny black leather Testament, with his name scrawled in the homely letters of a young boy, and a locket. Grandma never read the letters to me, but reminded me that someday I would know how to read them myself. Meanwhile, I just turned them and smelled them and laid them out in front of me.

"I was more the artist than the scholar even then, so I began copying them, imitating the curves and shapes of the letters, transcribing each one by the hours, although I had not the slightest notion of what the loops and curls meant.

"Some words and individuals of the alphabet were my favorites. I thought they were stunning in their grace and symmetry. Others I clearly disliked. As a result, my transcriptions were generally nonsense, made up of my favorite word pictures strung together to form a collage of my liking.

"Both Daniel and Ross, who were twelve and thirteen at the time, thought it was funny for a little kid to spend so much time writing stuff she couldn't read. Grandma always curbed their remarks by suggesting that I knew what it meant and that was all that was necessary. 'When it's important to her for someone else to know, she'll learn how to read and write like the rest of us.'

"So for years, I carried around my fistful of papers—my secret letters from my father, written on the insides of used envelopes. And at night, I laid the Testament on my bedstand, like Grandma did, and dreamed of the boy who had written his name inside. Although I could not read it, Grandma had helped me mark the Psalms. The Ninety-first I knew by heart, thanks to her tutelage.

"The other cherished object in my collection, requiring special care, was a chain and gold locket with the initials K. H., engraved in scrolled letters on the back. Inside was a tiny heart-shaped picture of my father looking very young and handsome, opposite a miniature American flag. My father had sent it to me before I ever saw him, along with a letter in a tiny square envelope, addressed to 'My Dearest Katie.'

"I would sit on Grandma's lap with the necklace clasped around my neck, holding the locket between my fingers until it was warm, and listen to his voice from the past, promising how much he loved me and looked forward to seeing me, and telling me that he would come home soon and make a home for me and my mother. It made me feel warm all over. Then we'd remove the necklace to its safe place in the envelope with the letter.

"Through the years I have been grateful for that collection and the stories about my father that went with it. The puzzling thing, though, was that unlike Daniel's mother, my father wasn't dead. He lived with my mother and little sister, and sometimes me, in North Carolina.

"As an adult, I can't help wondering if there was some hidden message in Grandma's collection. Perhaps my father had died to Grandma Henry when he married Janice. I always sensed that there was something amiss between them.

"Or maybe that wasn't it at all. Maybe. "Grandma felt she had lost her son to his job and his fancy life, that crowded out most of what she'd taught him. Maybe she really didn't know him anymore. It will never be anything more than conjecture on my part, because she never spoke of it.

"Janice, however, made little effort to hide her displeasure. She managed to avoid hearing from me anything about Grandma Henry, or anything we did during our time together. And when we got a letter from her, she grumbled that it was written on scrap paper, with carbon copies sent to all the other relatives. I didn't understand most of what Janice said about her when I was little. For that matter, I still don't understand.

"Grandpa Henry was a salt-of-the-earth man, admired and loved by everyone, the kind of person of whom it was said, 'If you can't get along with Ray Henry, you can't get along with anyone.' They farmed in a community adjoining the Hilemans' and knew many of the same people. But their worlds could not have been further apart.

"After the war, my father returned to my mother and me, then a three-year-old stranger. I think he intended to farm like his father and brothers, or maybe seek work in Ames, but Janice had other plans. She couldn't get out of the hokey rural existence fast enough, and on to bigger and better things. The need to escape propelled her with such ferocity that Daddy's farm-boy yearnings were turned to dust.

"Within months, he had 're-upped' for a career in the United States Air Force. She encouraged him to greatness, to make something of himself, and she was going with him.

"However, because they could not find suitable housing on base or off for a lower-ranked officer, they were forced to leave me temporarily behind. That was followed by a tour of duty in Germany, which further justified our separation. Leaving me with Grandma and Grandpa was a decision that would never be resolved. As the years unfolded, everyone was alternately frustrated and guilty as I was moved back and forth between my grandparents and parents.

"During the first six years after the war, and later, during the Korean conflict, Janice worked as a secretary to save money for a home when once Daddy was permanently stationed. With two working parents, it was nearly impossible to care for a preschool child. Consequently, they rationalized, it was best for me to stay with my grandparents. In the second year that Daddy was stationed at Wright Patterson Air Force Base, she became pregnant. Not in her plans! Since they had in the meantime secured the officer's quarters of married housing, it was decided again that I should return to my parents, because that was proper and because my mother needed help."

Katherine closed the journal and pulled the quilt up to her neck.

Katie hugged Grandm̃ ~~~~ tight, fighting the tears that threatened to spill from t̃ ̃ ̃ ̃ ̃ ̃ navy eyes. "There, honey, we'll see you at Thã ̃ ̃ ̃ ̃ ̃ ̃ ̃ ̃oner than you think." Grandma paã ̃ ̃ ̃ ̃ ̃ ̃ ̃ ̃ ̃ ̃ ̃ ̃ ̃ ̃ ̃ body off hers, but she kñ ̃ ̃ ̃ ̃ ̃ ̃ ̃ ̃ ̃ ̃ ̃ ̃ ̃ ̃ ̃ ̃ ̃ be ahead of the traffic. "Grañ ̃ ̃ ̃ ̃ ̃ ̃ ̃ ̃ ̃ ̃ ̃ ̃ ̃ ̃ ̃ about the kittens."

Katie held on, wishing she could magically blink ̃ ̃ ̃ ̃ ̃ time that must pass before she could return to this kitchen and hear her grandmother's familiar voice, "Oh, look what the wind blew in!" Then she would again be wrapped in security and kisses.

Preston brushed past with the black leather suitcase stuffed with everything she could take from the farm, including her clothes, which were of least significance to her. "Come on, Katie. We got to get going," he called over his shoulder. "We don't want to get caught in the morning traffic."

Grandma handed her a shoebox with a string tied in a bow on top, containing a little packet of oatmeal cookies wrapped in tinfoil, some stamped envelopes with the farm address, a picture of herself fishing up north, a feather, a nearly empty bottle of Grandma's Lily-of-the-Valley perfume (which Katie would never put on, lest she use up the only fragrance that reminded her of her missing life), some colored pencils, and other trinkets from the fair.

More important were all the precious items she'd left behind for safekeeping—the bracelet and letters, the amethyst ring Grandma had promised would one day be hers, golden sunsets, cricket sounds, sweet juicy fall pears, and the comfort of Grandma and Grandpa Henry's easy ways.

Preston hugged his mother briskly. " 'Bye Ma."

"Have a good trip . . . and drive carefully, you hear?" Grandma said as she walked them to the car.

Grandpa tousled Katie's hair and leaned over to kiss her cheek. " 'Bye Goose," he said and lifted her into the front seat opposite her father. "Take the south road, the other one is full of detours," he told her daddy. Then Grandpa pushed her door shut with both hands.

Katie could barely see over the edge of the window, to where Grandma stood with her arms limp at her sides, looking as helpless as Katie felt, tufts of gray hair blowing across her face. The morning air fanned her cotton housedress. Katie watched her for as long as she could.

As the wide black Buick made its turn in the circle drive, Grandpa put his arm around his wife, standing with her in front of the milk house. Grandma lifted her hand to shield her eyes from the sun. Slowly Katie's father steered the car past the silos and granary, alongside the long, white dairy barn, past the monstrous John Deere, and up onto the gravel road. Katie kept her wide eyes riveted on the couple, turning her body in the seat as necessary, craning her neck.

As the car swung left and rolled past the neatly trimmed farmyard, Preston waved with his arm out the window, grinning broadly, like he'd just won the prize. Grandpa waved back, as did the golden leaves on the ambling crab apple that stood by the mailbox.

The wind was already rattling the dry cornstalks, promising the cool autumn days of harvest, which Katie would miss this year. Purpose was lost to her, as the sense of familiar drained out of her onto the gravel road, leaving an empty spot in her stomach and an awkward child sitting next to a man she called Daddy.

They proceeded down the lane, the half mile to the paved road, until she couldn't see them anymore. Couldn't see her grandparents, or the white frame house with the blue roof, or the outbuildings. All that remained to be seen were the rows of corn she'd watched grow from the earliest tiny green spikes to the dense forest rows that towered above her head. She'd spent hours playing hide and seek with Matt and Sandy, giggling and racing over the mounded stripes of green poles. Now the rows stood mute in the morning sun, heavy with ears, sadly drooping their dark brown silks toward the ground.

"Crops look good," her father commented. "Should be a good year." Then he reached across the seat to pat her knee. "Bet you can't wait to see your mama. She sure misses you!" He pressed his foot to the floor, apparently anxious for his little family to be united again.

Chapter 14

The eight-hour ride "home" was boring and filled with embarrassed silence. Katie dozed against the seat, her head bobbing with each bump in the road. Daddy didn't talk much, so she was grateful when he turned on the radio and whistled along with the sounds of the big bands.

She liked to hear him whistle. The rifts and trills floating up and down the scale in lilting melodies sounded like the wild blackbirds that sang from the cattails growing in the dredge cut across the road from Grandma's. Grandma said she could always tell when it was Preston coming up the back steps by the whistle that went ahead of him.

After several hours, Katie announced awkwardly that she needed to go to the bathroom. He asked if she could wait till they needed gas. She guessed so.

Sometime around noon, both the car's needs and hers converged. Daddy took her by the hand and pushed her into the ladies' room. It was stinky, with pieces of wet toilet paper streaming across the perspiring floor. Katie tried not to touch anything. After she washed her hands, she couldn't reach the paper towels, so she dried them on her dress, which turned the cotton a dark blue. Katie hoped he wouldn't notice.

Just then she heard his knuckles tapping on the door, "Let's go, baby. Can't waste all day in there."

Back in the car, Katie saw that he had secured a semblance of a lunch, which they balanced in their laps and ate while they rode. When they jostled over a railroad track, she spilled some of the tuna salad sandwich down her front. Daddy's efforts to watch the road and swipe at her clothes at the same time only made it worse, broadcasting the mayonnaise spots over the ruffles Grandma had so carefully ironed.

Still hungry, Katie sighed and shook her head when he offered her more. He cleaned up her leftovers, gulping them down so as not to waste anything.

Together, they shared a quart of milk, drinking directly from the sweaty bottle, which they passed back and forth. Again they hit a bump, and Katie and the milk flew up, splashing her face, spraying up her nose, and of course, back down again to the skirt she was trying not to wrinkle.

As they headed southeast into the heat of the day, Katie began to perspire in little rivulets around her face until the wisps of auburn hair that had been so lovingly arranged in the morning stuck straight up when she tried to push them from her eyes. The back of her head looked as if it had exploded, by the looks of the matted hair that had crunched up from her fitful nap. And the little pink ribbon Grandma had tied in her too-long bangs had been sucked out the window when they passed a truck.

By the time they began seeing signs for Dayton, Katie was desperate to get out of the car. Except for the brief minutes in the ladies' room, she had been sitting in that seat for eight hours. But her boredom was overtaken by nervousness over seeing her mama again after over eight months. Her stomach felt like she'd swallowed a stone. She smoothed her skirt and hoped Mama would like her dress.

"Katie, we're almost there now." Daddy spoke with new enthusiasm. "See that sign?" He pointed to a large wooden billboard with the letter jumping out in three-dimensional patriotic colors. Katie picked at her cuticles. "That's where we live. That's the recreation hall, where you can play games and where we have parties for the grown-ups."

She peered over the edge of the window as they wheeled past a low warehouse-looking building with a large gravel parking lot. Some kids were riding two-wheelers out front.

"Oh, I should tell you . . . your mother is going to have a baby, so she'll be needing our help, 'cause she can't do all the things she used to do for us. You'll help, won't you? That's a good girl." He reached over and patted her knee again.

"Daddy, Misty's gonna have babies any day now." Katie looked over at his handsome face, peering intently through the windshield. "Grandma says she'll write to me and tell me about them. I hope there will be an all-black one. I'll name it Inky."

He mumbled, "Uh-huh," turning the steering wheel into a parking space in front of a two-story brown building with little bald porches missing their railings, evenly distributed, four abreast.

"Well, we're here, and we made good time—eight hours and fourteen minutes," he announced, looking at his wristwatch. "I'll get your suitcase. Can you manage the door? Don't forget your shoe box." He was out of the car, into the trunk, and halfway up the steps, second from the left, by the time Katie maneuvered the massive door and crawled out. She followed in the direction Daddy had disappeared, into a hallway that at first seemed like a dead end, very dark compared to the bright sunlight outside.

Then she saw the open door filled with her mother and father, embracing passionately. They must love each other a lot, Katie thought.

When Janice saw her daughter, she broke away, hurrying into the hall. She knelt and grabbed the tan little girl by her arms. "Oh, Katherine Henry! Let me look at you!" She smiled, turning Katie around so she could see her from every side. "My little girl is all grown up! But you haven't lost your big round eyes, have you?" She stepped back. "Well, give your mother a big hug," she invited, holding out her arms.

Katie set the shoe box on the floor and wrapped her skinny arms around her mother's neck. Over her shoulder, she could see her father smiling as he held the suitcase he was about to tote to some other part of the apartment. "Katie, Katie," she whispered, and Katie could see the tears in her eyes when she released her and, standing, took her by the hand. For a moment Katie wished mightily that her mother would lift her up, allowing her to straddle her body as she carried her through the door.

"Come. Let me show you your room." She led Katie through the kitchen and the living room beyond with its sheer swag curtains adorning the only window, and to a dark bedroom with bunk beds against the far wall.

Flipping the switch brought a startling glare of artificial light. "And this is your room, right next to ours." Daddy laid the luggage on the lower bunk, and Mama set the shoebox beside it.

"Oh, let's get you out of that dirty dress," she said pulling it up over Katie's head. "You'll feel better after you take a bath and put on some clean clothes." Katie watched as her mother stuffed the blue ruffles into a clothes hamper and slammed the lid shut.

Her mother ushered her into the bathroom, adjusting the water to the right temperature. Katie waited in the middle of a light pink shag rug in her panties.

"It's so good to have you home again, Katie. I really missed you." Janice kissed the top of her daughter's head and left the room, gently pulling the door closed behind her.

Katie stood planted on the rug and looked around. All the towels matched—fluffy, light pink ones—and were neatly hung over the chrome racks, their hems lined up perfectly, unlike the old washed-out, striped mismatches at Grandma's. A pink washcloth lay folded on the edge of the sparkling white tub, with a miniature bar of soap on top.

Cautiously Katie tiptoed to the door and peeked out through the crack. Her mother and father were sitting on the couch under the lovely window, Janice's leg draped across his.

"Why can't your mother at least send her home clean! She looks like a tramp! And carrying that shoe box! I'll bet her hair hasn't been combed in a month!"

Preston said something in a lower tone as Katie moved away from the door and slid into the tub.

"Let me know when you're ready for me to wash your hair," her mother called out from the other room.

Katherine rolled over, adjusting the old quilt over her shoulder. Then she buried her face in the pillow and sobbed, "John, Grandma, Someone!" Loneliness rolled over her with the weight of all the nights she'd stifled her tears, barely breathing, for fear they'd hear her and come for their explanation. Her ribs ached. "Lord, hold me!" she pleaded.

Chapter 15

When the sun topped the eastern rim, spilling molten rays down the other side into the weathered cabin below and across her face, Katherine opened one exhausted eye, refusing to venture from the warm spot in the middle of the bed. She could hear the birds marking their territory. But she wasn't interested in greeting the day. Her eyes felt like dry riverbeds. And she was quite sure that hot tears had continued to squeeze through her swollen lids long after she had lost awareness.

She really wanted to go back to sleep, but she couldn't ignore her thirst. She sat up, feet dangling over the edge. The night had been a wringer, leaving her flattened, void of substance. Her temples pounded and she had the sense of her face sagging in loose loops from the corners of her eyes.

This morning she was grateful for the absence of mirrors. It never helped to find out that she looked as bad as she felt.

Shuffling to the sink, Katherine made the effort to jerk the pump handle up and down till the cold clear water bubbled over her free hand. With it, she splashed her face and, gathering her unruly mane in a twisted knot at the back of her neck, scanned the room for the discarded hairpins, which she could have left anywhere. She found them on the arm of the sofa, next to a cold cup of coffee.

She wanted desperately to slide into a hot tub, but instead hauled her grinding stones and beans out to the porch. Dutifully, she retrieved the yellow flag from inside and hoisted the exchange up the pole as she had every morning since her arrival. Then she returned to her grinding.

When the coffee was brewed, Katherine sipped it in a stupor. Even this, her favorite beverage, tasted flat and uninspiring.

For some reason, all caring had drained out, leaving her without any inclination to do anything. She picked up the journal again and began to write:

"I wonder if I am feeling what I felt as a child when I awoke after that homecoming. Funny how many details I'd forgotten. They're finding their way back to me now, like the three little kittens who lost their mittens.

"I remember that year, when I entered second grade in North Carolina. We had to use 'sir' and 'ma'am' to address every adult, a custom which greatly endeared me to my mother, when I could remember to do it. And I remember that as my mother's belly grew, so did her impatience, until the day when she turned and screamed at me . . ."

"If you say 'Mama' one more time, I'll tear my hair out!" Katie's deep blue eyes widened, her lower lip trembling. Janice squeezed her arms, threatening to "shake the daylights out of her," pushing her away instead. Katie stared up at her.

"Oh, Katie . . . Mama's sorry. I didn't mean it . . . I just don't feel good today. Run and get my pillow so I can lie down here on the couch. . . . That's a good girl," she said, as Katie stuffed the pillow into the small of her back. "Now get up in your bed and take your nap."

Just as Katie turned to go, her mother caught her hand, pulling her back. "Katie, you're such a big girl now, why don't you call me 'Janice'? Wouldn't that be nice? Much better than 'Mama'—that's a name for babies, and you certainly aren't a baby anymore, are you! Why, you're already in second grade."

"Okay, Mama." Katie blinked, searching her mother's face, lowered in a coaxing gesture, to which Katie mouthed the strange word, "Janice." Janice smiled and fell back against the pillow.

"Janice!" Katherine spit out loud. "You couldn't even let me call you 'Mama' or 'Mommy' or 'Mom'! No! You had to be called 'Jan-ice.'" She forced the exaggerated syllables through her teeth.

Katherine poured herself another cup of coffee, recalling how miserable she'd been in the second grade, terrified of the big-boned, booming-voiced Mrs. Mercer, who could shrivel a child with a single glance. But it had all come to an end the night Daddy awakened her to take her back to Grandma.

"Where's Janice?" Katie asked, rubbing her eyes as her father threw her belongings back into the black suitcase from whence they'd come, his all-American features tense as he moved around the room in spastic jerks.

"Your mother's in the hospital."

"To have the baby?"

"No, she's sick. . . ." His voice trailed off. "Now hurry up and get dressed."

Katie couldn't imagine how her mother could be sick. Katie herself had dusted and washed the dishes, standing on a chair to put them away, and she'd folded the clothes, and had carried out every order Janice had dictated from the couch. How could she be sick? Even Daddy had come home early to cook and sweep. So how could she be sick?

As they were pulling out past the housing sign, she inquired, "Are we going to see Janice?"

"No, Katie!" His voice rasped with fatigue and exasperation. "Of course not! Grandma and Grandpa Henry are coming to take you home . . . back to their house . . . to the farm. We're meeting them at the hospital." Katie wanted to know why her mother was sick, if she wasn't about to have the baby, but she dared not ask.

The gravel spun beneath the tires as her father cornered and opened up. He gripped the steering wheel, driving very fast. From her vantage point on the front seat, Katie watched the clouds and treetops whiz by, now and then dreaming of fuzzy playful kittens and a black one named Inky.

Katherine dressed in jeans and a flannel shirt, pulling her hiking boots over the gray wool socks. She had decided days ago that this morning would take her on the other trail behind the cabin, the one that wound its way up the steep mountainside in switchbacks to ease the climb.

She threw some muffins in the canvas along with the thermos of coffee, slung it on her back and headed out, coffee mug in hand. She had no idea how long she would be gone or what she would find when she got there.

Rounding the shed, Katherine began the climb through a web of blackberry bushes, their long tentacles slowing her progress. She followed the trail leisurely, breathing in the heady air. The path was clearly marked, cutting back and forth on the diagonal so she was not even winded when she reached the tree line that afforded a stunning view of her wilderness world.

From the little gray cabin below, a soft curl of smoke wafted lazily on the air. The lawn, greening under late fall rains, rolled out toward the giant emerald firs, still wrapped in the leftover shadows of night.

Climbing higher, Katherine could see the river, could trace its silver journey through the earth. To the south the peaks pierced the morning mist that still clung to their tops, while the eastern slopes were gilded in sunrise. Here and there one mountain shadowed another.

Katherine sat down on a rock that grew through the crust and poured herself some coffee. Letting the coffee swirl in her mouth, she held it before swallowing its steamy essence. To her delight, the wonderful flavor had returned. She had to laud the vigor of exercise as a means of dousing the blues, a "quick cure" she had always resented as simple-minded.

Settling back on the rock, sipping coffee at an altitude that was breathtaking, she felt in charge and her thoughts wandered back to her mother and the autumn she had almost lost her baby.

While Grandpa milked, Katie sat on the barn floor in the straw, with Inky in her lap, purring as she stroked his throat and told him, "Janice's baby might die, Inky."

Grandma had tried to explain it to Katie, which prompted one of her letters, a collage of phonetic words and graphic pictures in which she flatly stated with all sympathetic intention, "I hope your baby does not die."

Grandma had encouraged her to take that part out, so she erased the words and replaced them with a line of tulips and butterflies. Had Mama looked closely and read behind the flowers, she could have seen what Katie was trying to say.

Katherine reflected on her present relationship with her mother, characterized by the fact that she still didn't know what to call her. "Janice" was so formal but was the name her mother preferred. "Mama" was childish. "Mother" might have been more realistic, but was not allowed.

Curiously, Katherine realized for the first time, she had always referred to Janice as "my mother" when talking about her, a term perhaps denoting an unconscious desire to connect with her. But when addressing her directly, Katherine still called her Janice.

"That about sums it up!" Katherine said with a note of disgust. "We have a postage-stamp relationship—a protocol of letters and phone calls—in which I pretend to be her sister or a friend . . . never her daughter. But just let us be together for more than an hour, and it's very apparent that she wishes I were Linda!"

Katherine pulled her journal from the backpack and began to write:

"Linda was the baby she almost lost that fall. I don't remember much about my sister as a baby. Probably that's because I wasn't around her very much. I surmise that Janice may have carried deep unresolved guilt over not wanting the baby, which resulted in years of devoted compensation and enshrinement. I don't really know this. It's only an educated guess.

"Still, she did always keep Linda with her, which is more than she did for me. I don't really know why she didn't want me. What I do remember about Linda leads me to believe she was not as easy to care for as I was. My sister was very active, talked and whined a lot. My mother often complained that she never sat still and rarely shut up. On the other hand, relatives tell me that I was quiet and compliant. Maybe it's just that I made my mother feel guilty because I had somehow fallen out of the nest too early."

Katherine looked up from her journaling and threw a pebble down the mountainside, watching it bounce its way to the blackberries at the bottom.

"So, okay . . . I lived without her! What's wrong with that?" she confessed to the clear blue sky. "I was loved and cared for by Grandma . . . she was my *real* mother. I hated it when I had to go and live with my parents." She touched the anger that floated easily to the surface whenever she thought of them. It was anger that grew as her own maturity increasingly revealed their lack of it. Their dealings with her, especially through adolescence, had often provoked her to wrath.

"So I understand the anger. But what's the hook? Why do I feel so responsible for her . . . so sorry for her?" Katherine put down the book and began pacing back and forth, gesturing with her palms up, like a courtroom attorney.

She returned to her rock again. "Maybe I'm just a nice person." John thought so. That was his explanation for why she could never do or say anything that might hurt her mother's feelings.

"No way!" she erupted. "There's something more." She had some trace memories which she trotted out to examine again. Maybe the altitude would help.

She returned to her writing:

"I recalled a night I lay in a crib, with Janice leaning over me, stroking my face, running her fingers through my hair. She was humming and her fingers felt cool against my skin. It is a delicious memory, sometime before I was a year old.

"It, like some of the others, clearly points to an intimate, bonded relationship between my mother and me, a bond that just as clearly was broken by the time my father returned, or shortly thereafter. Was it because I had to make room for him? Was I jealous? They often speak of my being jealous of Linda, but this was before that. Or were my mother and I estranged because she left me? Or was it something else?

"The memory of her is so vivid . . . so nice."

Katherine had closed her eyes to see it again when the subtlest drift of perfume floated through her head. Her eyes snapped open.

"Perfume! I don't remember my mother ever wearing perfume!" Katherine said aloud. "Once she even threw away Grandma Henry's perfume bottle in a rage . . . 'What? Is she trying to make me a streetwalker?' Janice said.

Yes! She was wearing perfume! Did she always wear it . . . or . . . was she going someplace special? Katherine's eyes glanced rapidly from side to side as they did when she was thinking.

Daddy was overseas then. Where would she go wearing per-

fume? Katherine thought. *What else was she wearing? How was she dressed?* She closed her eyes again.

All she could see was Mama's lovely face, framed in the moonlight, auburn locks falling forward. Katherine strained to see through the years, but it was too dark.

Opening her eyes, she thought, *My mother never wears perfume! And I never wear it when I'm with her!* It was another dead end . . . but maybe a new piece, like the spool on the parts door. Maybe it would still open to something important.

She picked up the pen.

"Then there was the other memory, a similar one. I lay in a crib, with moonlight softly bathing the white antique spooling. Through the rails, I can see my mother sleeping, the blankets of the double bed rising and falling rhythmically with each peaceful breath. I am engulfed in a delicious sense of well-being, the most poignant thing about this memory."

Katherine jumped up, throwing the pen in frustration, speaking her thoughts aloud. "Why remember that? What does that have to do with anything?" She exhaled slowly and sat back down to record her revelation.

"I'm sure both events took place when we stayed at Doctor Harris's. The Harrises had a big house on the edge of town. My mother cleaned it when they traveled.

"It was a good job, since it allowed her to be with me. We had a bedroom in the back. And at the same time, it was a supplement for the meager GI pay Daddy faithfully sent home every month, so they could have a 'nest egg' for the future.

"At about the same time, we also had the guest room across from the front door, at the Hilemans', which doesn't make much sense. I can't nail down a chronology. Like all prelanguage memories, the progression of events is scrambled and disconnected, like flashbulbs snapping pictures in the dark.

"But I remember many things about the Harrises, unusual recall for a child so young. Even my mother has confirmed that I can accurately recall the layout and much of the furnishings of that house. It was in that house, for instance, where my mother got cut."

Katie sat in a high chair at the end of a white enamel-topped table, pushed under a bay window. This window commanded a winter view of the field between them and the next house. The new-fallen snow matched the white sheer tiebacks that drifted to the corners of the window.

Doc Harris sat across from Mama. Between them was a white enameled basin that he had filled with cold water from the sink behind her.

Katie could see the blood, leaking in a curling stream of crimson into the water from the sterile gauze that had covered Mama's cheek. It swirled into the water like a red ribbon.

It was Katie's fault. Mama's lovely face had been cut when Katie threw the glass. She stared in silent shame as the doctor tried to repair the damage. It required stitches which made her mother wince in pain and bite her lip. Katie listened to the click of the hemostat as it grasped the curved needle and pulled it through her mother's skin. When he was finished a row of black knots with little tufts of thread ran across her cheek in the shape of a V.

Katie grew up looking at that scar on her mother's otherwise flawless white face, carrying the painful truth of how it got there. Although she had no memory of having thrown the glass, she never questioned her guilt.

And for a long while afterward, her mother would jump with alarm if anyone offered Katie a drink in a glass. "Don't!" she would shout. "She'll break it! Put it in a plastic cup. She throws glasses."

"But why," Katherine mused aloud. "Why does a kid throw glasses? Just heaves them across the room? And why is a baby terrified to sleep alone? Absolutely terrified! Why did I scream when put in a crib until they gave in and let me sleep with my mother? Was I just spoiled?" Katherine had covered this territory so many times she wasn't sure she'd notice it if she fell over a new insight. "Well, I'm not spoiled now, and I still have trouble sleeping!"

She gathered her thermos, stuffing it back in the canvas, and swung it to her back, resuming her climb. "Still . . . there is the perfume," she said to herself. "That's new!"

Katherine trudged on to the summit above the bathing pool.

Every difficult step seemed to fuel her frustration. She was angry that she couldn't get the past off her back, that it disturbed her tranquility, that she couldn't bury it or ignore it. The only path was through it.

Hot and thirsty, panting from the last uphill effort, she fought her way through the brambles toward a pool she could barely see glistening in the sparkling sun. She needed a machete. Sharp thorns caught at her clothing, letting go with a ripping sound, and pulled her hair loose, scratching her face and leaving tiny drops of blood in their wake.

She fought her way to the fern-lined pool—a place of solace amidst the moss-covered rocks. Its pristine loveliness was lost to her at this very moment. She was thirsty and mad—mad at the fight, mad at her mother, mad at the dead ends!

Katherine lowered herself to the water's edge and leaned forward for a drink, just as the thermos toppled out of the backpack over her shoulder, landing with a splash that sent the icy water into her face.

"Bingo!" she shouted, rocking back on her heels. "She threw water in my face! When I cried or was mad, she threw water in my face!" She lowered her voice to a whisper, narrowing eyes to a slit, "My loving mother threw water in my face! No wonder I threw the glass!" Her brain reeled with the revelation.

"I was never allowed to protest, to cry, to be afraid . . . just stuff it!"

There was a long pause as Katherine absorbed the pain. "Why didn't she ever let me talk?"

Chapter 16

The moon hung like a tear in the night canopy, a thin spot where a thumbnail had skinned the violet fabric, allowing the light from the other side to spill through in a yellow arc.

Katherine watched a thin white gauze float across the rip as if to bandage it. The stars faded in the wash of morning, as the eastern horizon waved amethyst clouds like sheets on a clothesline. One solo after the other, the winged chorus began, building to a full crescendo across the meadow.

Katherine loved the timeless evolution from violet night to lavender dawn. She thought of the mornings on the balcony with John, watching the sun reach across Lake Michigan to the towers of cement and glass, standing mute and unresponsive. It was the quietest part of the day, when they had sat together and shared in easy tones, praying for their needs and those of others whose lives were entwined with theirs.

It was a time between—the space when it is neither night nor day. That illusive moment when the day hides itself in the night and the night is diluted into day. That time when anything is possible and faith is easy.

In Chicago, Katherine mused, dawn seemed to come in answer to electricity clicking into the time card machines and newspaper carriers aiming papers at front doors, a signal to begin the cacophony and end the dealings of the dark. But here in the Northwest, tucked into the Cascades, the very stones seemed to cry out in celebration of the sun's arrival.

The landscape looked like a charcoal drawing, a moody day of purples turning to gray with the gathering light. Rain began in soft descent from a cement sky. Katherine moved back under the porch roof and listened to the droplets soothe the thirsty earth.

Summers in the Northwest were dry, with just enough moisture to keep life from sucking too hard on the reservoir deep within that sustained the giant trees. Katherine wondered if this were the onset of the fall rains, the relief from the drought of summer.

To Katherine, rainy days were peaceful days. She determined to keep a fire going and to make herself some wonderful soup and sourdough bread. She felt as if she had been running on reserve and was glad for the moody relief.

The past two nights had brought the familiar fight for sleep, which when it did come, yielded only fitful nightmares. Attempts to remember them were futile. All that remained were fading images of the toddler in high-top shoes, running, falling, as if in slow motion, never hitting the floor.

"I guess that's where I am . . . I never get to the bottom." Katherine exited into the kitchen, thinking about the revelation of the broken glass. She continued to turn all the pieces in her mind as she retrieved the vegetables from the cellar and started the chopping.

Descending the mountain yesterday, she had discovered some wild onions and vowed to include them, wishing she could as easily extract the ingredients of her past.

In the previous two and a half months, she had become quite adept with wood cooking and rather liked it. It assuredly took more concentration than she was used to, but tucked away here in the mountain retreat, she felt the necessity to be anchored to something.

Recently, she began to wonder what she would do if she really "lost it" and was here all alone. There would be no John to grab her back from the endless abyss. But some part of her had concluded that without John, she was not sure she wanted to come back anyway.

Besides, she reassured herself, she needn't worry about making a public display of herself, an idea which revolted her. She clung to the belief that her only concern was being found out. In that sense, this place had been an enormous relief, providing her the very freedom she sought.

But the past two nights, the old nightmares had returned

with a vengeance. Katherine felt her grip on seclusion weakening. She was about to pray for deliverance from the haunting images and the sick feelings when she found the words of her mouth and the meditations of her heart, "Lord, be with me in this. Show me what needs to be healed. Help me remember."

Katherine dumped the contents of the stirred bowl in a puff of flour dust and began the pushing and turning that would result in chewy fresh bread with an aroma that would surely call the raccoons. It felt reassuring to imagine she was baking for John. Kneading the bread brought remembrance of how John used to tease her about being antisocial.

"How long do you think you could go without seeing anyone?" he'd ask.

"Well, honey, I'd miss *you*," she had teased. "I'd miss you and the checkbook and all the long luscious arguments on the balcony in the lovely moldy smog of Chicago and . . ." at which point John would throw something at her.

"I do miss you, John. . . ." Her voice trailed off. "So, am I lonely here?" She turned the dough over. "I am lonely, but not here." Suddenly that struck her funny and she started to snicker. "Of course, I'm here. Where else would I be?" Now she laughed out loud, standing with her hands outstretched in front of her, the humor of it all rolling over her like a big joke. "Maybe I'm here but lonely someplace else. Oh, no, this sounds like one of the loony conversations I used to have with Adam. Like trying to prove to him that I was awake, not dreaming."

"Seriously," she said, recovering her composure, "you know what I miss?" addressing the room. "I miss the comfort of touch, of another body with heat of its own. I guess I never believed that I needed that." Crossing her arms, she rubbed her hands up and down.

"All the hours I listened to those battered and abused women. I never could figure out why they stayed. I wanted to scream at them . . . 'You idiot! Why don't you leave?'" She slapped the white dough. "'But, I love him,'" Katherine mocked their whining.

"I would have left. If John had *ever* raised his hand to me . . ."

Katherine knew there was something closed in her, some part of her being sealed off, unavailable to fellowship. A part of her that always protected itself. Never had she cast herself with abandon into the arms of another, not even her husband. It made her sad to realize that truth.

She surveyed the cabin. Fire spit and crackled in the wood stove; the propane lamps on the wall bathed the room with bright candlelight, replacing the daylight doused in rain.

"Of course it's because of my past," she said defensively. "Do I want company? Absolutely not! They never believed me when I told them I am a recluse at heart. Look at me! Do you believe me now?" She threw up her hands in a defiant gesture. "Do I miss voices and conversation? Or how about honking and beeping, or phones ringing, or Janice rummaging through my closet and finding *True Love* magazines.

"Oh, yeah. That's something I really miss." She covered the bowl and set it on an inverted flowerpot on the stove to rise. The old leaven began to work.

"That was a real moment in our relationship. No wonder I miss her so much!" She wiped her hands.

"Hey, Janice! You want to look under my bed!" Katherine shouted as she ran to the spool bed and pulled up the quilt. "What do you see?" she mocked. "Would you like me to read the dust to you?" Katherine fought the humiliation that rose with the anger until, sitting on the edge of her bed, face in her hands, she could hear Janice's shrill pronouncements.

"Okay. You think these filthy things are so great. Let's just hear what's so great about it. I've never read anything like this!" She flung the magazine at Katie. "Read it to me! All of it!"

Katie read through the tears, the sordid details of sappy romances and suggested sex. It seemed to take hours, during which time her mother's only reaction was a tongue clicking disgust and the injunction to read louder. "I want to hear every detail of your precious stories!"

When it was done, she paced the room and railed about how Katie could have subjected her to this humiliation. "And how do you think I will feel, watching you sing in the choir? Do you think I can forget this? And how would you like it if I told your saintly grandmother what I found? What would she think of you then?"

Katherine remembered the desperate longing she had felt then for Grandma Henry. She would gladly have taken her chances with the straight-laced matriarch.

She got up to check the bread dough before taking up her writing.

"There were so many memories, so many insensitivities, so much reason for anger. Yet, I could never confront Janice with it. All of my secret raging melted into a pool of misery whenever I should have opened up with my mother.

"Consequently, the years that followed were silent years, even to the present, years of taking the abuse without recourse, my own defense silenced. I am well familiar with why I am angry. What I do not know, cannot identify, is why I am afraid.

"And one seems to block the other. Sometimes I think that my rage is so intense that it is the cause of the fear. Perhaps I am afraid of what I might do to Janice. At other times, I am quite certain it was the other way around. Something is so terrifying to me that it keeps me from ever telling Janice how I felt.

"And, why does no amount of prayer or gesture or litany of forgiveness release me from this? Always the anger and fear lie just below the surface, waiting to devour me at a moment's notice."

The leaven had pushed the dough to the top of the pan. Katherine punched it down. Then shaping it into a loaf, she returned it to the warm spot on the flowerpot.

"God, what must I do to make it go away?"

It was Friday, the day of the drop. Over the weeks, Katherine had become quite proficient at dealing with that routine. She headed for the shed to get ready for the brief contact she had with life on the outside.

Having weathered six of these encounters, she felt a certain confidence in how it would go. There would be the trivial back and forth about how fine she was; he would offer to help; she would refuse, and he would send the precious cargo hurtling to the ground, then leave.

Katherine rummaged about the shed, checking for any last-minute needs. In one corner she noticed the pile of newspapers she had banished from the cabin, wondering if she would ever read them. For some reason, she had declined to burn them. Also, she sensed it was a small act of kindness on the part of the pilot to include them each time. Or maybe she was just imagining that he was trying to be nice because she was in this strange relationship with him, needing his skilled deliveries.

She felt the familiar vibration before she actually heard it. Within seconds the radio began to hiss.

"Ladybug. This is Ranger One . . . copy?" The connection was not the best today.

"This is Ladybug. I can barely hear you. Over." Katherine stood ready with her list.

"How's it going?" His voice was clearer now, as she could hear the plane rattling toward her.

"Everything is fine. Here's the list. Ready? Over." The radio spit something inaudible, which she assumed was the pilot asking for her requests, so she continued.

"Toilet paper. Garlic. Crisco. Paraffin wax and pectin for jam. And could you get me a new thermos? Over." Katherine flipped the switch, to a barrage of static.

"Ch . . . paper? Writing paper . . ." Katherine flipped it again.

"No! Toilet paper!" she shouted, "Bathroom tissue! Do you copy? Over."

"Chhh . . . issue? CHHHH . . . ab . . . aper?"

"This stupid thing!" Katherine sputtered to herself. "Now what?" She grabbed the microphone, articulating with precision, as if that would make the radio wave clearer, then flipped the switch several times.

"Do you copy? Can you hear me?"

"Ch . . . don't bother. CHHH . . . coming down!"

"That is not necessary! No!" Katherine felt helpless. The plane was approaching, aligning itself with the landing strip.

"No!" She threw down the microphone and ran toward the cabin, banging the shed door behind her. From the kitchen window, she could see the plane passing low over the trees.

"He's going to land!" She stared as the craft sank below the trees. "Well, he's going to wish he hadn't." Katherine stormed out and across the meadow toward the runway at full speed. As she reached the tree line, she could hear the plane coming down. The tiniest tongue of familiar fear licked at her ribs, but she shoved it down, rising to her full height, nostrils flaring, as she picked up the pace through the trees.

Rounding the bend, heels to the ground, she could see that the intruder had arrived but was not yet out of the cockpit. "And that's right where you can stay!" she spat, racing toward him.

Katherine reached the plane before he realized she was anywhere in sight. He had expected to have to find her or maybe even leave without seeing her. He'd long since figured that she was the most independent hermit he'd ever met.

"Just what do you think you're doing!" Katherine shouted, banging on the side window with her knuckles.

The man was leaning over, wrestling with something in the backseat. Startled, his massive body hurled around with such force that she jumped back. For a moment their eyes locked in standoff.

Then Katherine backed up a step. "I explicitly said, 'No visitors.' There is no reason for you to land."

The pilot opened the door. Stepping out, he held up his hands in a gesture of surrender. "Wait. Just wait. I can explain."

"I don't want your explanations! I want you back in that plane. Right now!" She was following him around to the other side, where the open door blocked her view of the cockpit.

He set a box on the ground, then lifted a small child from the plane. Katherine stared at her in disbelief.

"This is my daughter. Molly, say hello to Mrs. Allen." Molly smiled obediently.

Katherine cleared her throat and, embarrassed, dropped the short club she had picked up on the way. "Um . . . yes. Well. This *is* a surprise." Trying to collect her composure, Katherine knelt in front of the little girl, resenting her father for using the ultimate weapon against her.

"Your name is Molly. My name is Kate. How old are you, Molly?"

"Five and a half." Molly's brown eyes held her gaze, while the man unloaded the other items. "We brung you something . . . for a surprise."

Kate looked up to see Molly's father lift a squirming black puppy from behind the seat and hold it out like an offering.

Kate stared at him and at Molly standing beside him, smiling with tentative anticipation.

"We thought you might be getting lonely." The pup hung like a limp calf in his arms, its head drooping, its big brown eyes pleading. The three of them—Molly, with her tanned face, her homespun clothes, a barrette slipping from her silky blond hair; the father in cutoff jeans, logger style, suspenders over an open-collared plaid shirt, the irresistible puppy—looked like a poster with the subtitle, "Won't you please care . . .?"

Katherine was taken aback by their offer. "Oh, I couldn't."

"You can keep him," Molly butted in. "My dog had puppies, and he's the only one left. Papa said I could bring him up here to you . . ." she paused, "if you want him." Three pairs of soulful eyes bore down on her.

At that, the man put the dog down, whereupon the little animal became a squirming, furry ball of motion tumbling all over Katherine in a frenzy of greeting. The thick black fur blanketing his sixty-pound bulk was only the promise of things to come, she suspected.

"I guess he likes me." She grinned, watching helplessly, as the pup wiggled his way into her heart. "What kind is he?"

"Newfoundland."

"How old is he?"

"Nine months."

Katherine held the puppy's head still in her hands and looked at him. He represented an intrusion. But she could feel his body warmth penetrating her fingers . . . and her defenses.

His pink tongue reached out for her nose. Molly giggled.

Katherine slowly stood up. "Seriously, do you think this is a good idea?"

She watched as the pup bounded around the three of them. It was as if, after the unsteady plane trip, he was ecstatic to be on the solid earth again. She found herself laughing out loud. Molly lunged for him, then ran, with the pup at her heels.

"I guess I owe you an apology." Katherine shifted her weight nervously. "But I'm not sure I'm ready for a dog."

"Forget it. But we do need to find a good home for him. Look, if it doesn't work out, I'll pick him up later. Okay? He's a good pup."

"Pup! He's as big as a horse!" Her retort made him smile.

"Well, he'll be a comfort to you through the winter." The pilot leaned over to pet the wildly excited animal on one of his passes around their feet.

"Will he be okay here? I mean, in the cold?"

The pilot took off his hat to scratch his head with an exaggerated air of puzzlement. "Yeah, I guess. Newfoundlands like the snow. And they like water. They're still used on fishing boats to rescue men overboard, you know. So don't worry about the cold. He'll stand it better than you, I reckon."

"What will I feed him?" She had already guessed the answer.

"Oh, I brought along some dog food," he said, pointing to a large box on the ground.

Katherine shot him a sidelong glance. "Pretty sure of yourself, aren't you?"

The pilot smiled, a big sparkling white smile that reminded her of John. Molly and the dog joined them, both panting from exertion. The pup plopped his loose body down against her leg. Katherine leaned over and stroked his soft head.

"He has a head just like a bear."

"Can we see where you live?" Molly piped.

"Pardon my manners, young lady. Of course you may."

Molly held up her hand, which Katherine took. The child's father smiled and picked up the boxes. They fell in line, the second time Katherine had paraded to the mountain cabin. Only this time, she was in the lead, definitely on her own turf now.

She walked along holding Molly's hand, acutely aware of its warmth and the pressure of little fingers holding hers. It was the first human touch since Adam's embrace, which had fallen on numb receptors. It felt like a lifeline, like a stream of warmth melting something frozen within her. She wanted to pick the child up, hug her close, and bury her face in her plump neck.

Katherine blinked against the tears clouding her vision, grateful for the little chatterbox who danced beside her. She purposefully averted her eyes from the man's, pretending attentiveness to the roadside.

"We named him Cheyenne," Molly volunteered. "But Ben couldn't say it—he just kept calling him Ann. That's a girl's name. So Papa said we should shorten it to Chey." She pronounced it like "Shay." "You could keep that name if you want. Or you could name him your own name. Papa said I should tell you it's okay if you want to name him different."

Molly looked up at the pretty lady who walked beside her. "Mrs. Allen isn't scary, Papa. I think she's nice," she added matter-of-factly. With that, she proceeded to relax completely.

"Well, honey . . ." Katherine squeezed her hand, "I think I'll just call him Chey. That's a good name and it will always remind me of the sweet little girl who gave him to me."

They were near the clearing. Neither of the adults said much except the little it took to encourage Molly to keep talking.

When they reached the edge of the meadow, the pilot set the boxes down and lifted his daughter above the ferns so she could get a good view. "That's the cabin. See it way over there?" He pointed, holding her out in front, her feet dangling loose as she set her sights down his arm and off the end of his finger.

Katherine stepped back and observed the pair. He was a big barrel-chested man with a beer gut, probably in his late thirties. His giant fingers wrapped nearly around the girth of his delicate child.

"Yeah. I see it!" Molly reached for his neck and giggled into his face. "It looks like a hobbit house! Can we go see?" She wrapped her arms around his neck, her legs around his chest. He glanced at Katherine.

"Sure. In fact, I just made some bread. It should be about done . . . if it isn't burned to a crisp by now. Come on in."

Katherine was amazed that she felt so at ease with the visitors. In fact, all resentment seemed to have melted into the congeniality of the moment.

While Molly and the dog ran ahead, Katherine and the pilot walked in silence for a ways before he broke in to her thoughts. "I hope I didn't spoil anything. It's just I couldn't stand to think of anyone up here all winter alone."

They walked a ways farther before he added, "You know, once the snow comes, we can't get in. The strip isn't open enough for that kind of landing in the winter. So I just took a chance that you would like the dog."

"I don't know what to say except . . . thank you. I really do like the dog . . . and your thoughtfulness . . . and your daughter," who was waving from the porch, signaling her arrival with Chey, who stood patiently beside her, wagging his whole body.

"Well, she's not for sale." He waved back. "She's one little ray of sunshine I couldn't part with. Besides, her grandma'd be mighty upset if I didn't bring her back."

"Do you have other children?" Katherine asked, ignoring the obvious question about the mother.

"Just two. Molly and a boy—Ben. He's two."

They reached the steps, where the pilot unloaded the boxes as Katherine opened the door in a wide invitation. Without hesitation, Chey and Molly romped in. The fragrant aroma of fresh bread filled their arrival with warm hospitality.

Katherine went to the oven to inspect. "It's done," she said, lifting it up for admiration. "Care to join me? Have a seat by the fire. We'll give it a minute to rest and cool down a bit."

"This is just like our house, Papa. 'Cept it doesn't have a loft. And the furniture is different, of course," Molly chattered on.

He nodded, scanning the room, amazed at the transformation since the last time he had been here. "Everything okay?" he called over the back of the sofa to the woman who looked so at home in the primitive kitchen. "Everything working okay?"

"Everything is fine. Just fine." *Yikes,* Katherine thought, *we're back to that again!*

Chapter 17

"How about you? You got kids?" the man asked, poking the cold hearth.

"No. I don't." She felt slightly uncomfortable with the lie, but the truth was too difficult.

"The bread smells good. My mom bakes bread sometimes, too."

The space between Katherine and the pilot stretched like the Grand Canyon. She could not think of anything to say. Katherine was neither familiar nor comfortable with mutual relationships. In the past, she had found a reassuring hiding place behind her professional role, thus enabling the intimacy her clients so appreciated. Now, she tried to appear composed but was finding it difficult.

She cut and piled up heaps of steaming bread and carried it to the table. Molly slid easily into one chair. That left the other chair for the two of them. He immediately spoke up, "No problem. I can stand." Picking up a slice of bread, he leaned back against the wall, one foot across the other.

"When does winter come here?" Katherine asked, desperate to make conversation. "I mean, when can I expect the snow?"

"Hard to say. Could be any time between now and October." He spoke with his mouth full, "Good!"

"Did you say you can't get in during the winter?"

"Yeah. But it's not as bad as it sounds. If something happened, we'd come in on snowmobiles. But, yeah, it's impossible to land that crate in the snow. You need runners."

Molly sat quietly, chewing, and when they weren't looking, feeding Chey bits of bread.

"Hey! That's gonna teach him bad habits," the man said. "Don't give him food at the table, Mol." She raised her shoulders and made a funny face at him, like she'd just been tagged "it" in the game.

Her father moved toward her. "You done? Drink the rest of this milk."

"Papa, can me and Chey go back outside to play?"

"Sure. Just stay around. I don't want to have to look for you. And we gotta go pretty soon." Katherine heard that and wished she could somehow prolong the visit. At the same time she was ready for relief from the awkwardness.

Most of her adult life, Katherine had avoided people, refusing to answer phones and doorbells whenever she could get away with it, always finding excuses to decline invitations. As he took the empty chair, facing her with just the table between them, Katherine felt like a mute. She was bathed in self-consciousness, wondering how she must look, not having seen her own face for over two and a half months.

She could hear the child talking and humming on the porch, through the door left open a crack. And the man didn't seem the least bit off balance as he helped himself to another piece of bread.

"Where you from? Chicago?" he asked. Katherine nodded. "Big place, I guess. I never been there," he went on, spreading the butter. "I never been east of the Rockies, in fact. Oh, unless you count Nam."

"You were in Vietnam?" she asked, with a note of incredulity.

"Yeah. Just a working stiff—didn't have no deferment. There was no work in the woods, and I needed a job. Uncle Sam was gonna get me anyway, so I signed up." He looked up at her. "Crazy, huh?"

"Where were you in '68?" Katherine asked, trying to sound nonchalant.

"In the rice paddies, wading around like some lost duck! Why? Where were you?"

"I was in Chicago. In school. Trying to keep my nose out of politics. Trying to mind my own business." Then she added, "I got married then."

"You're married?" He stopped eating and stared at her.

"Yes, well, I was. . . ." Katherine cleared her throat. "My husband died last fall."

"Oh. Sorry." The awkwardness was back. Katherine could feel the tension laying bricks between them. She wished she had never told him about John. She felt she had betrayed something just to keep the conversation going.

Katherine got up to retrieve the coffeepot. Every step across the pine floor sounded like the echoes of eternity. She could not remember feeling so bumbling since the ungainly years of junior high. She sensed him watching her, which made the heat of embarrassment rise.

"What did you do in Vietnam?" she asked, hiding behind the coffeepot.

"I flew helicopters, when I wasn't tramping around in the muck. What do you do in Chicago, when you're not minding your own business?" he said, deftly throwing the conversation back to her.

"I listen to people."

He looked up in surprise. "You listen to people?"

"I'm a psychiatrist."

"Oh, man! Great! You're a shrink!" He squirmed in his chair, darting glances around the room as if he were looking for something to crawl under.

Katherine had always loved that reaction to the disclosure of her profession. The corners of her mouth took an upward turn. She was in charge again. "Oh, don't worry. We can't read minds," her grin widened, "exactly."

Feeling magnanimous, Katherine changed the subject. "Tell me about the dog."

"What about him?"

"I mean, what do I have to know about him? What do I need to do for him?"

"Feed him."

"Is that all?"

"Well, you could pet him now and then." Their words were now repelling each other like the similar poles of a magnet.

Suddenly she sensed she'd lost the edge again. *Men are so good at controlling conversations by what they don't say.* How was it they never seemed to mind the cavernous empty spaces in communication? What was there about some of the male species that never seemed embarrassed, that amazing ability to mark as their territory any place they happen to be? Katherine sensed that her only option was retreat.

She felt the room shrinking and the air congealing into a thick morass. Gesturing with her cup in the direction of the door, she turned to go, hoping he would follow. She could feel his eyes on her as she crossed the room. At the door, she shot a glance at him. He sat there like a still life, mug in hand, elbows on the table, the slightest hint of a smirk under his red beard, leaning back in the chair like he owned the place. Katherine wanted to admonish him, tell him that the chair was old and he might break it.

Outside, the dog was flopped on his side, dead to the world, while Molly played dolls with some pinecones. She looked up.

"Hi. We got pinecones at our house, too. And I make dolls out of 'em." She wobbled one back and forth in a pantomime walk.

The pilot joined them, sitting opposite Katherine on the step. "Sure is beautiful here, isn't it?" he commented.

Katherine looked across the meadow and thought, *Yes it is beautiful, more beautiful than you know,* but instead she asked, "What's your name?"

"Cyle."

Katherine chuckled.

"What's so funny?"

"Oh. I'm sorry. It's just that I knew a Cyle once. His mother went crazy."

"Maybe I'm him."

"I don't think so," she added. "You're too old."

Cyle stood up, his six-foot frame towering above her. "Come on, Mol. We got to get our bones in motion. Say goodbye to Chey." The pup popped his head up at the mention of his name. Molly hugged him with her whole body, which he patiently endured.

"Thanks." Katherine extended her hand in a gesture of peace. She felt his hand close around hers, a touch far different from the child's. His palm was padded with warm weathered calluses like a catcher's mitt that sent a warm signal rushing all the way to her blushing right ear.

"Thanks again," she said, stepping up two stairs till their eyes were level, "for the dog. And the company."

He held out his hands for the child, who jumped off the steps into his arms. With one motion, he swooped her up to his shoulders. "You don't need to walk us back. Appreciate the bread and the coffee."

"And thank you, Molly," she said, "for visiting me and for Chey. I'll take good care of him. You can come see him again, I hope. Don't you want to take your dolls?"

"No. You can have them. I got lots at home." Her elbows resting comfortably on her father's head, Molly pulled his knit cap down over his ears.

Katherine knelt to hold the dog who was ready to follow them. Molly called good-bye to Chey as they turned to go. Hands on his daughter's knees, Cyle strolled off across the meadow, whistling as he went.

Suddenly, Katherine remembered the list. She shot off the porch, running toward them.

"Wait! I forgot something!" Cyle turned. Katherine slowed to a fast walk, not wanting to appear too clumsy. He stood holding his daughter's knees and waited for her to close the gap between them.

"I'm sorry. I forgot to give you my list. I need a new thermos. Could you get me one? I dropped the other one . . . lost it in the water . . . up there." She pointed toward the hill behind the cabin, keeping her eyes on his. He just looked at her. "Is something wrong?"

"Uh, no. Guess I forgot all about it, too. So what do you need?" He pulled a small tablet from his flannel pocket.

"Like I said, I need another thermos. One with a wide mouth, so I can filter the coffee into it. And could you bring me a package of paraffin wax so I can seal jam?" Katherine rolled her eyes to the sky, recalling the list. "And, oh, yeah. Garlic and toilet paper."

"That it?"

"That's it." She turned to go, then turned back again, "And Crisco."

"Okay. Crisco. Anything else?" He stood with the tablet in one hand and a pencil poised in the other.

"No. That's all."

"See ya." He waved.

The dog stood between them, unsure of which way to go. Katherine called him, slapping her thigh. His response was immediate.

She reached the steps before turning to watch them go. Remembering how it had been the first time he left, she was thankful he didn't know. Cyle resumed his whistling. Suddenly a wave of loneliness struck her with such force she had to sit down.

The gentle morning breeze carried the melodious notes back to her from the place where they disappeared into the trees. She could not remember ever being carried on her father's shoulder.

A wet nose, with a fuzzy black head attached, lifted her arm, sliding it into her lap. She leaned over, drawing the dog to her, and buried her face in his soft coat, crying. She could hear the plane, following it up into the sky with her mind.

"Good-bye." She looked up and waved limply to the empty dome above her.

Chapter 18

Katherine had always wanted to feel that her father loved her, not just that she was part of his responsibility or his image. She had longed for him to see her, to respond to her, to be the man in the letters, the farm boy from Iowa, Grandma Henry's son.

In her journal she wrote:

"But he was always in a hurry, on his way to meeting with significant people, like senators and hunting buddies. I wonder what I would have had to do to earn the status of 'significant other.'

"As a child, he paid attention to me only when the opportunity arose for him to teach me something. He drilled me on the alphabet until I cried in helpless confusion, and he tried to teach me to play tennis until my knees were bleeding and I couldn't see the ball for the tears. Finally when I fell and broke one of his best rackets, he gave up on the lessons.

"His lessons usually ended in his total exasperation and my loss of speech. He'd yell at me, 'Why don't you talk! Why do you just cry all the time?'

"Somewhere along the years, I guess he gave up on me. Or maybe he was angry at something. It seemed that way.

"I know he was constantly worried about Janice, that she might work too hard or in some way be inconvenienced by my mere existence. It was as if he sensed that I could stay only as long as it wasn't too much trouble. I was always there on a trial basis, like I was a stray or something. Actually, I think he wanted me to take care of her so he would be free to play and be important. It was all a charade, their relationship. A grand charade!

"When I was a teenager, he rarely spoke to me, except to inquire about Janice's whereabouts or to enforce the rules or lecture about how irresponsible and lacking in self-discipline I was. There were never any letters, no phone calls or messages of care. And there still aren't. He leaves all that to his wife."

Katherine looked at the dog, with his head in her lap, and wondered how much trouble he'd be. Then she vowed to keep him regardless.

Stroking the soft black fur, she wondered how she could repay Cyle and Molly. It suddenly dawned on her that John was always right about another thing.

"Kate, you never let anyone give you anything. Why can't you just take it in?" he would say in exasperation. "You don't even let God give you anything! You always have to earn it!"

He was right. What she wanted so much—the affection and affirmation of her parents—she had learned to fear, to keep a healthy distance lest their "offerings" be too costly.

As a result, she would not receive either gifts or compliments from anyone else either. Clients often sent her cards of thanks and affection, the kind John said he could have savored for months. But she just noted the signature and put it in their file.

Instead, Katherine gave to others—mostly to her clients— what she had always longed to receive—acceptance, patience, unconditional love, esteem. Every gift to her, she held at arm's length.

She leaned over the dog as the sky opened, pelting the ground with water. The brambles trembled on the porch railing. Then the cloudburst ended as quickly as it had begun, replaced by the sun making diamonds of the trickles along the ground. Water droplets lay cupped within thirsty green leaves and speared on shafts of grass. The colors of the meadow glowed in the rich light that fell between the thunderheads.

Katherine leaned back against the porch post. Chey closed his eyes, drifting into a contented nap. The heavy rain clouds floated above in a rapid eastward direction. By afternoon it would be dry enough for her first walk with Chey.

A movement at the far end of the meadow caught her eye. Stepping from the trees was a sleek doe with her twins at her side. They nibbled their way along the edge of the clearing, then trotted casually across the grass toward the river. Katherine could hear the birds twittering, grateful for the shower. A spirit of peace had descended as mercifully as the rain.

"Maybe we'll go fishing." She pushed Chey from her lap. He followed her into the cabin, wagging his body, attentive to her every word, learning her language. He sat in the middle of the kitchen floor, so she had to walk around him as she cleaned up lunch. When she went to get the leftovers from the table, he followed her there and then back to the kitchen again.

It seemed odd to have another body in the cabin. Katherine had not had a dog since the farm. And farm dogs were never allowed in the house, except one very cold winter when Cameo was old and Grandma had let Katie make a bed for her just inside the back door on the landing to the cellar.

"I don't know very much about fishing, Chey. But my father took us fishing a couple times in Vermont." He snapped to attention when the pump handle squeaked.

"That was before Linda died," she said, wiping the flour from the counter. "I was twelve when Linda died. We didn't go fishing much after that." Chey cocked his head, sweeping his tail back and forth across the floor. "I guess when Linda died, a lot of things changed."

Katherine tended to the fire, with the dog right beside her. She liked that. Wherever she went, he followed. That seemed to allay her fears that he might decide to run off or be indifferent to her.

Quite to the contrary, Chey proved to be an extremely loyal companion from the very beginning. Any reluctance in bonding was not his. There would never be any question about his commitment to her.

"Anyway," she went on as if it were necessary to explain herself to him, "my mother went into a funk that lasted about two years. It was one of those times when I went back to Grandma Henry's. That's where I wanted to be . . . still, I felt like a failure leaving Janice.

"I think my father was disappointed that I couldn't make her feel better. After that, she spent most of two years in bed with various illnesses, until she was finally medicated."

Katherine settled back into the sofa. When Chey jumped up next to her, she pushed him off with a firm, "No. You stay down." After that, when she sat on the sofa, he was content to sit with his head in her lap.

"Poor Janice. She lost the daughter she loved. Linda was a bubbly little kid with golden hair who made them both feel good. I guess I always made them angry and guilty." She sighed. "I don't know what happened between my mother and me. We just never clicked after I was about two. But I can't figure it. Why did she leave me? . . . Why did she change?"

By late afternoon, Katherine had done all the inside puttering she could stand while the dog alternately watched and slept. She'd expounded in animated dialogue to him about her past, by way of introduction. It felt good to have an excuse to talk out loud.

At last it was time to leave the confines of the cabin, to venture out with her newfound companion, to see whether he would remain her companion or was just waiting for an opportunity to escape.

The sun fell in patches between the clouds as the two headed out across the meadow, Chey close at her heels. He had not come with a collar or leash. Katherine had not dared to inquire about such restraints, sensing that she would surely become the brunt of many jokes in a local tavern somewhere. So this was the test. If he was going to run from her, better he do it now, before she became attached to him.

The entire landscape glistened as if it had been dusted and polished. The greens were as iridescent emerald pools, holding tiny drops of sparkling water in solitaire settings.

Katherine stared up through the giant firs to the place where they pointed at the sky racing by. Her breath still caught in awe and wonder at such sights.

When they turned west along the river, Chey trotted on ahead, stopping here and there to sniff and mark. Chickadees and other winged residents flitted between the branches.

Suddenly, a rabbit caught his attention, leading him in a chase through the brush and out of sight. Katherine took a deep breath and called him back, not at all confident that he would respond. Then she saw his agile black form, clearing a fallen tree. He bounded toward her and plopped at her feet. Apparently he was more willing to be with her than even to chase rabbits. Katherine marveled and told him what a good dog he was.

They continued, threading their way along the path that led over moss-covered boulders, all but buried in compost. They walked under glittering yellow maple leaves trembling on the end of slender black fingers, reaching into the pools of sunlight. Over and over the same ritual was repeated. Chey would bound off in enthusiastic pursuit, only to abandon the chase in obedience to the sound of his name. He seemed to genuinely love the game.

They came to a place where the trail led through a small clearing. Katherine picked up a stick and threw it. Chey lunged ahead and grabbed it up from the ground. Stick in mouth, he stood looking at her, as if waiting for the rules to this game.

Katherine slapped her thigh. "Here, Chey! Bring it here!" He immediately romped toward her and dropped it in front of her. "Good dog!" she repeated, roughing his ears, impressed with how quickly he learned, even if only a game he had played with Molly.

As the weeks passed, Katherine enjoyed the dog more and more. She delighted in his companionship, was touched that he seemed so happy to be with her, to go where she wanted and to do as she asked. And all the while demanding so little, just that she feed him and let him be near her.

One cool afternoon, they were on the high trail, picking berries. Chey nosed around while she picked, humming a melody, the words to which she had forgotten, except for the line, "The only thing I require of you, is that you remember me loving you."

She wasn't sure, but she thought it had been sung by the Dominican Nuns, some recording that never made it to the pop charts in the sixties. The song had always seemed to her the most perfect description of unconditional love. She wondered if that could possibly be what God required of her. Did He ask nothing in return . . . only that she let Him love her?

Katherine looked out across the vast expanse before her— the valleys and emerald mountains. The scene was picture perfect, framed in blue sky and fluffy white clouds. A world that stood at His feet and received His grace—the grace of the wind and rain, of birth and life and death. She felt small on the mountainside, holding her bucket of blackberries, the sweet fruit He'd hung on the ends of the branches that clung to the vine.

On the way down, Chey flushed a covey of quail. The fat dawn-gray birds fluttered up in every direction. A ways further, they both heard the distant call of geese in flight. Far above them, she located the dotted line of birds, flying in V formation, moving south across the sky. She wondered what winter would be like.

Back home, the cabin was warm and homey. In no time she had the cookstove fired up. She dumped two large buckets of berries into the stockpot, filling it nearly to the top. When it was boiled down, it would become syrup, jelly, and juice.

She kept thinking about life without penance. What would it be like never to make guilt payments? What would life be like if she owed it no debt? If she didn't have to earn love?

Toward evening, the fruit had simmered to a thick crimson liquor, which she strained through a cheesecloth. The pulp bled into the white gauze as she tied the cloth in a bag that she would boil again, further extracting every drop of the flavor.

Katherine couldn't resist a taste. She poured a small amount in the bottom of a glass, grabbed a piece of bread to savor with it, and headed for the table to taste the labor of her day.

Her aching muscles sighed into the wooden chair. Her shoulders felt like they carried the weight of the world.

The bread and the juice lay before her on the uneven boards of the old table. A dying spear of sunlight found its way between the shutters. Striking the crimson contents of the glass, it sent a rainbow of refractions on the coarse, homely bread beside it.

Katherine stared at the juice and the bread, as strange but familiar words floated through her being: *This is My body broken for you . . . My blood shed for the new covenant between us.*

She ate the bread and swallowed the juice. "A new covenant, Lord?" she whispered. "Between You and me?" She bowed her head. "Let the work be Yours. . . . Let it be in my life as You would have it."

Chapter 19

Katherine retired to the sofa and pulled her feet up. Stretching out, she let the weariness take over, leaning into a cloud of sleep. For some reason, she thought of Linda's funeral, of which she remembered very little. Perhaps writing would help jar her memory. She reached for her journal.

"I do remember that Linda died of infectious meningitis the summer before she was to enter first grade. In my mind's eye, I can still see the pretty school clothes my mother had bought for her in preparation. And how angelic Linda looked in the pink-lined coffin with the pink rosets spilling down the side.

"Mostly, though, I remember Janice, like a violin string drawn tighter and tighter, her voice resonating in ever higher pitch. Once during the service, I reached over to hold her hand. Janice pulled away."

Katherine put down her pen and nodded off.

She was riding in a car, standing on the seat next to Uncle Sel. She could see them pull into a farmyard, with geese in the driveway. When Uncle Sel got out of the car, a dog ran toward him from the front porch. Barking, snarling, he lunged toward her uncle! Katie screamed!

Chey stood between Katherine and the fireplace, barking at her. Heart pounding, she raced back to reality. But not before ripping a scrap from the other.

"Oh God!" she gasped, as the flood of memory washed over her in horror. They had gone to a farm to collect a bill.

Selinus Hileman often went to get money from the "deadbeats" who owed him.

Uncle Sel slammed the car door shut, telling Katie to stay in the car. Across the yard, the dog advanced, his claws extended, hair bristling, hind quarters low. Uncle Sel headed straight for the front porch, oblivious to his violation of the invisible boundary the dog had set.

Then the German shepherd jumped. And what Katie saw caused her to gag!

Without missing a step, her uncle's huge hands caught the animal in midair, gripping its throat, squeezing the life out of it. He held it out from his body, shaking it. The dog pawed frantically at the air, wrenching its body from side to side in convulsions, emitting a liquid snarling sound. Then it went limp. Uncle Sel threw it in a heap under the porch.

"Dear God!" Katherine sat upright. Perspiration covered her trembling body. Her heart pounded. Chey stood at attention, staring at her as she swiped at her forehead with the back of her hand. But she could not wipe the memory from her mind.

"Lord, what kind of a man was he!" Katherine shot to her feet, shaking her head, nervously running her fingers through her hair. She half-ran to the door, jerking on it, desperate to escape. She could not erase the image of the dog, pawing and foaming at the mouth.

Once on the porch, she exhaled the long breath she had sucked in, in horror. Stepping into the sunlight, she threw her head back, trying to inhale a fresh reality. Her stomach turned with a wave of nausea she couldn't swallow fast enough. It erupted in painful force, spilling her insides over the porch railing. She clung to the post, heaving.

Katherine felt her legs dissolve beneath her. She slid down in a heap on the plank floor, muscles convulsing in released fear. Her ears rang with the snarling, foaming bloody sound.

Instantly Chey was in her face, nuzzling and licking her. For several minutes, she lay there, stunned, letting him minister to her lifeless being. Gradually, the violent trembling eased and she could breathe in even rhythm again. Grabbing her knees, she rolled sideways, curling herself into the smallest space.

For nearly an hour, Katherine lay like a stone, eyes wide, frozen in memory. Then a strange calm descended upon her. She hauled herself up on shaky legs and started for the meadow. She fell once, bloodying her knees, but tossed her hair and pushed herself on. Tears began to fall. It felt good not to fight them.

Chey walked resolutely beside her as they proceeded toward the river. Each rote step seemed a motion of someone else's body. Mechanically she pursued the river trail. The roaring of the water racing its course seemed to lure her, to entice her to a course of its own. Katherine walked the trail in a daze, turning and stepping with a precision learned of the past months. As her pace increased, Chey trotted along beside her, keeping his great brown eyes on his charge, as if her very life depended on him.

They came to the place where the river flattened and turned, cutting a deep crevice from the rocky bank. The glittering water sang an invitation to bury her face, to silence the pain and loneliness, to wash away the fears and the horror in its thick, cool, empty world.

Before her loomed the sickening picture of the helpless dog, his barking strangled in the death trap of her uncle's hands, squeezing, squeezing the breath from the animal. The ugly vision was unbearable. She wanted desperately to wash it from her mind.

Without a word, Katherine waded in. She opened her mouth to scream but stumbled and fell forward into the icy water. The water slapped her hard in the face, silencing her screams, shoving them farther down her throat.

Her limp body caught in the twisting current. Whirling, she could see the jade bubbles rising like jewels around her as she was drawn down into the murky darkness. Over and over she tumbled helplessly in the current. She could see the sunlight on the water, sparkling far above her, fading as the distant sound of the barking dog.

Deeper and deeper into the quiet, she sank. *I'm so tired. So tired . . . tired of fighting . . . tired of being afraid.* Katherine closed her eyes. *God forgive me. . . .*

She was moving upward, toward the light. Through a narrow tunnel, her limp body rose, drawn by a strength beyond her own.

Suddenly, in a liquid explosion, her head burst through the surface into the air, the dog attached to the knot of hair at the back of her head. Katherine gasped and choked, coughing and gulping the air, fighting to right herself as the dog dragged her backward toward shallow water.

He delivered her to the smooth warm river rocks. She lay beached, stunned, half-conscious, coughing and choking, shivering in another reality. When she opened her eyes, the sun burst in a blinding halo around the enormous black shadow that stood over her, like an eclipse, six inches from her face.

Katherine went wild with fear. In total frenzy, she scrambled backward, unable to escape. Throwing back her head, her body rigid, Katherine screamed. And screamed. Agonizing sounds vomited up the deepest terror, trumpeting through the empty halls of her being. Cold-blooded screams, sharp bleeding darts that sent the jays screeching into the air, joining her alarm. Chey jumped back, barking.

The woman's terror pelted the forest, jolting the serenity, richocheting from the mountain ridges and timbers, till it seemed the sound came from everywhere. Till the earth itself was screaming, crying out, as Abel's blood from the ground.

Every creature awoke from its sleep, froze in its tracks, lifted its head. The startled young doe sniffed the air, turning her great antenna ears, eyes wild in panic. Then it stopped.

Katherine's lungs burned with every labored breath. Her brain was a dull pounding, the veins in her neck swollen. For a long time, she lay still, registering nothing. Gradually, the smoothing rhythm of her own breathing brought the reassurance of where she was. When, finally, she reached up a hand to touch him, the dog lay down at her side, resting his head on her rising and falling stomach. She could feel the warmth of his body through the wet fur, holding her in the breach between himself and the sun-soaked boulders beneath her, cradling her in a safe place.

Katherine was dazed, confused about what had just happened. Had she wanted to die? Or had she merely slipped into a current too strong for her? Or . . . was she doing to herself what had been done to her—silencing—something she had learned from her mother so long ago?

Inside, she felt something snap, give up, yield. "Lord," she whispered, "I've always wanted peace . . . security . . . a way out of this misery. I have run and run. Now I ask . . . do what You must . . . to take me through this. Please, God, help me . . . give me courage."

Gingerly, she sat up, light-headed. The water lapped at her thighs, water warmed in the shallow tide pools out of the mainstream of the river. It gently patted her.

"Poor thing," she said hoarsely. "You got more than you bargained for." She was not sure if she meant Chey or the dead dog. Maybe both.

Chey whimpered and lay his head on her shoulder. Gathering him to herself, she gently rocked and comforted him, as she might have the four-year-old who had witnessed the grizzly scene. Tears softly washed her face. Holding the dog in her arms, with her face lifted for anyone to see, Katherine cried out loud, letting the wails roll up from the same sick pit as the nausea. "Oh, God! Oh, God! Are You there? Hold me!"

Chey licked the salt from her cheeks. Katherine didn't try to stop the flow. For once in her life, she didn't care. She cried openly, before the One from whom no secrets are hid.

Chapter 20

Back in the cabin, Katherine fed the dog, built a fire, and changed into dry clothes, in that order.

"Was I ever scared of him!" She shivered, settling into the sofa, facing the warm fire. She could see her uncle's hands—big powerful fingers, grimy with grease and the dog's life embedded in the skin and under the nails. With new resolve, she began to own her fear instead of hide it.

Even though she had been his favorite, and consequently appointed ambassador by her mother and grandmother, Katherine now realized how totally terrified she had always been of him.

"No wonder!" Katherine could not stop shaking. "And worse than that, I was always the one they hid behind! 'Katie go ask your uncle for this'; 'Katie, tell your Uncle Sel we want to go here or there,'" she mocked. Chey moved closer.

She jumped up, startling the dog. "Why were they so stupid! Didn't they see what was happening to me?"

Pacing back and forth in front of the hearth, she lectured Chey, who sat against the sofa, turning his head to follow her progress. "For some reason, I stayed with the Hilemans most of the time, till I was school age." She tried to piece together how the transformation had occurred from the Hilemans' house to the Henrys'. "I guess my mother wanted me with her parents. And, of course, Janice got whatever Janice wanted! But when I started school, for some reason, it changed and I went to the farm. Maybe they thought the schools were better in Gaston." Katherine kept pacing. "I don't know. Maybe it was just a miracle.

"But all the while I was in Vida, I was scared. I was scared of him, scared of the parts room. Dear Jesus, I was scared to death of everything!"

She started to cry again. "But I couldn't let on. There was nobody to protect me. Who? My mother? Pitiful Janice, who spent most of her life on the couch recovering from some ache or pain . . . who only saw her own needs? Or Aunt Elsie? She couldn't figure her way out of a paper bag!" Katherine kicked the rug.

She sat down again, watching the fire, and picked up her crocheting, but she couldn't concentrate. The thought of food was more than unappealing. It made her stomach turn. Her throat was still raw.

A restlessness pursued her around the room as she opened and closed shutters, thumbed through a book, emptied the drain water out the front door, threw her wet clothes over a line in the back, pausing to listen to the crickets and to notice the sun dissolving in a scarlet sky.

"Did I really want to die today? Or just escape the anxiety . . . or is it one and the same?" She considered the possibility that the only way to life might be through it. "Perhaps death must come to the hidden life, that what was done in the dark must be brought to the light. Perhaps I never really forgave them but merely succeeded in protecting the oppressors and thereby, I denied what happened. I tried to believe the myths about Uncle Sel. I was loyal to the family lies. I made a covenant with darkness. And it has been strangling me in this ungodly pit ever since!"

Chey moved to his favorite spot in front of the threshold of the front door, away from the heat of the fire, as if to soak up whatever minuscule draft might find its way through a crack.

"What else did I believe?" Katherine persisted. "What is the truth?"

She lit the lamps that bathed the interior in a gentle coziness. Something was happening to her . . . she was giving in . . . letting it happen. She sensed that something had broken within her. She knew she had never screamed before. And somehow screaming made her want to live again. She was finally protesting, letting the world know she was in it. Now there was a difference she could not explain. But she knew she would not resist it. God willing, she would ride it out to the end.

Out of the recesses of her memory, she called forth, imperfectly, the words of Grandma Henry, words from the Bible:

"He who dwells in the secret place of the Most High . . . He is my refuge and my fortress, my God, in Him will I trust." She got up and paced the room, as the familiar words tumbled unobstructed from the past. Only this time, they were not just a recitation to please her grandmother. They were truth!

"Surely, He shall deliver *me* from the snare of the fowler, and from the perilous pestilence. He shall cover *me* with His feathers and under His wings *I* shall take refuge. His truth shall be *my* shield and buckler. . . ." Standing in the middle of the room, her hands lifted up, voice strong, Katherine spoke into the stillness of the room. "And . . . *I* shall not be afraid of the arrow that flies by day, nor of the pestilence that walks in darkness, nor the destruction that lays waste at noonday."

Katherine sat down at the table, soft tears raining down her cheeks. "Because I have made the Lord, who is my refuge, even the Most High, my habitation, no evil shall befall me, nor shall any plague come near my dwelling . . . for He shall give his angels charge over me, to keep me in all my ways. Amen."

If John were here, she thought, *he would understand. He would celebrate with me and give me insight.* "The Lord is carrying me through those dark places, John," she said softly. There welled up within her a desperate longing to talk with him. It was physically painful.

"Oh, Lord, teach me to live without him!"

Then she remembered his journal. It lay undisturbed at the bottom of the drawer where she had put it for safekeeping that first week. Carefully, she lifted it from its resting place and carried it to the table.

Placing a lantern in the center of the table, Katherine seated herself precisely, as if to begin a very sacred ceremony. She opened the leather-bound volume, gently pressing its pages down. There before her, in black ink, lay the angular script of John's thoughts. It began simply:

December 1986

"My Dearest Katherine,

"I am resigned that what the doctors tell me is true. I have wrestled with the truth, as you know, but finding no peace in the deception, must finally give in. I suppose we only find the truth when we are willing to live it—to embrace it—to speak it. Until then, we are provided with all the deception our hearts desire.

"I suppose the most difficult part is the mere thought of losing control. And I must confess, I'd more gladly lose control of my life than to have you lose yours.

"How I wish I could be with you, even now, to hold you, to somehow reassure you. By the time of this reading, you will have found your place of safety. Or so I hope. It is unbearable to think of you alone and frightened.

"I hope this writing will be of some help to you. I fear a year may not be enough. I do not regret for myself—my life has been full to the brim—but I am unsure of you, your readiness to accept all this.

"Forgive me, Kate, if this is an affront to you. Perhaps you are stronger than I think. Perhaps it is some ego trip of mine, some reluctance in me to let you go, to think of you not needing me.

"One thing I do know about you, Kate, and trust—you will not read this until the time is right—your timing has always been perfect. You have never opened yourself up to me until you were ready to receive.

"As my life slips away, I shall lose the capacity to hold yours, too. I shall have to trust you to the Lord's care. I do believe implicitly that He will see you through—past all the deceptions and all the damage. Past all the rage to 'get even'—though God knows you have reason—to the true healing, forgiveness.

"In these final hours, by Grace alone, my heart is melted into His outrageous love! I find I, even I, can say of your wretched parents and uncle, 'God have mercy on them, they knew not what they did!'

"Katherine, forgive me for dying. For all the years we spent learning to trust, to overcome the fears, to come to this. If I have one resentment, it is this. It seems so unfair.

"And yet, Kate, it may be that in the final analysis, all that life requires of us is faith. Some knowledge that what is within our control is puny indeed. Maybe, being alive comes only in the exhilarating moments when we can throw inhibition to the wind—when we can ride it with abandon—like the secret moments we've shared with all self-consciousness set aside. Perhaps in those moments we have glimpsed Eternity.

"But life is easier when we give in to the truth—accept it for what it is, rather than what we want it to be—and trust that somehow in God's omnipotence, it's as it should be. At least for me. I find serenity in acceptance. It's easier.

"I can see you laughing now, your head thrown back. I can hear you saying, 'John, you're such a head tripper!' But it's what I do, Kate. It's what I do. . . .

Katherine closed the book softly. "I'm not laughing, John . . . I love what you do . . . need you." Tears squeezed through her closed lids.

His words kept playing in her mind, like a scratched record. *We only find the truth when we are willing to live it—to embrace it—to speak it. Until then we are provided all the deceptions our hearts desire.*

Katherine turned the insight. "I cannot know what I fear until I am willing to act on it," she whispered. She stared at the hazy reflection of her face in the window. "I cannot know the truth of myself until I am willing to live it—to defend it . . . until I stop hiding. But what does it mean to live it? What will it change? Am I willing to pay whatever the price?" For some reason, she thought of Janice.

Katherine sat in silence, hugging the book to her. Once again, she embraced gratitude for John.

Chey padded over to her. She stroked his head. "We'll go fishing tomorrow."

Chapter 21

Katherine awoke, thinking of Janice, aware that she had been dreaming again but unable to retrieve even a scrap of the dream from her subconscious. She had slept through the night, oblivious to the moon crossing the sky, pulling the sun behind it.

Chey still slept against the door, like her guardian angel. *Maybe he is,* she thought.

Katherine reached for the journal and sat up in bed, not wanting to lose her train of thought about how things had been after Linda died.

"It was decided that Janice should go abroad, while Daddy did a tour of duty in Korea. He thought it would be good for her to get her mind off things.

"That was his solution for everything—keep busy . . . get away. That attitude facilitated protocol social interaction. It seemed to me that their lifestyle had evolved into one long continuous cocktail party. It was extremely important to be at the right one and conversely to make sure that the right people—military and political—were invited to theirs.

"Daddy never allowed space for words. He kept everything moving briskly. His idea of intimacy was a tennis match—his first love—or golf, usually played for the politics of the game, or cards at the Officer's Club. As the life pain accumulated, he dodged it with more work, more time at the Officer's Club, tennis, and hunting trips.

"The only time I ever saw him slow down was when he would come in from tennis, with a white towel draped around his neck like a collar, and deposit his aching tan back in front of me to soothe. He loved to have his back scratched, 'like an animal,' Janice said. He would moan and fall into a stupor not conducive to conversation.

"Daddy didn't talk, he lectured. He didn't discuss, he debated. And he never listened. I was growing cognizant of the fact that he barely even listened to Janice. She was forever nagging at him to stay at the table when they dined at the club and talk to her, rather than sashaying around the room, backslapping and shaking hands with every man in a five-hundred-dollar suit or wearing military brass. At home at night, she would beg him to sit down for cocktails with her instead of rushing about, drink in hand, listening to the stock market report and the evening news at the same time. When she suggested a walk after dinner, he would ask why she didn't just take me so we could have some 'girl-talk.'

"I recall once asking my mother why *he* would never talk to me. Did it mean he didn't love me? 'Of course not!' she refuted strongly. 'If he didn't love you, he wouldn't let you do things for him. He lets you rub his back and help him in the yard, doesn't he?'

"So Janice went to Europe, finally doing what she had always wanted to do before Linda was born. Not that it was easy for Janice, after all she had been through. But, of course, her decision necessitated my return to the farm."

Linda died the first of October, the day before Katie's twelfth birthday. That summer, there was no celebration, no parental acknowledgment that a year had passed or that there was an older daughter. Two days later, they stood at the cemetery on a carpet of artificial grass, under oak trees rattling their bronze leaves.

Katie pressed her fingernails into her palms, trying hard to weep politely, not to cry out loud in such a way that might disturb the guests. Halfway through the droning message of comfort from the most Reverend Robert Kingston, Katie began to choke. She bowed her head in an attempt to muffle the agonizing convulsions in her handkerchief. Preston glared sideways, which was not enough to stifle her coughing.

Soon Katie felt his fingers biting into her shoulder as he reached behind Janice to signal her. "Back away," he whispered to Katie, giving her a gentle but firm shove backward. Clearly, he was concerned that she would upset Janice further, who was to this point rigidly resisting the urge to wail.

Katie stepped back through the crowd, her vision clogged with the sea of sorrow that threatened to suck them all under. Grief was everywhere. It hung in trees, clinging to the dry leaves. It skittered across the ground, waiting behind the tombstones. Then

*without warning, it would rush at her, clutching the flesh sur-
rounding her heart until she thought she would fold in half from
the weight of it.*

*It was not really the personal loss of her sister that gripped
her, since she hardly knew Linda, but an unnamed misery that
abided with her always. It was grief for the death of her mama's
gentle hands, grief for the loss of her fantasy father, grief for every
time she'd been pried away from Grandma and forced to feed
Preston and Janice until she was so dry even her tears were gone.
She was mourning her own life, too. Her own innocence lost in
Vida, her interrupted childhood, drained out on the gravel road
in front of the Henrys' place.*

*Standing behind other mourners at the gravesite, Katie won-
dered what would become of her now. She had never had any
control or even input into her destiny. It had always seemed
hopelessly entangled in her mother's whims. She would be returned to the farm, of course, where Grandma Henry would
resuscitate her again, until another illness or crisis called her
back to be the strange participant in the rituals of this counterfeit
family.*

"Through the years of back and forth, I watched my mother in a series
of chronological snapshots—the delicate young woman I'd known as
Mama; the bleached, brash socialite; and, finally, the pseudosophisticate I
now called Janice.

"Each season, upon my return, I could see Janice's face more deeply
etched in bitterness, eyes darting, gathering the evidence of what her mind
dictated was truth, her upper lip pressed flat as if she'd just smelled
something disgusting. Her once lovely fingers no longer caressed with
open palms, and whatever softness had existed in her body had been
replaced by rigid dieting. I was always aware of the scar, which required
great care and artistically applied makeup to conceal. But it was under
there. And lest I ever forget, Janice had a way of touching it whenever she
was distressed or upset, running her index finger over it as if it pained her
still. The scar pointed at me, accusing me, picking at me relentlessly,
reminding me of how much I had hurt her.

"Janice rarely wears any color except pink, or dusty rose, as she calls it.
She says it is her color, as if it had somehow been determined before time
and reserved only for her. No one else can own it, only borrow it. Pink is

an innocent and young color—quite inappropriate for Janice, whom I consider neither innocent nor young.

"The last time I saw her, at the Christmas party in Chicago, Janice looked painfully stiff in her dusty rose sequined cocktail dress, a fake smile painted on her face. With an extra-long slim white cigarette elegantly held between her fingertips, any hint that a real woman might live under there somewhere was successfully hidden.

"Being overweight, which she considers as having any flesh at all, is anathema to her. Consequently, she remains a tidy size five. But at that party, her whole body seemed as flat as a sheet of paper—a one-dimensional paperdoll, with an expensive designer creation hanging from her shoulders. She looked as if she had somehow crawled out from beneath the hem of her clothing, leaving the inside empty.

"Her peroxided hair, parted severely in the middle and pulled back above her ears, disappeared beneath a wide silk ribbon at the nape of her neck. Her other coiffure, for less formal occasions, is a tightly teased crown with a stiff flip at the length, resembling a Sandra Dee wig.

"And all her efforts accomplish a look that could not have been further from the one God created. The 'innocent' pink bows and youthful attire only add to the visual dissonance.

"At home, I remember that Janice was always wiping up, as if life were a dirty inconvenience requiring constant vigilance, lest there be any evidence of its having passed by. Even though she possessed the affluence to release her from this drudgery, she insisted on doing her own cleaning, except for the intermittent hiring and firing of 'help' and railing at me for their 'sloppy work.' No one can please her. No one is as clean as Janice.

"When I lived there, she fastidiously instructed me in how to erase any trace of myself. Bathroom tiles were dried right after a bath. Towels were used only once, new ones in their place, the used ones immediately placed in the washer. I had to make my bed with a military precision. Used dishes were to be washed, dried and put away, as were clothes.

"My room was as sterile as a motel unit, with no evidence that there had ever been a resident. It looked ready for the next occupant at any minute. Their entire house had the same vacancy, like a picture in *Better Homes and Gardens,* without the added touches of casual charm. It contained nothing handmade and nothing inexpensive.

"I guess my big sad eyes, tanned skin, and tattered self were always out of place. Even as an adult, dressed in an outfit I would wear to visit the Queen, I immediately unravel, when standing in my mother's living room, to a heap of shabby threads, inconsiderately cluttering up the decor."

Katherine uncoiled from the warm spot in the bed, and throwing back the covers, slid into the morning cool. Chey padded over to her and placed his great head under her hand. After properly greeting him, she puttered around with the usual rituals, aware of Janice and Preston occupying a back shelf in her consciousness.

That fall when she was twelve, the fall Linda died, had been a particularly difficult time. Try as she might, Katie could not keep from outgrowing her clothes, which sent Janice into rages.

"One thing I'll have you know, young lady, I'm not going to be spending all this money on you every month!" They had just ventured out in search of clothes for school, especially a new bra, since the surge of hormones had left her with nothing to wear. Janice repeatedly told her she could just wear the old ones. But the old ones were too tight, crushing her chest on the outside to match the crush on the inside that no one would notice.

But one progression of adolescence was definitely noticed. All the other girls at school were wearing light pink lipstick and shaving their legs. Katie knew better than to ask permission to join them, so she borrowed the lipstick from her best friend Kay Bealer, always careful to wipe it off on the bus home.

At school, the girls with the hairy legs were taunted, "If it gets any longer, you can braid it!" Katie tried to cover the evidence with a thick layer of lotion to slick down the hair. She also tried to pull her white cotton anklet socks up as high as possible, rather than neatly folded around her skinny ankles the way Janice wanted them. Her mother would never concede to the bobby socks that were in vogue.

But there was no avoiding the inevitable. It seemed that each day brought a new crop of fuzz and humiliation.

One day in English class, Nick, who sat in front of her, leaned back to whisper out of one side of his mouth, "Hey, Kate, I need you to do me a big favor. It's real important to me. Think you could help me out?"

"Sure, Nick. I'll help you." Kate was flattered that he'd ask, remembering her mother's advice, that when people love you they let you do things for them. Her pulse quickened, imagining in a split-second all her dreams coming true.

Nick motioned her closer with his finger. Katie leaned forward across the desk, till her ear was near his mouth.

"Stick your leg out . . . so I can pet your fur. I miss my dog!" Nick convulsed in laughter, along with Kenny and Rayme who were watching from the other row.

Katie pulled back, fighting the tears that burned at the corners of her eyes, wishing she could evaporate. It was one of the longest days of her life, one in which she felt naked as she walked through the halls, trying to hide behind an armload of books.

She envied Justine Carmela, another seventh-grader with a worldly air. Justine was at home in her body, never humiliated by anything the boys did. She shuffled through Central Junior High with a grin on her sticky mouth, her lashes thick with mascara and a switchblade in her purse.

Even though Justine failed every academic test, Katie would gladly have changed places with her. It seemed to Katie that she was a roaring success at life.

The half-mile walk from the bus stop in isolation was a welcome relief. It gave her time to recover before entering the world according to Janice.

When she eased into the kitchen, Janice was at the stove, stirring pudding with one hand and rubbing her neck with the other. "Hi, Janice." Katie stood in the center of the room and waited, scanning her mother as a sailor scans the horizon for a storm. Sensing none, she moved closer to see what was in the pan. "Pudding?" she asked. "For dinner?"

Janice nodded, without taking her focus from the thick bubbling mixture.

As Katie walked through the dining room toward her bedroom, Janice called out in monotone, "Straighten your bedspread—it's been that way all day."

Katie rattled through the house, still feeling the oozing sorrow welling up inside. She opened the closet to exchange costumes and place her books on the top shelf, out of the way. But seeing her stricken face in the mirrored door, she gave in to her latest grief.

Not wanting to be discovered, she stepped inside and shut the door. She sank to the bottom of the closet, under the dresses and coats, and pulled her legs up under her, pressing her face against her bony fur-covered knees. Over and over Nick's cruel laughter twisted in her spirit, hauling it down and down.

Suddenly, the door opened. "Why, Katie," Janice said. "Whatever is the matter?" She leaned forward as if to make sure it was her daughter hiding there in the back of the closet.

Katie felt the sobs still clogging her throat and dared not answer her.

"Come out of there," Janice said in a singsong tone. "I'll not have any little girl of mine hiding in a closet."

Reluctantly, Katie crawled out, looking away, hoping Janice wouldn't see the tears.

But she was not so lucky. "Why, you've been crying." Janice took Katie's limp arm and led her to the bed. "Has something happened? Is there something I should know?" Her face was uncomfortably close to Katie's, but her voice was unusually gentle.

Katie's mind raced down one corridor after another, searching for an explanation, one that would not make Janice feel that she was at fault nor would in any way question her mother's wisdom about not letting her shave her legs yet.

"I got teased today." Her complaint sounded puny and hollow.

"Who teased you?"

"A boy at school . . . Nick."

Janice put her arm around her daughter. Katie wanted to sob, but she held her breath. "Katie, why is it so important to you what this boy Nick thinks? Why do you care?" She was gently stroking her shoulder.

"I don't know. I guess I just want to be liked."

"Liked? By whom? Boys?" The stroking stopped. Without another word, Janice left the room.

Katie sat on the edge of the bed afraid to move, waiting for her mother to return, as if she'd been interrupted by something— maybe the doorbell, or dinner burning, or something—and would reappear at any moment. But she didn't come back.

After awhile Katie got up and picked up the list that lay perfectly centered on the French Provincial desk, her instructions for after-school chores.

At dinner that night, Preston picked up where Janice had left off. "Your mother tells me you have thrown quite a fit over not *being popular enough. Don't you think that's kind of silly?" He reached for the butter.*

Shame slid into Katie's wounds as easily as the butter melted into the slit in his baked potato.

"Don't you think you should be filling your time with more constructive activity than feeling sorry for yourself?" There was a long, empty silence. "Don't you have anything to say?" Preston was still arranging the contents of his dinner on the plate as Janice politely passed him each serving dish.

Katie could sense the edge of anger behind his composure. Desperately, she searched for the right answer—the one that would appease him. "No sir. I guess so."

"You guess so . . . what?"

"I guess I don't have anything to—to say," she stuttered, fighting the tears that really enraged him. "No. Yes. You're right. It's silly."

He leveled her a searching look. "Well, I hope we don't have to have any more performances like that. You gave your mother quite a fright. She thought there might really be something wrong."

"There *was* something wrong! Terribly wrong!" Katherine sputtered, carrying her coffee to the porch. Chey seemed grateful for the open door and to have her back again. She had sensed him watching her during her flights of memory, moving closer as if to be ready to grab her from some precarious edge.

Katherine felt the morass closing around her. She wanted to be part of the day, to join the land of the present, to soar with the wind. To race the dog to the river and laugh at nothing.

"Chey, there was something very wrong. You know, when I was thirteen she sent me a pink lipstick with a card that said, 'Congratulations, you're a teenager! We're so proud!' Can you beat that! And after she'd grounded me for a month when she found out I was using it at school, just weeks before, accusing me of being a streetwalker! 'You're a slut!' she'd screamed at me!

"I remember that everyone who saw the card commented on how sweet it was of her. I thought it was sweet, too. *Then.* Now I think it was nuts!"

She set down her cup with an emphatic thump. "Let's go fishing. I'm tired of this."

Chapter 22

They took the trail east, upstream. Katherine had never been fly-fishing in her life, so she tried to remember what she had seen in the movies about how to cast. She carefully scrutinized the landscape for a spot shallow enough to wade out barefooted and clear enough to practice her cast.

When she located what she thought must be the perfect spot, she sat down to assemble her gear. She removed her boots and rolled up her pant legs. She had already resigned herself to the unlikely prospect of actually catching anything. The water made her catch her breath as she tiptoed in, grateful that she didn't have an audience.

The dog jumped in with his usual enthusiasm. He splashed past her and paddled out to the main stream. Katherine was preoccupied with her pole and line when, from the corner of her eye, she noticed him in shallower water, snapping at the current. He jumped and turned like he was chasing something, plunging his head under the water.

Katherine felt her way closer to him to investigate. Just then, he lunged and came up with a wriggling fish, flapping its tail against his black muzzle.

"Chey! Good dog!" She splashed forward to see his catch, at which point he dropped it.

"Oh! Get it!" She slid to the spot where he'd let the fish go. Pointing to the water, she shouted enthusiastically, "Get it, Chey! Get it!" For a minute he stared at her as if he had no idea what she meant. Then in a flash, he came up with the fish again. Katherine laughed and reached for it and immediately it squirmed free, into the water again. Chey jumped around, snapping at the water and came up with it once more.

This time, Katherine splashed to the shore, calling Chey to her. It worked. Obediently, he followed her to the grassy bank and dropped the fish at her feet. It was a good-sized trout.

"Good dog!" She rubbed his ears enthusiastically. Chey responded by shaking his body, flinging a spray of water everywhere. Katherine put up her hands instinctively to shield herself. "Oh, for heaven's sake!"

With that, she turned and ran back into the river, yelling and waving her hands, splashing and jumping, laughing and calling Chey to join her. For a moment, he stood on the bank beside the fish, unsure what she expected.

Then he romped in, barking and jumping. The more he barked, the more she laughed, stumbling and falling, throwing water into the air. They played tag, lunging at each other and laughing until she fell exhausted on the smooth warm rocks on the edge. Chey flopped down next to her, panting. They lay there together for what seemed like a long time, soaking up the sun. Katherine had thought she'd forgotten how to laugh that hard. It felt good.

Finally, Katherine got up to find her boots and check the fish, which she was already planning for dinner. Just as she pulled on the last boot, Chey came trotting up with another fish.

"Good boy!" She stroked his head and took it from him. "But that's enough." She slapped the side of her leg. "Let's go. No more fish." Chey was heading back to the river.

"No! Chey, come!" He turned to look at her, stood for a minute as she knelt to coax him back.

"Come. Come, Chey. Come on, boy." He put his head down and came directly toward her, tail wagging.

With a twig she'd stripped from a bush, she threaded both fish and set off in the direction of home, the dog plodding along beside her. If she could have whistled, she would have.

Cleaning the fish was not her favorite thing. Especially since she was not at all sure what she was doing. So she just tried to remove all the parts that didn't look edible. She had two small potatoes left, which she fried with the fish.

When the meal was ready, Katherine sat at the table, facing the window. She glanced at the empty chair to her left. She felt like she was being watched again. Chey sat on the floor next to her, his eyes riveted on her.

She had the strangest urge to pray what she had prayed as a child, "Be present at our table, Lord. Be here and everywhere adored." She lowered her head and continued, "Thank you for the fish . . . and the dog . . . and for your wonderful presence with me. Amen."

The trout was heavenly. She could not recall any as good. Through the dinner, she talked to Chey, who now and then licked his chops, waiting for his turn.

When she was finished, she cleaned up the table and adjourned to the porch with a piece of bread spread with blackberry jam.

"Tomorrow, we're going up the mountain to pick up pinecones and whatever else we can find. This place needs some new dried arrangements. I think I saw some yarrow up there . . . that would be gorgeous on the mantle. And I wonder if there's any fish in the stream up there." She threw him the headcrust, which he swallowed in a gulp.

Pleasantly full and with her evening chores done, Katherine brought out her writing paraphernalia and began to journal her thoughts:

"In 1979 the snow came to Chicago, one storm following another, heavy on the breath of the former. Eighty-two inches of accumulation brought the arrogant city to a halt. A quilt of white crystals muffled the scraping sound of metal on metal. It shut the residents in their homes with the strangers they called family and made them work frantically to escape.

"Snow came out of the northern sky and skittered across the cement, lodging in the crevasses and incisions, piling up a pristine innocence. It was as if God spoke that winter. Everyone looked up. Some saw the beauty and were silenced to awe. Most swore and shook their fists, and, abandoning their entombed vehicles, rented another one.

"I loved that winter and the long liquid afternoons that slid into evening, as John and I were confined, snowbound, in our retreat above the streets. It was a wonderful time, my favorite time in all the years we'd spent there.

"While I lay half asleep, floating amidst piles of down pillows, John read to me—long complex treatises about the meaning of Scriptures and of the redemptive life in a fallen world. He tried his best to educate me to the wonder and necessity of the Greek language in any 'exegetical' pursuit, which made me laugh and tease him about his 'extra-Jesus.'"

Katherine turned another page.

"We ate omelets by candlelight and danced on the balcony in the snow and moonlight. And always I was dazzled by his smile. It started with a spark of mischief in his eyes that encouraged the upward turn of his beautiful mouth. It ended when he flashed a row of straight pearls in front of the resonating low male laughter that spilled over his lips.

"That winter was a private time. A time sealed away from the rest of the world. Once even the telephone went out, which sent the thrill of inhibition pulsing through my veins. And it seemed we fell in love all over again.

"These high times were ecstasy. I would have sacrificed any treasure I had for the secrets of keeping those moments. But inevitably, the spring thaw came, and with it the intrusion of the outside world.

"Typically Midwestern, particularly Chicagoan, the climate went directly from winter to summer. I sometimes suspected that spring had been lost under tons of concrete, too heavy for any tender green evidence to push through.

"Perhaps it was there, unnoticed. But it was always lost to me. Maybe because there were no activities that I associated with spring. No plows turned the earth, only the men in the highway department who came with jackhammers and roadblocks, and nothing was planted except the towers of glass and concrete. And it seemed to me that all that grew in Chicago was the noise and congestion and the knot in the pit of my stomach.

"So we were catapulted from winter to summer, until once again we were steaming in the heat and humidity, sitting on our balcony on the long summer nights, trying to remember our midnight waltz in the snow. Above the throbbing air conditioners and dying city sounds, John and I tried to recapture the quiet. We sat on the balcony late into the night, perhaps because it's what our schedules permitted, perhaps because it was the time when the cacophony was winding down.

"As the roar of the day folded itself into night sirens, echoing against the man-made towers and screaming through the neon canyons, we strained for the sounds of organic life and searched the sky for the strongest stars—the only ones loud enough to shout down the vaporous light that rose from the wounded earth they call Chicago.

"On those nights, John and I sipped our tea in silence, until the commerce ceased and decent folks slept, while others traded in flesh to the low hum of bodies, breathing hard, running from fear or loneliness.

"Chicago was a capsule, we believed, hurtling through the universe, where people were forced to live out their days according to artificial light and manufactured tomatoes, burning their souls in the fires of career, with the demented belief that it would heat their homes. And we among them. By day, each of us, according to what we thought was our calling, tried in our own way to reach some of them with the message of salvation, be it sometimes woefully diluted. At the end of the day, we crawled back to our compartment above it all, to compare notes and regroup.

"We knew there was a real retreat somewhere out there, beyond its reach, hours away—a refuge, a quiet place. We vowed to find it. Soon.

"Nights when I couldn't sleep, I would open the French doors, listening for the cricket song that wasn't there. By morning, the noise would rise with the sun again, a great metal dragon, stretching to scrape and lunge, to breathe fire—to lift its hoary head to the sky and belch the stench of steel and tar high into the sweet air."

Katherine had traveled three thousand miles and light-years away to a place where the sound of Chicago was only a memory. "I found it, John." She mouthed the words so softly that even Chey didn't hear.

She knew it was snowing outside. She could sense it. She had been awakened sometime during the night by the utter quiet.

Katherine got up and blinked at the windows. All she could see was a dim reflection of herself shining back against the emptiness. It was blacker than any night since her arrival. Every particle of light lay on the other side of the storm that had divided the heavens from the earth while she lay sleeping.

The windows seemed to have been sprayed black. Or someone had come in the night and stolen the landscape, leaving a gaping black hole in its place. There was a meager orange glow from the fireplace, facilitating navigation about the cabin. She was curious to see the outside, to see how much snow had fallen, and what it must be like. The first snow was special.

She reached for the matches to light a lantern. Suddenly, without moving, Chey lifted his head and curled his lip in a low steady growl. Katherine's hand froze in midair, her breath with it.

Again he growled, up on all fours. The warning rolled over his teeth, crawled across the floor, and climbed her legs to painful alarm centers up and down her spine. Prickly fear oozed through her shin as she listened to the liquid sound of his curled lip.

Leaning sideways, she could just see him, standing behind the sofa, with his head low, facing the front door. The heavy bolt lay across the entrance. Turning, she could see its twin barring the back door. But every window shutter lay open, spread like an invitation.

With neither sound nor breath, Katherine deftly moved about the room, closing and barring the shutters, till there were only two left. Those that hung on either side of the front door. *Those accessed by the porch.* Chey moved closer to the door, sniffing the draft.

Katherine reached above the counter, closing the shutter and securing the bar across the thick wooden enclosure. In one rigid motion, barking wildly, Chey suddenly lunged toward the other unshuttered window. She could see his fangs flashing as he snapped at the air.

"Oh, dear God!" Katherine pleaded, her heart beating in her ears as she slid forward behind the dog. Reaching for the shutters from her position along the wall, she hoped whoever or whatever was out there would not see her.

With a surge of bravery, she slammed them shut, banging the bar in place. Now perfectly sealed inside, Katherine felt trapped in a tiny box, remote from everything. She retreated to the center of the room as Chey moved back and forth between the door and the window next to it. Some ominous creature paced the porch, from door to window and back again, the dog's growl tracking its movement. Then he was still.

Chey stared at the door. After several moments, he stood up, paws against the planking, sniffing the wood. Then he began scratching at the door, asking to be let out.

"Chey! Come here!" Katherine slapped her thigh. He was immediately at her side, still watching the door but quiet now.

Katherine thought of the dusty guns that she so disdained. They were safely locked in the shed. She wished she had them.

What would make the dog react like that? She tried to convince herself that it was probably only a raccoon or opossum after a midnight snack. But she quickly dismissed the idea as absurd.

Her lungs still ached from the lack of oxygen and her ears were still at attention, capable of hearing dustballs roll across the floor. Chey sat down, relaxing into his pliable adolescence. For him, the crisis was over. But for Katherine, the alert had merely succeeded in lighting brush fires of anxiety all through her intestines.

Trying to produce some semblance of security, Katherine lit the lanterns and built a fire. But she could not chase the shadows from the corners of her mind. Every board that creaked, each time a log popped, Katherine jumped.

She reminded herself of something John always said: "Are you running because you are afraid, or are you afraid because you're running?"

Katherine pulled Chey close. She was unspeakably grateful for his presence. It made her absolutely shiver to imagine how she would have endured this alone. "You're a good dog." She rubbed his head and stroked his side. He looked up at her as if he deserved the compliment, glad she finally knew it. "You're a *very* good dog. I don't know how I would have managed without you."

She finally felt comfortable enough to cross the room to find out what hour of the night it was. According to her quartz watch on the bookshelf, it was 3:37.

"Another three hours till daylight," she calculated. It went without saying that she would not sleep. She would keep the vigil until morning.

Picking up her crocheting, which had progressed considerably under her steady daily discipline, she tried to concentrate on the design and stitches. Her stomach was drawn into a tight band, tied in a fisted knot in the middle of her back. Moving the crochet hook back and forth only seemed to tie it tighter.

"I hate feeling trapped!" Katherine shifted her position. "And I hate hiding!" Closing her eyes, burning from lack of sleep, she slumped, exhausted, to a half-reclining position on the couch as she had on her first night in this place. Sliding in and out of consciousness, Katherine dreamed.

Katie was hiding in the oil room at the top of the stairs, with Uncle Sel scuffing up the front steps, one at a time. Then she was hiding in the parts room, under the rocker, while someone sat there, rocking slowly. Then she was in her uncle's office, turning the key of his closet. All the while she could hear his shuffling footsteps . . . coming closer.

A little girl was running. Tripping over the edge of the braided rug, she stumbled, arms outstretched, falling . . .

Katherine's eyes flew open. That same dream. That toddler running, falling, in slow motion. From habit, Katherine turned to inspect both doors, watching. Watching for what?

She could hear Chey's steady breathing, nearly a snore, on the floor beneath her feet. Everything else was still. In the kitchen, she fixed some chamomile tea, an offering for her frayed nerves. She wished it would clear her head, allowing her to think through the meaning of that dream.

Katherine sat down on the sofa with her tea and journal and began to write:

"A child runs . . . and falls. The child is wearing high-top white shoes.

She looked up from the book.

"How old is the child?" She imagined her own calm professional voice asking a question, as she had asked fear-ridden clients many times. Maybe it would help if she could play an impersonal role in her own case, both asking and answering the questions. She picked up her pen and recorded the dialogue in her memory.

"It's all right to tell me. It will be okay. Now, how old is the child?"
"About two."
"Two years old?"
"Yes."
"What else can you tell me about the child?"
"She's wearing high-top shoes. White."
"The kind children wore in the forties. Is that right?"

"I guess so."

"Who is the child?"

"I don't know. I can't remember."

"I think you know. When you are ready, you can tell me. It will be all right. It's only a memory now, so it's okay to tell."

"But I can't remember."

"Where is she running?"

"In the living room . . . from the dining room to the living room."

"What causes her to fall?"

"She trips on the rug."

"So you know where she is."

"Yes . . . I think she's at the Hilemans."

Katherine paused, registering this new revelation. And, of course, she knew the child!

"But if she is falling, why does she not hit the floor?"

"Because she is stopping time."

"Stopping time?"

Hugging her knees, Katherine nodded in agreement and proceeded to write furiously.

"You mean . . . if she hits the floor, she will proceed to the next thing that happens?"

Again an affirmative headshake. Suddenly aware of pain, Katherine realized that she was biting her lower lip as she wrote. She exhaled slowly in a long whoosh of air. "So, that's why she never finishes the fall. It's her . . . my . . . way of stopping the progression!"

Kate . . . can we let her fall? Katherine's eyes widened over her face at the thought. *Is there someone who can catch her? Where's her mother?*

Suddenly Katherine was hugging her knees and rocking fiercely, whimpering and shaking her head. No. No! Chey raised his head in alarm as a purple blister formed on her lower lip.

Chapter 23

About the time the sun came up, the significance of Katherine's nocturnal discoveries had begun to dawn on her. Not that it should have been too difficult to figure out. But she was tired, and working on herself was like trying to ride an elevator up and down at the same time. She read and reread her journaled dialogue. She prayed and prayed, "Please, Lord . . . please . . . I've been stuck so long!" She paced and talked aloud.

"So the dream is about not seeing what happens next. And it happened in Vida . . . more than likely at Aunt Elsie and Uncle Sel's. It's the spot she can't get past." Somehow it was more comforting to speak of herself in the third person.

"And it happened to a two-year-old . . . and her mother," she mused. "Janice!" Katherine shouted her mother's name like a swear word. "She changed about then. Why? Before that, I remember her smiling and warm, loving me. What happened?"

Katherine jumped up, landing in the kitchen, as if propelled by some force other than her own. She jerked the pump handle till the water flowed. Then cupping her hands, she lapped the water. It sharpened reality, reassuring her that she was in the cabin, although still trembling.

Chey was right behind her, watching her. She forced herself to walk around the cabin, slowly getting grounded again, feeling her footing, the security of her legs under her. She did not want to probe anything more now. Her sanity felt brittle. She wanted to quit. She also wanted to push, to be through it.

"I always thought it was Daddy coming home that caused

the change in her. It was before Linda died. Maybe it was something else . . . before he came back."

Now Katherine felt the frustration of hitting that familiar stainless steel wall. She yielded this time, feeling her way along the smooth, cold surface. She had learned that it was pointless to attempt to crash through. That effort only produced more bruises over deeper wounds.

"It had to be before he came back. I was three when he came home. . . . And another thing," she went on, still pacing, "before that, I was afraid of the dark—terrified of the dark, absolutely would not sleep alone—before that!" The pieces of the jigsaw were moving, twisting, turning, passing close. She sensed it was a matter of time before one would fit. The tiniest beam of hope shone from the darkness.

"And Janice was afraid . . . of everything." Katherine picked up her journal.

"I remember the night Janice crept into my room and awakened me because she thought there was a prowler in the house. She was sure she heard noises from the kitchen. I stumbled out of bed and, half-awake, started down the stairs to investigate.

"Janice, as white as the fabric in her nightgown, remained at the top of the stairs. As I neared the bottom step, she suddenly called out in a hoarse whisper, 'Wait! Come back!' Obediently, I padded up the stairs, where Janice grabbed my hands. My mother's fingers were like icy bones!

"'Katie, I'm so scared!' Her voice was low and full of dread.

"That was the only time I can recall my mother making an honest statement about her feelings.

"It turned out that the prowler was Daddy, who had come home early from a meeting in Dayton in order to surprise his wife on her birthday. It was he who was rummaging around the kitchen, putting candles on a cake he had bought, and flowers in a vase. The whole thing might have worked if he had bothered to inform me so I could have run my usual interference. As it was, it resulted in a kind of family joke of which Janice was the butt. One that made her squirm a little.

"But for some reason, Janice tolerated our teasing. Daddy and I would erupt into howling laughter following the 'remember when . . .' phrase. Or we'd taunt Janice if she asked him when he planned to be home. 'Don't come home early!'

"'And for heaven's sake,' I would add, 'don't bang around in the kitchen in the middle of the night!' We'd both laugh and carry on as if we shared some juicy bit of gossip about Janice. 'Remember . . . no surprises, Daddy! Janice doesn't like surprises.' It was one of the only things over which we connected.

"Later, I realized it was a form of hostility we both aimed at her, maybe for all the other things we could never say. I also vaguely remember my mother's feelings being hurt by our relentless teasing.

"Just now, thinking about it, I wonder why Janice allowed it. Generally, she was not at all good-humored about anything that made her look foolish.

"But Janice remained terrified to stay alone. In fact, Daddy's trips were usually the occasion for me to pack up my belongings and 'spend time with your mother.'"

It was October. Katie had started her sophomore year in Gaston, Iowa, when the call came. Preston would be in Kenya for six weeks on a hunting trip, so naturally, Katie must "go home," as if she had been on vacation and must now return to her responsibilities.

Katie never thought of Preston and Janice's house as home. In fact, she had never been to the one they lived in now. Since her last visit the previous spring, they had built a new house in the suburbs of Arlington, Virginia. Katie was sure it was grander than the former.

With each visit, she could see visible evidence of their progress in the world. Carpets got plusher, bathrooms larger, more bottles appeared in the liquor cabinet as Preston ascended the ladder of military rank, finally winning himself a job at the Pentagon, serving his country from behind a posh desk in Washington. Janice was busy making the right friends at the country club, which they claimed was the only place in the area where he could get court time or play golf on a "challenging course" and where they could relax over a good meal. Besides, it was necessary for his job. Katie had learned that many more political decisions were made leaning over a putter than in the Senate chamber.

"What's the matter with your mother?" Matt asked when the summons came at Grandma's.

"What do you mean?"

"I mean, how come you have to leave now? Doesn't it matter

that school's already started?" He was exasperated at the thought of losing his cousin, a favorite playmate. The three of them—he and Sandy and Katie—did everything together, always had, since Katie's birthday was only five weeks after the twins'. "Why can't you go at Christmas or something?"

"Matt, shut up!" Sandy said. "You know how Aunt Janice is."

"Selfish, that's what!"

"She's not selfish!" Katie became defensive. "She's just afraid to stay alone!"

Janice was a sore subject, one they generally avoided. It was clear what Matt thought. He could never figure out why his cousin refused to see the obvious. Instead, she defended her mother against all his attacks.

So he wasn't surprised when she gave him a whole raft of reasons why Janice was Janice. Because Janice was very young when she and Katie's father were married. Because Janice loved Katie's father so much that having to be away from him during the war had been more than she could endure. Because Janice had to go to school. Because Janice was sick. Because Janice's favorite child, Linda, died. Because Janice had so many decisions to make with moving and all. But there was one excuse Matt thought held some credibility: Because she came from such a weird family, being raised by an older brother after her parents died.

With that, both Matt and Sandy openly agreed! Katie's Uncle Sel was frightening—not anyone they cared to spend much time around.

"Besides, I don't want to go at Christmas, that's why!" Katie retorted.

"Yeah, like you got a choice," he muttered.

Katie hated packing to leave. It was a matter of ripping away, of putting their relationship on a shelf—a process that always made them testy with each other, as if it would be easier to say good-bye if they were mad.

What made it even worse was that Katie never knew how long she would be gone. It would be only until Janice got fed up with her, then Grandma Henry would get her back. Katie was caught in a no-win web. If she succeeded in winning Janice's approval, she would not be returned to her grandmother. She wanted to stay with Grandma Henry, but she also wanted to please her father. Pleasing Preston meant pleasing Janice. So after an indefinite period of time, Katie knew she would be returned to the farm, a failure again.

"I don't know what you're harping about . . . at least you've got each other," she said, resenting the fact that Matt and Sandy were only a few hundred yards from their home.

Katie was sitting on the floor, leaning against the foot of the bed and sorting books. "I don't know what to take. Maybe I should take all this stuff and keep up on my own. Then if I get to come back after Christmas, I won't be behind. You don't think she'll make me start school there, do you?"

Sandy flattened her mouth, raising her eyebrows and shoulders in an "I don't know" gesture "What are you going to do about Chad?"

"I hope he'll write . . . and wait." Katie thought of her boyfriend and of Preston's letters, and felt as if she were going off to war.

"So when are they supposed to get here?" Sandy asked. They were driving this time because Janice thought it was a beautiful time of the year.

"Sometime before supper, Grandma says. Matt, hand me that notebook, will you?" Katie took it from him and began removing pages, which she then placed in her empty top drawer.

"What are you doing?" he wanted to know.

"Oh, it's just that Janice doesn't like me to get notes from boys."

"Let me guess!" he mocked. "Aunt Janice just doesn't know you're fourteen—she's lost track of time—and thinks you're still in the third grade." He stomped out of the room, leaving Katie and Sandy staring at the empty doorway.

Sandy, always the sympathetic one, carried a pile of folded clothes to the suitcase. "Don't pay any attention to him, Katie. He's dumb as a stump anyway."

They finished packing most of the clothes, and Sandy went off to help Grandma with supper. Katie glanced around the room, filled with so much of herself—the school pictures wedged into the mirror frame, her own drawings and sketches adorning the walls like a gallery, a basket of dried weeds and cattails, a stuffed bear that snuggled in the pillows of her double bed

The room opened to the sunporch, which made it the loveliest room in the house, to her way of thinking. The piano was on the porch, filling the room with the fragrance of aged music, something like sandalwood incense.

There was also a door to the outside—the official front door which was seldom used but which afforded her an exit any time she needed it. She was never sure whether or not Grandma knew about her midnight walks. If so, she had never said anything. It was impossible to believe she didn't know, though, since she seemed to know everything else. But somehow the idea that her grandmother knew things about her was anything but a frightening thought.

Grabbing a flannel shirt, Katie descended the front steps from the sunroom and darted across the lawn. Once past the apple trees, she couldn't be seen from the house. She just wanted to be alone. To say a leisurely good-bye to the farm, privately.

She slowed her pace, turning down the lane that ran between the fields—corn on her left, waiting for harvest, and brilliant green winter wheat on her right. It was like walking the path between fall and spring. It was like walking into the winter. Katie put her hands in her pockets and looked at the ground.

"I hate leaving in the fall," Katie confessed softly, to God or the land, she was not sure which. She had a need to touch something unchangeable, solid. It seemed to her that people were fluid. She had noticed new lines around her grandparents' smiling eyes. And last time, at the changing of the houses, Matt's voice had become deeper, still awkward with the male tones, sometimes skipping back and forth from child to man to child again. She and Sandy had tried not to laugh.

Only the earth stayed the same. She believed that only the earth would last forever, would never die or move away. Katie looked out across the green expanse of wheat. Green blades leaned with the wind. Winter was coming. There was a cold shaft of air slicing the Indian summer, a spear thrown down from the north. Katie slid her arms into the shirt.

The neighbors had picked most of their corn, so she could see forever to the west. Katie pulled her feet from her tennis shoes and slung them around her shoulders, the laces tied together.

The ground was still warm and dry. She needed to feel it

through her skin. It was like walking on a living thing. She loved this place which had absorbed so much of her sorrow.

Katie's life, it seemed, was destined to be a collage of days—bits of time spent with Janice and Preston, wired to the backdrop of Vida, with the twining vine of the farm growing across it and reaching into its crevasses.

Three years ago, on visitation weekends, after Uncle Sel's hands began prying into the private places in her body, Katie spent more and more time alone, walking this lane and letting her tears water the earth. She had never told Grandma Henry. Somewhere in the deepest part of her brain, lost to her own awareness, was lodged the image of the snarling dog that went after him. So she had never told.

According to Janice's wishes, the Hilemans periodically came for her. Usually, the visits were for weekends, since school was some concern. Katie hated the visits. But she dared not protest enough to arouse suspicion. Instead, she pretended a devouring boredom.

Those defenses were the best she could do and somewhat effective at keeping her safe from Uncle Sel—that and staying very absorbed in everything Aunt Elsie did. The worst times came when Janice and Preston were "home" and consistently left her alone with him, because "you are so close" and because "you're his favorite." He had only warned her not to tell once—the first time. After that, he was sure of her.

And Grandma Henry had never guessed. Not that she didn't see the distress. She cried out to God at night and sang to her granddaughter in the morning. She touched Katie and talked to her, cramming as much comfort as she could into the weeks or months they had together.

Maybe she had never guessed because she was blinded by the obvious. She had only to look at the behavior of her son and his wife to see reason for the pain she saw swimming in Katie's big eyes.

Grandma Henry had been silenced, too. Silenced by her caring. Tenaciously, Janice had woven an invisible threat. The brief mention of an "excellent girls' school" was all it had taken. Alta Henry knew that if she ever crossed Janice, Katie would be lost to her forever. She had long since accepted that her son had left *his mother and father and now cleaved to his own wife—and what Janice wanted, Janice got.*

It was a testing of her great faith. More than once, she had wept on her knees in helplessness, begging God's grace and protection for the child she carried so dear to her heart.

"I'll miss you. I'll be back by spring . . . I promise," Katie said out loud, probably trying to reassure herself. "Maybe by Christmas. Keep the first snow for me and the stardust that will dance upon the surface in the moonlight."

Katie had reached the end of the lane they called Goose Lane. She didn't know why it was so named. Maybe it had something to do with the nickname her grandfather had given her. Or maybe her nickname had come from the lane. But it had always conjured in her mind the image of a young girl walking a line of white geese, like the picture that hung in the stairway to the guest room.

It was time to start back. Preston and Janice would be arriving soon, and she had to get her heart tucked away, ready to greet them. One thing she knew. She could not face them needy.

A wave of dread swept over her. "Oh God, I can't this time. I can't do it . . . God help me . . . please . . . go with me." Katie always felt as if she was leaving God behind, too, even though Grandma Henry always said, "Go with God, honey." Katie never prayed for God to keep her from going. Perhaps it was because she didn't believe He was powerful enough to buck her parents.

Katie knelt with her face in her hands. "Please?"

Through the years, the earth had listened to her like a patient mother. Katie looked up into the face of the sky and followed it down to the line of the horizon. If she could somehow travel to that point—the exact spot where the earth and sky embraced—and peel up just enough sky to crawl under . . . or if she could shrink into a raindrop and sink deep into the earth between the warm particles of dust, she might feel safe.

Chapter 24

Rereading her latest journal entry, Katherine let the waves of nostalgia roll over her. It all seemed like only yesterday—those bright blue October days at Grandma's. But she knew her world would shift to shades of gray as soon as Preston and Janice collected her from the farm. She could just imagine the scene in their car on the trip over from Arlington.

The Olds 88 turned the corner from Gaston onto Edgerton Road. Janice held a compact in one hand and lipstick in the other.

"You're not helping," she commented, regarding the potholes in the gravel road. "You'd think they could at least grade this thing once in a while, never mind paving it." She jerked the rearview mirror toward herself, so she could add the finishing touches to her hair.

"By the time we get there, this car is going to look just like the other farm machines!" she complained, turning to watch the dust fly in a cloud behind them. Katie saw it, too, as she was rounding the corner of the cornfield.

"There she is!" Janice pointed excitedly. "Go on by and pick her up. Just look how much taller she is . . . not dressed any better . . . but taller."

"Janice, this is the farm. Not the country club. She's dressed like a farm kid."

Janice shrugged and rolled the window down to wave a white handkerchief out the window. Katie waved back and moved to the side of the road, as if they might accidentally run over her.

As soon as Preston stopped the car, Janice was out and engulfing her daughter in a big bear hug. Over her mother's shoulder,

Katie could see her father, leaning across the seat, smiling. Katie tried to smile back.

"Oh, let's have a look at you!" Janice studied her from head to foot. "You have grown. Look, Preston," she stood back to back with Katie, "she's taller than I am."

"Hi, Janice," Katie ventured at last.

"Well, don't just stand there. Get in the car." Janice pushed her into the backseat, slamming the door behind her. Then she climbed into the front, turning to talk over the seat as Preston eased the car toward Meyer's driveway where he could turn around.

"Daddy says we made good time," Janice chattered on. "I guess we did. You know how he drives! It took me a while, but I finally got myself on schedule with the car . . . if you know what I mean." She winked and pressed Katie's knee.

"What are you talking about!" Preston retorted in mock indignation. "I stopped several times. I even stopped at a dress shop. Now, Katie, don't you think that's above and beyond the call of duty?" He smiled at her in the rearview mirror.

"So what have you been up to? Do you like being a sophomore? Better than freshman, huh?" Janice didn't wait for an answer. "Looks like they added a new wing on Gaston. Don't tell me they needed more classrooms! Or are they just replacing the ones the termites ate?" At that, Janice threw back her head and laughed at her own joke. Preston laughed with her, or maybe at her. Katie couldn't tell which.

"Janice, don't start." He said it good-naturedly.

"Katie, just wait till you see our house . . . and your room! Won't she be surprised, Preston? You'll just die, honey!" her mother babbled on. "But I refuse to spoil the surprise. You'll just have to wait till we get there and you can see for yourself!"

Katie tried to remember if she had ever seen Janice so animated. She wondered what it meant. She kept her own smile permanently in place, her eyes moving between them, watching.

Preston brought the car to an abrupt stop in front of the milk house. Katie got out of the car on his side in time to meet his brief hug, her face pressed against the scratchy wool sports jacket. He smelled slightly of tobacco, although she was sure he didn't smoke. The odor had probably soaked into his jacket in one of those government meetings he was forced to sit through.

"Hi, Kate," he said softly. "Good to see you, baby." Then in one motion, he pushed her away by the shoulders and extended a hand to Matt, who had suddenly appeared at the back of the car.

"Matt, how ya doin', guy?" He pumped the boy's arm.

"Great . . . great. Just great, Uncle Preston. How's yourself?" He stuck his hands in his pockets.

"No complaints. Ready to be out of the car for a while, though." He had the trunk open by now, and Matt stepped forward to help with the luggage.

Janice had already gone in the house and was "freshening up" when Katie, Matt, and Preston came through the back door into the kitchen. Preston set the luggage on the floor and greeted his mother with a hug. Grandpa Henry shook his son's hand, holding it between both of his, as if to anchor him in one place for more than a moment.

"Everything looks good, Dad. Corn looks real good on Cal's place." Preston picked up the suitcases and filed into the other room, his dad trailing behind, leaving Katie standing in the doorway. She could hear them talking about the weather and what milk was selling for that fall. She could hear the familiar rattle of the china cabinet as the men passed by.

Slightly embarrassed, Katie joined Grandma to help her put the finishing touches on the supper. The meal would be served in the dining room because the kitchen table was too small and because, Katie suspected, you just didn't serve Janice in the kitchen.

"Put the good china on, and the pink glasses, Katie. And let's fill Great-Grandma's sugar service. It's in the china cabinet." Grandma Henry was turning the chicken. It was useless to argue. But she knew Janice didn't like old things—even if they were antiques.

Janice made her entrance in cool pink twill sport slacks with top to match, wearing satin slippers with a pink tassel on the toe, her gesture of informality.

"Can I do anything, Mother Henry?" Janice poured herself a glass of cider from the pitcher that sat waiting on the kitchen table. "Don't mind if I just help myself, do you? You know how Preston hates to stop when we're traveling! I just thought I'd die of thirst before we got here."

She sat down, as if exhausted. Glass in hand, she reached into her pocket and produced a small brown prescription bottle. She threw the tablet to the back of her throat and swallowed hard.

"No. Everything's just about ready. You just rest yourself." Grandma Henry watched her tuck the bottle away. "Janice, have you been ill?"

"Oh no. Just a little something for my nerves . . . nothing really." She waved off her mother-in-law's concern. The woman didn't miss a trick! "Have you done something different around here?" Janice asked, changing the subject. "Something looks different. I know . . . you painted." She glanced around the generous farm kitchen which had been the same for the past twenty years.

"No. I just washed the curtains. Maybe that's it." Grandma kept moving about the stove and counters. "Honey, would you get Grandma the pink serving bowl from the dining room?" she asked Katie. "And, Sandy, did you put on the napkins?"

"Hey! Look who's here!" Dan came through the door with Ross close behind him and walked over toward Janice, his dusty hands held up in apology.

Janice stood up to greet them but stepped back slightly as the fragrance of the barn arrived ahead of him. If Ross had entered first, she knew, he might not have been so polite. He might have hugged her for spite. Ross loved putting her on. "Good to see you, Daniel. And you too, Ross," she said, peeking around Dan's husky frame.

Ross gave a mock salute. "Aunt Janice."

"Supper's nearly on," Grandma announced. "You boys can eat with us before you milk. There are clean clothes for you at the foot of the stairs." They understood that they were to shower and dress in the bathroom built for that purpose just a few steps from the back door. It made the house infinitely more pleasant and much less odoriferous.

Food was carried to the table, the loveliest table Alta Henry could set. Katie knew it would be dissected later for about forty miles, as Janice gave Preston her rating. Within minutes, Daniel and Ross emerged again, just as everyone was being seated. They were spic and span, their hair slicked down wetly, revealing white foreheads that had escaped the sun's rays under the brims of AFM Dairy caps.

"Uncle Preston, you don't look too much worse for wear. Guess that fancy government life isn't gettin' you down too bad," Daniel jested.

"No. I'm holding my own. How about you?" He held the chair for Janice. "I notice you aren't exactly wasting away either." Daniel was twenty-two, just ten years younger than Preston, but they competed like peers, with some kind of running bet over who would end up overweight by age forty.

Ross both envied and admired Preston. He would alternately goad Preston into an argument or ask him leading questions, which allowed Preston to brag about his hunting prowess or new military hardware. Preston loved the effect when the boy would turn stone-faced over some "classified" project.

"Let us pray," Grandpa announced softly. They each assumed a quiet repose, bowing their heads, eyes closed. "Our heavenly Father, we thank thee for the blessing thou hast provided. Grant that we will use this food to thy service as thou wilt use us to thy glory. Amen."

Grandma handed the meat platter to Janice, holding it while she made her selection. Katie got up to offer milk or cider.

"Hear you're going hunting again. In Kenya. Is that right?" Ross had decided to throw out some friendly bait. Katie was grateful for the diversion, knowing that talk of her father's latest expedition would monopolize the conversation through the entire dinner.

"Yep. We leave a week from Monday. Should be a good trip. We're going back to the same place we went last year. And with the same guide. I hope we'll get most of the same porters, too. Those guys were really good." Preston nodded a thank-you at Katie as she filled his glass with milk.

"Dad," he asked Grandpa, "you ever see a guy who could carry a hundred-pound pack and walk all day? And I don't mean down a paved road. These guys walked up and down, through grasses over our heads."

Katie faded away as he launched into a detailed description of the last hunt. As he talked, Preston heaped the food on his plate as if he were still doing the farm chores. Janice tapped his hand and smiled at him as he was about to take the second spoonful of mashed potatoes.

But he was not to be deterred. "And with no shoes!"

"No shoes?" they all chimed in unison. Katie jumped, lost to the context. She glanced around quickly to see if anyone had noticed.

Her father was still engrossed in his tale. "Yeah. They go barefoot. You should see their feet!"

"Preston! Must we talk about feet at the table?" Janice smiled and was about to change the subject when Ross headed her off.

"So, Uncle Preston, would you rather hunt in Africa or North America?"

"Oh, here in North America. No question."

"What's the most dangerous animal you ever faced in America?"

"A holstein bull!"

That made everyone laugh, except Katie, who held her frozen smile and watched. Sometimes she could just kick Ross, but this was not one of them. Katie wished he could come to Virginia with them, just to keep the conversation going, and to keep Janice and herself out of it.

"Enough hunting talk." Janice wedged in a comment. "You guys can tell all the hunting stories you like in the barn. Now what's this I hear about Katie getting in an accident?"

"I didn't get in an accident," she said timidly.

"You mean when the tractor tipped over?" Grandma answered.

"Besides, it wasn't exactly an accident," Grandpa began to add his two cents worth.

"Yeah. We did it on purpose!" Ross volunteered, spitting mashed potatoes as he laughed into his napkin.

"For heaven's sake, Ross," Sandy said. "He's just kidding, Aunt Janice."

"It wasn't much of an accident," Grandpa began. "She and Cal just went over when they were coming down into the north field. There's kind of a dip there. And if you don't hit it straight on . . ."

"But it could have been real bad," Ross interrupted. "Last year, Sid Murry's kid broke his leg. Got pinned under the tractor. Laid there about a hour before they found him."

Janice stared at Ross, trying to figure out if this was one of his sick jokes. It was one of those times Katie wished she could have reached him with her foot.

"Ross, I think I hear our girls calling us," Daniel said, pushing away from the table.

"I'll be right out," Grandpa said.

"No hurry. We got plenty of time, Grandpa." There was a long awkward silence as Ross and Daniel left the room.

"It sounds worse than it was, Janice," Grandma finally spoke. "Cal was there. And you know he wouldn't let anything happen to Katie. Won't you finish that corn, Preston? Another biscuit, Janice?"

"I couldn't! I've blown my diet all to pieces on this trip. If I don't stop eating, I'll have to invest in a whole new wardrobe when we get back."

"Please, Ma, hide the biscuits!" Preston groaned. Janice giggled and kissed his cheek.

Matt asked to be excused for chores, adding that it was really good to see them all again. And Preston got up to change and join the men in the barn.

"Preston, be a dear, and bring me my sweater," Janice called after him. "It's on the bed."

Sandy offered Janice a cup of coffee, while Katie cleared the table, the usual routine, allowing time for Grandma and Janice to exchange small talk and pretend civility. But Katie was listening carefully, signaling Sandy to be quiet, fingertip to lips, when they were alone in the kitchen.

"How are your folks?" Grandma asked politely. "We haven't seen much of them this summer. Kate's been awfully busy with 4-H and all."

"They're doing well. Sel's had some ups and downs with his blood pressure, but Elsie says he's been better lately. I had hoped to take Elsie back with us. But I'm not sure she will if she thinks he's not okay." Janice stirred her coffee, although she liked it black. Katie was picking up glasses at the time and noticed. It was as if her mother thought it might not be thoroughly brewed or something.

"They wanted us to spend the night there tonight. I hope that's okay with you and doesn't spoil any plans you had," Janice said evenly. Overhearing from the kitchen, Katie rolled her eyes at Sandy.

"Well, Cal's family was planning to come over in about an hour . . ." Katie could hear Grandma stalling, helpless.

"Well . . . we could stay here tonight and there tomorrow," Janice hedged. Sandy and Katie held up both hands, fingers crossed. "I'll check with Preston," Janice said hesitantly as if she could not make the decision herself. Then, with sudden conviction, "Oh, I think that will be fine . . . as long as we get out of here by nine-thirty."

The remaining hours were drained away in small talk and innuendoes. Katie could feel her insides becoming hollow, her own voice trailing off. It was a numbing that sucked all the words from her brain, leaving her speechless, which she knew, would be an insufferable annoyance to both her parents. When she thought of how dumb she would seem to them, with nothing to say, it made her palms sweat. But Janice kept looking at her as if she couldn't wait till they could leave and start their wonderful life together.

Remembering Ross's inspired table conversation, Katie began to recite mentally a memorized list of captivating questions. She tried to imagine herself sophisticated enough to converse with Janice and Preston. Maybe . . . someday.

"Are you packed, dear?" Janice's question disturbed her reverie. "Your father will want your things ready to go in the morning."

Katie thought of her belongings, sorted in piles, pondering how to keep everything safe. She knew that every item would be scrutinized as it was unpacked. It must all be above suspicion, since nothing was sacred to Janice. Anything Katie wanted to keep was better left behind. But figuring out what might be objectionable required Katie to think like Janice. And when she did, it made her feel very small, rattling about in a large empty body. Sometimes, Katie wondered if Janice felt that way, too.

Uncle Cal and Aunt Nan and their baby boys arrived in time for dessert, after which the adults adjourned to the living room to listen to Janice and Preston tell about their glamorous and important life. Katie was glad for the two restless children who provided her and Sandy with an excuse to escape.

As the minutes continued to tick away, Katie checked the clock repeatedly. At eleven, Cal and Nan loaded the sleeping babies in the car and hugged Katie good-bye under the bug-infested yard light. Cal instructed her to "take care and hurry back." Nan whispered, "We love you."

Back in her room, Katie snapped the suitcase over her final decisions and placed her traveling clothes on top. Sandy was staying the last night, although Katie was rapidly fading in her capacity for communication, even with her favorite cousin. She just wanted to be alone.

Once the lights were out, Sandy's breathing became soft and even in no time. Katie lay on her back, tears trickling into her ears, watching the moon play tag with the dry leaves waving in the gentle night. Even the night sounds were no comfort; rather, a painful nostalgia she was already missing.

She waited until the house slept—no more running water, flushing toilet, squeaking floors. Then she tiptoed across the floor, through the dining room, avoiding the spots that creaked, listening at the stairway door for whispers from her parents' room. There were none.

When she reached Grandma's bedside, she found her still awake. Grandpa had already stretched out on the sofa, leaving a spot for her in the bed.

"I can't sleep, Grandma," Katie said, sliding under the covers.

"I know, honey. I wasn't asleep either."

"Grandma . . . I don't think I can do it . . . I don't think I can go with them this time." Alta could hear the tears in the child's voice, could feel the anger that stung her own heart.

"I don't want to go to school there. Are they going to make me start school there?" Her grandmother stroked her face in the dark. "I just can't do it," she sobbed.

"Shhh . . . there, there, honey. I know it's hard . . . very hard." She rocked her gently. "Come on. Let me show you something."

Pulling Katie up, Grandma led the way back through the darkened house and out to the front steps. "Sit down." She motioned Katie to sit beside her on the steps.

"Look." She pointed to the sky. The night was clear, studded with stars and a glowing moon. "This same sky that covers us here will cover you there. When you see those stars and that moon, I will be watching the same ones." She pulled Katie closer. "I'll be praying for you, honey. And God will be watching over you there, just like He does here."

Katie looked at the sky . . . and listened.

"I don't know why it's this way, honey, but I know the Lord

has a reason for it. In time, He'll make it good." Remember the Ninety-first Psalm?" Together they spoke the words aloud like a prayer and then sat in silence for a long time, watching the heavens and listening to the crickets.

Finally Katie sighed. "What does it mean to 'dwell in the secret place of the Most High'?"

"Well, honey, I believe there is a secret place in the heart of God just for you. A special place where the Almighty, Most High God will meet you. And the love He shows you there will help you face anything this fallen world may have in store."

"But, Grandma," Katie persisted, "what does it mean, 'no evil will befall you'? I think bad things happen sometimes."

"Yes, but if you live under the shadow of the Almighty, the evil will never crush you. Some things may hurt. But they won't keep you down forever. You'll be able to go on and love again."

Katie didn't always understand the answers the old woman gave, but she inhaled the lovely sense of assurance that Grandma always had about her and snuggled closer to the round, soft body, touching the long, loose braid that ran down her grandmother's back. And through the dark hours, Alta talked and prayed and soothed and encouraged until Katie was as ready as she could make her and they were both sweetly sleepy.

Back in her grandmother's bed, Katie closed her eyes, knowing that Grandma would be up with the sun, so she needn't fear being discovered by Janice. The moon inched its way across the crystal canopy, pulling with it the closing curtain on this chapter of Katie's life. In Grandma's arms, she fell asleep in the secret place of the Most High.

Chapter 25

Two days later, with the miles accumulating behind them, Katie slid deeper and deeper into a silent world, a world without words, where she could see Janice and Preston moving their mouths and gesturing with their faces, but where the sound was barely audible to her.

Katie was grateful that they had each other, and that at least for this part of the ordeal, little would be expected of her. She had the sensation, however, of being inevitably drawn to a fatal conclusion. Somewhere at the end of this white ribbon, divided by a yellow line, loomed a house. A house where she was expected to be the happy daughter, returned from boarding school, or whatever illusion her mother had spun for her friends. A house where she must follow all the rules, being careful never to voice an attitude or opinion of her own. Somehow she must pull this off without Janice ever being the wiser. It must be authentic.

Traveling past the burnished oaks, Katie felt herself coming down with a serious case of guilt over why she was so unloving, so unable to please her mother. After all, if Janice didn't really want her, she wouldn't have gone to all the trouble of getting her, would she? She would have just left her on the farm, wouldn't she?

The house was awesome. It had the appearance of a modern-day Colonial—brick with white pillars and a circle drive in front. The lawn was immaculately manicured and groomed. The place reeked of taste and prosperity. Katie's eyes were glued to the window as Preston guided the car toward the massive double door entry.

"This is it, your new home."

"Daddy was finishing the last-minute committee meetings and whatever else was required to free him of his government responsibilities so he could be off to Kenya. I thought it was a long way from the Midwest when I looked at the pictures in the *National Geographic*.

"My new room was all in shades of powder blue, like empty sky. The bed was huge, giving the appearance of a pool I could drown in. It did not strike me as a place of warmth or coziness.

"In fact, the entire house was wrapped in opulence—massive rooms, extravagant furniture and rigid pieces of art, and sculptures in brass and stone that reflected the lifelessness of the inhabitants of the house.

"My first impression of the living room caused me to shiver and want to reach for my flannel shirt. But I thought better of it, knowing it would stand out in the sterile surroundings like an invading insect. And I didn't want Janice to dispose of it.

"It had been decided that I would 'temporarily' start school, which I did, keeping my mind focused on the 'temporary.' I did the work, kept to myself, and waited.

"Actually, I was glad for the time away from Janice. And school became the great escape—the legitimate place to hide. I found I could beg off all kinds of invitations under the pretext of studying. And I had succeeded in locking my brain on the acquisition of facts, instead of the pit of despair that yawned beneath me at all times.

"As a result, I was rapidly becoming a star pupil, and that pleased Daddy. I was even finding some triumph in Math, although I still paid for low B's with a knot in my stomach.

"Janice was not so easily distracted. She thought I was somewhat dull and resented the fact that I was not more available. Perhaps it was too reminiscent of the years when Daddy was in OTS. Or maybe it was just her fear that I would learn more than she knew. In any case, she was edgy. My successes threatened our fragile peace, causing her to fly into a rage. 'You think you're so smart!' or 'Who do you think you are?' or even 'Do you think you can pull the wool over my eyes?'

"Weekends were spent following Janice up and down the aisles of the 'better' shops in Arlington, watching my mother search for the perfect image. I noticed that everywhere we went, the little brown bottle of pills went along, too.

"Sometimes, Janice was absolutely giddy, which would have been fun, if it hadn't made me so nervous. There were some lunches at the club when I remember being frozen in a combination of embarrassment and fear as my mother went on and on about some boring topic, or when she erupted into a tirade about the food not being prepared to her liking or the waiter having a bad attitude. It was apparent that if a person happened to appeal to Janice, all was well. But heaven help the person she didn't like! No effort on their part would ever change her mind. The frightening part for me was that I could never figure out what accounted for the difference. . . ."

Katie finished putting her breakfast dishes in the dishwasher and headed to the other end of the house to retrieve her mother's tray. She wished she did not have to rely on Janice to drive her to school. Katie would have preferred to ride the bus, but Janice had insisted that busses were the transportation of riffraff and that she wouldn't have any daughter of hers smoking in the back of a public conveyance!

Lately, it had been a struggle just to get her mother out of bed in the mornings. She was so tired, she said, begging for just a few more minutes of sleep. With Janice, Katie had to tread the thin line between coaxing and outright nagging to get her up. A few mornings, when it had appeared she would be late for school, Katie had managed to bum a ride with Preston when his meetings didn't start too early.

One thing that seemed to help was fixing her mother's breakfast and taking it to her in bed. Prior to that discovery, Katie had missed several days of school, covering with the excuse that she herself had been ill. But everything blew up the day Preston "ran into them" at the club and berated Katie for playing hooky, lying, and manipulating her mother.

Katie pulled open one of the double doors that led to her parents' suite. She could see the light streaming from the bedroom, beyond the sitting room. Katie paused for a minute and listened. Not a sound. That meant Janice had gone back to sleep.

She slowly pushed open the door of an all-white room that always reminded Katie of an igloo. The huge bed floated like a pink cloud in the center, the covers thrown back. Janice's pink slippers lay next to her silk robe, scattered in disarray on the floor.

Alarmed, Katie followed a trail of clothing into the bathroom, where she found Janice, clad only in her slip. She was slumped over the marble sink, fumbling with her prescriptions.

"Janice?" Katie moved closer.

"Oh . . . Linda . . . thank God, you're here. . . ." Janice reached for a glass, and Katie watched as her mother tried to locate the faucet. In the process, she stumbled and banged the glass on the side of the marble counter, shattering it into a million tiny pink slivers.

"Janice!" Katie rushed forward and caught her around the waist.

Her mother's face was ashen as she led her back to bed. Janice fell into the pillows. Katie lifted her feet in and pulled the satin comforter up under her chin. Janice's eyes rolled back, and her hand went limp.

Katie stared at her, trying desperately to think what to do. She started for the sitting room to call Preston's office. Maybe he hadn't left yet.

"No," Janice wailed. "Don't leave me!"

Katie flew to her side.

Janice clutched at her, erupting in tears. "Oh, God . . . don't leave me . . . please . . . Linda, don't go."

"Janice, this is Katie. What's wrong?" She rubbed her mother's wrist.

"Oh," she moaned. "Linda, this is God's punishment, isn't it!" She pleaded with Katie, clutching at her clothes. "God is punishing me. He is, isn't He. . . . Isn't He?" she insisted, pulling Katie's face down close to hers. "I know it! I must pay. . . ." Then she fell back against the pillows and moaned, "Linda, I'm sorry . . . oh, please believe me," she wailed, sobbing uncontrollably.

Katie tried to console her mother. "No. It's not a punishment. You didn't do anything wrong. You're just sick."

But Janice persisted. "It is . . . it is . . . I know it. . . . Linda, my sweet Linda . . . it's all my fault." Janice winced as if in pain. "I killed her! It's my fault . . . I killed her! I didn't want to . . . but what else could I do?" she whined, pleading with Katie for some sign of acceptance. "Please . . . you must understand. Please, Linda, tell me you understand!"

"No, Mama . . . it's Katie. Katie! You're here with me," she explained while Janice kept mumbling Linda's name.

Suddenly, Janice bolted upright, staring at Katie in wide-eyed terror. With both hands she shoved her backward and began inching her way across the bed. "Get away! Get away! No! Don't touch me!" In a frantic effort to escape, Janice hurled herself off the other side.

"Mama!" Katie screamed, scrambling after her mother who lay in a lifeless heap on the floor. Katie scooped her into her arms, rocking her, and sobbing, "Janice! Janice . . . it's all right . . . what should I do? Oh, God, help us!"

Laying her mother down gently, Katie ran for the phone. She could not remember the number for Preston's office. Somewhere there was a phone book. She jerked the drawer of the stand, pulling it out of its track and spilling its contents on the floor. Pens, tablets, pieces of paper . . . but no phone number.

Katie lifted the receiver and dialed the operator. "Help me! Send an ambulance. Hurry! Hurry!" The operator tried to calm her enough to repeat the address. Katie could barely remember what it was. At last she blurted, "5592 Burning Trail! Hurry!" into the mouthpiece and dropped it on the carpet.

Back at her mother's side, Katie rubbed her arms briskly and kept assuring her, "They're coming . . . they're coming! Oh, God, please don't let her die!"

Janice mumbled and rolled her head.

From far away, Katie could hear the sirens. "Janice . . . I'm going to let them in, okay? I'll be right back. . . ." She looked at her mother lying beside the bed on the floor, then raced for the front door, arriving about the time the paramedics were coming up the steps.

"She's in there," she screamed, pointing to the house. "Hurry! She's unconscious . . . I think."

The two men followed her through the house, asking, "Do you know what happened?"

"No. I just found her. She couldn't wake up. Then she got panicky and started screaming."

They entered the room where Janice lay, still and white, on the floor. Katie stood in the doorway and watched as they knelt over her, lifting her eyelids, listening to her breathing. "What's her name?" the man in navy blue asked, without looking up.

"Janice. Janice Henry."

"Janice!" He shouted at her, slapping her face on both cheeks. "Come on, Janice, wake up! We're going to take you to the hospital! Mrs. Henry, open your eyes! Come on, Janice, help us out here! Janice, wake up!"

The other paramedic, joined by two policemen, pushed past her with a stretcher and an oxygen tank.

One of the officers took Katie by the hand and led her to the love seat in the sitting room. "Do you live here?"

"Yes."

"Is this your mother?"

"Yes."

"Can you tell me what happened?"

"I don't . . . I'm not sure. I was getting ready for school. She usually drives me in the mornings. But when I took her breakfast in, I found her in the bathroom . . . and she was kind of stumbling. Then it was like she didn't know me . . . or what was going on. . . ."

The other officer came over to them and knelt beside her. He spoke sympathetically, "We're going to take her to the hospital. Can you show me where she keeps her medicine?"

Katie walked with him to the bathroom, glancing at Janice as they lifted her to the stretcher. A bottle of clear liquid, connected to her arm by a plastic tube, dangled above her head. Katie started to cry.

"It's okay," the policeman tried to reassure her, "they're just giving her something to revive her. You can ride with us so you can be with her. But first, we need to get her medication. Okay?"

Katie rode in the police car behind the ambulance, answering questions. It was a bright fall morning, which seemed to expand the world into nothingness. She felt numb and very small, as if she were on a conveyer belt heading for some inevitable destination.

Inside, her mother was whisked away to the inner bowels of the sterile world. Katie was left in a waiting room for what seemed like an eternity. Finally, a pleasant middle-aged woman escorted her into a small stuffy cubicle for more questions, the answers to which she recorded on a typewriter.

After what seemed like hours later, she was taken to her mother's bedside. Janice, still hooked up to the bottle of clear liquid, lay stiff in a hospital bed with the side railings up. Her face was devoid of color, her blond hair a disheveled mess, clinging in wisps to patches of dried tears. Katie sat down in the chair next to her bed.

The nurse who came in to take Janice's vital signs tried to be *encouraging. "She's going to be okay, honey. But she'll sleep for a while. The doctor will be in soon, and he'll explain to you. Okay?" Katie just looked at her.*

"How old are you?" she asked as she went about her routine, without looking up.

"Fourteen."

Katherine put down her journal and stood up to stretch. Three hours had passed since she had been spirited away into the past. She felt stiff.

To this day, Katherine did not know for sure what that episode was all about. Though they never spoke of it, she knew there was the possibility that her mother had been attempting suicide. At the very least, Janice certainly had muddled her medications.

From her training, Katherine suspected that anyone who lacks emotional health is living with a continual death wish. Some folks just try to kill themselves in more acceptable ways—overeating, working too hard, any form of addiction.

Still that scene had evoked a new sympathy for her mother that persisted.

Preston had finally arrived and had taken over. To all the medical personnel, he had been the epitome of the attentive husband and father. But in retrospect, Katherine now suspected that he had been deeply resentful.

He had barely spoken to Katie. And when he did, he had made it very clear how angry he was with her for failing to take care of Janice. The revelation came in one statement, which he delivered in the car on the way home from the hospital: "You'll kill her!"

"So I knew I was headed back to the farm again. But this time I was taking something with me," she explained to Chey and picked up the pen again.

"I was grateful for the brassy Arlington High School girls who took what they wanted from life (and retail stores) and didn't take any guff from anyone. I was much too timid to join them and too intimidated to let them know it, so I slid around in the murky space between genuine goodness and street sophistication.

"Those were the years of initiation rights. The trick was to convince them you'd already been through it. I recall my bravado when I'd hide the receipts from local stores and hope they would think I had stolen the merchandise.

The girls also taught me how to smoke, which I practiced in front of a mirror until I mastered just the right image. And the confrontation with Uncle Selinus came that summer—the summer between my sophomore and junior years—when my parents brought me back to the farm. . . ."

"Go on up to the office, Katie, I have something to show you," Uncle Sel had said with a sickly smile.

Now she waited, shivering inside, listening to the scuff of one foot and the other as he came up the stairs from the shop. She could hear the men talking and laughing below.

Wearing tight jeans and a black turtleneck sweater, Katie leaned against the closet door, a cigarette propped between her fingertips. When Uncle Sel lumbered in, she lifted the cigarette to her lips and lit it.

"What is that?" He pointed to the gray curl of smoke.

Knowing how strongly her uncle disapproved of nicotine and alcohol, Katie took a long drag and exhaled slowly in his direction. "You gonna tell my mother?"

That was the end of it. The molesting was over—three and a half years of it. It ended the moment Katie acted like Justine Carmela, sexy and streetwise. Uncle Sel never touched her again. But something had already closed inside her.

Whimpering to go out, Chey scratched at the door. Before opening it for him, Katherine parted the shutters, letting in the light. But all she could see through the frosted glass was a white world, shadowed in blue.

Gingerly, she opened the door for Chey. Snow blew into the cabin where it had piled up against the door. The dog pushed past her, out into the swirling whiteness. Katherine closed the door behind him and went to the window over the sink to watch.

Scraping away the frost from the pane, she could see a landscape draped in white, the sky still powdery. Gusts of wind sent white flakes dancing in miniature tornadoes across the meadow. The dark giant firs swayed with the snow heaped like frosting on their drooping boughs.

It was beautiful. But nothing about it was enticing enough to pry her out of the warmth and security of the inside.

Later, when she let Chey in, she stuck her head out just far enough to glance in both directions on the porch. Any sign of last night's visitor lay buried under several inches of drifting snow. Katherine felt safer as she closed the door with the dog inside.

She knew she must conquer this fear or be a captive until next June. She felt the steel presence of the prison within.

"God help me!" she prayed as she sat at the table watching the snow accumulate and trying to eat food with no taste.

She tried to recall the familiar words: "He that dwelleth in the secret place of the Most High . . . He is my refuge . . . in Him will I trust . . . Surely He shall deliver me . . . ."

She closed her eyes and listened to the still calm voice: *You shall not be afraid for the terror by night; nor for the arrow that flieth by day; nor for the pestilence that walketh in darkness; nor for the destruction that wasteth at noonday. . . .*

By sheer force of will, bolstered by an unseen arm, Katherine settled into a winter of resolution. The dam had broken and the memories were flooding in. The tide would carry her to freedom.

"Let it come," she whispered.

Chapter 26

"Roe versus Wade slipped through while the country wasn't looking!"

"That's politics, John. What do you want?" Adam plucked a square of cheese from the toothpick, knowing he would regret playing devil's advocate. But it was a good show for the students. They could watch their professor in action. "You can't expect the government to pass laws that favor one particular religious viewpoint. You're not that idealistic!"

"We're not talking about idealism here. At least, I'm not." Finding an opening, Katherine wedged into the conversation. "Adam, listen. It's something more. It's more than a Christian issue. Something is happening here, something insidious, yes, political!"

"Okay, okay. So you hold your beliefs strongly. But politics determines whose strong beliefs and ideas become policy," Adam interjected between cocktail shrimp. "Do you really think you're going to win? Do you really think you can make the world one big happy family? With no more rapes, no incest, no more children getting pregnant? What happened to 'live and let live'?!"

"Well, if you must know . . . it's not right!" Now she was bearing down on him with that intensity with which she could nail a person to his own argument. "That point needs no discussion. My point is not about winning but about consensus-building. How can we educate the public and how can the politicians listen to the public, if the media persists in reporting us as a minority of nuts! And if they do that long enough, we will be! Public opinion will side with those whom they believe to be the majority. America likes to be on the winning side. Right *or wrong, they like to win! But this is not about winning. It's about a fair hearing."*

"When this whole thing started, public opinion was against abortion," a young grad student piped in.

"Exactly! But I don't suppose it is now." Katherine paused just long enough to catch her breath, before poking her finger back into Adam's lapel. "And what's become of those gutless wonders we call colleagues? They know abortion is harder to counsel than rape. If they can't stand up for what is godly, then why don't they take a stand for their own ethics—to work for the good of their patients? They see the devastation of it, the resulting promiscuity, the denial. Women whose psyches are saying, 'If you can't defend your baby, you aren't worth defending either!' How many women are trashing themselves following this 'medical procedure'?"

"Please, please. . ." Adam held up his hands in surrender. "I'm not the enemy, remember?"

"I didn't know that, Dr. Allen," the student said earnestly, ignoring Adam's playful rejoinder and addressing Katherine. "Is it really more difficult to recover from abortion than from rape?"

"Yes, because the woman must direct her anger at herself. We call that 'depression.' It's as if she volunteered to be raped. How does a woman recover from killing her own child? Outside of Christ, there can be no recovery."

"I suppose that's why the secular community maintains that there is no issue," John interjected, sensitive to the broader implication. "Because they have no solution."

"And there is the height of hypocrisy!" Katherine threw up her hands in exasperation. "If Jesus is the answer—a premise the world rejects—then there is no problem!"

Two more of John's students joined the discussion. "So, do you pray first? Or do everything else and then pray?" Before he could answer, the other asked, "What do you think, John, will this be the issue that brings on the Christian backlash . . . the persecution?"

"It is a concern. The last time our country went through this kind of 'civil war' was over Vietnam. And we've not settled that one yet. What concerns me here is that these issues are being drawn around lines of identifiable creed. We are already seeing a massive shift away from Christian values. Now there is increasing intolerance of anything bearing His name."

"Even of Christians themselves," Adam added.

"You think the issue of abortion might be that divisive?"

The student watched both the professor and his friend nod in agreement.

"And there is something behind this deception. What explains the feminists supporting abortion, when worldwide its female babies are being killed?" Katherine rolled her eyes.

"Still, in the providence of things, if indeed 'all things work for the good,' this may be the very issue that God uses to bring this nation to its knees," John countered. "After all, the Faith has always flourished under persecution."

Katherine's mind wandered off. She did not like to think of the possibility that she might be part of a group singled out for attack. Adam was a constant reminder of the fact that God's people have always been persecuted. Her throat constricted at the thought. Somehow, it reminded her of those awful nights in '68, when they had watched the local news and realized hell was all around them.

"Why can't we deal with the truth?" someone asked.

Adam joined in, "Because it isn't what we want to hear. It doesn't validate our virtue. For most people, truth is whatever makes them feel good . . . not what makes them look at the skeletons in their closet!"

"And truth must be lived, not just believed," John said. "It may require taking on the system." He put his arm around his wife.

"Yeah, and I'm about ready to take on 'the system' in my biannual pilgimage to Virginia, to pay homage to motherhood and apple pie and all that sort of thing." Guiltily, Kate glanced around to see if her mother was within earshot. She wasn't. "God help me," she whispered, smiling good-naturedly.

"What if Jesus had worked in the system?" asked a bright young woman who was not ready to let the dialogue end.

"He didn't," John said over his shoulder, heading for the food. "He said, 'I am the system . . . the Way'."

Kate slid out of the group, aware that Janice would be thinking these were inappropriate topics of conversation at a Christmas party. Certainly they were not acceptable subjects between mother and daughter, since her opinions could not have been further from Janice's.

Kate threaded her way through the living room stuffed with holiday cheer, acknowledging compliments and sharing anecdotes with friends. She inched toward her mother. Janice was perched on the ottoman in the corner, talking to Eleanor, the wife of the chairman of John's department.

"Janice, you've met Eleanor Boyd?" Kate slid alongside the woman, joining their conversation dutifully, not wanting Janice to feel as if she had been deserted. There was an awkward pause during which each of them played with the ice in their punch cups. A pause that made Kate consider a graceful exit.

"So, will you be staying for Christmas, Mrs. Henry?" Eleanor addressed Janice, breaking the silence.

"No. I think we need to get back. My husband can't stay away that long. He's just returned from Africa, you know," Janice hinted, leaving Eleanor to figure out why he had been there. "I had hoped Katie would come home with me for these two weeks, but I guess she couldn't see her way clear to take time off."

Katherine winced at the childhood name her mother had used, signifying her private ownership, labeling her daughter as a child still—small, inept, inadequate. It was a further aggravation to Kate that her mother dismissed her profession as insignificant. Janice seemed to think that her daughter could just pick up any time and fly off to attend to her needs. Oh well, what's new? Katherine thought.

She knew that Janice considered people who went into ministry or religious study to be frauds. The fact was, she knew that her mother was threatened by their message, since it was about people and not things, and most frightening of all to her, about God. So she simply discounted the messengers as "unrealistic."

Katherine was aware that she could not have selected a more threatening career than psychiatry, so far as Janice was concerned. Nor could she have chosen a more grating identity than "Christian." Janice hated the terms "born again" and "Christian counseling" because these somehow defined her as an outsider. Therefore, rather than deal with her feelings of insecurity, Janice simply ignored them.

Glancing up, Kate saw her father on the other side of the room, looking competitive and stern with his arms folded across the brass on the front of his uniform. She could guess from the individuals gathered around him that he was getting an earful of "prayer in the schools" or some other pressing issue of Christianity. That made Kate smile slightly. Let someone else try to take him on, she thought.

Lest she feel guilty about engineering this event where her parents were outnumbered, Katherine reminded herself again that it had long been obvious that both Janice and Preston lacked both the internal security and the social grace to acknowledge either her career choice or John's. Both of them, on the other hand, had endured endless hours of palaver regarding the political maneuverings of the defense department, where the men at the top—the real movers and shakers, so her father maintained—secure the world for those who concern themselves with things of the spirit.

Kate mentally rejoined the conversation at hand. Janice Henry was a gallery of carefully hung self-portraits, always on exhibit. Now she was telling how she had gotten a steal on a vacuum cleaner by persuading the salesman to sell it to her at the sale price. Like all her carefully rehearsed stories, this one was designed to demonstrate her guilelessness, as if people were just waiting to reward her for her goodness. Then she went on to tell Eleanor about certain risqué remarks the salesman had made.

"Why, I didn't know what on earth he was talking about!" Janice said innocently, sipping her punch.

From the way her mother slurred her words, Katherine could tell that she had spiked her drink and might be on the verge of causing an embarrassing scene. But before Kate could intervene, Janice continued with the portrait.

The remaining impression she conveyed was a familiar one—how much she was valued for her integrity, her "down-to-earth honesty." "Oh, I'm not one to put on airs," Janice was saying, "but it seems someone is always after me to chair some charity function or other."

Janice also prided herself on being a superb judge of character. "No one can pull the wool over my eyes," she went on. Katherine knew that simply meant that she would not be moved once she had formed an opinion of someone. Kate's attention wandered as her mother rambled.

"I didn't know you had a sister," Eleanor said to Katherine when Janice finally paused for breath, lifting her glass to her lips.

Kate looked at her mother in disbelief. She had never known Janice to bring up the subject. "Ye—es," she said a little hesitantly. "She was six years younger than I. She died when I was twelve."

"Janice was just telling me about her. That must have been a very hard time for all of you." Eleanor was a warm and sensitive woman, one whom Kate had liked from the beginning of John's tenure with the department of Religion twelve years ago. "I suppose anyone would suffer some damage from that kind of trauma."

Kate began to wonder what Eleanor was talking about. She had never been aware that her mother cared anything about the damage to her life, let alone the reasons behind it.

At that, Janice stood, wished Eleanor a "Merry Christmas," and headed for the bedrooms.

Kate excused herself and followed her mother. "Is there something wrong, Janice?" she asked, finding her sitting on the bed, removing her shoes and jewelry.

"It's just that I find these people very different . . . from our friends, I mean." Janice rose and stood in front of Kate, her back to her. Kate unzipped her dress and carefully unbuttoned the sequined collar, lifting it over her mother's head when Janice held up her arms.

"What do you mean, different?" She hung the lovely dress in the closet.

"Just . . . different. Sort of 'holier-than-thou,' I suppose. Don't want to get their hands dirty in the real world." Katherine chose to ignore that. Janice went on. "They're not . . ." she searched for the word, "very well-informed, I guess. I suppose that makes them the way they are."

"Not well-informed! Janice, that room is full of very well-educated people. What do you mean? What makes them the way they are?" Kate felt a slow burn rising, the heat penetrating her defenses. She regretted the lateness of the hour. Her insides were churning, and she really needed to finish this before it made her sick.

Katherine had always carefully refrained from losing her temper or in any way confronting her mother. Only recently had she even begun to be in touch with feelings of anger toward her. But she maintained a constant vigil, lest she reveal her true feelings. The past two weeks had been a strain.

"Take John, for instance. I don't want to say anything against John. His ideas are just different from ours, that's all. But if he's been good to you, that's all that matters."

"Janice, what are we talking about here?" Kate stopped in the middle of the room, hands on hips, and turned to face her mother.

"Well, I'm sure if there was a better way to handle things, your father would be doing it."

"Are you talking about Christian politics? That John is a committed . . ."

"Oh, yes, that—that religious stuff, too. Well, it's just plain embarrassing for me. I'm not used to bleeding hearts who sit around and talk things to death. I prefer people of action."

Katherine was incredulous. "What! Those are very committed and informed people out there! Committed to the cause of Christ. Doing their level best, in the trenches, to bring a message of hope. What I do every day makes a difference, Janice!"

"Well, I think those people just need to get hold of themselves. Stop feeling sorry for themselves and . . ."

Katherine interrupted her "Janice! Have you no compassion?"

Janice whirled around to face her daughter, "What kind of compassion is it that tells a poor impoverished girl she must bear a child, while 'bleeding hearts' like John sit around and talk about it?"

"The kind of compassion that reaches out a hand and says I'll help you, feed you, clothe you, take you in. We're doing more than the media gives us credit for, you know." Kate's voice was escalating. "Besides, John is not a bleeding heart!"

Janice slipped into her wounded little-girl role. "It just bothers me, the crass way he talks. I suppose I've always been too thin-skinned." She wrapped herself in a pink silk robe, as if to shield herself.

Kate set her cup on the dresser. "Oh, brother . . . like you've never heard anyone use a crass word!"

"Well, I'm not used to it. Our friends don't talk about . . . that," Janice insisted.

"Like what? You mean your friends don't talk about abortion?" Katherine was genuinely confused and thought she might have missed something. But reading Janice's face, she could see that the word abortion brought a grimace of disapproval.

"Abortion is not a swear word, Janice. Nor is it a subject we must never mention, as if that would make it go away. It is a real issue . . . a very nasty issue."

"I see no reason why it must be discussed at a Christmas party, or why he has to be so crude."

Janice was fiddling with her watch clasp.

Katherine restrained the urge to help her. "John is not crude!"

"Maybe not to you. But I think it's crude to show those pictures. I've always been a pretty good judge of character, and he simply does not know the proper topics to bring up at a social gathering."

Katherine gasped. "What pictures? You mean the pictures of mangled babies the protestors are holding up? Of course, it's crude! It's more than crude, Janice, it's sick! Evil! That's why we want it stopped. Maybe we need to show the world what is being done in secret."

"All this preaching! It's just so . . . upsetting. It makes it very difficult for us to spend time with you. I'm not used to it." Janice was beginning to whine again, which annoyed Kate more than her sharp tongue. "Your father is . . ."

Without thinking, Katherine blurted, "What about your brother? Now, there was a man of gentile dialect!" She stared at her mother, aware that she had just collided with an invisible wall.

"Why are you doing this, Katherine? Now I'll always remember the Christmas I spent with my daughter as a time of pain and upheaval," she complained.

Kate felt her anger turning to liquid rage and was helpless to prevent its eruption. After all the years of avoidance, she felt drawn into this, attracted as a moth to flame. Some part of her wanted to flee. But perhaps because she was on her own turf, or because of the years of emotional anemia, Kate sensed the inevitable and let it happen. "I'm not ruining your Christmas. This isn't Christmas, and I did not start this!"

"Oh, Katie, you've always been the one to bring difficulty into my life. What was I to think of all your antics? I never know what message of disaster you're going to bring next. I just wish Linda were here." She started to cry.

"Antics! Linda! What does she have to do with this?"

"Linda was such a pleasant child. I always knew what she was thinking. She was honest. Not like you. You were always lying . . . deceitful from the beginning. I never knew what to believe!"

"Honest! Linda's not honest, Janice, she's dead! And I wasn't lying to you. I was trying to protect you. You never wanted to know the truth . . . because you were always sick!"

Both women knew they were skating dangerously close to the open water in the ice between them—an area never before approached, though they both knew it was there.

"You should have told me when it was happening. Now I can't do anything about it! My brother is dead. I can't do anything about what happened now!"

"You don't have to fix it. Just care!"

"Oh, Katie! You know I've always loved you. Everything I have done was for you. I always wanted you to have the best. Katie," she moaned, "why must you ruin everything? This is making me sick. I don't know why you're always saying things! I suppose you get all this from that meddling grandmother of yours!" Janice's eyes, white with hatred, bore into Kate.

"Are you saying I should not have told you about it?"

"Yes! Why did you have to ruin my memories of him? He was all the family I had!"

"Janice, that's outrageous! He's the one who violated your trust when he violated me! I was the victim, Janice, remember? Three long years . . . while you looked the other way!"

"I still don't see why you had to tell me. Didn't you ever think about how I would feel? Some things are just better left unsaid!" Janice stood in defiance, her angry face thrust forward, spitting words like darts at her daughter, who for the first time was not backing down.

In the challenge, Janice began to feel the cold fear rising. It wasn't working—the intimidation was not working.

Janice ranted on. "But no! You have to be free . . . feel good . . . 'get things out,'" she mocked. "You are the most selfish person I've ever met! And you always have been!" She turned her back as if to indicate that was an end on it.

Then whirling around, Janice screamed, "Katie, can't you just leave it alone?" With her eyes closed, she shook her head and flailed the air with her fists. "It was over! Let well enough alone!"

"Janice! It was not well enough . . . it was a nightmare! And . . . it . . . is . . . not . . . over! I'm still hurting!"

"You're hurting! What do you think you've done to me . . . and your father!"

"Oh, pardon me for getting myself molested!" Katherine retorted. "For not thinking about how you would feel! And I enjoyed it so much, too!" She was shouting at her mother, while Janice glared back, jaw locked, lips thinned.

"What other little secrets do you want me to keep?" Katherine screamed, pulling out all the stops. "What else, Janice? What else am I not supposed to say? That you never loved me . . . that you have never once cared anything about me or my needs . . . that you shuffled me back and forth when it was convenient?" Katherine drew a deep, steadying breath. "I was a little kid trying to take care of you! Shall I keep it to myself when you tear down the people who really do love me? When you make one snide remark after another about a woman who is more loving than you ever thought of being . . . and John!"

Janice covered her ears with her hands and squeezed her eyes shut. But Kate would not be deterred. "Shall I keep to myself the real truth—that you were an outrageously abusive parent, that you brutalized me emotionally?" Janice headed for the bathroom, with Kate on her heels. "That the lovely innocent Lady Janice is . . ."

"I don't have to listen to this!"

"Oh, no, you've never had to listen to me . . . I just listen to you! That's how it goes, isn't it? Isn't it, Janice! But I'm not through! I'll tell you what is the best-kept secret in the world— how on earth you got this way! That's the . . ." Katherine's head snapped back, gasping and sputtering as Janice's hand shot out of nowhere with a full glass of water and threw it in her face.

"What is going on in here?" Preston had appeared as mysteriously as the water.

Seeing him, Janice suddenly wilted, as if she were on the verge of collapse. With his arm around her waist, he helped her past Kate, to the bed, where she fell back into the pillows, dabbing her face with tissue.

"I don't understand," she whimpered. "All I've ever wanted was for her good. Now she's attacking my relationship with Linda. I just don't understand it."

Preston stroked her scarred cheek, speaking in low, soothing tones, oblivious to his daughter as she stumbled out of the room.

Chapter 27

Kate raced down the hall, through their bedroom, to the den which adjoined the living room, before she collapsed. John found her sitting on the floor beside the love seat, drowning in tears, her hair and the front of her dress soaked.

"What happened?" John knelt beside her.

"I don't know what happened . . . I just blew up at her!" Kate put her head down and cried. "I couldn't stop myself . . . I said awful things to her." Between sobs, she poured out the conversation.

"Sounds to me like it was a long time coming," John said, his hand on her shoulder.

Actually, John wanted to cheer. He'd spent their entire married life keeping a tight rein on his responses to Janice and Preston, both of whom he respected less than the neighbor's poodles although he did fear them for their power in his wife's life. So, for Kate's sake, he had tolerated the emotional turmoil they left in their wake, painstakingly picking up the pieces.

"I've got to go to her . . . to apologize," Katherine said, drying her tears. "This is the most unchristian thing I have ever done!" Pulling herself up by invisible bootstraps, she began to smooth her hair.

"Wait." John stood in front of her, blocking her way. "Kate, listen to me. Give it some time. At least wait until morning."

"But, John, you don't understand . . . Janice is really a very fragile person."

"She's okay . . . your father's with her." John enfolded her in his arms, pulling her close. "But what about you . . . you're fragile, too."

"I have resources. I have you . . . and the Lord. She only has

Preston, who avoids everything." She looked up at him, through stricken eyes. "I'm so sorry . . . I didn't mean to hurt her like that. She must feel just awful right now."

"You think she's hurting. You want to know what I think?" John sucked in his gut. "I think she is the coldest, most insensitive, poorest excuse for a mother I've ever seen!"

Kate pulled away from him. "So what do you want me to do . . . become as cold and unloving as she is?" She bristled visibly.

"Is that what you're trying to prove, Kate, that you're loving . . . that you're a decent person . . . that you are . . . not . . . like . . . your . . . mother?"

"I'm not trying to prove anything. I'm just trying to be me!"

"Kate, why do you have such a blind spot? You can see the truth in other families. You see how victimized other kids are. Why can't you see this? Why can't you hold her accountable?"

"She's already been hurt enough! She's lost a child. . . ."

"Two children!"

"She's lived through the fear of losing a husband. . . . "

"Whom she has lost to tennis and hunting, not war!"

"And look at the family she comes from."

"Yes, look at them," John protested. "Take a good look. And look at her! Kate, she's got to choose to be different. It isn't enough just to be the victim. She needs a Savior, not a scapegoat."

"How can she choose to be different? There were no therapy sessions available for her. Only bad medical advice and Valium."

"What? So you think therapy is the savior! That if people don't have therapy as an option, they aren't accountable? Kate, she's never wanted to be different!"

"Well, how can she? No one has ever loved her . . . witnessed to her. . . ."

"You have. The Lord has. And maybe He's using this! All her expensive dresses and perfect houses and charity balls can't erase who she really is! And only two people in this whole world know who she really is—you and your father. Do you think he's going to tell her the truth?"

Katherine ignored his question and paced. "I'm all she's got!"

"Kate, you're helping her live a lie!" She glared at him as if he'd spoken the unforgivable heresy. "You're treating her like one of your victim kids. You've changed places with her. You've become her champion, her mother . . . she's the child!"

"Well, when did you hang out your shingle, doctor!"

"You know I'm right. Get your friend Adam in here. See if he doesn't agree with me. You're the one who needs a champion. But you won't let me be one for you!"

Kate stood for a long time, staring at the floor. John knew she was either assimilating what he'd said or dismissing it. And he knew the dialogue in her head would not be shared.

Finally, she looked up. "Okay. You're right."

"God be praised," he muttered.

"I feel like such a fool! How can I counsel others when I'm as enmeshed as they are?" They both felt the coin turn, the coming collapse into the morass of incompetence, insecurity, and depression.

John tried to head it off. "Maybe because you know how they feel. Maybe you should take your own advice." He was desperately searching for the words that would hold her above the dark pit that he knew could swallow her for months at a time.

"Do you really think I'm trying to prove I'm loving . . . by never getting angry, never confronting her?"

"I don't know. You're the shrink. But it makes sense to me. There's got to be some reason why you always protect her."

"Other than the fact that I was taught to? Daddy protects her from everything."

"From you, Kate. He protects her from reality, and from you!"

"Maybe so. Maybe in the morning I can talk to her. But I'm not sure I can say anything profound."

"Kate, I think you already have. I think the ball's in her court now. You told her the truth. You can tell her again, but the message will be the same. I think she owes you the apology. Or at least something indicating she's heard you. She's never given you so much as a word of comfort for what her brother did to you."

"She can't help it that he's her brother."

"There you go again . . . defending her! I'm not blaming his behavior on her. I'm saying she is responsible for never comforting you or showing you she's sorry that it happened. And look what kind of a home you came out of, yet you're not like her. She could be different, too."

John could see that Katherine was exhausted. "Why don't you lie down?" he asked, helping her to the love seat and propping the pillows for her. "I'll go make excuses." He gently pulled the afghan over her.

"You all right?" Kate asked, looking up at him. John nodded and kissed her forehead.

Surprisingly, she relaxed and began to consider what she would say to her mother at breakfast. The toddler in white high-top shoes raced through her head.

Sometime later, John returned to check on her. She nodded when he asked her if she wanted him to leave the door open. Everyone was gone now except Adam. The two of them would just finish cleaning up.

Kate felt safe and protected in the room lined with books, listening to the conversation between her husband and Adam through the open door. She heard Adam say he guessed there had been a problem, not that John would have cared if the entire North Shore had known what jerks his in-laws were.

"So the Imperial Mother strikes again!" Adam leaned back and lit a cigarette.

John slumped in the chair opposite him, his feet on the coffee table. "What is the matter with that woman?"

"She's keeping secrets," Adam said matter-of-factly.

"Secrets?"

"Sure. Nobody tries to exercise that much control unless they're hiding something."

"Like what?" John got up. "You want some coffee?"

"Sure," Adam said, ignoring the late hour, then addressed the question John had raised. "I don't know. I can think of hundreds of things it could be. But it's something that protects the thing she is most afraid of losing."

John left the room and returned with two saucers, rattling cups, and a half pint of half and half tucked under his arm. "What do you think she's most afraid of losing?"

"I couldn't say. But if I had her in my office for an hour, we could sure find out. I can only guess—her reputation, her home, her husband?" Adam leaned forward to reach the ashtray, twirling the cigarette to remove the ash, aware that Katherine would have told him to put it out. "And another thing, whatever it is, it's taking a fair amount of medication to keep it down." He exhaled the smoke toward the ceiling. "The woman's definitely overmedicated. Also, she'd better watch mixing drugs and alcohol, or she'll cease to be a problem . . . for herself or anyone else."

"Alcohol! Where did she get that?"

"What world do you live in?" Adam said sarcastically. "What do you think she carries in her traveling case—makeup?"

"So that probably accounts for her scrambled thinking, huh?"

"Could be some of it." They sat in silence finishing the coffee. "So how's Kate?" Adam asked.

"Worn out. I'd think she would get tired of this whole thing and just let go. But she's more of a saint than I. I'd tell those two to take a flying leap!"

"She's not a saint, John, she's enmeshed." Adam tamped the butt, crushing the glow.

"Great. What's enmeshed?" John's face, framed in the distinguishing gray sideburns, sagged in weariness.

Adam felt a camaraderie with him, wishing they could somehow lift Kate out of the muck, avoiding all the pain that went with it. "Well, we hang on until we get our needs met. But it's hard for Kate to realize that her parents are never going to meet her needs. And to make it even more complicated . . . in order to get her needs met, she's figured out, at least subconsciously, that she must first meet theirs . . . classic role reversal." Adam shoved some glasses out of the way and crossed his feet on the coffee table between them, a gesture that seemed to say I'm in this, too. I'll help if I can.

"It's not a virtue, John," Adam went on, "it's a neurosis. Kate's hooked on trying to make them better. Like a little kid always thinking what she can do or say that will make her folks finally approve of her, love her."

John stared at him while he continued. "And she's trying to meet needs that they, especially the mother, won't admit she has. The result is this incredible struggle between them—Janice, trying to cover up; Kate, trying to bring it out in the open. Whatever it is."

"So what do they want from her?" John leaned forward.

"They want her to maintain their image, their myth system. And she's their scapegoat child, the one they blame for everything, so they want her to continue to be at fault."

"And the dead sister is their perfect, fantasy child who can do no wrong?" John added. Adam nodded. "Then there's no way out of this?"

"Yes, there is. But no way out that keeps the system intact. She can't change and stay the same. Kate's going to have to decide, 'It's them or me!'"

"She'll never do that," John replied flatly.

"But wasn't your Jesus confrontive? Doesn't He call upon you who claim His name to speak the truth?" These seemed to John like strange words coming from an orthodox Jew. "Hey, John, don't underestimate her. People who are loved grow. And look what she just did."

"You think this fight is progress?"

"Sure it is. She's finally willing to risk getting angry and letting them know she's hurt."

"Do you think they'll respond to her? She's going to talk to them in the morning."

"What do you think?"

"Not a chance in a million!" John set the cup down hard.

"You're right."

"But maybe this time she'll see it. Isn't that what we're hoping for?"

"Yeah. And something is changing. It might pop something loose . . . in Kate. Maybe she'll remember what they have agreed to hide."

"You think she knows Janice's secret?"

"Yup! And Janice thinks so, too. Why else would she go to such lengths to silence her?"

"Have you told Kate all this?"

"She knows. Be patient, John."

The two men got up and began to clean up the after cheer. Glasses and hors d'oeuvres plates were stacked and teetering on top of every possible piece of furniture. It took them about an hour to return the apartment to its former state of order. John walked Adam to the door and said good night.

Kate dozed until John roused her and adjourned with her to their room. Opening the other door to check the lights in the hall, he looked down its length toward the room occupied by his in-laws. A yellow glow streamed from beneath their door. It was 2:37 in the morning.

Kate awoke early, with a fist in her stomach, her eyes feeling like a gravel driveway. She tiptoed into her dressing room, assembling herself for the day, rehearsing what she was going to say to her parents at breakfast. She wanted to tell them that she really did love them and was sorry for causing them grief and for blasting her mother. She also wanted them to understand that much of what had gone on during her childhood had been very hard on her, that it had caused her to do the things she had done. She wanted them to acknowledge that she had reason for her feelings, that she wasn't just bad or selfish. She needed them to say they loved her, too, and to indicate that they were concerned for her welfare. Above all, she wanted to be heard—without rage, without intimidation, without fogging—with just understanding and compassion.

Kate took a deep breath and headed for the kitchen, closing doors behind her as soundlessly as possible, not wanting to disturb John or her parents. Everything was still. She was grateful for the early hour and the time to compose herself.

Through the French doors, she could see newly fallen snow on the balcony. A clean white blanket had drifted over the soot-soaked street beneath, covering the filth. The sky was thick with flakes descending silently, like the quality of mercy into her own heart.

In the kitchen Kate reached for the coffee ingredients as she did every morning, started the pot, then set a one-cup filter over her mug and filled it with boiling water. That was the cup that revived her while she waited for the rest to brew.

Kate turned to the table at the end of the kitchen under the windows. Propped against the bowl of apples, was a note.

Dear Katie,
　　We woke up early. Knew you were tired, so will just grab something on the way. Thanks for everything.
　　　　　　　　　　　　　　　　Love, Daddy

The hall clock chimed six.

Chapter 28

"It was a blowup we never finished. The top blew off the mountain, the dust settled, and we went on as if nothing had happened. Janice sent lead crystal as a Christmas gift. I responded with the solicited thank-you and pushed the crystal to the back of the hall closet.

"The only remote reference to the painful exchange came between the lines of a Christmas card, which read:

> May you share the Joys of Christmas
> And may the New Year be a time of New Beginnings.
> Love as always,
>
> > Janice and Daddy"

The warmth of the coffee cup cajoled her back to her mountain retreat. Katherine finished her coffee, threw another log on the fire, and set about opening shutters.

Since that terrifying night some weeks ago, she had moved the guns from the shed to the top of the wardrobe and had dutifully closed and barred the shutters every night. As time passed without any repeat of the terror, Katherine's fears eased enough to allow her to keep the shutters open above her bed. Watching the moon play games with the clouds helped her pass the hours when she couldn't sleep.

Since that night, snow had fallen steadily, accumulating to a thickness of several feet. The lush green that had greeted her arrival had been transformed into a pristine white world, even more silent then the one before. Now even the slightest sound carried for miles.

Watching the fire blaze, Katherine's mind wandered up and down the hallways of her history. But she kept falling over that awful night with Janice. There was something about John's words at the party that night: "Roe versus Wade . . . abortion . . . more difficult than rape" . . . and Janice. What did the two have to do with one another? Katherine reasoned that her feelings had a lot to do with Uncle Sel. He certainly was an authority; a trusted one, turned enemy. But Janice?

Chey stood in front of her. Tired of the confinement, he was ready for his morning walk. She sighed and tugged on her parka against the chill wind outside, then opened the door a crack.

Seeing his chance, Chey wriggled his way through. The mere presence of snow caused him to lose all semblance of grace and dignity. And, with a running leap, he sailed off the porch, landing in a drift of snow piled at the foot of the steps. His shining black body swam in a sea of white, joyfully and with abandon.

Katherine stood in the doorway, watching him, aware that she had never liked snow. As a child, she had bundled herself so warmly that her body was too stiff to play. Matt and Sandy had loved the snow. . . .

Matt and Sandy loved to sled down the haystack beside the barn—the only elevation in the flattest county in Iowa. They went up and down the hay mountain for hours with the sled, alternately carrying and being carried, while Katie stood at the bottom. She did not like heights. She liked cold even less.

When they were finally worn out—faces red, noses running, on their way to the hot chocolate in Grandma's kitchen—they would lie down in the snow, waving their arms and legs to produce angel patterns.

Once Matt got the idea that if they each helped, they could make a circle of angels all around the house. Katie declined, having no desire to get any snow down her neck or in her boots. That was the day Matt called her an "old poop!"

Chey rolled in the snow, twisting his body back and forth as if extinguishing fires, his legs pawing at the sky. He yipped, bit at the snow, romped and lunged. Periodically, he looked up at his mistress, totally baffled that she wasn't participating, a look that made her think he thought she was an old poop, too.

Then he took to running in circles, his nose to the ground, a black furry plow sending the white powder in a flurry of celebration. As she watched, Katherine could not contain her laughter.

A sudden impulse seized her and she hurled herself off the porch after him, landing face down in the snow. Chey raced toward her as she rolled to her back, laughing out loud. Over and over she tumbled through the snow, feeling its fluffy support and invigorating cold.

Chey jumped and twisted and barked around her. She lunged and slapped at him, running through the deep snow in slow motion.

Finally spent, she fell back as if into a heap of pillows, and waving her arms and legs, Katherine created her first angel.

"I made it! I made it!" she shouted, pointing to the lovely angel print. Then, throwing her arms wide and twirling around and around, she laughed with her face to the sky. Chey watched her dance of celebration. The firs watched. The jays watched. And God watched.

Chey's ears perked to attention. He turned to the west. Then Katherine heard it, too. The plane.

She waited for it to circle in view, then ran in her own circles, waving her arms and laughing. Chey looked at her, looked up at the circling plane, and joined their dance.

In the cockpit, Cyle was really confused. He could see her on the ground like a small brown mouse on a sheet of white paper, running and jumping around, waving her arms. And the dog racing around her. He knew it was useless to call her on the radio. The more he watched, the more alarmed he became.

"God, help us . . . she's flipped her lid!" He circled the craft, knowing he couldn't land.

Cyle slid the window open and stuck his head out. Maybe she could hear him. The wind grabbed his knit cap, floating it earthward with the rest of the flakes. He saw Chey retrieve it.

"Get to the radio!" he shouted, then banked the plane sharply again.

"The radio!" Katherine composed herself somewhat and ran for the shed. Inside, the shed was alive with his insistent pleas. "Lady! Come in!"

"Yes. This is Ladybug . . . it's me!" She giggled.

"What's the matter? What the deuce is going on? Over."

"Nothing. I mean everything is . . . great! Over." Katherine could see the plane through the open door. "Are you there?" She switched the breaker up and down.

"Yeah. I'm here. What are you doing! Are you okay? Over."

"Just fine. . . . I just made my first snow angel! Over."

"What? You made your what?"

"An angel. Didn't you ever make angels in the snow? Well, I never did. Till now! Over."

"Man, she's lost it!" he mumbled, his mind calculating how long it would take him to get back here on the snowmobile. "Can you just hang on? I'll be back. But it'll take a couple of hours. Over."

Katherine suddenly recognized how this must look from the air. The idea doubled her over in a spasm of laughter. "You don't have to come back. I'm all right. Really. Over," she managed between snorts.

Oh, brother, he thought, *here we go again.* "What were you doing?" he spoke carefully into the microphone. "Why were you flagging me down?" He banked again.

"I wasn't flagging you down. I was just having fun! Over." There was another long pause.

Cyle didn't think of her as someone who had fun. "Great Scott! Would you please not have fun on my Fridays!"

"Roger. I'll try to restrain myself on Fridays." Katherine giggled again. "I'm okay. Really." Then she added, "It's good to hear another voice. Over."

"Are you ready to quit?"

"No way!"

"I lost my hat down there! Try to get it from the dog. Over."

"Hey, the dog's wonderful. I love him. How's Molly? Over."

"She's doin' good. She sent you something in the package. If you're sure you're okay, I'll drop this stuff. Over." He knew he couldn't fly over this cabin all day, much as he might like to.

"I'm fine. . . . Cyle? Could you and Molly come for a Christmas dinner? Over." There was a long pause.

"When?"

"Name it . . . you're the one with the schedule."

"We'll come the day before Christmas—the twenty-fourth. How's that? Do you know when that is? Over."

"Of course I know when the twenty-fourth is! I have a calendar. See you then. Over."

"Yeah. Thanks. Here comes your stuff. Over and out."

She could hear the plane turn, the engine rattling westward.

Katherine pulled an old toboggan from the shed. She had made a harness of rope and rags for the dog. This was the day she would find out if he could really pull his weight.

"Here, Chey." She knelt to accept his friendly licks. The animal was patient as she adjusted the contraption around him. Standing back, surveying him, Kate could not contain herself. What a ridiculous sight he was! He looked like a four-legged mummy, who'd lost part of his bandages. Chey's ears drooped in humiliation at her laughter.

"Oh, I'm sorry, boy," she said, roughing his ears. "It's all right." She took hold of one of the rags tied across his back. "Let's go. Come on, Chey," she called, urging him forward.

It took some coaxing before he was willing to walk beside her. She could tell he didn't like it. And, she had to admit, the ragged harness was an insult to his dignity.

In the few months she'd had him, the Newfoundland had matured to as handsome a dog as Katherine had ever seen, weighing, she guessed, nearly one hundred pounds now. She had found him to be an invaluable companion and could not imagine what life in this frozen wilderness would have been without him.

Everything was draped in white, like a bride waiting for her groom, Kate thought. The last remnants of the night drifted on a brisk breeze that sent billows of white powder swirling from the treetops. As they walked through the tree line, miniature avalanches cascaded from the trees, as their topmost boughs yielded to the weight.

The sky was a Pacific blue, the color that only God could have thought up, Katherine mused—majestic, intense, clear, and fathomless.

When they reached the runway, Katherine immediately detected a problem. The packages were nowhere in sight. They were buried somewhere under the snow, somewhere in that two-hundred-yard strip.

Beyond the runway, the river glistened like a silver vein through the earth's flesh. Together Kate and Chey walked toward the river's edge.

Icicles hung from the lower branches that had been splashed with water. Even the shallow, smooth rocks were shellacked in crystal. In every direction the world was a winterscape in bold relief.

Katherine sat down on the toboggan to strategize the most efficient way to hunt for their supplies. She knew she must find them, if for nothing else than the dog food. Chey's reserves were all but gone. She also knew she did not dare leave it overnight, lest some other woodland creature make off with his sustenance.

Suddenly, Chey stood up, fangs bared, a low growl issuing from deep in his throat. Katherine grabbed him. Hugging his side, she crouched next to him and looked wildly about. Across the river she spied the object of his alarm.

A brown bear, easily ten times the size of her dog, had ambled out of the trees and was sauntering along the bank, dipping his paw in the water's edge. He had not seen them nor had he yet picked up their scent.

"Shhh. Chey, quiet," she whispered, closing his muzzle in her hand. Her heart pounded as she watched the great animal mosey along, not more than a hundred feet away. She could see white frost encircle its jowls with each breath, its powerful body moving in suspended animation. All that lay between them was a shallow expanse of river.

He was moving to their right, when suddenly he lunged into the river and came up with a fish, which he carried in his mouth toward shore. Lumbering up the bank, he dropped it, just as Chey growled again. Katherine gripped his mouth tight and watched wide-eyed as the bear stood on his hind legs, sniffing the air in their direction. He snorted.

"Oh, dear God . . . I hope it's true that bears don't see very well," she prayed. She held the dog in an iron grip, not trusting what Chey, the lionhearted, would do if she let him go.

Apparently the bear's eyesight was less than keen, for he dropped to the ground, attending to his meal of fresh fish. It seemed to Katherine that she and Chey, crouched there in the snow, watched him for hours before he ambled into the cover of trees.

After he was out of sight, Katherine remained paralyzed in the snow for several minutes, clutching her dog. Mentally, she raced through the instructions she had read in the manual: "Don't feed the bears. Don't panic; they're more afraid of you than you are of them." She doubted that! Nor could she fully believe the last entry: "Bears won't bother you as long as you don't get between them and their cubs." Besides, how was she supposed to know where their cubs were?

For a moment, Katherine considered going back to the cabin to get the gun before resuming her search for the supplies. But she had never shot a gun in her life! Then she weighed the wisdom of just running back to the cabin and staying there. *What? Till spring?* she thought.

The only reasonable course of action seemed to be to start looking for the packages but be ready to run should the bear show up again. She faced a dilemma, however. She knew that if she released Chey, he might quickly locate the supplies, but he might also go charging across the river, starting an altercation she did not care to finish.

So, holding Chey by his harness, Katherine began tracing a path back and forth across the runway, keeping her eyes peeled toward the river. Once when the jays screamed out of the trees, she hit the ground, like a combat soldier in an artillery attack.

About two-thirds of the way, she found them—three twine-wrapped packages wedged in the snow. Quickly she anchored them on the toboggan and ordered Chey to pull. He balked, not understanding the directive.

Katherine was about to give up, feeling frustrated with him for the first time, when he caught on. To her great relief, he trotted effortlessly to the cabin with the cargo. It would have taken her two trips without the toboggan and one long one with it. She was even able to fall in line behind him, allowing him to break trail for her, making it much easier to navigate through the deep snow.

When she tore into the packages at last, Katherine found that Molly had sent along some shells she'd picked up along the coast near Yachets, and a drawing of herself and Ben. But she was really thrilled with a school picture of Molly, mounted in a cardboard frame and wrapped in aluminum foil. Kate smiled at the likeness of the little girl, grinning her toothless grin. Her hair was tied in a bun on top of her head, and she was looking very pleased with herself.

The short letter read:

> Dear Mrs. Allen,
>   We went to the ocean. It was cold. I got shells and sent you some. Also, see my hair is like you.
>   Love, your friend.
>   Molly Sterling

Katherine set the picture on the mantel, next to the pine-cone dolls and spent the rest of the day in the safety of the cabin. She baked bread again, sending a fragrant invitation up the chimney. When it was cooked to a golden brown, she curled up on the sofa with the photo album she had brought with her and John's journal.

As the days passed and the hours of daylight grew short, Katherine found more and more time to read or crochet. With all but three of the pieces now completed, the lace coverlet was nearly ready for assembly.

From time to time, when the mood was right, she read John's journal. The last year of her husband's life was here recorded, a gift he had wanted to give her. Only now was she able to receive it.

During that last year, Katherine had studiously avoided discussing his death or what he was learning and thinking. Instead, she had kept trying to cheer him, to kindle life within him. It had been perhaps her bravest performance. John had watched, at first in great frustration, then in quiet dignity and resigned appreciation.

In the end, he had become too weak to fight her resistance, to push through her walls of denial. He had wanted to give her the faith to accept his death when it came. But when John felt the strength of his body ebbing, he found, amazingly, the peace to pass the torch to Jesus. He could only trust that someday she would understand. And, for the first time, John believed she would. It was all here in the journal.

While the winter gathered on the outside and her heart warmed within her, Katherine read.

She continued to marvel that he had found this very intimate way to touch her even now. These hours had become a time she looked forward to spending with him. It was good to sense his presence and the reassurance of the understanding between them. It was good to feel again the familiar touch of his words, the way he thought, the way he turned a phrase. Finally, even missing him felt good, and the tears became sweet.

She turned the pages, inhaling John's wisdom once again, sensing that he was coming to the end:

"My dear Kate, it will be so hard for me to let go of you, more difficult for me than even releasing my own life. To think of never touching you again, of never seeing how the sunlight catches in your hair, to never lie with you and lose myself in you. Death is so final.

"Worse than all of that, my greatest struggle has been over your healing, your freedom. Through our years together, all the things that mattered and were dear to me—the causes, the ambitions, the ministries—have fallen away, one by one, till all that is left is a burning desire for you to be who you were created to be. To be well. Healed of the dark fears and solemn grief. To see you abandon yourself to life. However poorly, I have done all that I knew to facilitate that. But I have failed. It has been a source of rage in me to realize I would not live to see the harvest. I felt so cheated—so out of time!

"At first, I was overcome with the fear that without me, you would be lost, might never make it. But that was my own fragile ego talking. Then, just as I might have rested in peace that you would be okay, I began to feel the bitter realization that you would go on without me. That the laughter and the joy would be there for someone else to see, to share. A part of me wanted to say, "Please, Kate, never smile again, never walk in the sunshine, never again go to the country and let down your hair. Please, Kate, need me always, never leave me." (All the while it was I who was leaving you—who would have thought it? As if your needing me could or would keep me alive.)

"So all these years, while I've seen myself as the strong one, the one who must be there for you, now I see how much I have needed you. Loving you has given reason for my existence. It was a script God graciously let me play to the last curtain call.

"I wanted to be everything for you, to be the one who met every need of your life. Ironically, had I succeeded, you would most assuredly not be okay, or have any life past this. Thank God for failure—for His greater wisdom!

"As I lie here, helpless, barely enough strength to push this pen, somehow God is giving me the assurance that I am not your source of wellness, that you shall indeed be healed. That I can trust Him with you. And I am relieved.

"I weep with gratitude that all I am called to do is to love you, not to fix you or protect you, not to control you or even guide you . . . just love you—to celebrate who you are and to rejoice in the memory of our celebrations. What moments of love and majesty we have shared! And in love there is no failure, my Kate, no failure! We have loved each other. However imperfectly, we have loved. And our abiding Christ Jesus, who blesses every human act of love with His divine presence, making it eternal, has surely gathered every moment unto Himself.

"Every moment will somehow remain because it was created of God. All our efforts at atonement (the other sacrifice) have fallen short of the glory of God. Only the sacrifice of praise celebrates the joy. It alone is worthy of Him. It alone glorifies. And loving is the most supreme sacrifice of praise.

"Remember always, I have loved you well, do love you, my Kate . . . go with God. Embrace Him with all your heart, and allow Him into your life . . . not His rules . . . Himself! Celebrate your life . . . and mine, too . . . for we are as one . . . as we shall be for all eternity.

John"

Katherine closed the book. Holding it to her face, she breathed in its essence. It smelled of the sunporch at Grandma Henry's, of sandalwood and security. It smelled of loneliness melting into peace.

"John knows Grandma's God," she whispered. "A God who is alive. Who acts, touches, reaches out. Who does not need us to do anything but is the Author and Finisher of everything." She remembered the night under the stars on the farm. The same stars had lit the sky that wonderful night weeks ago, when something had touched her. Someone. She had felt the warmth of it. She knew she had not made it up or imagined it.

"He is real—not just a concept thought up by scholars and theologians—and He is not far away. Not a set of rules or

Sunday school attendance—but real—living, breathing, passionate, real! And He has not left me orphaned."

Leaning against the stones of the fireplace, Katherine surveyed the simple room, her place of refuge for the past seven months, now bathed in peace. A gentle spirit had moved in. Katherine felt the safety. And somehow in that moment, she believed with John that she would be all right, that whatever she must face, she would come through it.

"You are here, aren't You?" Katherine spoke softly, reverently, "Jesus, I need you. I have been so damaged, so hurt that I have inflicted much pain. I have been too afraid to love." Katherine slid to the floor, holding her knees, "Thank You for John, who tried to tell me. But I pushed him away—would not share with him—would not be comforted." Katherine listened. The wind stirred the trees outside, scraping the low limbs against the roof. "Just please stay with me, as You are now," she whispered. "I don't want to be alone anymore."

Chapter 29

Out of the seedbeds of pain, new life stirred. Katherine found herself singing the songs of her grandmother, and she felt His smile.

No reality of her life had changed. John was still gone. She was still alone in the Cascades—she and a dog—trying to make sense of things. But somehow it was all right. If nothing ever was any different, if there was no resolution past this point, Katherine knew that this new assurance of God's presence was enough.

According to the calendar she kept, in which she marked off the days so as to be sure she knew when Friday drops were due, it was now one week before Christmas. Suddenly aware of this deadline, she and Chey left the cabin and followed the deer trails up the slope at the rear. Here there was an abundance of wild rosebushes, adorned with festive red rose hips, not yet devoured by the hungry deer. She intended to pick and string these for Christmas tree decorations. It was a reenactment of a piece of childhood. After the holidays, Grandma had used the dried rose hips to add vitamin C to soup and tea.

Today Katherine and Chey spent the afternoon searching out and plucking the shiny red fruits like miniature apples. When she had a bag full, they trudged back down the mountainside and retrieved the ax, then set out in search of a Christmas tree. The invigorating cold seemed to flood her body with energy. Or perhaps it was the anticipation of Christmas.

It was very quiet in the woods now, except for the crows. There remained some small birds, flitting among the branches, but they were silent. She didn't remember the day they had stopped singing, but thinking about it made her look forward to spring.

She wandered around in the low growth, looking for the perfect tree, just as she had on the Christmas tree lots in Chicago with John. The physical effort was made greater by the depth of the snow, now about three feet.

Finally the choice was made. Katherine dug out the snow from the base of the tree, her body wedged sideways into the branches, and began chopping. It was harder work than she'd imagined, marveling at what it must have taken to cut down one of the really big trees like those that formed the walls of the cabin.

Then with a tremendous sense of accomplishment, she headed for home, dragging the tree in a wide, sweeping path across the white surface, the dog trotting beside her. At the back door, Katherine leaned the sturdy fir against the woodpile.

Inside, the stockpot of water was simmering on the stove. She carried it to a large metal bucket she'd rigged with a bundle of small logs, split kindling-size, standing on end. Into that she poured the hot water. Chey sat beside the sofa and watched.

After stamping the tree on the ground to shake off the traces of snow, she dragged it in and, with both hands, lifted it into the bucket of logs and water. Its smooth round trunk slid tightly down between the logs which held it securely upright. Chey cocked his head in bewilderment.

Katherine stood back to survey her prize. After selecting the best side, she slid it into place in front of the window next to the fireplace.

On the log bench that served as the coffee table in front of the sofa, she had assembled the things she had been collecting and making for decorations. With artistic precision, she arrayed the tree with lacy crocheted stars and snowflakes, pinecones, sprigs of dried grasses and weeds, a long string of popcorn, three delicate bird's nests she had picked from the bushes along the river, and eggshells she had carefully hung like bells.

The tree that appeared so small in the forest reached almost to the ceiling and spread out in a glorious circumference, releasing into the room the wonderful smell of fresh-cut pine.

Katherine felt festive and was excited about her invitation, even if a little nervous. With a cup of hot cider spiked with cinnamon sticks, she sat down to string the rose hips into the final touch of a primitive Christmas.

She had gathered some pinecones in a variety of sizes, resembling a family, for which she'd crocheted tiny clothes. She hoped Molly would be pleased. Some red wool yarn had been looped and knotted into a new cap to replace the one Chey chewed up that lovely afternoon of the angel prints.

The contentment of the evening created a funny sensation in her stomach, like butterflies on a summer day, like the first night home at Grandma Henry's, like dancing with John in the snow on the balcony. Blue and orange tongues licked the logs, spitting glowing sparks, as she sat with her feet propped against the sleeping dog, his great head on his paws.

For a moment, she fantasized that her father—Grandma Henry's son—and her mama—the young lovely woman with the soothing hands—were coming for Christmas. How delightful it would be to sit before the fire and sip hot cider and talk to those people. They'd tell funny stories and laugh, and she'd tell them how much she loved them and how she appreciated what they'd done for her through the years. Then they'd exchange gifts, special tokens that would make them hold their breath as each gift was opened.

How wonderful it would be for Grandma and Grandpa Henry to come, too, and Dan and Ross, Uncle Cal and Aunt Nancy and their boys, and Matt and Sandy. And John . . .

They would sing carols, some so lovely that their eyes would grow misty. Some funny and off-key.

In her journal she wrote,

"But Christmas has never been like that. The reality has never matched the anticipated fantasy. Instead, it has always been a string of tension looped around the holiday, threatening to break into irreparable pieces and ruin every pretense.

"Whatever else the year has held, it has always concluded with a big get-together with my parents. After all, isn't that what families are all about?

"When Janice and Daddy opened the gifts I'd selected, I always held my breath, hoping they would like them, accept them, that they would be enough to elicit their love and approval, which was so reluctantly and judiciously handed out. They never were enough.

In some ways it had been easier when Linda was alive because she was the focus of attention, the one on whom Janice showered material displays of affection, carefully explaining to me that it was because Linda was the baby.

"In other ways it was harder because the comparison was unbearably embarrassing for me. I felt decidedly inferior and jealous of my sister at those times, especially if the festivities took place in Janice and Preston's home rather than on the farm. And I always felt guilty for the sin of envy.

"As an adult, I dreaded the annual search for the perfect gift, the perfect act of contrition or atonement to make up for all that had gone before. John would chide me, saying, 'Kate, you're not looking for a gift, you're looking for a payment or a statement that says God knows what . . . please love me . . . accept me!' I am certain he was right and just as certain it would have been easier if I had been able to figure out just what I was trying to say to them. Now, for the first time in nearly half a century, there will be no pretense."

Katherine shoved down the slightest pang of guilt that pushed against her freedom. She knew that her parents would be lonely without her. In fact, she had been so certain of Janice's reaction and so uncertain of her own ability to resist her mother's disappointment that she'd chosen not to explain in person but to notify them by letter of her plans for this year, including this Christmas. Her timing had been such that the mailman had delivered the letter to Virginia the same day her plane had landed in Portland.

She knew it would be one more unforgivable brick in the wall between them. This one, too, might never be resolved. But silence had become her only means of communication with Janice and Preston. Perhaps in the silence they would begin to listen, to wonder. Perhaps they would notice the silence, like Katherine had always noticed the dark.

Katherine marked off the days until the twenty-fourth, realizing, somewhat stupidly, that she had failed to clarify what time of the day she expected her guests to arrive. She guessed they would arrive by snowmobile.

She passed the days in preparation—cleaning and scrubbing, changing menu plans, alternately looking forward to and dreading the event. In her mind, it was a kind of benchmark, a test of her own growth. She kept reminding herself she lived under the shelter of the Most High.

Katherine awoke the morning of the great day just as the first shaft of dawn pushed its way through the east window. She lay there for a moment, listening to the quiet, letting the unfamiliar well-being flood her insides. It had been six months. And in all that time, she'd had only one real face-to-face conversation with another human being, since you could hardly call the radio interchange a conversation.

Out of bed, she dressed in brown wool slacks and a dark green sweater. Unraveling the loose braid she usually wore, she fluffed her hair. It was still damp from washing the night before. She made her bed, stoked up the fire, and set water to boil for the coffee.

Chey pushed past her when Katherine opened the door for her coffee-grinding ritual. He had launched himself off the porch and was bounding into his winter delirium before she had closed the door behind them.

The morning was cold and still and brilliant white. With the broom, Katherine swept the steps and cleared the landing of the inch of snow that had fallen overnight. Her waist-length brown hair fell like a cape over her shoulders, the sun igniting red sparks. If she'd had a mirror, she would have noticed the new silver strands mixed in.

Katherine left Chey to his games and went inside to make coffee and get organized. While the coffee dripped, she took down the rest of her clean laundry hanging from the rafters. Everything was folded and out of sight in the bottom of the wardrobe by the time the coffee was ready.

The rest of the morning, she hummed and made a chicken potpie of some canned chicken and vegetables. She fluted the crust, confident of this decision—she was a good baker, like her Grandma Henry and her Aunt Elsie.

She could put it in the oven whenever they were ready to eat, along with a dish of candied sweet potatoes and baked beans. It was the strangest Christmas dinner Katherine had ever cooked, but without a doubt the most fun.

Katherine dug out her makeup and, as best she could, created the artwork that made her eyes as soft as doves and gave her face expression. The one-inch mirror on the eyeshadow case never allowed her to see her entire face at once, so she was guessing it was okay. Also, she was surprised at how clumsy she'd become, not having practiced in six months. The lipstick was especially difficult, requiring several attempts before it was straight. All this only added to her sense of being about as competent as a school girl.

When she was finished, she wound her hair in a bun and secured it at the back of her head. Then she sat down to wait.

Funny how slowly time passed. Time, which had meant nothing to her for the past months, now seemed stuck in place. She let the dog in and out several times, crocheted, and stirred the soup at least a hundred times. She rehearsed what she would talk about, very grateful that she could count on Molly to fill the empty spots.

Just as she was putting the lid back on the soup kettle, Chey lifted his head with a half bark, half whine. Then she heard it, too. The unmistakable buzz of a snowmobile.

Katherine scraped the frost from the window in time to see the shiny black vehicle sail into the meadow, fanning a trail of white powder behind.

This is it! She opened the door. Chey raced past her toward the familiar man. Katherine watched from the doorway as her dog whined and wriggled his greeting upon his long-lost master. For several minutes Cyle knelt beside the animal, hugging him and receiving his affection.

Then Cyle stood up and unhooked a box from the backseat as Katherine stepped out to the porch. Molly was nowhere in sight.

"Where's Molly?"

"Aw . . . she was real disappointed she couldn't come. She's got a bad earache . . . so I promised her I'd bring her up another time . . . if it was okay with you." He came up the steps toward her as if it was an everyday occurrence, stomping the snow from his boots as Katherine opened the door.

All her composure seemed to have evaporated with the revelation of Molly's absence.

Cyle set the box on the counter next to the sink. "Some

things my mom sent along—Christmas cookies and candy. And there's some ice cream, too. I'll just set it outside. . . ."

Katherine watched him open and close the big door and deposit the ice cream in one motion.

Then he unzipped his parka and stepped out of his snow pants. "Where should I hang these?"

"Oh . . . I'll do it." She grabbed the heavy things and found a peg across the room. When she turned around, he was warming his hands in front of the fire with Chey at his side. "Well . . . hello." She headed for the kitchen. "Can I get you some coffee or anything? You must be cold."

"Coffee would be great . . . black."

Katherine poured him a steaming cup and handed it to him. He accepted it and sat down on the sofa while she pulled up a chair by the hearth. "How long did the trip take you?"

"It's not too bad . . . about an hour and a half. But it's beautiful country, so the time goes fast." Cyle sipped the coffee, holding it in both hands. "You ever been snowmobiling?"

Katherine shook her head. There was one of those lulls in the conversation when she could have used Molly.

"You have this place really looking good . . . and Christmasy . . . even a tree."

"I like it here." Her voice sounded strange to her ears. Lowering her head, she said, "You'll have to excuse me . . . I haven't exactly been practicing the art of conversation lately."

"What's it like?"

"You mean being alone . . . not having anyone to talk to?" Katherine poked the fire, then sat down again. "It's quiet." That made them both laugh, which helped, even though she wasn't trying to be funny.

"Yeah, I'll bet. I don't get much of that around *my* house."

"Tell me about it."

"You mean my house . . . or me?"

"Well, tell me about you and your house." Katherine folded her hands and waited.

"Okay . . . my house. My house is a log cabin like this one only newer and bigger—it has a loft. I live there with my mom and my two kids and two dogs and a rabbit. When I go to work, which is most of the time, I work in the woods on greenchain, or, when we're shut out, I work for the Forestry Department, or I make runs like this one to you. I was in Vietnam . . . that's where I learned to fly. But I already told you that. Now you tell me about you." He put his cup down and stared at her.

"Well, you already know what I do for a living . . . although maybe not anymore. I'm not sure I'm going to keep practicing."

"How come?"

"A lot of things I guess. For one thing, it's hard." She glanced at him. His gaze was still steady on her. "Well . . . see, my husband died a year ago . . . over a year ago and I wanted, needed a change. I found it very hard to go to work after that. To think about other people. I just wanted to cry all the time . . . but I couldn't find the tears."

"So did you come here to cry?"

"Yeah. I guess I did." Katherine shifted position. "Do you want some more coffee?" He shook his head. "What about your wife?"

"My wife decided she had better things to do than change dirty pants and cook for me. So she took off . . . a year ago."

"And you don't know where she is?"

He shook his head. "And I don't care to know," he answered flatly.

"Do I detect a note of bitterness?"

"No. Just plain anger."

"It's hard to lose . . . "

Katherine was mid-sentence when he interrupted. "Yours was a loss. Mine was a relief!"

Not knowing how to reply, Katherine walked into the kitchen and began stoking the cookstove while Cyle stared at the fire. "Would you like to eat soon?" she called to him. "We're having potpie that will take about forty-five minutes."

"Sure. That will be great. Hey, I didn't mean to dump my problems on you. I bet you get real tired of hearing other people talk about their miseries, huh?" Cyle got up and walked to the kitchen. "If we've got nearly an hour, what do you say we go for a ride?"

Katherine had always had about as much enthusiasm for snowmobiles as she did for motorcycles, probably because of the noise. But within minutes, she found herself roaring along the river, holding tight to a man she barely knew, and loving it.

They raced the river, bounded over hills, and spun in circles until she screamed.

As the time for the potpie was approaching, Cyle slowed the machine for a more scenic tour of the area. He pointed out things to her she would never have noticed and told her what was on the other side of the mountains and how it would be when spring came.

When at last they pulled up in front of the cabin and he cut the motor, Katherine felt exhilarated, charged with energy. "That was great! I can't believe it . . . I never thought I'd like winter sports!"

"Do you ski?" Cyle was stomping the snow from his boots.

"Oh, no! You're not going to push me down a hill somewhere on those things. Just forget it."

Inside, they threw down their coats and stood by the fire.

"But you can come back and give me a ride anytime . . . that was marvelous." Katherine's hair had sprung loose and she was trying to get it under control again. Cyle just smiled.

The cabin was filled with the aroma of dinner. By the time she had finished the last-minute details, the sun was setting. Cyle lit the lamps and helped carry food to the table.

When they sat down, she said, "It's Christmas Eve. . . ."

"Yeah. I gotta play Santa tonight."

"Do you believe in God?"

"I didn't use to. But you know what they say. 'There are no atheists in foxholes.'"

"You mean you were converted in Vietnam?"

"Weird, huh? That little shoot-out was enough to cause most people to lose their religion. It helped me find mine."

"I know what you mean. I was never in Vietnam . . . but I guess I've been going through my own private war zone. And I had a believing grandmother whose lessons have come back to me. Would you say grace?"

He bowed his head and spoke softly, "Lord, bless this home and all that happens here and this food to our use. Amen."

They ate in silence for some time. Cyle seemed to enjoy his meal.

"What does a psychiatrist do?" he asked at last.

Katherine cleared her throat. "Well, I try to help people understand themselves, to learn to enjoy life, to get over phobias and dysfunctions. But I'm unusual, I guess. I do more therapy than medications."

"How do you do it . . . make people feel better, I mean?"

"Oh, by looking into their childhood—examining traumas . . . that sort of thing."

"Well, I had a good childhood," he said with his mouth full. Katherine stared at him, believing him. "But I guess you didn't, huh?"

"Why do you say that?"

"Because why else would you be a psychiatrist?" He set his fork down. "And why else would you be so testy?"

"I'm not testy!"

"Lighten up, Mrs. Allen . . . lighten up!" Cyle chuckled and went for the coffeepot in the kitchen. He filled her cup and sat down. "You know what I think? What shall I call you? Kate?" He leaned close to her. "Kate, what you do is real important. I've seen guys come back from Nam who really needed help . . . and it's a kind of miracle what people like you can do. But you can get lost in it. You can forget there is any life outside all those problems. I think you are a very sad lady. Now, don't take this wrong, but I've thought about you lots since I first dumped you off up here. Let's go sit by the fire."

Carrying the two full cups, he led the way and continued. "First, I thought you were crazy!" They settled on the sofa, facing each other. "Then I thought you were probably the bravest woman I'd ever heard of . . . coming up here all alone. Didn't it scare you?"

Katherine chuckled. "No. To tell you the truth, the only thing that really scared me was *you*."

"Me!"

"Well, not you personally. Just you as a person. See, you were right about my childhood. Mine wasn't so great. I suppose you're also right about why I do what I do. But I am good at it, by the way! Anyway, I guess I always believed I could be happy if I didn't have to deal with anyone. There has never been anything in the streets that hurt me half as much as what was in the house."

"So you just pulled away. I saw guys in Nam do that. Like they got so scared they just pulled away from everybody."

Katherine nodded. "But the bad thing was it made them even more scared. . . . By the way, what was in the house?"

For a minute she didn't follow him. "You mean what frightened me?"

"Yeah. What was in the house?"

"I wish I knew. . . ." Her voice trailed off. "Well, I know some of it . . . but not all."

"Do you want to know? Can't you just forget it?"

"I think I want to know . . . and unfortunately I did forget it. I'm hoping to remember."

"You lost me there. But I guess you know your business." Cyle looked at his watch. "Hey! Molly will have a fit if I don't get you to open these presents so I can tell her how you liked 'em." He thrust two packages at her.

Molly's was a necklace she had made—a laminated heart with her smiling picture on one side and I LOVE YOU printed on the other. Katherine's eyes filled with tears as Cyle tied it around her neck with the length of yarn running through it. "She thinks you need some faces to look at, she said."

The other package was a pair of heavy fur-lined deerskin mittens. "I didn't know if you had any . . . these are real warm."

"Thank you, Cyle. I don't know what to say to Molly. . . . Tell her it means so much to me—" Her voice broke.

Cyle reached over and touched her cheek. "She'll be glad."

He stood up, and Katherine knew it was over. Now he would leave. She didn't want him to go.

"Wait! I have something for you, too. But I didn't have any wrapping paper." She handed him the red crocheted cap. "It's to replace the one Chey ate."

"Great! This is just great!" Cyle adjusted the cap on his head. Then he cocked it forward over his forehead. It looked right.

"And this is for Molly." She handed him a cereal box with a red yarn around it, tied in a bow. "Something I made for her."

"She'll love it . . . she loves handmade stuff."

Katherine watched Cyle put on his leggings and the parka, listened while he complimented her cooking and her house. She threw on John's tweed jacket and walked him outside, hugging the sleeves close, her hands pulled up inside the cuffs. "Thanks for coming, Cyle."

"Well, hey. Let's do it again. I promised Molly, you know."

"I'd like that."

"We're gonna have to wait for the weather to break for her, though. She's kinda prone to earaches. But I'll come back any time for another dinner like that."

"Maybe week after next?"

"Sure . . . let me know Friday." Cyle turned the key and revved the motor. He turned the machine with his foot out, put up his hand to signal good-bye, and buzzed off into the night.

Katherine stood on the porch for a long time, listening to the sound of his leaving. Then she put her fingers to the place on her cheek where he had touched her and went inside.

Chey joined her by the fire. She closed her eyes, basking in the warmth. *Merry Christmas, Lord.*

Chapter 30

It was a small, red leather book of black pages, tied with rawhide. Inside were the aging, black and white images of childhood. It was one of those pieces of memorabilia, compiled by her own hands and kept through the years.

The captured moments ranged the years of grade school. The photographs had not been entered in chronological order. The composition was arranged according to a child's logic, by shape and size rather than by date.

Rarely had Katherine looked through the album. Never had she taken the time to really study its contents. As an adult, she was uncomfortable with the gawky images of herself, conveying such hopelessness against the backdrop of despair.

It was one of those items she kept in the back of the hall closet, along with the manipulative gifts sent by Janice, gifts eliciting some payment of loyalty. It shared the shelf with pieces of crystal and silver—all lovely, but not the sort of thing that graced her table. She and John were not fond of such traditional fare. Their tastes ran to the artistic—pottery and sculpture—believing it their duty to support as much of the starving artists' community as possible.

Janice, on the other hand, saw herself making a feeble effort to provide a touch of class or culture to her hopelessly inept daughter. This silent warfare irked Katherine to the edge of her tolerance.

Whenever she had occasion to come across the album, when either looking for something else or cleaning out the closet, all that had ever registered were big lonely eyes, peering over the black half-moons that hung beneath them. Katherine would sigh and close the book, promising that someday it might have some meaning. Until then, it was one of those things she didn't know what to do with, so she just kept it. It was packed and hauled along on several moves. She didn't really want the homely thing, but it didn't seem right to throw it away.

It had been in a sheer moment of spontaneity that made her dig it out of the back of the closet for this trip. At that time, she'd entertained the possibility of burning it and scattering the ashes to the mountain wind in some kind of symbolic gesture of breaking with the past.

She could no longer postpone it. Katherine sat at the table, with her hand on the album. "Jesus, help me. Give me eyes to see . . . whatever is here."

She opened to the first black page. Centered on the page was a portrait of herself and her mother, the only professional photograph she had. Janice never allowed her to keep any of the "good" ones in her picture book.

A round-faced, big-eyed baby clung to a beautiful young woman, whose long auburn curls framed a gentle smiling innocence. It was a picture Katherine had always liked, this portrait of Janice when she was Mama. In a dark plaid, double-breasted suit, accentuating a graceful neck and slender, straight shoulders, the toddler standing in the circle of her arm, Janice was the image of gentle grace.

Katherine leaned forward, focusing on the child. The little girl appeared full of wonder, somewhat shy, like the wisps of baby hair curling softly in dark rings to match her mother's.

Scrawled in white ink on the black paper under the portrait, in the homely cursive of a ten-year-old, were the words, *Katie Elizabeth Henry's Photo*. A light blue colored pencil had later been used to add an s to complete the word *Photos*.

Katherine turned the page. On both sides the array of pictures of herself and her Vida friends stared out from the dark pages. There was Frankie, a gangly kid who was the son of the elevator operator on the east side of town, the boy Uncle Sel had humiliated, calling him a "sissy." Frankie stood with his arm around Alice Mitchell, a faded strawberry blonde with buck teeth, who had been his girlfriend for as long as Katie could remember. She smiled when she saw them standing together. Probably not more than eleven years old, they were in this romantic pose following their performance in an amateur talent show for the rest of the kids. Katherine remembered them singing "Walking My Baby Back Home," complete with theatrical gestures, the nearest thing to Broadway most of the Vida kids would ever see.

There were some kids standing on top of the well cover, in the circle of hollyhocks. She could barely remember their faces, and the names were gone. One was a Mexican kid, Sanchez, she thought, who came up with his parents to work in the fields in the summer. Others she could not place at all. But apparently she had been quite taken with them, since there were about two and a half pages of them in various poses and activities.

Some shaggy-haired, tanned farm boys were captured forever, riding by on two-wheelers, one trailing a long willow branch. Then she noticed the kid riding the back fender, her skinny legs stuck out wide. It looked like her. That made her vaguely recall having helped them put cards in the spokes to make the bike sound as if it had a motor.

There was a picture of Katie, sitting on the brown couch in Aunt Elsie and Uncle Sel's living room. Flipping the pages back and forth, Katherine located what appeared to be a series of her, taken by someone else. At first glance, they were just silly pictures of a child caught in the spontaneous antics of clowning.

Several were of Katie, clad in shorts, biting her toe, knees bent and outstretched, body curled, her hair shielding her face. There were three others, stages of a somersault, as she recalled—leaning forward, head down, bottom up. Another showed Katie turning a cartwheel, her shirt slid down to her face, revealing her flat chest.

The last in the series showed her posing with one hand on her hip and one behind her head in a distinctly sexy gesture. She was wearing the same shorts, but the shirt had been replaced by a black and white, strapless halter top with bone stays that filled out the empty cups. Katherine did not remember posing for any of these.

Carefully, she removed each of this series from the corner tabs that held them in the book and lined them up on the table in front of her. She closely examined each picture, paying attention to every detail. Obviously, they were taken at the same time. Her clothing was the same in each—light shorts and a light sleeveless shirt to match, and the one with the halter top. In each one she was barefooted. She must have been seven or eight at the time, for Katherine recognized the Hilemans' living room in each one.

Something about them made her distinctly uneasy. She wondered again who had taken them.

Turning back to the album, Katherine noticed that there were no pictures of the other kids inside the house. And most of the snapshots that included her were taken outside. They were group pictures, usually of children standing together, grinning their toothless grins. Except for the tumbling photos, they seemed to be a hodgepodge of snapshots the children had thought were significant, trading the camera back and forth to capture the images of one another.

Katherine scrutinized each one of herself—the same hollow expression, the same forlorn, skinny girl. The only exceptions seemed to be of the pictures taken at the farm. These included pictures of Matt and Sandy, holding kittens, fishing in the dredge cut, eating raspberries. There was a picture of Katie poking her head out of a hay bale, face streaked with dust and perspiration, giggling.

Another was a favorite of hers, an enlargement of which had hung for years in her bedroom. It was a photo of Grandma Henry holding one of Cal's babies. She was holding the baby like an offering in front of her, smiling and talking to him, as he waved his little arms. It was so lifelike she almost expected to hear Grandma's voice whenever she looked at that picture. It was one of the only bits of memorabilia she had, since Grandma Henry had left this fallen world in September, twenty-five years ago.

Grandma Henry died singing. She had lain four days in a dimly lit hospital room, surrounded by flowers and prayers and her closest family. Other family members were on their way, Matt from California. Ross and Sandy were en route and should appear momentarily with Cal and whomever might be with him. They all knew the time was short.

They had taken turns in alternating vigils for the past days and nights, during which the old woman sometimes slept, sometimes spoke in halting deliberate words.

That morning, she had awakened and smiled when Kate kissed her forehead and took her hand. Her skin was soft and cool and transparent. The salt of the perspiration from her forehead lingered on Kate's lips.

"Can I get you anything, Grandma?" Kate saw the flash of mischief that danced across her face, sparkling in her tired eyes and lifting the corners of her mouth.

"You can get me a new life!" she answered with a touch of her old spunk.

Okay . . . I'll bite, Kate thought as she said, "What kind of a life do you want?"

"One that will guarantee me a place in heaven."

Kate smiled. "Oh, Grandma, you already have that."

The old woman patted her hand. "Then I don't need anything else, do I?"

For most of the rest of the day she slept while Kate watched and held her hand. Twice she asked for water, which Kate gave her through a straw, with her finger over the end, one drop at a time.

Midway through the afternoon, Dan arrived for his shift. Kate went to the hospital cafeteria and sat quietly sipping vegetable soup that was anything but gourmet, but it was soothing. She decided to stay.

It seemed strange to Kate how completely at peace she felt, as if everything was just as it should be. Perhaps it was because Grandma Henry was so at peace herself. Or perhaps it was because she had a way, even as she slept, of making Kate feel that all was well. The hospital was quiet, and a spirit of peace seemed to hover in the hall.

Back in the room, Dan was glad for her company. Mostly they sat in silence, waiting. Around seven o'clock, the hospital chaplain stopped in for a "season of prayer," he called it, of which Grandma seemed unaware.

At five minutes to nine, she again asked for water and to have her bed cranked up to a sitting position. Then, with Dan on one side and Kate on the other, Alta Henry raised her hands and began to sing in halting phrases:

"Amazing grace . . . how sweet the sound . . . that saved a

wretch like me. I once was lost . . . but now I'm found . . . was blind but now I see. . . . T'was grace that taught my heart to fear . . . and grace my fears relieved . . . How precious did that grace appear . . . the hour I first believed.

"When we've been there ten thousand years . . . bright shining as the sun . . . " Suddenly she clasped her hands and dropped them to her chest. Then she leaned back and closed her eyes. And was gone.

Tearfully, Dan and Kate finished, *"We've no less days to sing God's praise, than when we've first begun."*

They held each other and cried and thanked God for her.

Ever after, her grandmother's death had remained one of the truly magnificent moments of Katherine's life. Quite different from what she had expected, from the previous deathwatch over Uncle Sel. He had died, paralyzed from a stroke, unable to eat or take care of himself.

Kate had expected him, in his last days, to make some reference to his violations of her, perhaps even to ask for forgiveness. So she had been somewhat shocked the day the preacher came and asked if he was ready to meet God, when Selinus Hileman responded that he was.

One night when they were alone, while Aunt Elsie slept, Kate thought he might be wanting to talk. He reached up with the hand he could still maneuver and held her arm as she was about to administer the insulin shot, which he'd needed for the last year.

"Give an old man a break. Forget the insulin," he slurred.

"Uncle Sel, I can't do that!" Kate protested, unsure whether out of compassion or as the result of years of therapy to heal the damage he'd inflicted.

"Nobody will know." His words drooled from one side of his mouth, and his grip on her arm was feeble.

"No!" Kate said it forcefully enough that he never asked again.

At the funeral visitation several weeks later, Kate overheard one of the local school board members whisper, "Most of these people are here to see for themselves if he's really dead!"

Katherine laid aside the pictures. From the chill of her coffee, she guessed that more than an hour had passed. She hoped a fresh cup would give her some fresh insight . . . into what, she wasn't sure.

"Okay, where were we? Oh, yeah." Katherine picked up the photo album and stared at one of the pictures she had not removed. It was of two little girls, sitting on the bottom step of the great expanse that led to the Hileman dwelling. "Oh, this is LuEllen. I had forgotten all about her . . . she moved away. We must have been about five, maybe four here."

She turned the page. "Oh, and this is the dress I wore to court," rolled out as easily as a Freudian slip.

"Court? When did I go to court?" Katherine suspended the steamy cup in midair, trying to remember. "I did go to court . . . but I can't remember why. Why would I be in a courtroom?"

Katherine took her cup to the front of the fireplace, as if pacing might jog her memory. Chey joined her.

"So what do you think, Chey? Why would I be in court?" She ruffled his ears, to which the dog let out a lazy moan. "I can vaguely recall something about being asked if I knew what it meant to tell the truth. . . . I suppose it might be a lawyer who would ask something like that."

I was with Uncle Sel floated through her head, like a message from the distant past. "I was with my uncle," she said out loud. "I was with Uncle Sel? Where? Doing what? Why would I be in court with Uncle Sel . . . or . . . saying I was with Uncle Sel?" *God, help me to remember!*

"Or maybe . . . it meant that Uncle Sel was with me . . . that he wasn't somewhere else!" Katherine shivered and returned to the photo album.

She removed four pictures of LuEllen, recalling that when she was four and five, they had been best friends, laughing and playing and sharing what little girls share. It was LuEllen who had taught her how to make the hollyhocks dolls.

Then she noticed something else. All the same faces—Frankie and Alice, Carol somebody, the Mexican kids, the Williams sister and brother, whose dad ran a dairy farm within walking distance, and some others she could no longer name—were evenly sprinkled throughout the three or so years. All, that is, except one. LuEllen!

"LuEllen just disappears!" Katherine studied the picture of

herself standing in the driveway, wearing a cotton, ruffled dress her Aunt Elsie had made, the one she had worn to court, and realized that there were no pictures of LuEllen after that. "That's when I went to court." Katherine spoke the words very slowly, letting the meaning sink in.

"LuEllen went to court, too! I remember her sitting across a room. . . . I didn't know what was going on. . . . They told me I must never play with her again!" Katherine's mind raced. "What happened? What is this about?"

She knew she was in new territory, dusting memories that had been shelved a long time. Dread and excitement vied for the upper hand as she carried the photo of LuEllen to the window for better light.

In the picture, LuEllen was scantily clad, with limp blond hair and the same hollow eyes peering out from some dark place far away. Katherine stared. Then she looked at the gymnastic poses of herself. Then back to the picture of LuEllen. Then at herself in the oversized halter top.

"Oh, dear God." Katherine's fingers began to sweat, sticking to the picture of the two little girls with the same sad eyes. The ladies in the parts room flashed before her. They were photographs, too! *"Uncle Sel* took the pictures of me . . . tumbling," she moaned, looking at the photographs that now revealed something slightly indecent, just the angle of the camera, aimed, visually prying, where his hands later followed.

Katherine was seized with a wave of nausea. "Oh, please God, help me," vividly remembering the last time she had felt this way. It was the day the dog pulled her from the river. She had sensed this same suffocation.

She felt Chey's soft head under her hand just as a new image floated to the top of her consciousness. She recognized it immediately. It was the closet door in the office. She could almost smell it—the strange musty odor that had crept from the space beneath the door. Katherine took a deep breath and slowly exhaled into the past.

It was Katie's eighth birthday. Janice and Preston were visiting. They had gone for a ride with Aunt Elsie and Uncle Sel, to show off their new car and to pick up Matt and Sandy for the party. Katie was left to baby-sit Linda, who was sleeping in the crib in the room at the end of the hall.

Katie had begun the afternoon watching TV. That was before she got the daring idea to look for her birthday presents. She looked in Aunt Elsie's closet, a narrow alcove in her bedroom, covered by a drab green drape. Inside, she found nothing but clothing and shoes that smelled like cheddar cheese. And all that hid under the bed were dust balls.

With the stealth of a detective, Katie rummaged through the trunks and closet of the back room storage. Nothing but the stuff that had been there forever. She was considering looking in the closet in Linda's room, when another thought grabbed her, more daring than anything yet.

The office closet! It was locked, but she knew where the key was. It hung on a nail at the top sill, behind the door in the oil room, along with the keys to other secret places.

As if it were inevitable, Katie retrieved the large key ring from the oil room. Her pulse pounding in her ears, she closed her eyes and chose one from the dozen that tinkled together like tattling little bells.

Her first pick was right. As she turned the chosen key, she felt the lock slip. With a slight turn of the handle, the door popped opened to what Katie knew was the most secret and forbidden room in the house.

Frozen, Katie listened. Nothing. In slow motion, she stepped forward, swinging the door in a wide, deliberate arc, exposing a narrow walk-in closet. The odor—a dusty blend of old papers and something medicinal—reached for her, luring her in.

Never before had Katie dared to venture into the inner sanctum of Selinus Hileman. Tiny sparks skittered across her pelvis and up and down the edges of her ribs. Sparks she could not decipher, fear or excitement or both.

An antique oak file cabinet to the right was piled high with official-looking file folders and boxes, decorated with fake marble-ized paper. Shelves from floor to ceiling—holding papers, shoe boxes, bundles bound by rubber bands, camera and the tiny canisters that contained the film, boxes of flashbulbs—built a wall of secrets. Uncle Sel's secrets.

Katie forgot she was looking for a birthday gift and began to search for an explanation, a clue to the identity of these people who carried her fate in their pockets. In the corner stood tripods, projector screens, and some strange objects that looked to Katie like umbrellas of net and tin.

Rolling her eyes up and down, from side to side, Katie saw nothing resembling a birthday package. But she pushed on, searching, prying.

She lifted the lids of the shoe boxes. They were crammed with strips of developed negatives and developed pictures of wrecked cars, wind-damaged trees, and snowdrifts. It was a pastime of her uncle's to visit the sites of natural and unnatural disasters. Katie often rode with him on these excursions.

Standing on one of the boxes, filled with what appeared to be receipts, Katie began rummaging through the faux marbleized boxes and folders on top of the cabinet. The assortment of forms and papers held no message for her other than the confirmation that adult life contained much of what was incomprehensible.

Katie turned her attention to the oak file cabinet. It took all her strength to pull the top drawer free. It was so tightly stuffed with receipts and papers that she judged it would be impossible to insert even one more sheet. Leaning her weight into it, she managed to close it again, with an alarming squeak.

The bottom drawer, housing only a few files, no more than six inches deep, yielded easily as she pulled with all her might, expecting it to be as heavy as its twin above. It was only luck that kept the thing from coming off its track and landing on the floor at her feet.

Had it not been super-extended, Katie would not have noticed the two boxes wedged behind the files, one on top of the other. The smaller one was an ornately carved wooden box with a small brass latch on a lid that lifted like a cigar box. Yellowing news clippings, brittle with age, lay folded on top of another box.

Katie carefully unfolded the leaves of paper, reading the article with a date scribbled across the top, May 24, 1916. It reported the heroism of a local boy, Selinus Hileman, who was in critical condition in a French hospital, having lost his right leg below the knee.

The paper was the front page of the Herald. Seeing the bold headline—"Soldier Returns Home—Walks Down Main Street!"—she read about the miraculous recovery of young Hileman, who, although losing his leg, had worked his way back with the aid of a prosthesis and sheer grit to walk again. Hileman would be returning soon to his loved ones and to his faithful fiancée, Elsie Carlson, oldest daughter of Lars and Viola Carlson, of Ames.

There were other articles on the front page, lauding him for his heroism and mentioning the parade in his honor to be staged down the main street of Gaston. In the center of the page was the picture of a young man in doughboy uniform, the flat brim hat shading his face, arm lifted in smart salute. It was Uncle Sel.

Katie lifted the lid on the smaller box. Inside, pinned to the satin lining, was a purple ribbon with a bronze heart dangling from the bottom.

Carefully and with precision, Katie reassembled the contents just as she had found them, placing the news clippings in the memorized order on top of the purple heart medal.

The tin box wedged at the bottom of the drawer was more resistant to her prying hands. She had to work to wrestle it from its hiding place.

It was a rectangular cash box, locked. Katie shook it, feeling the contents shifting back and forth like loose cards. She tried to turn the lock with her fingernail, then remembered the other keys that hung on the nail in the oil room, tiny ones that might fit this lock.

Box in hand, Katie moved quietly across the porch toward the oil room. She set the box on the floor and ran to check Linda. Reassured by her steady, rhythmic snoring, Katie pulled open the massive front door and closed it behind her.

Inside the oil room, by climbing the scaffolding that had once held the fuel oil barrel, she reached the nail at the top of the doorsill again. Retrieving a dirty string loop with several miniature keys, Katie jumped to the floor. Squatting before the tin box, she tried one key after the other. None released the lock.

Back on the scaffold, she reached for one more key, hanging from a rubber band. All the others were clearly too large for this opening.

Katie inserted the tiny key in the lock, metal to metal, and turned. It clicked. Katie listened. Jumping up, she peeked through the crack of the door and listened for any sound of their return. Nothing.

The tin box was warped. She pried it open with a key. It was a box of photographs, shiny prints, trimmed in odd sizes and shapes. At first she did not recognize what she was seeing. Several layers deeper, however, revealed the same brash ladies that danced on the walls of the parts room.

Toward the bottom of the box, she came across some weird, contorted poses of skinny arms and legs, attached to flat bodies . . . naked bodies . . . children's bodies! Bodies doing strange things that made no sense to her. Katie flipped from one to the other, numbed, stunned, as all the air was sucked from the room.

Then she saw a face. LuEllen's face! She was barely recognizable. Her face looked like a mask. A weak smile hid behind bright-red lipstick, her deep, sad eyes hanging on the upper half of her face!

Staring at LuEllen's face, Katie heard the ominous crunch of tires on the gravel driveway. They were back!

She grabbed the box and raced for the office. She could hear the car doors slamming as she jimmied the lid down. She forced it into the drawer, put the wooden one in its place on top, and slammed the cabinet shut. Quickly, she slid the makeshift stool back to the spot where she remembered it had been and closed the closet door.

She could hear them coming up the stairs, their voices and laughter carrying to her pounding ears. Katie looked around anxiously. Where was the key ring to the closet? She couldn't leave it unlocked!

She could hear Janice hushing them as they turned toward the front door. What if Uncle Sel came into the office? Katie stepped into the closet and softly pulled the door shut. And waited.

She could hear her mother in a loud whisper, trying not to awaken Linda. Katie stood in the closet, barely breathing.

"Katie," Janice opened the office door, "are you in there?"

Katie held her breath. After what seemed like an eternity, she could hear her mother's high heels, tapping across the porch toward the house.

Katie carefully opened the closet door and looked out. The room was empty. She dropped to the floor, frantically passing her hands over the dust in the closet. At last, her fingers closed around the key ring that lay wedged against a box on the floor. She put the old key in the lock. The bolt scraped into its hole in the doorjamb.

Katie still held the keys which belonged on the nail in the oil room. Mentally, she wildly retraced her steps to that room. She had left the other string of keys on the floor! Had she closed the white door behind her? Had anyone looked inside?

She had to get back there! Those keys must be in place the next time Uncle Sel reached for them. But how was she going to get to the oil room without anyone seeing her? She knew it wouldn't be long before her mother was searching again.

Katie stuffed the little key in one pocket and the key ring in the other, and went out to face her birthday guests, hoping that no one would notice her trembling knees or hear her racing pulse . . . or the jingling keys.

"There she is! The birthday girl!" Preston looked up from the TV.

"Where were you?" Janice asked, looking up from the table. "Didn't you hear me calling you?"

Before she could answer, Sandy jumped up and ran over to hug her and wish her a "Happy Birthday." Matt rolled over on the floor from the magazine he was engrossed in.

Through dinner, Katie did her best to act natural. Janice sent her to the bathroom to wash her face, muttering about how any child could get so filthy watching television that she looked like a dust ball! The food stuck in Katie's throat, halfway down, her mouth dry as dust.

Opening gifts was agony. The keys bit into her hips, producing little droplets of perspiration across her upper lip. She feared that someone would see into her head and discover the secrets she held, even if she didn't exactly know what those secrets meant.

But as time passed, the meanings solidified and a portrait of herself emerged, framed in guilt. She was clearly a liar and a very naughty girl who had nasty images dancing in her head instead of sugarplums, like "good" children.

Katie was especially thankful for Sandy that day. Her cousin chattered like a squirrel, keeping the adults in stitches. She was even more grateful when Grandma and Grandpa Henry arrived for dessert and then to take the children home with them so Janice, Preston, and Linda could get an early start for home in the morning.

After all the good-byes and thank-yous were said, the three cousins piled into the back of the Dodge to head for the farm.

Katie put her hand in her pocket and fingered the old closet key and the little key on the rubber band, which she imagined was expanding like a noose around her neck.

It was only a matter of time before she would be discovered, Katie knew. Probably by Uncle Sel. The evidence still lay on the floor of the oil room. All she could rationalize was that maybe she could say she found the keys and just dropped them there. Maybe she would never have to admit that she had opened the closet door, or the hidden box. But how would she ever account for the missing keys?

"Katie, did you get your good shoes?" Grandma Henry asked as they were backing out.

"No. I forgot them!"

"Stop, Dad. She'll have to go back in and get them. She'll need them for church tomorrow."

Katie bounded from the car and up the steps, two at a time and into the oil room. She scooped the keys from the floor, elated to find that they were still where she had left them. She scampered up the scaffolding and thrust them on the nail, along with the keys from her pocket.

It was not until much later that she was quite sure she had never locked the tin box. There was the remote possibility that he would never realize it, she thought. For many nights, she turned it in her mind. Would he notice? Would he get the key first? Then he might never find out that it had been left unlocked.

But it was never mentioned, and Katie never opened that door again. She grew up believing that her life depended on keeping it closed. And . . .

Until now, Katherine had had no understanding of what she had discovered in the closet on her eighth birthday.

"Dear Lord!" she gasped, the revelation whirling in her head. She stood up. Dropping the picture she'd been holding of LuEllen, Katherine backed away from it as if it were alive, as if it might bite her. "That's why we went to court. That's why I couldn't play with LuEllen anymore. He . . . got caught!"

Chapter 31

Katherine forced herself to breathe. "Oh, God, I don't want to know this." Tears pooled across her bottom lids. "It was Uncle Sel and that guy who lived behind them. Delbert Russell. LuEllen must have told on them. She didn't move away! She went to court! That's right, I remember being told that I couldn't play with her because she told lies. Lies!" Katherine shouted, sweeping the photos from the table.

"She was telling the truth!" Katherine threw back her head and bellowed, "LuEllen was telling the truth! Do you hear me! It was the truth!" Chey started to bark furiously.

Clenching her fists, Katherine held herself together by sheer force of will. "Lord, this is a nightmare. And it's getting worse."

Deliberately, she tried to calm down and piece together what she "knew" and what she remembered and what she understood now, arranging the pieces to fit. "Uncle Sel was not prosecuted. Delbert was. And Uncle Sel paid his legal fees. That's another story of my uncle's generosity to the downtrodden! Of course he was! Because Delbert took the fall! Selinus Hileman could muscle his way out of anything! And I was the alibi! I went to court and told them he was with me!"

Katherine's head fell against the back of the sofa. "I didn't even know what they were talking about. I no doubt said whatever he, they, told me to say! And that's why they let me go to the Henrys'—to keep me away from any place where I might say the wrong thing or find out something or have some contact with LuEllen again. I probably even lied in court!" Guilt squeezed her conscience.

Katherine lifted her hands from her face and spoke in a clear voice. "But it wasn't my fault! I was just a little kid!" She could hear Janice accusing her of lying all the time, and now she wondered if Janice had been there. "Is that why Janice always thinks I'm lying? Is this the secret I know . . . that she doesn't want me to tell?" She pondered this new thought.

"But they never knew I had found this out. And I never knew the meaning of the secrets until now. I put the pictures back just as I found them. I'm sure of it. If I hadn't, they would have said something . . . I would have been in trouble.

"I wonder what happened to poor LuEllen? What was her last name . . . Manny? No . . . Massey, I think." Katherine went to the kitchen for some water. "When I get back to civilization," she decided, "I'll find out. It must be in the newspapers or court records somewhere. I'll find her."

She thought of the numbers of patients she'd seen who had experienced invalidated horrors, who had to cling with fragile courage to their own perceptions, struggling to believe the truth. Maybe she could be that validation for LuEllen. *Or maybe she can for me.* Katherine sat down to rock and think. The images of herself as a guarded, withdrawn child, hiding, protecting herself from unknown threats, floated back to her. As the years turned, she had believed the worst threat lurked in the dark places buried in herself. She began to write:

"Childhood curiosity and abandon, that delightful ability God gives to children to carry them through the uncertainties to adulthood, stumbled that day and has until now lain buried under heaps of secrets—things I had to pretend I didn't know. As I accumulated the bits and pieces which were not to be disclosed, which I could never discuss, which I could never ask for help in understanding, my own anxious feelings clung to the secrets like wrap on a birthday gift, and I buried myself with the strange memories.

"Pretending I didn't know has required hours of daydreaming rehearsal to concoct a child free of this knowledge, an innocent child, an imagined child, a public child who would cover the dark truths. And if the act was good enough, no one would suspect—that I was becoming increasingly terrified, lost to myself, confused about what life meant and unable to accept the tickling, warm sexuality that spread across my pelvis and into my being as the days of childhood ticked away toward the inevitable.

"I pushed down my fears of Uncle Sel by allying myself with him. I tried to pretend a special closeness to him. I even ate Limburger cheese and raw hamburger sandwiches with him to prove my loyalty, and watched Texas Wrastlin as an act of camaraderie, which even then I knew was fake. I didn't comprehend until years later, though, that people didn't watch professional wrestling because they believed in its authenticity.

"Through those years, I gingerly slid over the razor's edge of loyalty and terror, hoping my identification with him would keep the tyrant from turning on me.

"When thoughts of LuEllen crept in, I tried to convince myself that she was different. Surely my uncle had a special love for me. He would never hurt me or be mean as he was to other kids. After all, he was family, my benefactor, the one who took me places, who gave me candy, and black and white sodas on hot days, and nickels for pop. And he was the one person in the world who could call Janice down. He was the benevolent dictator, whom my mother stroked and placated when she was unavoidably in his presence.

"But it didn't work. One day, he crossed the line as easily as he took the second piece of pie. It happened about the same time my body gave evidence of my entrance to womanhood. Betrayal came from the same thick fingers that had choked the life from the dog. Those same hands choked the joy from my developing.

"The pleasure nerves of my skin collided with the wall of condemnation in my brain. I learned to experience pleasure and guilt as one and the same. Hot fudge sundaes became sweeter when eaten alone. Mouthfuls stolen from the refrigerator were infinitely more delicious than the same food at the table. Sexual feelings could be produced under cover, in the dark, alone . . . but never shared, never admitted, never in love.

"It was the same time that Janice's indifferent rejection turned to active disgust. As desperately as I tried to avoid any confrontation with her, I could not keep my hips from widening, or my breasts from expanding, or my lips from fullness, or my eyes from turning to a beguiling soft sadness. I felt my own body was betraying me. I hated it!

"All indications of the life that pulsed beneath the budding womanhood were a personal affront to Janice, to which she reacted with rage as if I were a disobedient sinner, challenging everything my mother held sacred. As my bra size surpassed my mother's, Janice had words for it—'streetwalker' and 'slut'—words I did not understand until I was educated by the girls at Arlington High. Justine Carmela, they said, was a 'slut.'

"But the most tragic wound left in my molested puberty came from the invisible veil that severed the flow of security from the arms of Grandma Henry. I feared more and more being discovered, anticipating an all-out war between Uncle Sel and Grandma Henry, a war I was certain Grandma would lose. Consequently, the battles raged within me. To whom did I belong? Which genes stamped my being? I would look at Grandma sometimes, certain that her goodness, her godliness, could contain none of the corruption that lurked in my own dark thoughts.

"That which God had created as a place of wonder, of tender bonding and mysterious coupling, had become a pit of darkness, of shame and loneliness—a place invaded, but never invited.

"By thirteen, I was as silenced as the retarded Putney girl. Inevitably, I began to believe that if the truth were ever known, if my real self were ever exposed, I would be that girl—just as unlovely, just as unlovable.

"Increasingly, the only time I ever aired my true self was when I walked in the undeveloped woodlot behind my parents' Virginia home, or through the midwestern fields. Then I would feel the pain, the tears—all that remained of the dying child."

Katherine looked up from her writing and rocked herself, struggling to continue, aching as the pieces fell together.

"When I was a teenager, I was hired as a baby-sitter by Janice's friends. I would wait until the children were asleep and then begin snooping, compulsively searching drawers, closets, shelves. I never consciously knew what I was looking for.

"Now I know. Did they have secrets, things that couldn't be talked about, things that explained them, or cautioned me, things that could tell me if I was different, or like them? I was desperately looking for reality, some indication of whether or not mine was a normal life, the same life experienced by everyone else.

"In all of my searching, I never found anything resembling my own darkness. I concluded that Janice's friends were as good as she said. They were people with whom Janice was comfortable. Therefore, I must be what Janice had called me—a slut—explaining why she was so uncomfortable with me.

"Through it all, I kept Selinus Hileman's secrets. I never told until years later, well after his death. I told John. And then I only told what I could remember of my own violation. LuEllen's story, had, by that time, been buried beneath years of fear and ignorance.

"That was about the time I finished my residency and began professionally searching the lives of others, groping in the darkness for other forlorn and forsaken children of the shadows, like myself. Perhaps, through their stories, I was trying to find my own.

"Finally, years later, I told Janice, too, hoping it would penetrate the barricade between us. I so wanted my mother to understand why I was the way I was and give her quarter to forgive me. I secretly hoped that it might call up, from some buried depth, the mama who smoothed my hair with graceful cool fingers. It didn't work.

Katherine put down the book and turned her attention to the cabin, the primitive room in which she rocked, the room where it had become safe to remember. It was as if this one key piece had caused all the unidentified pieces to shuffle and magically slide into place, revealing for the first time a part of her life that made sense.

She rocked, grateful for reality, for coming through the darkness that had in previous years taken the very floor from beneath her. When her mind had closed against the truth, it had lost its capacity to self-regulate, to maintain any reasonable outlook on life. The result had been like wandering aimlessly in a circus house of mirrors—a hopeless maze of grotesque distortions. She took up her pen again.

"Nineteen sixty-eight in Chicago triggered an avalanche of fear, necessitating countless hours of talking to John, listening to him describe reality and what was normal, followed by nightmares and day terrors, and finally two months lost to hallucinations of black swirling triangles above my bed and outside the window. Even in the crib, awaiting the birth of our child, the ugliness stalked me.

"At the end of it, the child was stillborn at six months. Janice's words of consolation—'everything turns out for the best'—left me limp with depression.

"It was a long climb up the steep slopes of sanity, from the two most terrifying months of my life, when whatever I did or said was lost to me, lost in horrifying black triangles. I was locked in silent screams. When gradually I began to emerge to face the death of my baby, I was the shell of a person—not only afraid, but afraid to be afraid.

"For most of a year I clung to John like a helpless child, afraid of the dark, afraid even of my old refuge, solitude. With a lot of help, I have been able to play the notes of anger that drained the depression. But no amount of persuasion could entice me to unearth the roots of the terror. Those horrifying black triangles—whatever they are—must never again be allowed to gain strength of expression."

Katherine sat back, her palms dripping, the flesh of her body in a cold fear just thinking about it. She knew she needed to somehow face this. But it filled her with dread. She wrote on:

"As a psychiatrist, I know this is unsound doctrine. We do not work to keep things buried. How many times have I had that argument with Adam? I know I am no exception, but I wish there were an easier way. I wish we could walk away from our damage, our sin nature, without having to look at it. But how would we know what needed to be healed? How would we ever know any forgiveness? 'Search me, O God, and know my heart. . . . See if there be any wicked way in me and lead me in the way everlasting.'"

Katherine stretched before the crackling fire. She looked at the pages of insight scribbled hastily in the journal and felt the ache in her hand from writing as fast as the thoughts came. The last paragraph was a speech she had made numerous times to her patients. Now it was for her ears. Consciously, she pulled herself into the healing presence of the One who had promised never to leave her.

She could feel the gripping fear releasing its icy tentacles from her gut. Her shoulders, rigid from years of alarm, dropped, relaxing into a dull ache. If she'd had a mirror, she would have seen the tight lines of stress around her eyes soften and her mouth again yield to a hint of the youthful fullness anticipating life.

Now, after forty-nine years, Katherine Elizabeth Henry Allen was beginning to understood why she was who she was. It felt odd and somehow tragically wasted. At the same time, she sensed with some curiosity the question of who she was meant to be—God's dream for her. Had the fallen world not so ravaged her, what would her image have reflected of His likeness? And had she not sinned against herself and Him, refusing the integrity of her being, who would she be now?

Katherine lifted John's journal from the shelf, leafing the pages until she found the passage which read:

". . . and perhaps salvation means from the condemnation of the fallen world, if eternity begins now, from the separation from God in whom we have our true meaning and life. Perhaps it is never too late to be healed, reconciled to the truth of who He created us to be. Perhaps, Katherine, it is really true that His word that goes forth does not return to Him void, but does accomplish that which He sent it out to do. Perhaps, as He says, we 'shall go out with joy and be led out with peace; and the mountains and the hills shall break forth into singing before us, and all the trees of the fields shall clap their hands.' And where there was a thorn, 'there shall come up the cypress tree, and instead of the brier shall come up the myrtle tree; and it shall be a name for the Lord, a sign that shall stand forever.'

"I conclude, Kate, that anything less is hell! And here is Jesus, His Christ, who through whatever torment, humiliation, or assault to His person, never gave up being who He was. He remained to the end Himself, as God made Him, God's will and His identity one and the same, without sin! In His life He never separated from God, and consequently, He never placated anyone—became who they wanted Him to be—never pretended, never lied, never was or has been other than who He says He is. . . . "

Katherine closed the book. "I, too, am who I am. I have an identity, not through my own efforts but by grace, and somehow that is a creation, the work of God."

Katherine returned to the table of photos, now in disarray as she had left them several days ago. Stuffing them back in the book, between the pages, loose, she came at last to the first—the one of her mother and herself. She looked again at the picture. The child's side seemed clear and sharp, the mother's still dim and out of focus. She was making sense of her own life, but not Janice's. When it came to her, Katie still felt the orphan, searching for her birth mother.

Can we ever really know ourselves until we know whence we came? Until those primary to us make sense, can we ever know their imprint? Can we erase or enhance it? And, as John is telling me, we must know our Creator if we are to ultimately know ourselves. To be free, John said, we must know the truth of ourselves and of God. Chey interrupted her thoughts with a paw against the front door.

Katherine called him to the back door and let him out. It was snowing again, silver-dollar flakes twirling earthward. She could tell from the new layers of firewood that were exposed since her last trip for wood that several inches had fallen in the past few hours. Round white mounds stood like marshmallow caps on the fenceposts between the cabin and the shed and on the ax she'd buried in the tree stump, where she had chopped the last bundle of kindling.

All was quiet. She let the stillness seep into her ravaged spirit. She called Chey back and closed the door.

Chapter 32

The days were uneventful, passing peacefully as the wilderness settled into winter. Katherine and Chey hiked, ran, and rolled in the snow, and once Katherine even rode the toboggan down the east hill. She cooked and crocheted, cut kindling and kept fires going.

The coverlet was assembled, all but the final piece, then the design would be complete. Away from the prying eyes of evaluation and hovering shadows of criticism, Katherine began to feel more alive and healthier than she ever had. She found herself in almost continual awareness of the Lord with her, blessing her with that abundance of life that was her birthright as His child.

As the snow deepened, she returned with her dog to her favorite trail almost daily, the one that flowed westward along the riverbank, walking the four miles unhurriedly. It was completely transformed in white now, bearing little resemblance to the dark path she'd followed to her near destruction last summer.

She felt stronger now, too, not so intimidated by her own fearful discoveries. On sparkling white days, the river sang a celebrating praise in rushing water and tinkling icicles. And Katherine found herself singing along. At last she was healing. It was real.

The bond between Katherine and the dog grew tighter, as they learned each other's language and shared a common routine. Her hearty companion continued to coach her in the sport of winter games, and the invigorating cold became a friend, not something she must shelter herself from but a thing she could revel in.

Cyle came as he had promised, racing her through the trees at breakneck speed, leaving her exhilarated and wanting more. They'd shared meals by the fire and long conversations. He had invited her out to "civilization," an invitation she was thinking about. Spring was coming, he'd told her, citing the increasing daylight hours, even though the snow was still deep and continued to pile up.

Chey had grown and filled out to his adult size but still played like a puppy. She fully enjoyed his strength and enthusiasm, thinking of him more as a friend than a canine companion.

Sometimes their excursions revealed that they were not the only occupants of this corner of the world. The proof was left in the snow—the tiny stick tracks of birds, the unmistakable paw prints of coyotes, dainty foxes, and similar small mammals.

From time to time, they came across the evidence of a struggle. Red stains in the snow, feathers, or clumps of fur told the story of how it had ended for one creature and provided for the other.

One day, about a mile from the cabin, they came upon a place where a very large animal had bedded down, packing the snow in a diameter of several feet. The dog carefully sniffed the area and the stained yellow spot a short distance away. Then he lifted his leg to mark their territory. Katherine's instincts leaned toward a low profile, thinking it more discreet not to announce their presence. But Chey had other ideas.

These months of watching the Newfoundland's reactions had led Katherine to the conclusion that only one thing in the forest alarmed him. Bear!

She shuddered to think that it might have been the huge brown bear they'd spied across the river that had invaded the space of their cabin and walked up on their porch that night a few months ago.

It was then that she began to notice the trees that had been clawed about three feet above her head, strips of bark hanging loose, exposing red flesh beneath, bleeding clear amber pitch. She tried to console herself with the manual's pronouncement: "Bears are more afraid of you than you are of them!" She didn't want to test the theory.

Seeing these signs, Katherine began to seriously consider the wisdom of carrying a gun. She was certain she could never hit anything but imagined that the noise might be intimidating. At such times, it was reassuring to catch the fragrant scent of her own cozy hearth, filling the clean air with the knowledge that she was close to home.

It was strange to be truly on her own, with no one to call— no police, no constant friend, or rescuer—only the great black dog on whom she relied more and more.

Katherine had searched her entire life for the liberating relief of not having to take into account any other person or fear invasion, physical or verbal. Her life had been a process barring discovery, until she finally lost the ability to trust anyone or the spontaneity to interact with the truth of herself. She had always been on guard, as she practiced the art of reading others, until their feelings and needs were more obvious than her own.

Never had she been free enough of the restraint of family or friends, or work, to find the bottom line within herself—to make her own decisions, to find her own needs, to own her own wants, to live, without having to justify herself. Sermons on justification always baffled her. How could Jesus be all the explanation we would ever need to make? But John had insisted it was so.

One thing about the wilderness she had learned: Nothing here made an excuse for itself. It merely existed, living out its appointed being as long as it had life, never doubting itself, its impact, or its right to be here. Sometimes at night, a sound distinctly different from the shrill bark and wail of the coyotes, echoed from the ridges. Wolves! The dog heard it, too, causing him to lift his head, ears perked, and sometimes whimper softly as if he knew their language. Or perhaps he envied their freedom as opposed to his duty inside a hot, suffocating human shelter. In any case, neither held any cause for alarm for him. He would simply roll on his side, sigh, and go back to sleep against the door draft.

Of all the animals in the woods, Katherine had heard that wolves were the most elusive. They were heard but not seen. The mournful sound left her awake and alone in the dark, aware that there was no one to call and no one to answer if she did.

Lying in the dark and listening to the wolves, Katherine realized she was beginning to look forward to the static conversations on the radio and Cyle's visits. For all the magnificent sounds of the North woods, none struck the chords of her own being like another human voice, words and language she understood. All the other animals in these woods had someone to hear them. The wolves spoke a familiar dialect and the coyotes and the jays. A dull longing was taking shape—the desire for fellowship—for the sounds of a person other than herself.

She found herself trying to imagine her grandmother's voice, but try as she might, her memories were only monotones. The sounds did not reach her ears. Increasingly, Katherine longed to be touched, to feel human warmth. And she spent hours on the floor in front of the fire, curled up with the dog. After ten months in this wilderness womb, Katherine was beginning to feel the isolation of a lifetime.

On the morning when she heard a bird singing, Katherine flew from her bed and ran barefooted onto the porch. A cardinal perched in the fir tree was singing to the heavens that spring was coming. Katherine lifted her nightgown to her ankles and danced a jig while Chey stood and watched.

That night she dreamed of spring. Of flowers and warm breezes and singing.

Some time after midnight, the peace was shattered. As she lay sleeping beneath the homely quilt, Chey erupted in wild barking at the back door. Alarmed and disoriented, Katherine bolted to her feet and froze in place. By the amber light of the hearth coals, she could see his hair in upright bristles lining his spine. White flashing fangs signaled all-out alarm. The dog stood stiff-legged, claws extended to the floor. Deep, fierce warning pounded her eardrums. The bear, she thought! It must be the bear!

Katherine's brain snapped to attention as she inched toward the wardrobe, reaching for the loaded twelve-gauge shotgun that lay across the top. It shook in her hands as she aimed the barrel in the direction of the door.

She could hear the logs out back, crashing against the cabin like boulders in an avalanche, splintering under the swipe of the lumbering bear. The beast growled a low rumbling threat, as Chey answered him point for point.

There was a ripping sound that she guessed must be his claws against the log wall. Chey went wild. The door rattled against the bar that was the only barrier to his entrance. Over and over the animal shoved at the door.

The wrought-iron latch handle moved up and down spastically

as he clawed the wood. She could feel his breath hot and with the stench of terror, seeping through the cracks. The noise was deafening.

Slowly Katherine backed toward the kitchen, expecting the massive door to give under his attack. In her mind's eye, she could see the monstrous black form filling the doorway, invading, overpowering, consuming. She was trapped.

Chey barked and barked as the split logs rumbled and the door rattled and wood splinted and ripped beneath the powerful claws. Suddenly, the door slammed against the bar hard, opening a crack. Chey raged with ferocity. Katherine knew she could not contain him or call him off now.

She lifted the cellar door, ready to make an escape should he come through the door. Her fingers gripped the gun, the butt shoved into her armpit. She must aim high, to miss the dog.

Then with one deafening tear, the bolt gave and the door flew open. With a swirl of white, like exhaust from hell, the colossal dark beast stood on the threshold, filling the frame. Chey attacked.

She squeezed the trigger. The gun fired, blazing the dark in a streak of flame. The sound exploded in her ears, echoing off the walls like the inside of a bomb. Katherine jumped, fell, into the cement hole as the trapdoor banged shut above her.

Buried in the dark beneath the floor, Katherine trembled violently. Above were the sounds of crashing and glass breaking, snarling and scraping.

Katherine feared she had hit the dog. All at once, Chey was barking again. *He must be all right,* she thought with immense relief. The sound was coming from outside and moving away from the cabin.

Katherine stood mute in the hole, listening. More barking. Suddenly the dog screamed in pain. Then silence.

She clutched the gun, cold and hard in her hand, and waited. Minutes passed. Nothing came but the moaning wind. Her ears strained against the silence for any minute indication of either animal.

Chey! Where was Chey? Why wasn't he barking? The darkness was as engulfing as blindness. Katherine stumbled forward, groped her way up two rungs of the ladder, and pushed against the trapdoor overhead, lifting the weight of hiding.

A draft of cold air hit her across the eyes as a shaft of firelight speared the hiding place.

"Chey," she whispered, repeating his name into the crack. There was no answer.

Cautiously, in slow motion, she crept up the ladder, the weight of the door on her shoulder. Half emerged, she was high enough to see into the empty room. What she saw was horrifying!

The back half of the cabin was a disaster, the front half untouched. The back door hung wide open against the wall. Firewood lay helter-skelter in the doorway, with feathery snow blowing through the opening. The nightstand lay on its side, the glass lamp shattered, bleeding kerosene across the floor. The table and chairs were in a rubble against the wardrobe. Her bed was overturned, the bedding strewn like discarded laundry.

Propping the cellar door open, Katherine lit the kitchen lantern before tiptoeing into the room to survey the rest of the damage. The massive door hung from one hinge. The arm that had held the bar had been ripped out from the wall and lay on the floor, screws exposed like an amputated paw. All the damage was confined to the back half of the cabin. Chey had stood his ground.

Barefoot, stepping lightly around the glass, Katherine felt something warm and sticky under her feet. Lowering the lantern, she could see large drops of blood on the floor and her own footprints where she had walked through it.

Mechanically, Katherine pulled on her clothes. She had to find the dog. She knew he must be hurt . . . or worse, but she had to find him. She owed him. Her numb fingers trembled as she laced her boots.

Pulling on her parka, she grabbed the lantern and the gun and crawled over the logs that littered the once neatly stacked tunnel out back. Once clear of them, Katherine began calling, "Chey! Chey!" Nothing. The north wind bit into the exposed flesh of her face, as the mountains moaned with winter. "God help me," she pleaded, "help me find him. Oh, God . . . please let him be alive!"

Waving the lantern back and forth, she detected tracks in the snow. There seemed to be two trails. She reasoned one must be the incoming bear and the other, his tracks as he left. Trying to discern one from the other, she knelt, aiming the light.

Telltale drops of red pointed up the steepest grade behind the cabin. The trail was clear, with two sets of prints visible. Katherine followed the trail, stumbling and clawing her way up the mountain.

About a hundred yards into the trees, she could see the evidence of a struggle. Bright red stains in the snow, more blood crying from the ground.

Holding the lamp above her head cast the light forward, revealing the spot where they had separated. One set of tracks went north. One west. Both bloody.

Katherine leaned closer. She put her finger in the print she determined was Chey's. Now she was certain he was injured. The snow was stained every few feet. She could only hope he was alive.

Through the dark she followed the trail, pleading with God. The wind was relentless, as cold as the blood that froze in her own veins. Her hair flew around her as if attempting escape, whipping across her eyes and into her mouth. After several hundred feet, she came to a spot where the snow was packed down. The red stains bled into the snow in three places, where he'd lain down. She could see the evidence of Chey's life in thick black pools, connected by bright red ribbons melting into the snow. Steam still rose from the last pool of blood.

His trail turned in a wide circle, heading back toward the cabin and downhill. Katherine could see he was dragging his hind legs now.

She pressed on. Wolves mourned behind her, high up the mountain.

"Chey! Where are you? Chey?"

Then she saw him . . . there, ahead, at the edge of the circle of light. The large black form lay crumpled and bleeding in the snow.

Katherine threw herself beside him. He was still warm. He was breathing, barely. A deep gash in his belly was oozing blood and what looked like intestines.

"Oh, God!" Katherine scooped snow and packed it against his wound to stop the bleeding. Chey lifted his head, whimpering. She knew she couldn't carry him, and she couldn't leave him here. The wolves sang their threat across the night.

Looking down through the trees, she could see the cabin below. Somewhere out there was the monster who had done this. And he knew her whereabouts. Suddenly she felt more anger than fear.

Lantern in hand, she raced for the bottom. Running, falling, white. Tree limbs with sharp fingers scratched her face and tore at her clothes as she cascaded down the mountain, lungs burning like dry ice.

At the back of the cabin, out of breath, she frantically dug through the firewood, throwing logs out of the way. She had to find the toboggan. Her gloves were torn, exposing the ragged, bleeding flesh to the splinters of firewood.

Freed, she grabbed the toboggan rope and without stopping to catch her breath, she began the climb on all fours, back to the place where her friend lay dying in the snow. Through her tears, Katherine kept calling him, coaxing him, "Chey, I'm coming. Hang on. I'm coming!"

When she finally reached him, he made no response. He was weaker than before. Katherine positioned the toboggan next to him against his back. Then grabbing all four feet at once, she pulled with all her strength, rolling his lifeless body over and onto the sled.

His head hung limp. She put her mouth close to his. She could barely feel his shallow breathing. Pulling his weight in a circle, she headed down toward the cabin, begging God for his life, as she deftly threaded the trees.

She knew she would have to go through the back door where there were no steps. That would require clearing the entrance of the scattered firewood.

Once at the cabin, Katherine clambered over the heaps of wood to the inside. She ripped the quilt from the bed and returned to the dog and tenderly covered him. Tearing into the scattered logs with a vengeance, Katherine managed to quickly clear a path through which she pulled the sled and dog. Across the floor, Katherine pulled him on the toboggan to the hearth, where she piled new wood, setting it ablaze. The room was icy, sucking the warmth from both of them.

Katherine ran her fingers into the heavy black coat, touching Chey's skin. It was cold, too. "Oh, God. Please!" Katherine rubbed his limbs and head. "Chey! Chey . . don't die!" Tears streamed her face.

Then in a ferocious effort, she threw herself against the back door, wrestling with it as if with death itself, to shut it, at least against the cold. The massive door scraped the floor and finally rested on the splintered frame. It was the best she could do.

She went back to check the dog. He was still breathing, however feebly. She rubbed his body again, forcing circulation.

Katherine shed her parka and sat helplessly beside him, stroking his ears, whispering his name, calling him back from the edge of death.

She was alone. Her mind raged at the impotence. There was no phone, and the radio was useless until the plane came, which would be sometime tomorrow . . . or actually today, in a few hours. She could put up the alarm flag, but it wouldn't be seen until daylight.

Was there nothing to do but wait—for Chey to die, for the bear to return, for her own breath to freeze within her?

Then she remembered the fire tower. Maybe she could make them believe the cabin was on fire. She flew through the front door.

For the next hour, Katherine worked in a frenzy, hauling armloads of wood into three huge piles across the front of the cabin. Then with the aid of the entire supply of kerosene, she lit them, and one more at the east end of the cabin, near the shed. It had occurred to her that if nothing else, it might deter the return of the bear. Katherine then went back inside to wait and watch the windows glow as if the woods were ablaze.

Holding Chey's head in her lap, leaning against the sofa, she drifted in and out of exhausted consciousness, half dreaming.

A dark form looming in the doorway. Swirling black triangles chopping the air in wide arcs. A toddler running . . . falling. . . . Far off she could hear a little girl crying, "Mama . . . mama."

Katherine awoke with a start and, for a moment, could not tell if she was in Vida or Chicago. Then she heard the low droning of the aircraft. Katherine raced for the shed in time to hear the static, "Lady . . . this is Ranger! Come in."

"Oh, thank God, Cyle!" she screamed. "Help me!"

"Okay! Okay! We're on the way. What's wrong?"

"Chey's hurt! A bear! Got in the cabin! Hurry!"

"They're on the way . . . with snowmobiles. Are you hurt?"

"No! Just hurry!"

Cyle got there ahead of the snowmobiles, by helicopter. The light of dawn was just piercing the darkness over the east ridge, when she heard the chopper's rhythmic whirling out front.

Within minutes, he'd loaded Katherine and the dog and they were flying west ahead of the sun. Katherine sat with Chey, unable to communicate in anything more than monosyllables and nods.

The landing, the drive through the city streets to the veterinarian, who stood in surgery for four and a half hours over the dog, checking into the motel room—it was all a blur. Katherine felt like her mind was on overload, all circuits fried. She dumbly reassured Cyle she would see him in the morning. She collapsed on the bed, with the homely light still glaring overhead.

Katie opened her eyes. It was dark in the guest room. Moonlight streamed through the open window. White sheers floated softly at the window, caressed by the warm summer night. In the moonlight, white high-top shoes glowed from the top of the dresser opposite her crib, and she could barely make out the dark profile of the fighter plane flying above the double bed.

Suddenly an icy presence seeped into the room. A dark form filled the doorway. Katie peered through the bars, eyes wide. A cold empty phantom brushed past her, with raspy, rancid breath.

Katie buried her face in her bed. Then the shuffling sounds. She looked up to see her mama fall backward on the bed with such force that her arms and legs flew up. Mama . . . in a coral dress, trimmed in embroidered daisies around the neck, and black stack heels. Katie could smell the sweet, strong aroma of flowers, Mama's perfume.

Then the immense black triangles hovered over Mama, raising and lowering, pounding her, covering her in blackness. Katie stared in horror, sucking her blanket, hearing the raspy breathing and ripping cloth.

Mama rolled sideways between the bed and the wall as the fighter plane hung helplessly above the scene. The little girl whimpered, "Mama . . . Mama." The dark figure moved toward her.

Katie felt the cold hands around her own body, squeezing, thumbs digging into the small of her back. She screamed into the blanket. Screams echoed down the corridors of her past as the fingers bit into her flesh.

Chapter 33

Katherine awoke to pounding at her door. Recovering her bearings, she opened the door a crack.

"Lady . . . you okay? We heard screams. You okay?" A graying woman in hair curlers hid behind a balding man with bewildered brows. Alarm covered their faces as they stared at the woman with sunken wide eyes, her face badly scratched and bruised, her hair tangled with twigs and debris.

It took repeated explanations and reassurances before the worried woman gave up her efforts to see past her husband into Katherine's room. They finally left with furtive glances over their shoulders.

Shaken and heavy with the events of the past twelve hours, Katherine filled the tub with steaming water. She sat on the floor and watched it pour from the spout as if it were a miracle she'd never before experienced.

As she slid under the hot water, she was seized with pain. Every open cut stung and the bruises burned, muscles throbbed. Katherine tried to yield to the comfort of the water but began to cry. She did not know what she was crying for—the pain, the wounded dog whose life was anchored by a thread, John, whose life thread had snapped, letting him float away from her. . . .

Katherine sat up with a jolt! In her mind the image of the bear in the doorway and the dark form that became the black triangles, flashed back and forth. Slowly she registered the dream, the flashback that had brought the neighbors. A strange awareness dawned. It was as if the earth stood motionless in orbit, and she could hear the pieces of unconsciousness sliding into place, like metal gear bits. Katherine gingerly lifted herself out of the tub. Every part of her body screamed at the agony captive in it.

Wrapped in a towel, she padded into the bedroom. It was her own reflection in the mirror that caught her attention. There, on her cheek, a V-shaped scratch! Or was it Janice?

There was a TV but no clock. Sitting on the edge of the bed, she lifted the receiver from its cradle.

"Front desk," came a voice.

"Can you tell me what time it is?"

"Nine-thirty seven."

"Can you place a long distance call for me? Area code 708. 252-2757. This is room . . . uh," Katherine looked around the room for the key, "twelve." Katherine listened to the clicks and beeps, resulting in the monotone rings.

"Hello?" said the familiar voice.

"Adam?" she spoke softly. There was a brief pause.

"Kate!" his voice excited. "Kate, is that you?"

"Yeah. Hi, Adam. It's been a while." Her voice was worn and exhausted.

"You okay? Where are you?"

"I'm in Klamath Falls . . . in a motel. It's too long to tell. A lot has happened. Listen, Adam . . . I know her secret." There was silence from Chicago.

"Whose?" he asked. "Janice's?"

"I think she was raped . . . when I was a baby . . . and I was there."

It all made sense. The black triangles—sleeves, moving up and down in the moonlight, fists pounding. The raspy breathing and the perfume. After that night, Janice had never worn perfume.

Preston was flying bombers somewhere in Europe when Katie's lovely young mama donned a coral summer dress and fragrance to match and went out. Here was the secret she must never remember. Here was the answer to the unspoken riddle, the barb that lay at the center of the twisted tangle of mother and daughter.

"I didn't cut her face! *He* did!" Katherine jumped up and slapped her palm to her forehead, like she'd known it all along, which of course she had. "She had to make some explanation . . . and I was it!"

Katherine eased herself into the pillows against the motel headboard, melting into the bed, welcoming the softness and the warmth. Just as softly dawned the next realization.

"Oh, dear God! That's why she kept crying and saying, 'I killed her . . . it's a punishment'! That's it—when Linda died, she got it all mixed up with . . . Was she pregnant? Did she have an abortion?"

Katherine buried her face in her hands and wept for her mother. "Poor, poor Janice! God forgive her. She did not know what she was doing."

She lay very still, listening to the traffic go by on the street outside. It was a comforting sound. She closed her eyes, too exhausted to hold them open but not sleepy. Her mind was numb.

The phone rang. She hauled herself upright, sending a sharp pain down her neck, and answered it. Cyle's familiar voice requested that she meet him at the café across the street for breakfast. She begged off for an hour to get herself together.

Katherine ambled back into the bathroom, this time for a shower. With shampoo, compliments of the motel, she washed her hair, letting the soap and hot water run down her back for the first time in seven months. It felt delicious.

When she got out, she dried her long hair as best she could, then peered into the steamed mirror. Clearing a spot, Katherine blinked as the foggy reflection of an old woman stared back. Her skin looked aged and leathery. Dark eyes retreated into the skull, and deep hollows inhaled the flesh beneath her cheekbones. Her face was a series of scratches that looked as if she had just been in a fight. And Katherine did not remember her hair having that much gray.

She had no comb, no makeup, no clothes other than the torn ones she'd worn, no means to secure her wild hair, which hung most of the way down her back. So when she entered the café across the street, heads did turn. She looked like the ghost of a logger who had fallen down a mountainside, through the brambles, and been left for dead.

K Fall Café was a fifties-style diner that smelled of hash browns and coffee, inside and out. Through the door, Katherine could see the row of low counter stools, split and frayed around their shiny red vinyl tops. A line of window booths offered what privacy was to be had. A bell over the door announced her arrival.

Here and there, shaggy loggers in flannel shirts slumped over coffee cups, waiting for spring. Cyle blinked when he saw her.

In spite of her appearance, he grinned politely as she approached the corner booth. She swallowed hard from a glass of water that tasted of bleach, as he poured her a cup of coffee from the thermos on the table. Katherine sipped the cup, holding it with two hands.

"How's Chey?" Her eyes were riveted on the dark pool in her cup, to avoid the answer.

"Hanging in there." His voice was gentle.

She looked up across the table. "Really? He's not dead?"

"You sound surprised." He watched the strange woman he'd flown in here from Chicago, the old stirrings of compassion tugging at his awareness, but he had no desire to do battle with her. Besides, he didn't think she could take it.

"Yeah, well, most good things in my life die."

"Well, hey. Maybe it's time for your luck to change."

She gave him a vacant stare. "Maybe."

He continued. "Doc says he has a good chance. He lost a lot of blood, but no vital organs. Newfoundlands are tough."

"Did I shoot him?"

"Shoot him! Oh, no. But you did hit the bear. The guys went up and tracked him. They put him out of his misery."

"Good!"

"You must have got him at close range." He added more coffee to her cup.

The waitress came for the order. When Katherine didn't respond, he ordered for both of them.

After the waitress left, she added, "He came through the door. He was in the cabin. I shot him . . . from the kitchen."

"Well, I'll have to give it to you. And darn smart to set all that wood on fire, too. Around here, fire is the best way to raise an army, even if it is off-season. You got every logger from here to Coos Bay. I thought the cabin was on fire. 'Course you burned up a five-year supply of wood!"

Katherine smiled, breaking a scab on her lip. Their breakfast arrived. At first it tasted like boiled paper. But after a few more bites, Katherine could feel her appetite revive. By the third cup of coffee, reality was setting in.

"Cyle, I have no money," she said.

"Oh. No problem. It's on me."

She tilted her head to the side and furrowed her brows. "I have traveler's checks in the cabin. I have no clothes. I don't even have a comb. And when can I see Chey?"

"Okay, here." He threw a twenty-dollar bill on the table in front of her. "There's a dime store around the corner. I got some errands to do." He stood up to go. "Meet you back at the motel. Then I'm at your disposal."

They left the K Falls Café. He went one way. She went the other, in the direction of the dime store. The climate was totally different at this lower elevation—warmer, wetter.

Katherine looked out at the surrounding mountains, drenched in a moody purple. The sky looked like cement. A cold mist drizzled down, giving the passing motor vehicles a swishing sound as they went by.

A few people smiled as she passed them on the street. Katherine tried to ignore the questions in their eyes and pretended she didn't hear the little boy who asked his mother in a loud whisper, "What happened to her!"

As she collected the items in the dime store, the intercom pealed out "Joy to the World," even though Christmas had passed. Katherine smiled. The thought registered. Chey was alive.

Within an hour, there was a firm knock at the door. Katherine opened it, letting Cyle's surprise register as a compliment. A handful of makeup in the hands of an artist could do wonders.

Her auburn hair was caught back in a low ponytail. The scratches had all but disappeared under the camouflage. Softly enhanced dark purple eyes were the same misty color of the mountains.

They rode in silence in the cab of his pickup that was easily as filled with rattles as the plane had been that first day. Only this time, it sounded to Katherine like music—the sound of life, a way of getting from here to there.

He drove down streets and past landmarks that were totally

foreign to her. They had come this same way only hours before, but Katherine had absolutely no memory of it. Even when they pulled into a wet parking lot in front of a converted brick house, with a sign that read "Michael Barth, DVM," Katherine could have sworn she'd never seen it before.

Cyle pulled the emergency brake with a jerk. They got out and slammed both truck doors with a simultaneous metallic thud.

Inside, she could hear dogs barking from a back room. The waiting room was small and unremarkable, with pictures of dogs and cats hung too high on the walls. The floor and wall corners held traces of their patients' last brave efforts at marking their territory.

A man in his mid-thirties appeared from behind one of the doors and shook her hand. "Ah, Mrs. Allen." He pumped her hand up and down. "You've been through a real ordeal. And so has your dog." He stood aside, holding the door for her to enter the hospital room of cages, stacked two high in the center with treatment area around the perimeter.

Katherine peered sideways into the cages as they passed animals in various stages of recovery—some lying limply on their sides, others jumping and yipping at the wire, begging for any scrap of attention.

On the far side of the hospital square, in a large cage on the floor level, Chey lay on his side, swathed in a wide strip of white tape around his midsection. The hair was shaved on his right front leg. His tongue flopped to the side.

"He's still pretty much out of it." The vet opened the door and tapped the area at the corner and just above his eye. Chey reacted with a blinking reflex. "He's coming around," he said, pulling the dog's tongue farther out of the dog's mouth. "Color's good.

"Your dog probably would have bled to death if it hadn't been that cold. As it was, he nearly did anyway." The vet backed away, allowing Katherine to kneel beside her friend.

Chey smelled medicinal, but his breathing was deep and regular. She spoke his name and touched his head. His tongue moved in a slight licking motion.

"He should be fully awake in an hour or so. That bear really sliced him. All the way through the peritoneum. But he made it through the shock, so I think he's got a good chance."

Katherine looked up. "How long will he need to be here?"

"Oh, we'll keep him about a week just to make sure all the plumbing's back where it should be and working right . . . and there's no infection. He'll be pretty sore. But after that you can take him home."

Katherine wondered where that was. She thought about Chicago and couldn't imagine Chey ever feeling at home there.

The bear was dead! They had fought and won!

When she next saw Chey, he was alive with affection, covering her hands and face in celebration.

Cyle took her back to the cabin to gather her things and to say good-bye to her hiding place. As they entered the clearing, it looked the same—pristine white, glittering in the morning sun. Snow had covered all traces of a struggle, as well as the charred ground around the cabin. *Like love covers a multitude of sins,* she thought.

Inside, the men had replaced the door frame, rehung a new door, and set the furniture upright. Everything else was as she had left it.

Cyle waited outside while she packed her personal belongings back in the boxes from which they had come three seasons before. As she closed the last box, folding the flaps over the two journals laid on top, she noticed the lace coverlet, still crumpled on the arm of the sofa.

Picking it up, Katherine shook it out. Spreading it over the back of the sofa, she fingered the delicate lacy pattern that was revealed with all the pieces together. It was beautiful!

Katherine folded it twice and gently laid it on top of the old blue quilt that covered the yellowing fabric. And left.

Cyle loaded her boxes on the toboggan. Katherine looked back only once when he circled the meadow before heading west along the river.

"Sure you don't want to stay?" he couldn't resist shouting above the motor as they headed into the band of giant trees.

Katherine looked up as she always did. The emerald giants, swayed gently against the crystal sky . . . still pointing. "Safety is not a place . . . it's a Presence," she answered softly. When

Chey was ready, they might take a place in Klamath Falls so she could see spring in the mountains. Or maybe she'd buy a little house at the ocean, in Yachats, where Molly gathered shells. The dog loved the water so.

Katherine thought of the reflection she'd seen in the mirror at the motel—the gray streaks in her hair, reminiscent of Grandma Henry's—and realized who she had become. She could hear the relatives at the reunions, "Katie, you favor the Henry side of the family."

Poor Janice, she thought, *she doesn't know the God who can forgive even that.* Katherine didn't know if Janice would ever admit the need for comfort, if she would ever drop her pride and repent. If not, Katherine would shake the dust from her feet and move on. *But I will no longer be part of the pretense,* she thought. *It's over. And, I will call her Mother,* she added triumphantly. *I will reach out with a healed hand, but it must be received. God Himself cannot heal where He is not received.*

And John was right. Forgiveness and reconciliation were different. Reconciliation and comfort require repentance. Forgiveness requires compassion. Finally, Katherine felt the compassion. The anger was gone.

"Lord, bring her to repentance, that she might find comfort," she whispered. "I do forgive her. Poor Mother, she truly does not know what she has done!"

They sped along beside the river. Even now she could hear it singing,

> Through many dangers, toils and snares,
> I have already come.
> 'Twas grace that brought me safe thus far,
> And grace will lead me home.